"You came to court, ████████████████████████
your part of our ba████████████████████████
think I'd use force, b████████████████████████

"I can't, not now. ██████ I saw you last week, everything's changing. Rokeby's always at my side. He won't leave me alone. He wants me."

Dirk ran his eyes over Melora, a hot light kindling in their depths. "What man wouldn't want you?" He pulled her against him, but this time he was not trying to comfort her. His body pressed against hers, bending her backward. She could feel the hard muscle of his thighs against her legs. He lowered his head, his face poised above hers.

She tried to turn away, to twist her body out of his arms, but she managed only to free one hand. Filled with helpless rage, she drew back her arm. He caught her wrist; then, slowly, he drew off her glove. He raised her hand to his lips, palm upward, and his tongue flicked lightly over the bare skin. She was caught up in a rising tide of passion.

He released her hand, and now his mouth covered hers. This was no gentle kiss. She was shaken to the depths of her being by the fierce hunger she felt in him—as fierce as the hunger surging up in her.

DIANA HAVILAND

Stolen Splendor

PINNACLE BOOKS
WINDSOR PUBLISHING CORP.

PINNACLE BOOKS are published by

Windsor Publishing Corp.
475 Park Avenue South
New York, NY 10016

The P logo Reg U.S. Pat & TM off. Pinnacle is a trademark of Windsor Publishing Corp.

First Printing: April, 1994

Printed in the United States of America

Prologue

The chill October wind swept in from the sea, across the moors of Northumberland, bending the leafless, twisted oaks, and flattening the withered gorse and heather. Dirk Grenville glanced at the darkening sky above the moors, and spurred his stallion to a canter. The first drops of rain stung his face and he brushed them off impatiently, without slackening speed.

Dirk, born and bred in this rugged country, knew the autumn gale would strike in full force long before midnight; the driving rain would turn the Great North Road into a morass. Though he might urge on his powerful mount with whip and spur, he would not reach London tonight.

He would have to take shelter at the Leaping Stag. There, at the inn, over a hot dinner and a bowl of mulled wine, he would devise a new plan to soothe King James's displeasure and win his way back into the royal favor.

His lips tightened and the tanned skin drew taut over his angular cheekbones as he bent forward, urging his horse to the gallop, his russet velvet cloak streaming out behind him; but the breakneck pace did little to ease Dirk's seething tension.

Damn Uncle Nicholas. And Aunt Jessamyn, too.

Why the devil had they pushed Rosalind into marriage with that prosperous, fat-bellied merchant? In their haste to rid themselves of a daughter whose small dowry had so far hampered her prospects, they had unknowingly upset Dirk's plans for his pretty cousin—and for himself. Now it was impossible for Rosalind to take her place as lady-in-waiting to Queen Anne, a position Dirk had managed to win for her after tedious months of complicated maneuvering.

Dirk's hard mouth twisted in a grim smile. It was fruitless to brood over past disappointments. Since Rosalind could not play the part he had chosen for her, he must find another way to gain access to the inner circles at James's court.

The sooner he reached that goal, the sooner he would be free to leave the court behind, to sail from the nearest port without a backward glance or pang of regret. He had already had his fill of Whitehall Palace—of the jockeying for position, the efforts to gain the monarch's nod of approval.

Even the perfumed, white-bosomed court ladies, skilled in the pleasures of the bedchamber, had lost their appeal for him. Gripped by the familiar restlessness that was a part of his turbulent nature, Dirk longed to be on his way again.

He had left Northumberland in his fourteenth year as cabin boy on a ship bound for the New World. With any luck, he soon would set out on his roving again. But this time, he would not sail under the command of another—not even a captain as great as Sir Francis Drake, his former master. This time, he would command his own ship, and carve his own settlement on the shores of that wild, uncharted land beyond the sea.

Abruptly, he drew rein, his dark eyes narrow and alert. What was that sound he'd heard, half lost in the rising storm? He turned the stallion off the road, and down the rocky slope to his left; then he drew rein beside an ancient oak whose wind-twisted branches stretched out over a deep ravine.

Were his senses playing tricks on him? No—for now he heard the sound more distinctly than before. Here, in this desolate spot, a girl was singing, her voice blending with the early twilight, weaving an unearthly magic.

He's gone . . . he's gone away,
To stay, a little while . . .

But he's coming back to me,
Though he ride a thousand miles . . .

Dirk guided his horse closer to the edge of the ravine. Peering down, he glimpsed the ruddy firelight. The wind shifted, swept aside a veil of mist. Now he saw the singer.

His strong hands tightened on the reins. An icy, prickling sensation touched his spine. Although he was not given to flights of fancy, he was caught in the spell cast by the girl's voice.

She sat on the edge of a flat rock, her fine-boned, oval face gilded by the firelight. Her head was tilted back on the slender white curve of her neck. The wind whipped her long, jet-black hair across her cheek and she brushed it away impatiently. Then her fingers returned to the strings of the lute she held in her lap.

Was she alone in this desolate spot? Dirk leaned forward in the saddle and caught sight of a small figure standing close beside her. A child, perhaps . . . no, a dwarf. The long, narrow visage under the peaked cap was a man's face.

On the other side of the fire, a white-haired crone, wrapped in a long gray cloak that was embroidered with curious symbols of tarnished gold, crouched close to the leaping flames; she was rattling a handful of stones, then casting them on the ground and examining them intently.

Dirk sat motionless in the saddle, his eyes drawn back to the dark-haired girl. Her high, clear voice, the music of her lute, wove a spell about him. Years before, his nursemaid had filled his mind with tales of witches and spirits who dwelt in lakes and streams; of fairy folk and hobgoblins. Here in Northumberland, not only humble folk, but the gentry, too, believed such legends.

But even as the girl's spell drew closer about him, a more mundane sound startled him back to reality. It was a bear's deep, menacing growl, rising from the depths of the ravine.

His stallion pawed the ground uneasily. Steadying the animal, Dirk leaned farther forward. Now he saw the bear and its keeper, a huge, shaggy man who held the beast by a heavy

7

chain. Behind them stood a canvas-covered wagon with crude multicolored pictures painted on the cloth.

Dirk mocked himself for his flight of fancy. He had come upon a small band of traveling performers, the kind who tramped the roads, seeking to earn their bread by entertaining the country folk at a fair or an innyard. Poor devils. There'd be slim pickings for them in this bleak time of year.

Dirk's eyes lingered on the dark-haired girl. Eighteen, perhaps, scarcely older than Rosalind. But Rosalind would lie warm beneath a feather bolster beside her stout merchant husband. The singing girl would not be so lucky. Her canvas-covered wagon would give scant shelter from the wind and rain.

Would she lie alone tonight? Perhaps the bear leader would share her bed. What of it? The wench was no concern of his. He spurred his horse away from the ravine.

But when the stallion's pounding hooves thundered along the road once more, Dirk could not forget the singing girl. The white oval of her face, the curve of her throat, her dark, wind-tossed hair and lithe, slender body remained with him, even as he caught sight of the lighted windows of the Leaping Stag.

Chapter One

Melora Standish rose and tossed the waves of her dark, wind-ruffled hair back from her face. In the firelight, raindrops glittered like diamonds in the thick, dark waves, and clung to the long, curving lashes that set off her violet eyes.

She slipped her lute into its worn cloth covering and handed the instrument to Osric, the dwarf. Drawing her worn shawl about her, she crossed the ravine to her wagon. With one swift, graceful movement, she swung herself up onto the board at the back.

She pushed aside the flap, but even before she was inside, she flinched at the sound of her father's racking cough. Quickly she made her way to his straw-filled pallet in the corner. The canvas that served as a makeshift roof was torn in several places, so that rivulets of rain came dripping through. The flame from the overhead lantern flickered in the wind that penetrated their flimsy shelter.

Her father ought not to spend another night here in the wagon. If he was to survive the winter, she needed to find him a snug roof and sturdy walls, and hot, nourishing food. Maybe with luck she might even earn enough to pay for the services of a physician.

Edmund Standish had never fully recovered from the lung fever that had laid him low four years ago. It had robbed him of his wife, wrecked his career, and sent him traveling the roads with his daughter.

During the summers, he had managed to eke out a bare living, performing at fairs, in the courtyards of country inns, or in market squares. One week last spring, he had been hired to entertain at a manor house; afterward, he and Melora had dined off pigeon pie and roast lamb left over from the betrothal feast of the squire's daughter. More often, they made do with bread, cheese, and ale.

Since the end of summer, even such meager rations were in short supply. Melora had spent the last of their hoard of coins two nights ago, for a few scraps of mutton, a cabbage head, and a handful of onions to make a pot of broth. Later, when Osric had handed her a small jar of honey and half a bottle of wine, she had not asked the quick-fingered dwarf how he had come by such luxuries. She had heated a soothing drink for her father, hoping to ward off another bout of fever; but to no avail.

Now she bent over his pallet, forced a smile, and drew the worn blanket up around his bony shoulders.

"I'll heat the rest of the broth for your dinner," she said.

"I'm not hungry, poppet."

"Is my cooking not to your taste?" She tried to speak teasingly. "You've not eaten since morning."

"Neither have you, nor the others, I'll warrant."

The clear, ringing voice that had held London's audiences enthralled now sounded hoarse and weak. And even in the dim light, she could see the flush of fever on his gaunt cheekbones.

"It's share and share alike—for Lord Wilmot's Men," he muttered.

Melora searched his haggard face in dismay. Was his mind wandering, so that he thought himself still the manager of Lord Wilmot's Men?

A pox on the irascible nobleman! He had lent Papa his patronage and had raised him to the heights, as actor-manager of London's leading theatrical company, only to cast him down when he could no longer satisfy his lordship's demands.

10

The few loyal players who had followed Edmund Standish into exile had long since deserted him, one by one. Young Robin, the player's boy, had hung on through the past summer; then he, too, had gone. And who could blame him?

The slender blond youth had realized he would not be able to act in female roles any longer. Even the country louts had laughed each time Robin's voice had cracked as he had spoken the lines of Titania, Juliet, or Ophelia.

And I cannot perform in a play on any stage in England, Melora thought. It was a senseless law that forbade women from acting in public. A gust of wind rocked the wagon, reminding her that this was no time to brood over her frustrations.

She bent over her father's pallet. "We can't stay here tonight," she told him. "Osric says there's an inn not far away."

Osric, the dwarf acrobat and juggler, had not been a member of her father's original troupe; neither had Caleb, the burly bear leader, nor Bronwen, the soothsayer. These three had fallen in with Edmund and Melora last July, shortly after Robin's departure. Only a few years ago, her father would have scorned the notion of performing with such people. But without Robin to play the female roles, he could no longer present the scenes from the plays of Shakespeare, Jonson, or Kyd.

Although Edmund Standish was slow to admit it, he needed each one of his new troupe. Country audiences were drawn by the dwarf's nimble antics; by the spectacle of Old Bruin, the bear, capering on his shaggy hind legs. And young girls were easily lured into Bronwen's wagon to hear of their marriage prospects. Who would the young man be? How soon would he declare his intentions?

When Melora first began performing, her father protested. He did not like the notion of his daughter displaying herself before the rough audiences at the fairs and innyards. But they needed her earnings.

At least the law did not prevent a female from singing, playing the lute, or dancing.

When the lung fever had laid her father low again, Melora

11

had gradually assumed responsibility for the troupe. So far, the others had not questioned her authority.

Now she hurried to the back of the wagon, lifted the flap, and called out, "Osric, come and hitch up our horse. Caleb, get Old Bruin inside your wagon. We're going on before the storm gets any worse. We'll get a warm welcome at the Leaping Stag, I've no doubt." She tried to sound confident, but she knew, as the others did, what dangers might await them.

Soon after she and her father had taken to the road, she had learned all about the harsh laws that governed the lives of traveling performers. She had listened wide-eyed to other wandering players, who had told of the brutal punishments meted out to them.

Even now, she remembered the night she had fled into the shelter of her wagon, sickened by the sight of a livid brandmark on the shoulder of a girl scarcely older than herself.

"The constable said it was because I showed too much of my tits when I was dancin'—long-faced, psalm-singin' Puritan, he were. Incitin' evil, that's what he called it. But the mealy-mouthed bastard ripped my blouse clear down to my waist and took a good long look before he left this mark on me."

Respectable farmers and merchants were deeply suspicious of wandering entertainers, deeming them little better than gypsies and vagabonds. In towns where the new Puritan sect had taken hold, a local constable might refuse to allow any sort of performance at a fair or marketplace. In others, the law required that all players get a license from the magistrate.

But tonight Melora refused to consider the risks they might have to deal with. She knew only that it was raining harder by the minute. Soon her father's pallet would be soaking wet.

"Bronwen, gather up those rune stones," Melora called, her lips curving in a faint semblance of a smile. "Maybe if you promise the serving wenches a bright future, they'll feed us more generously."

"The stones fall as they will," the white-haired Welshwoman

said, with quiet certainty; but she scooped them into the pocket of her long, tattered cloak, and headed for her own wagon.

Osric hitched up Melora's sway-backed nag. The dwarf's agility more than compensated for his small stature. He leaped onto the seat, wrapped a torn sack around his shoulders, and took the reins. Melora bent her head and slipped back under the canvas.

As the small caravan went jouncing out of the ravine, she sat beside her father's pallet, her hands clasped tightly in her lap, her jaw set.

Bronwen's words echoed in the rhythm of the turning wagon wheels: *the stones fall as they will.*

Melora ran her fingers over the strings of her lute, and turned a dazzling smile on the men gathered around her in the tap-room of the Leaping Stag. A few were local farmers, but most were pack mule-drivers forced to take shelter from the storm. She knew the kind of song most likely to win favor with such an audience.

I bought myself a bonny cock,
The biggest I did see,
I fed him 'neath the tree, boys,
And the cock, he pleasured me.

A mule-driver at the next table grinned up at her. His eyes lingered avidly on the seductive rounds of her high breasts, the curve of her slender waist, the long, shapely line of her thigh. He drank deep from his pewter tankard, wiped his mouth on the back of a grimy hand, then ran his tongue over his lips.

Concealing her revulsion, she launched into the next verse. The men nudged each other and beat time on the tables with their tankards. Tobias Abernathy, the red-faced, pot-bellied innkeeper, made his way to the table on which Melora sat, and gave her a nod of approval.

She had persuaded Abernathy to allow her to perform in

13

exchange for food and lodging. Now her father was sheltered in the stable loft with Osric and Bronwen. Caleb and his bear had been sent to a nearby shed.

"We got us a handsome thoroughbred stallion in the stable tonight," Abernathy had said. "High-spirited beast, he is. The stink of that bear'd have him kicking down his stall."

Melora glanced over the denizens of the taproom again, but she saw no one who looked as if he might be the owner of a fine horse. A coarse, hard-bitten lot, they would throw coins to her, if she pleased them; but they would prove difficult to handle later. No matter; she would have to get them to open their pursestrings, then escape to the sanctuary of the stable loft.

In the meantime, Osric, Bronwen, and Caleb were dining on hot pork pie and ale, and the cook had sent beef broth for her father. When she had finished the ballad, maybe she could charm Abernathy into providing a mug of hot spiced wine with honey.

Even as she sang, she shaped her plan. She would insist that she alone could persuade her father to drink the healing mixture. Osric would take her place in the taproom and perform his feats of acrobatics and juggling.

But she had scarcely finished the song when the landlord ordered: "Give us another!" He made his way between the tables and stopped beside her. She stiffened at the touch of his hand on her bare arm. The hot reek of his sweating body and the unconcealed lust that flickered in his small, pale eyes sickened her.

She hesitated, then launched into the first verse of "Pricked by Cupid's Arrow." She had learned the words, with their lewd double meanings, from a blowsy strumpet who had performed at the Dorset fair.

Abernathy bared his broken yellow teeth in a grin. When she saw the bulge at the front of his tight breeches, her insides lurched with disgust.

She must give the best performance she could, while trying to ignore the landlord and his drunken guests. From her perch

14

on the side of the long oak table, she looked over the heads of the crowd.

It was then that she first caught sight of the tall, lean man who had paused on the landing halfway down the wide staircase. Even seeing him in the dim light from the single lantern over the landing, she sensed something commanding about him. He might be the gentleman who owned the fine stallion, she thought. He wore a close-fitting doublet of cinnamon-colored velvet, the full sleeves slashed with gold; his long, well-muscled legs were sheathed in tight black breeches and high leather boots. One hand rested lightly on the jeweled hilt of his sword.

Like every other man in the room, the stranger stared straight at her, but she saw no lust in his look. He was observing her with a cold intensity that she found even more disturbing. Why should an elegantly dressed gentleman stop to stare at a ballad singer that way?

She bent her head over her lute, her long, slender fingers moving skillfully over the strings; her dark lashes cast crescent shadows on her cheeks. But although she got through the rest of the ballad without stumbling over the words or plucking a false note, she was still acutely conscious of the stranger's eyes upon her. It was as if she could feel his gaze tracing her every feature, from the curve of her cheek to the delicate molding of her small, square jaw. She felt flickers of awareness burning into her, spreading through the taut nerves of her body.

Scarcely had she finished the song when a mule-driver called out, "Can you dance as well as you sing, wench?"

"Kick up yer heels for us, girl!" another shouted.

Others joined in. "Let's see what's under yer skirts."

"If yer legs are as fine as yer tits, I'll pay a farthing fer a look."

But the landlord took the lute from her hands, set it on the bench, then lifted her off the table. He pulled her against him. She was overpowered by his rank smell, sickened by the hard pressure of his arousal against her thigh.

When she tried to pull away, the landlord tightened his grasp.

His breath was hot against her cheek, and his booming voice carried through the taproom.

"This little doxy'll do her dancing for me—up in my private chamber." He jerked his head toward the stairs.

Melora had fended off such crude advances before, at fairs and innyards along the road. But her father had been nearby to protect her then; or if not, Caleb had driven away her unwelcome pursuers. Few men, however hot with lust, had wanted to tangle with the burly bear leader, or the beast, with its great yellow teeth and formidable claws.

But now her father lay in the stable loft, weak with fever; and if she called out to Caleb for help, her cries would not reach him.

I am on my own now. The realization made her heart speed up, her breath catch in her throat.

"I got a soft feather bolster on my bed," the landlord boasted, tugging at her arm. "Better than what you're used to, I'll warrant."

"Take your hands off me!"

He gave a derisive snort of laughter. "What d'you think you got under them rags that's so special? Let's find out." His thick, hairy hand reached into her bodice, and she stiffened with outrage and disgust as his groping fingers found the swell of her breast.

When Melora fought to free herself, he caught one of her nipples between his thumb and forefinger, and pinched down hard. She could not keep back her cry as the fierce pain shot through her.

"Come along, nice and quiet-like," he warned.

She tried to claw at his face, but she was beginning to feel dizzy. The room swam around her and spots began to dance before her eyes. One of her flailing hands knocked against a tall tankard on the table beside her. Her fingers closed around the pewter handle. Driven by instinct born of sheer desperation, she drew back her arm and swung with all her strength.

The heavy tankard struck the landlord on the side of the

head. She heard his yelp of pain, saw a trickle of blood streaming down his cheek.

He let her go abruptly. She staggered backward and nearly
fell. Recovering her balance, she lifted her skirt and headed
for the back door. Once out in the yard, she would scream for
Caleb. But the others, spurred on by the spirit of the hunt,
closed in around her. "Stop the doxy—don't let her get
away!"

"Abernathy'll have fine sport with 'er tonight!"

"To hell with the landlord—I want 'er myself!"

"We'll take turns when he's done—plenty there for all of
us."

A hand caught at Melora's skirt. She heard the worn cloth
tear as she freed herself and kept going, dodging, panting as she
headed for the door.

Another moment and she would be outside.

A muddy boot shot out, tripping her. She fell to her knees,
scrambled up again. But not fast enough.

Abernathy, close behind her, got his heavy arm around her
waist. Holding her in an brutal grip, he dragged her through the
crowd.

"Don't keep 'er up there all night, Tobias—"

Melora writhed in the landlord's grasp, tried to kick his legs,
knowing all the while that resistance was useless. Even now, she
had to go on fighting as long as there was an ounce of strength
left in her body.

She heard Abernathy's startled grunt, and felt his grip loosen
slightly. The tall, velvet-clad gentleman stood blocking the way
upstairs, his long legs in their fine boots planted apart. The
lantern's light glinted on the jeweled hilt of his sword.

"Stop right there, landlord." His self-assured tone brought
Abernathy up short. The shouts of the others trailed off into a
half-audible muttering.

"Sorry we disturbed you, sir," the landlord said, with a
placating smile. "A real hellcat I got here. Tryin' to raise her

17

price, actin' like she never spread her legs for a man before—"

"Let her go."

Melora felt a faint stir of hope. Might she still escape the landlord's bed?

"You goin' to let 'im give you orders in your own taproom, Tobias?" Ned Bascomb, a local farmer, jeered at him.

The landlord knew if he gave way before the unknown gentleman he'd be the laughingstock of the countryside from now on. But he could not ignore the strong hand that rested on the rapier's hilt; the powerful body beneath the velvet doublet and breeches; the stance of the practised swordsman. All his instincts warned him to retreat before the stranger's commanding stare.

"No need to trouble yourself over the strumpet, sir. We have our own ways of dealing with her kind here."

"I am no stranger to Northumberland." The man's icy tone silenced the landlord. "Grenville's my name. Dirk Grenville. Nephew to Sir Nicholas Grenville of Ashcroft Hall."

Abernathy swallowed and tried to speak, but could make only a wordless croaking sound. He stumbled back hastily, dragging Melora with him. Like the others in the taproom, he, too, had seen Ashcroft Hall, with its battlements dark against the sky, its tall towers topped by menacing stone gargoyles, its heavy iron gates. He took another step backward. "I didn't know—it's an—an honor to have you under my roof, sir."

"The king's law forbids the taking of a maid against her will. In any part of his realm."

The landlord's broad face turned the color of a ripe plum. "A maid? What sort of maid is it who roves about with a troupe of traveling performers—who sings lewd songs in taprooms?"

Grenville's hand tightened on his sword hilt. The gesture and the look that accompanied it silenced Abernathy.

Was it possible that no man had ever tumbled the black-haired wench under a hedge beside the road? Yet she had fought him fiercely when he'd tried to get her upstairs. His head

18

ached where she had struck him with the tankard. If he could not bed the little trollop, he'd get his revenge.

"You, Bascomb. Ride to town. Bring back Constable Pratt."

"I'm not ridin' out on such a night. An' what ye want with a constable, anyhow?"

"This slut attacked me. It's your duty to see the law's carried out—or land in jail along with her."

It was no empty threat. Every able-bodied Englishman was required to help bring a criminal to justice, or suffer punishment himself. The landlord turned on Melora. "Belike you'll get a few dozen lashes to mend your manners."

Before she could take in the full impact of his threat, he went on, his pale eyes vindictive. "And the rest of your crew'll go with you.

"The dwarf—and that hag—a proper old witch, I'd wager. And your father."

"No!" Melora cried out. "They've done you no harm." Abernathy shrugged, unmoved. "My father's ill—he—"

"You should've thought of that before, doxy."

"Bridle your tongue," Grenville ordered. "You'll beg the lady's pardon at once."

"The—the lady?"

"My cousin, Lady Rosalind Grenville."

"Your—your—" Abernathy croaked. He released his grip on Melora.

"I'm escorting Lady Grenville to London, where she will attend upon her majesty, Queen Anne. We ride out at dawn."

The landlord swallowed hard, then managed to speak. "Your pardon, my lady. And yours, sir. How was I to guess that a—a lady—would be traveling with those ragtag players?"

"This lady's inclined to be headstrong." Grenville remarked. "Now she's learned the dangers that lie outside her father's gates, she'll make no more foolish attempts to escape my protection." He turned a faint, icy smile on Melora. "Isn't that so, my dear Rosalind?"

He took Melora's hand and drew her to his side. She stared

up at him, her violet eyes wide with bewilderment. A gentleman like Dirk Grenville, moved by the injustice of her plight, might go so far as to help her. But what possible reason could he have for claiming her as his own kin?

Chapter Two

"Come along, my sweet cousin."

Melora heard the irony in Dirk Grenville's tone, and caught the mocking glint in his dark-brown eyes. Had it been a chivalrous impulse that had moved him to protect her from Abernathy? Or did he want her in his own bed tonight? Her ballads had been bawdy enough to arouse even a highborn gentleman, no doubt.

But if Dirk Grenville wanted no more than a quick tumble on a bed, why should he say that she was his cousin? Why invent the ridiculous tale that they were bound for Whitehall, where she would attend upon the queen?

No matter, she told herself firmly. This was no time to try to fathom Grenville's motives. At least, she had escaped the landlord's lechery, and the threat of jail, as well. Her father and her friends were sheltered, warm and dry, in the stable loft. They'd sleep soundly tonight. Now she had only to convince Abernathy that she was the headstrong Lady Rosalind.

Dirk Grenville had taken her completely by surprise, thrusting her into the role of his cousin, without the slightest warning. Could she carry it off?

She drew a steadying breath, and stiffened her spine. She was Edmund Standish's daughter. Her mother, Adrienne, had been a talented actress on the Parisian stage, where there were no laws forbidding women to perform in the theater.

21

And she herself had grown up in the company of actors. She had watched them rehearsing, had memorized their lines and copied their gestures. Now was her chance to prove her skills.

"I'll not go to London with you," she told her "cousin." She tossed her long, jet-black hair, thrust out her chin, and hoped she looked and sounded like a rebellious young aristocrat. "I told you that, even before we set out from Ashcroft."

"You little lackwit! You should thank your stars for the honor his majesty has bestowed on you—choosing you as one of the queen's ladies-in-waiting."

Melora caught her breath sharply, and her heart began thudding against her ribs. What madcap charade was Dirk Grenville playing now? She searched his face, but she saw no trace of amusement there.

Lady-in-waiting to Queen Anne. Any young noblewoman in England would be delighted by the prospect of living at court, decked out in gorgeous finery, flirting with handsome young gallants at the royal banquets, balls, and masques.

But I am not a noblewoman. I'm the daughter of a traveling player. For a moment, her confidence drained away, leaving her weak and shaken. If only her father's illness had not driven her to seek shelter here at the Leaping Stag.

It was too late for such futile thoughts now, she told herself. She must go on improvising until she discovered what game Dirk was playing. "I escaped you once—I'll do it again."

"I'd advise you not to try it." There was no mistaking the warning in his voice. She opened her lips to speak, but he silenced her with a hard, level look. She saw the gold flecks that glinted in the depths of his dark eyes, and she felt a warm, unfamiliar sensation awakening within her. Heat tingled in her breasts and went rippling down along her thighs. What was happening to her?

"Come with me." Dirk's implacable tone startled her back to reality. "I've a good, hot dinner waiting in my chamber. If you behave properly, I may share it with you."

"Not yet, cousin Dirk." The mention of food reminded her

22

that she was responsible for the needs of her father and the others in the troupe. Since she was trapped in this dangerous charade for now, she would make the most of it.

She turned an arrogant look on Tobias Abernathy. "I demand your word—whatever that may be worth—that none of the players will be turned out tonight. Or harmed in any way."

"To be sure, my lady," the landlord agreed hastily. "If it is your wish."

"Why concern yourself with the treatment of these players?" Dirk asked her. Was he daring her to produce a plausible explanation?

"They sheltered me in their caravan, and shared their food with me." Her lips curved in a slight, mocking smile. "Would you have me disgrace the name of Grenville by forgetting my debt to those who befriended me?"

"The players may stay the night," the landlord said. "And I'll see they're well fed tomorrow morning, my lady."

He tried not to think what would have happened to him had he mounted the wench on a table, right here in the taproom. That hard-eyed cousin of hers would have gutted him like a flounder. Or ordered him hanged from one of the towers of Ashcroft Hall.

Eager to mollify Dirk Grenville and turn a profit at the same time, the landlord asked: "Shall I have a chamber prepared for the lady, sir? It will take but a moment—"

Grenville cut him short. "Now I've found my kinswoman, I'll not allow her out of my sight. She'll share my bedchamber tonight. And I want a second horse fitted with a lady's saddle ready and waiting. Lady Rosalind and I will ride out at dawn."

"Another horse," Abernathy repeated. At least there'd be profit in that. As for Grenville's sleeping arrangements, maybe he would tie the girl to his bedpost to keep her from giving him the slip again. It'd serve the skittish bitch right, the landlord thought, his loins still heavy with unsatisfied lust. Let her cousin take his riding crop to the soft, white skin of her back. Abernathy felt a surge of obscene pleasure just thinking about it.

The gentry had their own ways—damned peculiar, some of them. And the Grenvilles were known for their unpredictable, sometimes violent behavior. Since the wench had chosen to defy her family's wishes, she must pay for her folly.

"Guard me as you will, Dirk Grenville." Melora's slanting brows drew together; her eyes flashed violet sparks. "You'll not deliver me to Whitehall like a calf to the market!"

With one swift movement, he silenced her by lifting her off her feet. He tossed her over his broad shoulder and started up the stairs. Her head lay against the hard muscles of his back, her dark hair cascading about her face in heavy silken waves.

Her mouth went dry, and she fought to draw her breath. She had escaped Tobias Abernathy only to fall prisoner to this man, a hard-eyed, arrogant stranger who might do as he wished with her. No one would dare to interfere on her behalf. She had seen how the landlord and his guests had reacted at the mere mention of the Grenville name.

Her first instinct was to struggle against Dirk's powerful grip. Common sense told her that it would be wiser to save her strength until she might use it to some purpose.

He had reached the top of the stairs, and now he was striding along the dimly lit hallway. With her face pressed against his doublet, she breathed in his scent—a blending of warm velvet, horseflesh, and his own potent masculinity.

He paused only long enough to kick open a heavy door. She caught a brief glimpse of the large chamber, aglow with candlelight. A moment later, she gave a cry of indignation as he tossed her onto the wide, red-curtained bed.

Raising herself to a sitting position, she brushed her tangled hair back from her face. Her eyes moved to the stone hearth with its blazing fire, then to the table before it. Steam rose from the wooden trenchers, giving forth the delicious promise of quail, venison, roasted apples and onions, and fig pudding. Her mouth watered and her insides contracted with hunger.

After she'd spent weeks sleeping in the wagon, trying to satisfy her healthy appetite with bread, cheese, and watery stew,

24

Dirk's warm chamber, with its soft bed and lavishly spread table, was a paradise. If only Papa and the others could share such luxury.

Then she caught Dirk's eyes flicking over her torn skirt, which had fallen open to reveal her long, shapely legs. She glared at him, and quickly covered herself with the tattered cloth as best she could. Her roving life during the past few years had left her with no high opinion of men. It was likely that Dirk had rescued her from the landlord because he meant to bed her himself.

What else could she have expected? A girl who traveled with a troupe of players was fair game for any man; and no doubt her bawdy ballads had convinced him that she was a free-and-easy wench who would be his for the taking. Maybe he thought she'd be grateful that he had spared her the landlord's crude embraces.

He started to unbuckle his sword belt. Melora's eyes widened, and she froze, like a deer confronted by a hunter; then she moved swiftly to the far side of the bed and leaped to her feet. Her gaze shifted toward the chamber door.

"Stay where you are. Unless you'd rather share the landlord's chamber instead of mine."

"Certainly not!"

He inclined his head slightly. "Thank you for the compliment, my lady."

"It wasn't meant to be a compliment," she retorted. "As far as I am concerned, there's little to choose between you."

But she was lying, and she knew it. Even as she spoke, her breathing quickened. Heat stirred deep inside her, spreading through her body, tingling all the way to her fingertips. She was startled by the tumult he had aroused in her with no more than a glance.

"I want to join my father in the stable loft." To her dismay, her voice sounded unsteady.

"You will stay here as long as I wish it."

He turned a hard, searching look on her, his dark, gold-flecked eyes probing deeply. "Is that actor fellow in the stable really your father?"

"Of course he is." Her voice shook with indignation. "Why would I lie about—"

"Maybe you hope to fend off overeager males by pretending to be the sheltered little virgin, under her father's protection."

"Edmund Standish is my father! And I am a—" She felt her skin go hot, from the top of her low-cut bodice to the roots of her hair. Her cheeks burned crimson under his searching stare.

"A virgin," he said softly. "Even better than I'd hoped."

Bronwen had told her that some men took special pleasure in deflowering a maid. Was Dirk one of them?

"Queen Anne demands that her young ladies-in-waiting be virtuous." His mouth twisted in a brief smile. "Of course, most of them learn to keep up the appearance of chastity, while taking their pleasures discreetly. Whitehall Palace has many out-of-the-way chambers and hidden corners—as you'll discover when you learn your way around the court, Lady Rosalind."

Melora stared at him. He seemed sane enough, but until she was more certain, she must use caution in dealing with him.

"I am *not* your cousin. I have *not* been summoned to court by the queen." She spoke quietly but firmly, as if to a fractious child.

"You gave a most convincing performance downstairs." A smile crossed his lips. "Indeed, I've seldom seen better on the London stage."

"That's as may be." The familiar resentment surged through her. "But you'll never have a chance to see me on the London stage. And all because of a ridiculous, unjust law that forbids women to act in public."

Dirk threw back his head and laughed. It was not the laughter of a madman, Melora would have sworn to that. "I agree that the law's unjust, Mistress Standish. By the way, what is your given name?"

She pressed her lips together in stubborn silence.

His eyes moved over her, lingering appreciatively on the thrust of her enticing young breasts against the worn bodice, the curves of her rounded thighs beneath her tattered skirt. Then he looked toward the bed. "Under the circumstances, there's no need for formality."

Best to humor him, she told herself. "My name's Melora."

He cupped her chin in his hand, tilting her face upward. What was he seeking there? A shiver ran through her.

She took a deep breath as she tried to prepare herself for the moment when he would carry her to the bed. She'd heard the bawdy talk of the women at the fairs and marketplaces. When she had questioned Bronwen, the Welshwoman had explained in blunt, honest words what happened between a man and woman in the dark.

But this was different. Soon she might be lying naked beside this dark-eyed, sun-bronzed stranger, his strong hands moving over her, exploring her body, stroking her skin, probing each curve and crevice as it pleased him. She shrank inwardly, not daring to imagine how it would feel to bear the weight of his broad chest and well-muscled flanks . . . to part her thighs to receive the hard, searing thrust of his manhood . . .

Fear threatened to engulf her, but she fought against it with all her strength. She still might manage to get away, if only she could play for time.

"The landlord promised me a dinner," she said quickly. "I've not eaten since morning."

"And little enough then, I'd wager." He took her arm, led her to the table, then drew out a chair for her. "Will you do me the honor of dining with me, Melora?"

Her knees trembled as she sank gratefully into the high-backed chair. He took a seat at the other end of the table, and lifted the cover from one of the trenchers.

She eyed the golden-brown quail hungrily, then hesitated. "I should like a plate."

"I wasn't expecting a dinner companion." He passed her his own plate. "I'll make do with one of these other trenchers." He

27

pulled a wooden platter to him, pushed aside the heap of roasted apples that filled its hollowed-out center, and helped himself to a thick slice of venison.

Melora lifted a quail onto the plate with a large, double-pronged serving fork. He handed her his knife, then drew a jeweled dagger from his belt. Long and sharp enough for him to wield as a weapon, it could also serve as a table utensil.

Hungry though she was, Melora restrained her avid appetite. She broke off a wing from the quail, nibbled it daintily. She caught Dirk's look of surprise. Had he expected her to tear at her food like a starving animal? Her delicate features hardened. Dirk Grenville was a gentleman and probably had little respect for the lower orders.

He filled the single goblet with hot mulled wine from the steaming pewter bowl. "We'll share this," he said.

He handed her the goblet. The mixture of Burgundy wine, laced with brandy and spiced with cinnamon and cloves, stirred a delicious glow inside her. All her taut muscles relaxed, right down to her toes. She was feeling a trifle light-headed.

Dirk reached out. "My turn now. We'll make it a loving-cup." He drank, passed the goblet to her again, then moved his chair back from the table, his eyes fixed upon her.

"Must you watch me like a—a tomcat, stalking his prey?"

"Your pardon, my lady." His dark brows drew together in a puzzled frown. "You do have the manners of a lady; you speak like one. Yet you travel the countryside in a broken-down wagon pulled by that sway-backed nag."

"How can you possibly know what sort of wagon we—"

"I caught a glimpse of you and your companions back in the ravine," he interrupted. "You were singing a bewitching ballad there, altogether different from those verses you sang in the taproom. Little wonder the landlord tried to drag you up to his chamber."

"I choose my songs to suit my audience. I'm sorry if I offended your delicate sensibilities."

"I've heard such ballads sung before. But never by a girl with

28

the bearing of a gentlewoman and the face of—" All at once, he found himself at a loss for words. He'd sound addlepated, indeed, if he were to say that when he'd first seen her, he had thought of dryads, of wood-nymphs; of all such fanciful creatures from half-forgotten legends.

Deliberately, he turned the conversation to more mundane matters. "You were half-starved when you sat down at the table, yet you ate as carefully as any lady in the king's dining hall."

He stood up and strode to her side. "I wish to know more about you." It was not a polite request, but a command. "Who is your father? A juggler, perhaps? Or a rope walker?"

"Edmund Standish is a great actor." Her voice shook with indignation.

"Yet the two of you travel the roads with a bear leader, a dwarf, and a witch."

"Bronwen's no witch. She is a wise woman who reads the future in the rune stones. She can see a man's fate in the cards, too—or in the palm of his hand."

"To the devil with Bronwen. It's you and your father I must know more about."

She fought down the hot resentment that rose inside her. So long as she could keep Dirk Grenville talking, she would be able to delay the moment when she would have to choose whether or not to lie with him.

Quickly, she began telling him of those happier days when her father had been the actor-manager of Lord Wilmot's Men. As she spoke, Dirk paced before the fire, pausing from time to time to look down at her with his disconcerting stare.

Her voice shook slightly as she told him of her mother's death from lung fever. "Papa was terribly ill, too, and though he recovered, he did not regain his strength. He has never been really well, not since my mother died. He loved her dearly."

Her father's illness had left him with a bad cough and a low fever. He had been grateful when Magnus Verney, one of the players in his troupe, had offered to take his place onstage.

29

"Magnus Verney always grudged Papa his success—but my father never imagined how jealous Verney was, how far the man would go to replace him as leading actor and manager of the company." Even now, she felt a stab of anger as she went on to tell Dirk of the catastrophic performance that had put an end to Edmund Standish's career on the London stage.

Lord Wilmot had sent an message to her father ordering him to present a new drama, a command performance at court, where the aged Queen Elizabeth was to honor the troupe with her presence. His lordship had insisted that no one but Edmund Standish play the leading role. Verney had taken her father to a tavern before the performance, saying that a cup of good wine would ease his lingering cough and raise his spirits.

Dirk interrupted with a mirthless laugh. "Verney made sure your father was in no condition to go on that evening, I'd wager."

"My father's performance was—a disaster. He missed his cues, forgot his lines. He stumbled over one of the props and fell down. Lord Wilmot was furious. That highborn popinjay felt that my father's failure reflected upon his own reputation as a patron of the stage."

"And so his lordship tossed your father out," said Dirk.

Melora nodded. "No other courtier would offer him patronage after that. There was nothing to do but take to the roads."

"And he dragged you with him?"

"I wanted to be with him. Besides, we had no relatives in London to offer me a home."

Dirk studied her in silence, strode to her side, and pulled her to her feet. She could delay no longer. If she refused to share his bed, what then?

Once more, his dark eyes traced her features carefully. She clamped her teeth together, determined to conceal her fear. "You do bear a resemblance to Rosalind." His words took her by surprise. "The same square chin," he went on thoughtfully. "Even the same little cleft right here." He touched her chin lightly.

"Black hair, thick and glossy. The eyes aren't quite right. Hers are azure. Yours are darker, violet, I'd say. An unusual shade. And tilted at the corners."

Why should it matter to him whether or not she looked like his cousin? If he went on this way much longer, Melora was sure she would scream.

"You should do," he said. "Yes, it's quite possible you will suit my purpose."

His purpose? What was he talking about?

It was possible that Dirk Grenville, although outwardly sane, might be afflicted with some hidden mania. What would he do to her, once he got her into bed? She had to shake off the lingering effects of the wine, to ignore her rising panic and try to think calmly.

If she refused to lie with him, perhaps he mightn't take her by force. But he would ride off at daybreak, leaving her to face the wrath of the landlord. And when Tobias Abernathy discovered he had been deceived, that she was no kin to Dirk Grenville, his fury would explode. He'd hand her over to the constable, along with her father and the rest of the troupe.

Visions of the branding iron, the slash of the jailor's whip, sent waves of terror sweeping through her. Even if she could bear such agonizing punishment, her father could not.

She drew a deep breath, and sought some small measure of reassurance. Dirk was completely unpredictable, frightening in his swift changes of mood—but he wasn't a raving madman. Whatever demands he might make of her there in the wide, curtained bed, he would be done with her by morning. He'd go on his way to London, and she'd be free.

And what then? Her mind began to race. If she hoped to convince the landlord that she was Rosalind Grenville, she would have to ride out with Dirk tomorrow. Perhaps if she pleased him tonight, he would agree to take her away with him at dawn, and leave her on the road a few miles from the Leaping Stag. Then she'd get word to her father, telling him where to find her. One night with Dirk, and afterward, she'd put all memory of him from her mind.

She waited for him to lift her and carry her to the bed. Instead, he moved away from her. "Walk across the chamber, as far as the door. Then back here to me."

Too surprised to question him, she forced herself to obey.

"No, not like a marionette on strings. Move with dignity. Hold your head high."

What else would he ask of her, even before he got her into bed? And when she lay naked beneath him . . . No, she wouldn't allow herself to think about that.

She walked to the door and back again. He rewarded her with a nod of approval. Then he spoke abruptly. "You boasted that you could act, given the chance. Prove it to me."

"You mean—right now?"

"Surely you can remember a few lines from one of the plays your father's troupe performed."

His challenge swept aside her fears. "I can speak parts from the works of Will Shakespeare, Beaumont, Fletcher, Thomas Kyd—"

He folded his arms across his chest and leaned against the bedpost. "I am waiting."

For one instant, her mind went blank. Then she heard herself speaking the first words that came to her.

> *Oh, you beast!*
> *Oh, faithless coward! Oh, dishonest wretch!*
> *Will thou be made a man out of my vice?*

She knew by heart this speech from Master Shakespeare's play *Measure for Measure,* and it served as an outlet for her mounting indignation.

> *Take my defiance!*
> *Die! Perish!*

"You've proved your claim," Dirk interrupted. He reached out and drew her to him. She felt the hard pressure of his thighs against her legs, and she could no longer restrain herself. "Bronwen didn't tell me a man with fire in his loins would ask so much before bedding a girl for a night. Shall I dance for you as well, my lord?"

Her indignation overpowered her fear. "Take me to bed, if you must. I've never lain with a man—but I'll try to satisfy your desires, however outrageous they may be. Only—" her voice rose shrilly, "Only stop this damn mummery, Dirk Grenville!"

"Have I asked you to lie with me?" A slight smile tugged at the corners of his lips.

"Not in so many words, but I—you certainly—"

"You have beauty of a sort, I'll not deny it. But I have no designs on your well-guarded virginity."

She tried to collect her whirling thoughts. "You expect me to believe that you'll share your bed with me tonight and never touch me?"

He laughed softly. "Perhaps I shall be tempted. But you'll have the bed to yourself, I give you my word on that."

"And tomorrow?"

"You heard what I told the landlord. We'll ride for London together at dawn."

"But why should you—what do you want with me?"

There was no trace of laughter in his voice now. "I promised King James that I would return to court with my cousin Rosalind."

"And she has refused to go with you." Little wonder, Melora thought. What girl would trust herself to a man like this one, rational one moment, mad as a Bedlamite the next?

"Let us say that because of certain unforeseen circumstances, Rosalind's unable to serve as the queen's lady-in-waiting. That is why you will take her place."

This wasn't happening. Fear, exhaustion, and the effects of the strong wine had addled her wits. Or he was still playing his outlandish games with her. But when he spoke again, the level look in his dark, gold-flecked eyes told her that this was no game.

33

"From the moment we leave this chamber tomorrow, you will no longer be Melora Standish. You will be Lady Rosalind Grenville, daughter to Sir Nicholas and Lady Jessamyn Grenville. And you will wait upon Queen Anne at Whitehall, for as long as your services are required."

Chapter Three

Melora drew her frayed shawl about her more tightly, and followed Dirk out of the inn and across the stable yard. Although the rain had ceased over an hour ago, the dawn wind still blew down from the north, carrying a raw, penetrating chill, a promise of early winter. It ruffled her dark hair and tugged at her torn skirt, even as she picked her way between the puddles left by last night's storm.

"That rag will do little to keep you warm," Dirk said. He removed his heavy cloak, draped it over her shoulders, and fastened the jeweled clasp beneath her chin. She felt a swift current of sensation move through her, for the fine garment held the warmth of his body, the male scent of him. Bewildered by her disturbing response, she drew a deep, steadying breath. Then she quickened her pace to keep up with him. The cloak was far too long for her, and she had to hold it up with one hand so that the hem would not drag in the mud.

As they neared the stable, she heard the whinnying of the horses, the stamp of hooves, and the voices of the hostlers, who were already hard at work, feeding and currying the beasts. "I hope you have some skill in riding," Dirk said. "We've many miles to cover before we reach London."

But Melora stopped where she was and turned to look up at him, her jaw set at a stubborn angle.

"We're not leaving yet," she said. She hoped she sounded

more self-assured than she felt. "If I am to go with you to London, we must strike a bargain here and now."

"You are scarcely in a position to bargain, my lady. Or have you forgotten what awaits you if you remain behind?" He gave a short, mirthless laugh.

She forced herself meet Dirk's hard gaze. "I've not forgotten."

She flinched beneath the folds of the heavy cloak, as if she could already feel the jailer's whip cutting into her bare flesh, the heat of the branding iron burning into her smooth white shoulder.

Her father could not defend her now, and her friends were equally powerless before the law. It would not matter that she had struck the innkeeper only in self-defense. The local magistrate would be sure to take the word of Tobias Abernathy over that of a traveling singer.

But she must not let Dirk see her fear. She had to keep up a bold front, no matter how great an effort it took.

"From what you said, Master Grenville, you have need of my services in London."

"You could be useful to me," he conceded. "If you are as quick-witted as you seemed last night. And if you know how to obey orders."

"My wits are as keen as your own," she told him. "And I have already proved my acting skills to your satisfaction, haven't I?"

She caught the faint gleam of approval in his eyes. "You have courage even when you're cornered," he went on. "A distinct flair for mimicking your betters. And you will follow my orders, if you know what's good for you."

Melora nodded, dropping her lids to hide her swift flare of anger at his last remark.

"Then speak out, my lady, and quickly. What are these your terms of yours?"

"First, my father is to remain here, warmly housed and well

fed, until he has recovered from his fever and may take to the road again."

"Go on," he urged.

"Bronwen will remain here to care for him. She knows much of herbs and nostrums. But if her potions do not help him, you will leave enough coins to pay a physician's fee."

"Is that all?"

"The others in our troupe must be fed and lodged, until they are ready to move on."

Dirk's mouth curved in a half-smile. "That includes Caleb's bear, I suppose."

"Bruin works hard for his keep," she said.

"No doubt he does. All right, my lady. Your father and the rest of your troupe will be fed and sheltered at my expense." He held out his gloved hand. "My word on it."

She hesitated, then took his hand, feeling the strong fingers close about hers. The bargain was sealed and she would have to trust him to carry out his part. Forcing down whatever lingering doubts still nagged at her, she allowed Dirk to lead her inside the stable.

A moment later, Melora started at the sound of the landlord's harsh voice. "Master Grenville must be on his way by sunrise. Get moving, you good-for-nothing louts!"

Then, as Abernathy caught sight of Dirk and Melora, his tone changed instantly. "Master Grenville—my lady." He touched his forelock. "I trust you slept soundly. We don't often have the honor of serving such distinguished guests, but we do our best. The dinner—the wine—all was to your liking?" He gave them an ingratiating smile. Melora guessed that he was toting up the bill, deciding what extras he might add without incurring Dirk's displeasure.

The soiled bandage around the landlord's head reminded Melora of the blow she had dealt him yesterday evening. She kept her spine straight, her head high, as she tried to conceal her uneasiness. She was not out of danger yet. If, even now, Dirk were to expose her as an imposter, if he were to ride off without her, she and her father would find themselves in jail this very day, along with their friends.

"I've a fine gray gelding for the young lady. A swift mount, yet easy to handle," Abernathy was saying. "And a decent enough saddle." He glanced down doubtfully at Melora's small feet in their worn slippers. "There's a good bootmaker in Lamington. No doubt he can supply more suitable footgear."

"I'll see to it," Dirk interrupted. He turned to Melora. "Now, if you are quite ready, Cousin Rosalind."

"Not yet. I must speak with my—" She caught herself in time. "—With my friends before I go."

Dirk's mouth tightened in an impatient frown. Then he shrugged and helped Melora up the narrow ladder leading to the stable loft. The low, sloping roof had been carefully thatched, so that the straw underfoot had remained dry even through last night's fierce storm.

By the light of the lantern that hung from the oaken beam, Melora caught sight of her father's pallet. Bronwen and Osric had been keeping watch beside him. The dwarf hurried forward and cast a quick, searching glance at Dirk, then at Melora.

"My fa—" She corrected herself instantly. If she was to play the role of Dirk's cousin, she must begin to practice at once. "Master Standish—he rested well?" Melora asked anxiously.

"Better than he would have done in the wagon."

"And the landlord sent the broth as he promised?"

"He did. Good, nourishing stuff, it was. Master Standish drank most of it." Osric jerked his head in the direction of a cracked earthenware pitcher. "He took some ale, too. It eased the thirst from his fever."

"And you and Bronwen. You both supped your fill?"

"That we did, thanks to you, mistress." Osric glanced briefly at Dirk, then back at Melora, with a hint of sadness in his pale blue, deep-set eyes. Maybe the dwarf believed that she had given herself to the tall stranger in exchange for food and lodging, and protection from the punishment of the law.

Her cheeks grew hot. Would she have lain with Dirk last

38

night if he had demanded it? She forced her treacherous thoughts away from such dangerous ground, as she knelt beside her father.

"Master Edmund's not himself yet," Bronwen told her. "The fever's still working on him. But as soon as the sun's up, I will go find a bit of comfrey and a few shoots of sweet briar, if there's any growing hereabouts. I'll make him a fine, healing brew."

"Hot broth and sack posset will do him more good, I've no doubt," Dirk told the Welshwoman. "The landlord'll see he gets as much as he needs. Now, take yourselves off, both of you."

But Bronwen and Osric held their ground until Melora nodded; only then did they move to the far end of the loft. She was touched by their loyalty, and vowed that it should be well repaid.

Melora leaned closer, anxiously searching her father's face. As if sensing her presence, he opened his eyes and his fingers closed around her hand.

"What a fine cloak, poppet." His breathing was labored, and he brought the words forth with difficult.

"It was a gift," she assured him. "A token of appreciation for my singing." It was not uncommon for a prosperous member of an audience to show his approval with such a gift.

"The performance went well, then?"

She nodded. No need for her father to know what sort of guests she had been forced to entertain. Or of the blow she had struck the lecherous Abernathy.

Now he caught sight of Dirk, who stood beside the pallet, his booted feet planted apart. "This gentleman is not the innkeeper, surely?"

"This is Dirk Grenville. He wishes to engage my services. He wants me to—"

She broke off, then glanced up at Dirk. What did he want with her? Could he have been serious when he had spoken of bringing her to London to take the place of his cousin, Rosalind, to serve as lady-in-waiting to the queen? It was all too fantastic. Yet why else had he ordered a horse for her and led her out here to the stable at dawn?

How was she to explain Dirk Grenville's audacious scheme to her father when she scarcely believed it herself? While she was still seeking an answer, Dirk dropped to his haunches beside her father's pallet and spoke quietly, but with his usual self-assurance.

"I have need of your daughter, Master Standish. As soon as our horses are saddled, she will accompany me to London."

"To—London?" Her father raised himself, his eyes fever-bright, his bony frame taut beneath the blanket. "Melora, what is he talking about?"

"I am prepared to pay well for her services," Dirk went on calmly.

Color flared along her father's gaunt cheekbones. "My daughter's no trollop, to be hired by any passing stranger." A fit of coughing racked his lean frame.

Melora quickly poured a draught of ale from the earthen-ware pitcher into a dented cup, and held it to her father's lips, while Dirk steadied the older man so that he might drink.

"You do me an injustice, Master Standish," Dirk said. He waited until her father had drained the cup, then eased him down again. "I wish to engage your daughter as a performer," he went on. He spoke with the same courtesy he might have offered a gentleman of his own rank. "Last night, I was privileged to hear her singing in the taproom."

Her father shook his head. "Taproom of an inn—no place for Melora."

"I agree," Dirk said. "She is gifted with a most enchanting voice, and is skilled at playing the lute. She should be allowed to display her talents where they will be properly appreciated."

"But Melora's a child," her father protested. "For all the heavy burden she's had to carry these past weeks—I cannot allow her to go to London without my protection."

"Her performance will add luster to the Christmas festivities at Whitehall Palace."

"Whitehall Palace!" Her father stared at Dirk in disbelief. "Melora is to perform before his Majesty and Queen Anne?"

"With your consent. King James means to entertain his guests with a splendid masque."

"Is it a new custom that hired performers should appear in his court masques?"

For an instant, Dirk hesitated, then went on quickly. "The court ladies will lend their talents, as always. But not one of them is as gifted as your daughter."

Standish nodded. "She comes by her talents naturally. And not only through me. Her mother was a great beauty—much admired in the theaters of Paris . . ."

Dirk followed up his advantage swiftly. "Melora will do you both credit," he said. "And have no fear. She will treated with the respect due the daughter of the illustrious Edmund Standish."

Melora saw the proud memories stir to life in her father's eyes. When he spoke, his voice rang with a trace of his former vitality. "There are those who remember my performances in London, even now?"

"Talent such as yours is not quickly forgotten," Dirk assured him.

Her father nodded, then sank back against the pallet. "This damned fever—a passing indisposition. Once I have recovered, I shall return to London. Find a new patron—organize another company. We shall have a great playhouse, in Southwark, or Moorfields . . ." He went on, creating his vision of a brilliant future, oblivious to his surroundings. "Splendid costumes— taffeta—velvet—the best scene painters—"

Melora stroked his cheek. "Hush, Father. You'll have your theater. But first you must get your strength back."

"And your daughter's services will provide you with all you require," Dirk said. "Has she your permission to leave for London, under my protection?"

Edmund Standish turned to his daughter. "It is for you to say, poppet."

Melora was sure that if her father had been in full command of his senses he would have questioned Dirk more closely. But the fever kept him dazed, drifting in and out of consciousness. Perhaps even now he was seeing a vision of the splendid future that lay ahead for him, once he returned to the London stage.

She shot a suspicious look at Dirk Grenville. What did he really want of her? He had said nothing to her father about using her to impersonate Lady Rosalind; to serve as lady-in-waiting to Queen Anne. Instead, he had offered a far more plausible excuse for taking her to London.

Her father had taken Dirk at his word, but she was still racked with uncertainty. Dirk was a stranger to her, after all. Why should she trust him?

And yet he had kept at least one promise: he had not tried to share her bed. Instead, he had slept in the chair before the fire.

But what might he demand once she was far from her father and her friends? It was a long way to London, and they would be forced to stop for the night before they reached their destination.

Her lips tightened as she reminded herself that she had more to worry about than guarding her virginity. She tried to put her thoughts into a semblance of order. Why had he given her one reason and her father another, to explain their trip to London together? If his only purpose was to have her perform in the Christmas festivities, why had he talked of passing her off as his cousin?

Rising to her feet, Melora crossed the length of the loft to the far end, where Bronwen and the dwarf crouched on the straw.

"Stay here with my father until he is well again. Your food and lodging will be paid for."

Osric cast a knowing glance at Dirk. "Our humble thanks for your generosity, sir."

Melora still hesitated. Was she making the right choice?

Once she and Dirk had ridden off together, that greedy rogue of a landlord might keep the money and turn her father, Bronwen, and Osric out on the road. She tried to reassure herself that Abernathy stood too much in awe of the Grenvilles to risk cheating any of them. If only there were some way she might get word of her father, when she was far away, in London.

"Come along," Dirk urged impatiently. He jerked his head toward the shuttered square that served as a window. Through the wooden slats, the first rays of the sun already slanted down on the straw. "I've no more time to waste."

"Not so quickly, sir," Bronwen said. She took the pouch of rune stones in her hand, shook it, then whipped open the strings. The stones fell to the straw, where the narrow bars of light picked out their curious markings.

"Save your mummery for Bartholemew Fair," Dirk growled, but she paid him no heed.

"We should have the cauldron and the candles," the old woman said, shaking her head slightly. "But since your fine gentleman is so eager to set forth, we will make do with the stones."

"A man can shape his own future, if he knows what he wants and is willing to take what risks he must to reach his goal," Dirk told her.

"Have you found it to be so, sir?" Bronwen's laugh was soft and melodious, like that of a far younger woman. "Then how does it happen that you journeyed this far north, only to find your plans thwarted by events you could not have foreseen?" She stared at the nearest stone. "The unexpected wedding of a pretty young noblewoman. Your kinswoman, I believe."

Dirk started, and fought back the primitive fear that stirred in the depths of his consciousness.

"And was it not by chance that you heard Melora singing over the sound of the storm? What made you stop to listen?"

"By all the powers of darkness, how could you know?" His eyes hardened. "His majesty has decreed severe punishment for witchcraft."

43

"I am no witch," the Welshwoman told him calmly. "I do but follow the teachings of my mother, and her mother before her. They, too, could sometimes see the future."

"Then tell me, Bronwen," Melora urged. "Shall I trust myself to Master Grenville's protection? If I ride with him to London—"

"You believe in this foolery, Melora?" Dirk demanded. But even as he spoke, he could not take his eyes from the rune stones.

Bronwen's long, bony finger traced the markings on one of them. "The Great Mother will protect you in your travels, young mistress. Rhiannon, the warrior maiden, will ride before you on her great white steed. Both will give you strength and courage. And you will have great need of them, for you are setting out on a perilous path . . ."

Melora remained motionless, hypnotized by the slow, measured tone, the invocation of the ancient, half-forgotten deities that had been worshipped by Bronwen's people, long ago.

"You go to a royal hall where danger holds court, where deception lies coiled in the shadows, like a serpent," the voice went on. "Your eyes will be dazzled by the light of a thousand candles, but you must watch the darkness beyond . . ."

Dirk's lean, hard-muscled body tensed. He knew all too well the ruthless struggle for power that was a part of daily life in the court of King James. But he played for high stakes, and now this dark-haired, violet-eyed girl had become necessary to his plan.

His voice was hard-edged as he interrupted the Welshwoman. "Melora and I have made our bargain. I mean to see that she keeps her part of it. She will be well paid for her services."

"She may trust you to pay what you have promised," Bronwen said calmly. "You will be generous enough in providing for Master Edmund, and the rest of us. But the risk will be hers. Should she not know what may await her in London . . . in the shadowed corridors where all is not as it seems . . ."

"Enough, you croaking hag!"

It was as if Bronwen had not heard him. She bent over the stones again, tracing the arcane lettering upon them, nodding from time to time. Then, all at once, she drew a sharp breath and fixed her gaze on Melora. "The night of the winter solstice." Her wrinkled hand closed around the girl's slender wrist.

"The longest night of the year . . . the night when the dark powers seek ascendancy over all mankind. You will be far away by then. There will be those who seek to do you great harm. Guard yourself well on the night of the solstice, Mistress Melora . . ."

"Hold your tongue! I'll not warn you again." Dirk's voice was hard with anger. He had too much at stake to allow the old woman to terrorize Melora with her senseless maundering.

"No need for threats, Master Grenville. Melora will go with you." Even as she spoke, Bronwen gathered up her rune stones, slid them back into the pouch, and tied the strings. Then she rose to her feet with a swift, graceful movement that belied her white hair and her lined face.

"We will care for your father," she assured Melora. "All that may be done to restore him, we will do. Trust us." She touched Melora's cheek lightly in a gesture of farewell.

The autumn sunlight was already gilding the rooftop when Melora, mounted on her gray gelding, rode out with Dirk. She drew rein briefly, as she caught sight of Caleb, who had emerged from the shed, leading Bruin by his heavy iron chain. She longed to take proper leave of the burly bear leader, but Dirk was already spurring his stallion into a canter. She raised her arm and waved goodbye to Caleb.

She longed for a glance, a nod of reassurance from Dirk. She bent low in the saddle, urging her mount forward. But even as she matched her pace to her companion's, she saw that his eyes were fixed on the road that led from the bleak, furze-covered hills of the borderlands southward to the teeming city of London.

Chapter Four

The manor house, with its magnificent stone facade topped by six crested towers, was set amid the smooth green expanse of the wide park. The late-afternoon sun struck sparks from the mullioned windows; the golden light lingered on the intricate stonework design of the towers. It gilded the leaves of the ancient oaks and beeches surrounding the house, and glittered over the smooth surface of a pond, where a flock of regal white swans glided by.

Dirk led the way up the wide drive, and slowed his horse to a walk. Melora brought her gray gelding up beside him, and tilted her head back to get a closer look at the mansion.

This was the third day of their journey. Until now, Dirk had set a hard pace, never stopping until the darkness had forced them to take shelter at the nearest inn. Yet now, when they had already reached Hertfordshire, no more than twenty miles from London, he halted, and said, "We'll stop here for the night."

Melora, although surprised, gave a small sigh of relief. Her father had provided her with riding lessons during those prosperous days when he had been one of the most celebrated actor-managers in London. Riding was a necessary accomplishment for the well-bred young lady, as were dancing the sarabande and playing the lute and the virginal.

But coming down from Northumberland, Dirk had ridden as if pursued by unseen demons, and after the first few hours on

47

the road, Melora's muscles had begun to throb in protest. The boots he had bought for her in the shop back in Lamington had been made for a larger foot; even when stuffed with rags at the toes, they had not fitted her snugly.

Long before they had dismounted at a roadside inn, her thighs and calves had protested against the unfamiliar strain, while the ache in her rump had given way to merciful numbness.

Although she had grown more accustomed to the pace during the next three days of their journey, it had been rough going all the way. They had traveled south over rutted roads, some of them little more than cattle paths, through marshy woods, and across rickety bridges.

Tormented by her sore muscles, brooding over her father's illness, fearful of what might await her when she and Dirk finally reached Whitehall, Melora had given little thought to her appearance. But now the stableboy who hurried down the elm-lined drive to take their horses gave her a glance of wide-eyed surprise. And who could blame him?

She felt the limp strands of her hair clinging to her forehead. Her face must have been splattered with traces of mud from the puddles along the road. Dirk's fine russet cloak covered the shabby bodice and torn skirt underneath, but once inside, she would have to remove the concealing garment. She flinched at the thought of how she would look to those who lived here at this splendid manor house.

But before she could protest, Dirk lifted her down from the grey gelding. Her legs were stiff, and she clung to him for a moment before she regained her balance. When he gripped her around the waist, she felt the hard strength of his tall, lean body beneath his close-fitting doublet of russet velvet and his linen shirt. He also wore fine Spanish leather boots. Although he, too, was disheveled by the swift, relentless pace of their journey, his fine clothes, his whole bearing, proclaimed him to be a gentleman.

"What house is this?" she asked uneasily.

48

"Netherwood's its name. It belongs to Pembroke."

"Pembroke?"

"William Herbert, Earl of Pembroke." He reached up, removed her canvas-wrapped lute from her saddlebag, and handed it to her. Then he took her arm and led her toward the front door. But she pulled back. "No, wait! We can't stay here tonight."

"I'd have thought you'd prefer it to those inns along the road. The beds will be far more comfortable, that's sure."

"You can't introduce me to the earl and his family as your cousin. Once I take off your cloak, I'll look like a—"

"A hedgerow drab."

She flinched at his bluntness. "Then how can you—"

"Pembroke's not here," he went on calmly. "He's at court in Whitehall. You'll have only the steward and his wife to deal with. And the underservants. They are too well trained to pass judgment on the appearance of Lady Rosalind Grenville."

She tried to draw reassurance from his words.

"And I promise you, my dear cousin, by the time we leave Netherwood, you'll look the equal of any of the court ladies."

"And how do you hope to manage that?"

He did not reply. Instead, he raised the massive iron knocker. It struck against the door with such a loud, metallic ring that the swans on the pond stretched their necks and beat the air with their powerful wings, while a flock of starlings took to the air from a nearby elm.

Melora fought back her impulse to turn and run back down the drive. Her fingers tightened on the canvas bag that held her lute.

The door swung open. Pembroke's steward, a plump, balding man in dark blue livery, stared at her and Dirk for an instant, then bowed and ushered them inside.

"Master Grenville. His lordship did not send word that you and—" His eyes flicked over Melora. "—and the lady would be arriving. I fear we are unprepared."

"Don't vex yourself, Haywood. Lady Rosalind is fatigued

from her journey," Dirk said. "I trust you and your good wife will be able to provide us with the necessities for tonight."

The steward peered out through the half-open door, and down the drive. "No doubt her ladyship's maid is on her way."

"My cousin is not traveling with her maid," Dirk told him. "Surely you have a serving wench or two who are suitably trained to attend her."

"Mistress Haywood will be honored to perform whatever services her ladyship requires," Haywood assured him. "The footmen will take her ladyship's baggage, and yours, up to the west wing."

"We carried no baggage," Dirk interrupted.

Haywood did not blink an eye. Dirk had been right, Melora thought: Pembroke's servants were far too well trained to ask questions of their master's guests.

Haywood led the way up a wide flight of stairs and into a high-ceilinged drawing room hung with Flemish tapestries. Quickly, he lit a fire in the marble fireplace, stirring the coals until the flames leaped up.

"May I take your cloak, your ladyship?"

Melora swallowed, shook her head. "I prefer to—keep it on."

Haywood kept his features carefully expressionless. After telling them that refreshments would be brought promptly, he bowed again and hurried off, plainly determined to do credit to his master, even at short notice.

"You won't be needing the cloak now," Dirk told her.

Before she could protest, he unfastened the clasp and removed the heavy garment. "Don't stand there, cringing like a frightened housemaid applying for a situation," he ordered brusquely. "And don't offer any excuses about your appearance to Mistress Haywood. Remember, you are a Grenville."

"But I'm not!"

He seized her by the shoulders, his fingers biting into her flesh. The gold flecks in his brown eyes took on a metallic glint. "Don't say that again. Not even when we're alone."

But they were alone no longer, for now Mistress Haywood

came bustling in, carrying a tray. Dirk kept his hold on Melora's shoulders. "Steady, my dear," he said smoothly, and now he was smiling down at her. "A little wine will restore your strength."

What a clever rogue he was, pretending that he was supporting her because she had been overcome with exhaustion from the journey. With his arm around her shoulders, he led her to the high-backed settle and drew her down beside him.

The steward's wife poured the wine and placed a plate of cakes before them, chattering all the while.

"The chambers in the west wing are being made ready," she told them. "The queen's chamber for you, my lady. And the one across the hall for you, sir. Shall you be wanting supper in the small dining room?"

Dirk shook his head. "Her ladyship will dine in her chamber, Mistress Haywood." He turned and headed for the drawing-room door, then paused on the threshold. "I have business to attend to in the village. I will have my meal there."

The steward's wife curtsied. "We'll take good care of her ladyship," she assured him.

Melora stared at him, panic surging up inside her. What possible business could he have in the nearby village, immediately after their arrival? Before she could think of a way to detain him, he bade her good evening and departed.

Her palms went damp, and a trickle of perspiration traced its way between her breasts. She had thought she would not have to assume her role as Lady Rosalind until they reached court. Yet here she was, thrust out of the wings and onto the stage. She would have to rely on her as-yet-untested acting skills, her own quick wits, to give a convincing performance.

I'll never be able to go through with it . . . not without Dirk to back me up.

The queen's chamber had been so named, Mistress Haywood had explained, because Queen Elizabeth had spent a night there during her royal progress, years ago. But although it was nearly midnight, Melora lay beneath the downy silk-covered comforter, staring at the canopy above her.

Hours ago, two of Pembroke's serving wenches had helped her out of her torn gown and shabby underclothes. As Dirk had predicted, neither of them had shown the slightest surprise at seeing a lady dressed in this disgraceful fashion. No doubt there would be gossip aplenty below stairs, however.

Then Melora had let her worries slip away as she settled into a tub of hot water, and felt her taut, travel-sore muscles begin to relax. One of the wenches slathered her long, dark hair with castile soap. The other carried off Melora's clothes, and returned with a linen nightdress, lavishly trimmed with Venetian lace. Mistress Heywood rummaged through the tall carved-oak armoire and found a purple velvet robe and matching slippers.

"No doubt you'll be ready for bed early, after your long journey."

Even as the steward's wife spoke, she was busily brushing Melora's damp hair over her shoulders until the heavy, dark waves glowed in the firelight. "We must be sure your hair is thoroughly dry, my lady," she said. "We can't have you taking a chill."

Mistress Haywood's words, the concern in her voice, stirred a rush of memories. Melora's mother had spoken to her that way, when she had come in from play with wet slippers and damp clothes. Her mother had brushed her hair carefully, until every strand was dry and shining.

Tears stung Melora's eyelids. In spite of the hardships she had endured traveling with her father, the strain of the weeks after he had fallen ill, and she had taken on the responsibility of managing the troupe, she had not given way to weeping. She could not allow herself to give way now. She blinked and brushed the back of her hand across her eyes.

"There, now. What you need is good food and a night's rest to put you right, my dear," Mrs. Haywood told her. "Such a long, hard journey you must have had, and your feet bruised and swollen from those boots! I myself can't abide ill-fitting footgear." She gave Melora a comforting little pat on the arm. "I've a salve in the stillroom, my lady. With your permission, I'll rub a bit into your feet before you go to bed."

Melora nodded, afraid to trust herself to speak. Gratefully, she gave herself over to Mistress Haywood's maternal care.

But although Melora had dined well and climbed into bed early, she could not shake off her uneasiness. She needed to talk to Dirk before she could sleep, for there were still too many unanswered questions between them.

She shifted restlessly and her body stiffened at every sound: the crackling of a log in the fireplace; the tapping of a branch against one of the tall windows; the gruff hooting of an owl, as it wheeled through the autumn night, seeking its prey.

She sat up, her breath quickening. In the time they had traveled together, she had come to recognize Dirk's booted tread. And now at last she heard him striding down the hallway, stopping at the door across from hers.

She did not delay long enough to put on her robe or thrust her bare feet into her slippers, before she ran across the deep carpet, and flung open her chamber door.

"Dirk." Her voice was low but urgent.

He turned and looked down at her, his mouth curving in a faint smile. "I thought you'd be asleep by now."

"I can't sleep." Her voice shook slightly and her hand closed on his sleeve. "You must come inside."

"As you wish, Cousin Rosalind."

He allowed her to draw him into the firelit chamber, then paused, his eyes moving over her. He had called her "cousin," but she realized, with a tightening in the pit of her stomach, that he need not treat her with the respect he would have given the real Rosalind Grenville.

During the past two nights, although they had shared a single room, he had followed the precedent he had set at the Leaping

53

Stag. He had not attempted to get into her bed, but had stretched out on the floor, wrapped himself in whatever coarse blanket the innkeeper had provided, and gone off to sleep almost immediately.

But now she sensed the change in him. His gold-flecked eyes lingered on her, and she realized with a start that the borrowed nightdress was of sheerest linen. The firelight shone through the delicate weave, revealing the thrust of her firm breasts with their pointed rosy nipples, her flat belly, the dusky triangle of her womanhood. Quickly, she moved away from the fireplace.

"You've been well cared for, I see." He lifted a shining strand of her hair and ran it lightly between his thumb and fingers before letting it fall over her shoulder. She took a step back, but he was not ready to let her escape so easily. He advanced, then flicked at the lace ruffle that edged the bodice of her nightdress. "Most becoming." His hand brushed the curve of her breast, left bare by the low-cut neckline. The warmth of his touch against her skin sent a swift current racing through her.

Sternly, she forced herself to ignore her response, to remember why she had insisted that he come into her bedchamber.

"I must talk to you," she began, hoping he would not hear the slight tremor in her voice.

"You invited me into your chamber only for conversation? And here I was, thinking you might be restless, all alone in that fine, wide bed."

"Don't flatter yourself, Dirk Grenville." She glared at him. "I left the Leaping Stag with you because I could see no other way to save myself, and those who depended on me." She drew a deep breath, and her voice grew steadier. "But before we ride through the gates of London, I intend to know the real reason you're taking me to court."

The teasing golden lights flickered out, and his eyes went hard. His lips clamped down in a tight, thin line. For a moment she shrank inwardly. What weapons could she use against such a man?

54

Then she reminded herself that he had brought her this far because he needed her. But why?

"The night we met, you said I must pretend to be your cousin. But you gave my father a far different explanation. You told him I was to be no more than a hired performer for a court masque."

"Your father was ill, feverish. I had to put his mind at ease so he'd agree to allow you to leave with me."

"You lied to him."

"Not really," Dirk interrupted. "King James is determined to impress his court. He longs to outshine Queen Elizabeth with the splendor of his entertainments. It's likely you'll get a chance to appear in a Christmas masque along with the other ladies."

It was acceptable for highborn ladies to show themselves in a masque, whether at court or in a country manor house. But she was still not satisfied with his smooth explanation.

"Then why did you find it necessary to deceive Master Haywood and his wife?"

"I have my reasons. And you, sweeting, were able to carry off your role with conviction, even in those wretched rags you were wearing." He gave her a slight bow. "You're a skilled performer, indeed."

"But when I have to face King James—the queen—the whole court—" The prospect filled her with rising panic.

"You will play your part without a mistake. The stakes are too high for you to back out now." He was not flattering her. He was giving her a direct command. "You will serve as the queen's lady-in-waiting, for as long as I need you to."

"But why does it matter so much that I—"

"That Rosalind Grenville," he cut in.

"Rosalind Grenville, then. Why is it so important that your cousin act as lady-in-waiting to Queen Anne?"

"Because it will serve my purpose."

"To the devil with your purpose!" Melora's taut nerves were strained to the breaking point. "Maybe the name of Grenville will protect you, should their majesties discover our deception. But what about me?"

"You're afraid." His brown eyes challenged her to deny it.

"And why not?" Melora fought to control her rising anger. "There are surely courtiers who know the Grenvilles, their names, their family history. If I make a single slip—"

"You must make sure there are no slips."

"But I know nothing about your family. Does Rosalind have a brother, or a sister? If so, what are their names, how old are they?" She had to bite down hard on her lower lip to keep her mouth from trembling.

"That's why I chose to stop here, instead of riding directly on to London. Before we leave, you'll know all you'll need to know about the Grenvilles."

"You plan to tell me all about your family history in one day?"

"Two days, then. But no longer." She caught the impatience in his voice.

"I'll never be able to—"

"Losing your nerve?" His smile mocked her fear. "Can this be the bold piece who sang those bawdy ballads at the Leaping Stag? And nearly split Abernathy's thick pate with that tankard?"

"I'd have paid dearly enough, even for that, if you hadn't stepped in when you did." She felt as if an icy tide was swirling around her, engulfing her. "But to deceive the king himself!" The enormity of it threatened to sweep away every vestige of her self-control. "Only a fool or a madwoman would have no fear of the Tower. The rack—the thumbscrews—the—"

"The headsman's ax," Dirk finished obligingly. His words drove the color from her face. Her slender body went rigid beneath the linen folds of her nightgown.

"I saw a man's head—severed by the ax—impaled on a spike atop London Bridge. Papa said the man was a traitor who'd plotted against the queen—"

She had been a child then, on the way to the theater with her father. She had cried out in terror at the gruesome sight, and buried her face against his shoulder. He had spoken softly, trying to calm her, but the horror had etched itself into her consciousness.

Even now, a shudder ran through her at the memory. "The ravens had plucked out the man's eyes—there were only two empty sockets—"

Strong arms closed about her. For a moment, it was as if Papa held her again.

"Forgive me, sweeting. I didn't know." Not her father's voice, but Dirk's. She clung to him and his arms tightened about her. She did not try to draw away, but pressed her cheek against the hard muscles of his chest, like a frightened child seeking solace.

He cradled her in his embrace, then carried her to the bed. He sat down, holding her in his lap. His breath was warm against her face. He stroked her hair, as her father might have done.

"That happened years ago, during Elizabeth's reign," she heard Dirk saying.

"But King James lives in fear of treason, too," Melora reminded him. "Since Guy Fawkes and his followers tried to blow up parliament, his majesty thinks he sees traitors lurking in every corner. Even in the court itself."

"There is danger at Whitehall," Dirk interrupted. "Your witch woman, Bronwen, was right about that. And if the king is suspicious of those around him, who can blame him?"

"Yet you plan to bring me to court, to betray the king's trust."

"I have no designs on the life of his majesty. My future depends on doing all one man can to keep James and his consort on the throne."

For a moment her taut body began to relax, and she rested against him trustingly. But only for a moment. His tone, his reassuring touch, must not put her off her guard. She, an actor's

57

daughter, knew well enough that even a mediocre performer could feign sincerity on demand.

What real reason did she have to trust Dirk Grenville? She had known him for only a few days. He had lied to Abernathy, deceived her father, introduced her into Netherwood under false pretenses. He had admitted that he needed her to serve his own as yet undisclosed purpose.

She tried to draw away, but his arms tightened about her.

"If you do exactly as I say, no harm will come to you. I give you my word."

He was stroking her hair, his fingers moving slowly, sensuously. Then, pushing aside the dark, gleaming waves, he traced the long curve of her neck.

His hand cupped her breast. Through the sheer linen, she felt his palm moving, circling. Her nipple began to tingle, then harden. She made a soft moaning sound deep in her throat as his touch stirred a swift, answering response.

Moved by her own instinctive need, she dropped her head against his shoulder. He lifted her breast, his fingers curving around the white roundness, and bent his head.

He drew her nipple into his mouth. Warmth spread out in ripples, radiating to every part of her body.

She moved in his lap, then caught her breath, feeling his hardness under her rounded bottom.

"Let me go."

Even as she forced the words out, she knew how powerless she was. He had only to push her down on the bed, to hold her immobile beneath him, and thrust her thighs apart.

She tried to twist away, then heard him draw in his breath sharply. She sensed that the friction of her buttocks against him was stimulating his urgent need.

"Are you no different from Abernathy?" The words sprang unbidden to her lips. "Do you mean to take me against my will?"

With one swift movement, Dirk pushed her off his lap. She tumbled back across the bed. He got to his feet, his lean body rigid. His broad chest rose and fell under the tightness of his velvet doublet. Then, gradually, she saw the naked hunger in his eyes give way to icy self-control.

With shaking fingers, she arranged her nightdress so that it covered her breasts, then pulled the coverlet up to her shoulders.

"Forgive my lapse in manners, my lady. Now, with your permission, I'll take my leave."

"Not yet, Dirk."

"If you take pleasure in leading a man on, then playing the outraged virgin, you'll have to find a man who enjoys that kind of sport. One of Pembroke's footmen may still be somewhere about."

She flinched, then set her jaw. "This is no sport," she said. "If you want me to go on to Whitehall with you, you'll answer my questions before you leave this room."

His eyes narrowed and the skin drew tighter over his cheekbones. "Suppose I refuse?"

"Then you will have to tie me to this bed for the rest of the night. And drag me to the palace in fetters."

"I wouldn't hesitate, if it were necessary," he said. "But you will go to Whitehall with me of your own free will. You'll smile and curtsy to their majesties. You'll thank Queen Anne for doing you the honor of choosing you to be one of her ladies."

"And risk my neck for your mysterious purposes? Don't wager on it, Dirk Grenville."

"And if you break your bargain with me, what then? Do you mean to slip out while I sleep, and ride back to the Leaping Stag in that linen nightshift?"

Melora flinched under the cold mockery in his voice. For the first time she realized the strength of his hold over her. True, he had handed a bag of coins to Tobias Abernathy, as he had promised. But he had given her no money. She did not have the price of a meal of bread and cheese at the meanest wayside tavern.

And how was she to clothe herself for the return journey? No doubt Mistress Haywood had ordered one of the maids to burn her tattered garments.

In desperation, Melora struggled to force her whirling thoughts into some semblance of order. She could wait until Dirk was asleep, cover her nightdress with his cloak, and slip out of the house.

And then? How could she get the grey gelding out of the stable without waking Pembroke's hostlers? As for the horse, it did not belong to her. Dirk, if he chose, could have her pursued and arrested as a horse thief.

"You are beginning to see how useless it would be for you to try to break our bargain." His gold-flecked eyes challenged her while his lips curved in an ironic smile.

Still, she refused to admit defeat. She drew on the small, hard core of strength deep inside her.

Dirk Grenville could not force her to be a pawn in his dangerous scheme while he kept his own purpose hidden from her.

Chapter Five

For one reckless moment, Dirk was strongly tempted to tell Melora to go back to Northumberland. There was nothing to stop him from throwing her out of the house right now, clad in only her nightdress. Let her make her way back to the Leaping Stag as best she could.

She was trouble, and no mistake. Beneath her ladylike facade was a stubborn determination that matched his own. She might be afraid of him, but stronger than her fear was the unmistakable determination in her eyes, the firm set of her chin.

"We're close to London now," she reminded him. "There'll be plenty of farmers out on the road, bringing crops to market. I'll ask a ride of the first one I see." She leaned forward, as if preparing to spring from bed, and the coverlet slid down to her waist.

His gaze raked over the swell of her firm breasts, and a corner of his mouth turned up. "I don't doubt that any man will be eager to oblige you, dressed as you are."

"I'll wrap myself in a bedsheet and walk to London, if I must. But I'll get there without your help, Dirk Grenville."

"And once you're in London?"

"I'll play my lute and sing in a tavern to earn my keep."

He gripped the bedpost so hard that the carved wood bit into his palm. It was all he could do to keep from grabbing her by the shoulders and shaking her until her teeth rattled.

"Do you plan to entertain your audience with that ballad about the bonny cock?"

"A rooster! That's what it means. It's about a country maid and her pet rooster."

"I hope the tavern louts give you a chance to explain that, before they throw you on your back across the nearest table. Or maybe you think you will only find such crude behavior among the ruffians of Northumberland."

"My travels have taught me that there's little difference between a randy blacksmith and a drunken country squire." Her dark-lashed violet eyes taunted him. "Or a courtier in velvet, when the mood's on him."

He felt a tightening in his groin as he remembered her fragrant warmth, when he had held her a few moments ago. True, he had taken her in his arms only to comfort her, after she had shared the terror of her childhood memory. But the firm thrust of her breasts against his chest, the scent of her hair, had wrought a swift change of emotion. A searing hunger had gripped his loins and coursed through his whole body.

Even now, with the length of the bed between them, he searched her face, wanting to understand what lay behind her fine-boned features, her violet eyes.

Who was the real Melora Standish? The fey, otherworldly singer he had first seen in the mist-shrouded ravine? The bold vixen who had sung her bawdy ballad at the Leaping Stag, and creased the landlord's skull with a tankard?

Or a girl on the threshold of womanhood, innocent yet passionate, and still a virgin? He would swear to that . . .

He managed to wrench his thoughts away from such speculations. He had brought her this far because he had a need of her. A need that had nothing to do with her pliant young body, her silken skin. And he would get her to go the rest of the way to London with him, even if it meant revealing more about his plan than he wished to.

"I did not ask you to come with me because I lusted after you," he said. "London's full of pretty, ambitious young girls

62

who'd leap at the chance of playing the lady at court. But you are different, special."

She eyed him warily.

"You have the breeding and wit to serve my purpose."

"To help you curry favor at court? You'd have me risk my neck so that you might be rewarded with the title of First Lord of the Royal Bedchamber? Does it mean so much to you, to tie the ribbons of the king's taffeta tennis drawers?"

"To hell with the king's drawers!" he shot back. "I've no wish to remain at Whitehall one day longer than necessary. I'm going to set sail again for the New World. And this time, I won't be coming back."

"This time?"

Dirk's eyes were no longer fixed on her, but at some distant place, far beyond this firelit room. "I was not yet fifteen when I sailed with Sir Francis Drake," he said, and she heard the intensity in his tone.

"It is a new world," he went on. "No one who hasn't seen it can imagine those endless miles of untouched land, rivers teeming with fish, great forests filled with game. And none of it the property of the lord of the manor. All of it free for any man's taking."

Melora's eyes widened as she caught a glimpse of his vision. "And are there really savages who worship pagan gods? Who go about decked out in gold and precious gems?"

"There are. But I've no need of gems, and as for gold, I want only enough to pay for ships and supplies," he said, impatient at the interruption. "It is land I seek. Acres of land waiting to be cleared, rich soil to be planted with crops."

"There's land enough here in England," she said. "Your uncle owns a great estate in Northumberland, doesn't he?"

"My father was Uncle Nicholas's younger brother—he inherited no more than a horse and a sword." His lips tightened. "The sword he used to fight for the cause of Mary, Queen of Scots. And the horse he rode across the border, up into the

Highlands to find refuge, when Mary's cause was lost." A slash of resentment tore through him.

Sir Nicholas Grenville had never forgiven his brother for choosing the wrong side, not even after that disastrous choice had cost him his life. Dirk's uncle had grudgingly allowed the boy and his widowed mother refuge on his estate; but he had missed no opportunity to remind them that they should be grateful for the food they ate, the beds they slept in.

Dirk had stood it until he was nearly fifteen; then he had turned his back on his uncle's estate and gone to sea. And he had discovered a world in which a man could shape his own future.

"Does your uncle still blame you for your father's mistake?"

Melora's words brought him back abruptly to the present, to Pembroke's manor and this herb-scented bedchamber.

"He does. But even if he did not, his estate would go to his own son, Hugh."

"Rosalind has a brother? How old is he?"

"That's no concern of yours, since you lack the courage to keep your part of our bargain. You're heading for London on your own, to seek your fortune."

Her eyes wavered slightly.

He had her off balance now. Ruthlessly, he pressed his advantage. "No doubt you'll find a tavernkeeper who'll hire you. And if you make yourself agreeable to every taproom customer who wants you, you should earn a few extra coins."

She stiffened with indignation. Her lips parted, but he gave her no chance to interrupt. "You'll get along. But what about your father?"

Melora caught her breath and looked away.

"How long will he last, tramping the roads in winter, without you to care for him and keep up his spirits? He needs you, Melora. By early spring you could return to him, with a heavy pouch of gold. You could help him start over again, to hire a new company of players, to build a theater of his own."

Her eyes glowed at the bright picture he was painting. "My

father could do it. Oh, I know he could, if only he had the chance."

"If you believe that, then believe that I am offering him the only possible chance he'll ever have. A few months at White-hall, where you will be surrounded by every luxury. And then you'll be free to go."

Her eyes turned wary. "You will sail off to the New World. But what of me? Am I to stroll out of Whitehall without a word of explanation to the queen?"

"I will provide her majesty with a plausible excuse for taking you back to your doting parents in Northumberland."

"And my brother, Hugh," she reminded him, with a touch of irony. "We mustn't forget him. You've not yet told me his age."

"Hugh's fourteen."

"What's he like? A pale, bookish lad? Or sturdy and fond of sport? Obedient or rebellious?"

Dirk repressed a smile of triumph. His instincts about the girl had been right, after all. Her devotion to her father was stronger than her fear for her own safety. She would go through with her part of the bargain.

Melora's spirits rose as she and Dirk joined the jostling throng that surged over London Bridge and moved on into the teeming city. Although she not yet cast off her misgivings, she felt a stir of hope for the future. Her father had made a great name for himself only a few years ago. With her help, he would climb the heights again.

She sat erect in the saddle. Surely all who saw her riding at Dirk's side must believe that that she was a highborn lady. The breeze from the Thames ruffled the plumes of her jaunty blue hat and tugged at the folds of her matching cloak. Beneath the cloak, her midnight-blue riding gown sheathed each line of her body to perfection.

Now she knew the reason for Dirk's hasty departure from

Netherwood so soon after their arrival at the manor. He had set forth on a swift search for the most skilled seamstress in the vicinity, and had found her. The woman had arrived promptly the following morning, attended by her apprentices.

At Dirk's orders, Mistress Haywood had looted the cupboards of the bedrooms and attics for silk stockings, scented gloves, and fans; and for gowns of the finest velvet, taffeta, and silk. The dressmaker and her helpers had set about cutting and stitching, to refit the garments to Melora's slender young body.

"Won't the earl mind?" Melora had asked Dirk anxiously.

"Pembroke'll be only too pleased to oblige when I explain the circumstances. We share many mutual interests at court."

When her fittings were completed, he had taken her off to the drawing room, where he had trained her in her new role. He had made her go over and over the information about the family she would now claim as her own.

She had learned that Nicholas Grenville had a slightly crooked left arm, the result of a hunting accident. That Dirk's aunt, Jessamyn Grenville, had come from Cornwall, and had been affianced to Nicholas years ago, through the arrangements of Sir Richard Grenville, a member of the Cornwall branch of Dirk's family, and one of Queen Elizabeth's boldest naval heroes.

"Richard was one of the queen's favorites. A daring and successful sea raider. Both he and Nicholas supported Elizabeth's cause. If my father had chosen the winning side—"

"Why didn't he?" Melora interrupted. "Why did he support Mary of Scotland instead?"

"No doubt he was cursed with a streak of gallantry. I suppose he was moved by the sad plight of Mary, imprisoned by Elizabeth for all those years."

"But now, with Mary's son on the throne, surely your father's loyalty should be rewarded."

"I intend it should be," Dirk had assured her. "Now, back to your lessons, sweeting."

He might call her "sweeting," but he was a strict tutor who

reviewed those lessons over and over, and sternly corrected her smallest errors.

"When I'm presented at court, am I to mention my musical skills?" she had asked.

"Not at once. But when you take up residence in the queen's chambers, be sure that she hears you singing, and playing your lute. Be modest, but if she praises you—and she will—tell her you will be only too pleased to entertain her. None of her other ladies has any special talent in music. The winter afternoons at Whitehall can grow tedious."

He had given Melora a teasing grin. "No doubt you have better sense than to favor her with one of those taproom ballads." His eyes grew thoughtful. "I recall a song you sang about a maid whose lover had gone far away. *'He's coming back, though he ride a thousand miles.'*"

"I know many more, equally touching and proper enough for the queen and her ladies."

"The queen's proper enough," he had said, "but as for her ladies, most are as eager for a quick tumble as any taproom wench."

Now, as they left the bridge, Dirk turned to Melora and nodded with approval. "You'll do," he said.

She stiffened in the saddle. Damn the man's arrogance. By his look, his tone, he might have been buying a new sword, or a hunting hound. She fixed her eyes on the crowd ahead of them, and her gloved hands tightened on the reins.

It was no easy task for her to guide the gray gelding through the narrow, crowded streets. Orange sellers, vendors of eel pie, women hawking fresh milk, flowers, vegetables, cheap trinkets, called out to prospective customers. A carter, his swaying wagon dangerously overloaded, jerked his horse to a stop, and climbed down to retrieve a heavy crate that had fallen to the cobblestones. Pewter cups and plates went rolling in all directions.

67

Melora's horse shied, then reared, nearly unseating her. Dirk caught hold of her reins, and spoke soothingly to the frightened beast.

Ragged mudlarks, homeless children who managed to survive on London's streets, grinned at the carter's predicament. The carter ignored them, until one of the urchins, bolder than the rest, sidled forward, his sharp eyes fixed on a burnished cup. The outraged carter loosed a stream of hair-raising oaths, and seized his whip. He struck out, but the mudlark dodged away, unscathed.

"We'll head for the Strand," Dirk told Melora. "I'll hire a boat there, to take us on to Whitehall."

She nodded, but her attention had shifted to a juggler, in a threadbare shirt of blue and orange. Torn hose covered his skinny legs.

He tossed the brightly painted wooden balls in the air and caught them again. His lips were set in a determined grin, but Melora saw him shiver.

The autumn breeze from the river felt good to her, clad as she was in a heavy velvet gown and warm cloak; but she knew from experience that the juggler, in his thin garb, must be chilled to the bone.

"Dirk! See that juggler in front of the tavern? Throw him a coin, please."

His gold-flecked eyes mocked her. "We'll see a score like him before we reach the landing. Along with acrobats, bear leaders, and street singers."

"But he looks half-starved. How can he show his skill, when his fingers are stiff with cold? A penny will buy him a hot pie and sup of ale."

Dirk shrugged, reached into his cloak, and tossed the juggler a few small coins. With incredible dexterity, the man dropped the wooden balls into his pocket, caught the coins before the mudlarks could get them, and doffed his shabby peaked hat in Dirk's direction. Then he hurried into the tavern.

Dirk eyed her with amusement. "How little it takes, sweeting, to change you from a ragtag tavern singer into a fine lady. A borrowed cloak and gown, a plumed hat, and behold—Lady Bountiful."

Her gloved hand itched with the sudden need to strike out at him, to wipe that mocking grin from his face. "That juggler reminded me of Osric. Even after a whole day without a bite to eat, he would keep up a brave front, while he did his somersaults in a muddy innyard or market square."

And Osric had made use of all the skill in his undersized body to scrounge food for her father, and the rest of the troupe.

"It was you who gave me the title of 'Lady,' and I shall play my part well, never fear."

"See that you do."

"But I won't ever be ashamed of my friends—Osric, Bronwen, Caleb," she went on evenly. "Or Old Bruin, either."

She saw a brief flash of admiration in his eyes.

"I admire your loyalty," he said. "But I can't go about London scattering coins to every stray beggar."

"That man is no beggar! He is a performer—doing his best to please this crowd."

"As you wish, Melora. Once you've done what I expect of you, you'll have enough to spread largesse among every performer, every crossing sweeper and mudlark in the city."

The carter, at last, had retrieved the cups and plates, hoisted the crate back on the wagon, and tied it in place with heavy rope. The wagon jerked, then rolled forward. Now Dirk and Melora were able to get moving again.

They rode in silence to the river landing on the Strand. Here, Dirk helped her to dismount. He led the two horses to a stable, where he gave orders to the hostler.

The man pocketed Dirk's coins, bowed, and assured him that these fine beasts would be as well cared for as if they had belonged to the king and queen.

"Not but what you look to be a far better horseman than his majesty," the man told Dirk. "They do say he gets himself

69

thrown regular. Took a bad spill before he got to the city to sit his royal Scots' arse on Elizabeth's throne, he did."

The man shook his head. "Now, she was a fine rider, was our queen. We'll not see her likes again, more's the pity."

"King James is our ruler now," Dirk told the man sternly. "Anne of Denmark's our queen."

The man hastily protested that he had meant no harm, but Melora guessed that he would not waver in his adoration for the late queen. Elizabeth Tudor, like her father before her, had known how to hold the loyalty of her subjects. Such a gift could not be bought; it was bred in the bone. A hundred years hence, thought Melora, Londoners would still speak of Elizabeth with unshakable devotion.

Melora and Dirk walked along the Strand in the direction of the boat landing. Great mansions lined the Thames, their carefully tended gardens still bright with autumn roses. The afternoon sunlight struck diamond sparks from the ripples of the river. But Melora was too preoccupied with her coming ordeal to fully appreciate the surroundings. She must learn all she could about the new monarch before she stood in his presence.

"Is it true that King James is a clumsy horseman?" she asked.

Dirk nodded, a slight smile touching his mouth. "But no courtier would be so rash as to mention it—not in his majesty's hearing."

"I suppose it is necessary for the king to ride nonetheless."

"Necessary?" He threw his head back and his laugh rang out. Then, although the passersby appeared intent on their own business, Dirk lowered his voice. "He chooses to ride and hunt as often as possible, like the stubborn Scotsman he is."

Melora realized that he was taking no chance on being overheard. She remembered how Bronwen had warned her of the treachery at court. Was it dangerous to speak one's mind about the new king even here, in the midst of a hurrying, jostling London crowd?

"James would sell his soul to gain the admiration of his subjects," Dirk went on, in the same low tone. "But he knows well enough that he has not yet replaced Elizabeth in their hearts. Not for all his costly masques, his hunting parties, and banquets.

"Of course, the courtiers try to outdo one another, heaping flattery on him for every gaudy display. Why shouldn't they, when he rewards his honey-tongued favorites with great manor houses, titles, monopolies on the trade in wines, in French silk, in Venetian glass?"

"And what about you?" Melora could not quite keep the irony out of her tone. "Do you, too, fawn over him and praise his hunting parties and masques and—"

Dirk stiffened as if she had struck him, and his mouth tightened. She longed to take back her words, but it was too late.

"I do what I must." She flinched under his hard stare. "And I'd do far more if it meant getting my ships and my land grant across the ocean."

He lapsed into frigid silence, but the tension crackled between them. She searched for a way to distract him. "Will I be presented to their majesties as soon as we arrive at Whitehall?"

"Certainly not. A lady does not enter the royal presence in a riding costume, no matter how becoming it may be. And those fine trappings do suit you well, sweeting."

He stopped, turned to her, and cupped her chin in his fingers. His gaze caressed her upturned face, and she felt a surge of warmth flooding her body.

His look eased her tension, and her spirits began to rise. He did not see her only as a possession, then; a tool to be used in his elaborate scheme. Once more, he was seeing her as a desirable woman. The woman he had held last night. He drew her against him, molding her to his body.

Her nipples raised and puckered against the bodice of her riding habit. Her body went hot with the memory of his mouth suckling her, his tongue flicking at the sensitive pink peaks. Her flesh remembered the rock-hard thrust of his manhood against

71

her bottom as she had sat cradled in his lap, with only her nightdress a fragile barrier between them.

Now, standing with him on the riverbank, she felt the same fiery glow begin to spread through her body.

"Sweeting . . ." He bent his face to hers. Her lips parted as she awaited the delicious invasion of his tongue.

But he released her abruptly. He hailed the nearest river craft, took her hand and led her down the slippery landing steps. He helped her aboard the boat. "To Whitehall," he told the boatman.

She settled herself beside him, and arranged her velvet skirt, then glanced at him from beneath her lashes. His face was set, and he leaned forward slightly, as if unaware of her presence. The brief intimacy between them was gone. Once more, she had become no more than a weapon he could use to further his plans.

She felt a slash of outrage. Then her own innate honesty made her admit that she, too, was driven by ambition. But there was one difference between them. If his plans succeeded, he would get what he wanted most—a land grant. The freedom to build a colony in the New World.

But she would have to take her satisfaction from her father's return to the London stage. Never would she know the triumph of giving a magnificent performance before a public audience; of hearing their applause, their shouts of approval.

She caught her breath sharply. If she and Dirk carried off their dangerous scheme, he would leave England forever.

She gripped her gloved hands together. Dirk's leaving didn't matter to her. She would not allow herself to fall in love with the cold-eyed adventurer who sat beside her.

That would be the greatest risk of all.

Chapter Six

William Herbert, Earl of Pembroke, had summoned Dirk to his spacious private apartment at Whitehall Palace, and had listened closely to his account of his meeting with Melora at the Leaping Stag. But although the earl had remained silent, his deep-set black eyes had reflected his growing disapproval, and as Dirk was finishing his description of Melora's assault on Abernathy with the tankard, Pembroke broke in.

"Have you considered the risk in trying to pass off such a creature as your cousin?"

"Since Rosalind's no longer available, what choice did I have?"

Pembroke shook his head. "It won't do, Grenville. Pay the wench off and get her out of here."

Although only a few hours had passed since Dirk and Melora had arrived at Whitehall Palace, he had already arranged for her temporary quarters. Even now, a maid would be helping her to remove her riding costume, while others would be carrying buckets to fill her tub, unpacking her borrowed trunk, laying out a costume suitable for Melora's presentation to the king and queen.

As for Dirk, he had not taken time to wash off the dust of travel before answering Pembroke's summons. Having convinced himself that Melora would be able to assume the identity of Rosalind Grenville, it now was necessary to win the earl's approval for his plan.

"Melora's no common wench, my lord," Dirk told Pembroke. "I made sure of that before we left the Leaping Stag. Believe me, she will serve us well. Better, perhaps, than my own cousin."

The earl was an imposing presence, with his long, lean body, his heavy-lidded onyx eyes, his aquiline nose and thin lips. Dirk sensed the controlled, unwavering alertness in the other man. Even now, seated at ease beside the marble fireplace, with a goblet of wine near at hand, Pembroke did not allow himself to relax completely.

"You mean to present her to their majesties—this singer of bawdy ballads, this daughter of a strolling player?"

"No ordinary player, my lord," Dirk interrupted. "The girl's father is Edmund Standish."

Pembroke's eyes narrowed slightly. "Edmund Standish. I remember him well—a most talented performer. He played the role of a villainous nobleman and a lovelorn shepherd with equal skill."

"So Melora has told me." Dirk had counted on the earl's enthusiasm for the theater to help win his support. "And she has inherited his talent," Dirk assured the earl. "What is more, she is well spoken, she moves with grace, and her manners are impeccable. She has an excellent singing voice besides, and plays the lute with great skill."

The earl's lips curved in a brief, ironic smile. "She seems to have made quite an impression on you, Grenville." He paused and took a sip of wine, then set down his jeweled goblet on the polished marquetry table that stood between him and Dirk. "Are you sure your judgment of the girl wasn't swayed by certain of her—other talents?"

"I didn't bed the wench, if that's what you mean." Dirk saw no reason to add that he had come close to it, during that first night in the earl's manor house. Even now, his loins stirred with a sudden, fierce surge of heat at the memory of Melora's body, cradled on his lap; he remembered the sweet perfume of her dark hair, the smooth white curve of her throat. His palm began to tingle as if he could feel, even now, the swift hardening of her nipple under his touch. With an effort, he wrenched his thoughts away.

"Melora's clever," he told the earl. "She can keep her wits about her, even under great stress. When I first claimed her as my cousin back there in the taproom, she slipped into the role quickly enough to convince that scoundrel of a landlord that she was Lady Rosalind."

The earl's black brows drew together. "If she's all you say, perhaps she can be of more use than we thought. Do you think she would want to risk her safety to serve as a member of my organization?"

Caught off-guard, Dirk spoke impulsively. "Melora would risk anything to help her father. She wants to see him win back his fame on the London stage."

"It's been years since Wilmot cast off Standish. You believe he still has a chance to climb to the top of his profession even now?"

"I suppose it's possible. It's true that I left him back in the stable loft, shivering with ague, and half out of his head with fever. No doubt he was worn out with tramping the roads. But I gave the innkeeper a generous sum, and, who knows? With rest and good food, and with his motley friends to care for him, he may recover."

"And suppose he does. What then?"

"Melora means to bring him back to London and help him to organize a new company of players."

"Her devotion to her father is commendable," Pembroke said.

"She's more than a dutiful daughter," Dirk assured the earl. "She has inherited her father's acting ability. You should hear her tirades against the law that keeps her from appearing on the stage herself."

"A female performing in a public playhouse?" Pembroke

shook his head. "Surely you didn't promise to persuade the king to change the law to satisfy such a farfetched ambition?"

"Hardly, my lord. And Melora would not have been foolish enough to believe such a promise. But I did suggest that she would be able to use whatever acting talent she has to convince their majesties that she is my cousin Rosalind. She took up the challenge. Even now, she's getting ready to make her first entrance tonight, with the great hall for her stage."

Pembroke did not reply at once, but stared into the leaping fire, his sharp features immobile. He was studying the plan as a master weaver might study a length of cloth, seeking for the slightest flaw, before giving his approval. Dirk knew from experience that it would be useless to say anything more.

At last the earl nodded. "It's possible this scheme of yours may work." Coming from Pembroke, this was praise indeed. "And it would surely be to your advantage to have the wench win favor with Queen Anne."

Dirk stretched out his long, booted legs, raised his goblet and savored his wine. It was the finest Malaga, from the earl's private stock.

Pembroke, one of the king's most favored courtiers, already had reaped a harvest of rewards: an import monopoly in Spanish wines, another in Flemish lace, yet another in Venetian glass. An estate in Scotland, to add to those he had inherited from his family. This spacious apartment, one of the finest in all the palace, with its tapestried walls and elaborate plaster friezes, its inlaid chest, marquetry tables, and carved cupboards, its oaken chairs cushioned in purple and dark green velvets. Nothing was too good for Pembroke who had managed, during James's brief reign, to win the king's trust, no small achievement, considering James's suspicious nature.

His majesty was never free from the fear that he might one day meet the same fate as his luckless father, Lord Darnley, who had been assassinated by his own followers. Or of his mother, the beautiful, reckless Mary, Queen of Scots, who had been executed by Elizabeth.

And James's fears were well founded, Dirk had to admit. Although the Guy Fawkes plot had been thwarted, thanks to the efficient machinations of Pembroke's elaborate spy network, the earl had hinted at a dangerous new plot that was taking shape even now.

"Exactly how much does the girl know?" The earl spoke abruptly.

"I told her only that she is to serve Queen Anne." Dirk felt an unfamiliar twinge of guilt. "I said I needed her to help me win favor with the king, so that I might get ships and a land grant."

"I was thinking about more important matters," The earl spoke with a touch of impatience.

"There is nothing more important to me than to return to the New World and establish a colony there."

"If you can put aside your own narrow interests for a moment, Grenville, perhaps you may be able to give some thought to affairs of state."

Dirk felt a sudden tightness in the pit of his stomach. In trying to convince the earl that Melora would make a suitable lady-in-waiting, had he gone too far?

"We agreed that she might be of some trifling use to you, by carrying an occasional tidbit of gossip from the queen's chambers," he said carefully.

"But that was when I expected you to return from Northumberland with the real Lady Rosalind. Once Melora Standish is settled here at court, I will have ample opportunity to observe her, and decide for myself if I wish to make greater use of her." The earl gave a short, mirthless laugh. "If she's as quick-witted as you say, she might serve our purposes better than the real Lady Rosalind."

Dirk's throat had suddenly gone dry. "How so?"

"This little adventuress, this player's daughter—if I were to enlist her as an agent in my service, surely you would not object to her taking whatever risks might be necessary to ferret out this new plot against his majesty."

77

Dirk drew in his breath and gripped the stem of his goblet so tightly that the raised design bit into his fingers. He was startled by his response to Pembroke's suggestion.

"Naturally, I would be prepared to pay the wench generously out of my own coffers," Pembroke went on calmly.

With great effort, Dirk managed to keep his voice even and impersonal. "If she lives long enough to collect her reward."

The earl shrugged. "I choose my people carefully, Grenville, and I don't send them into unnecessary danger. In any case, Melora Standish is no kin of yours. So you will surely agree that she is expendable."

The words struck Dirk with the force of a blow. He did not know all the intricate workings of Pembroke's spy network; perhaps no one else did, either. He certainly had never troubled himself about the possible fate of any of the earl's agents.

How many hirelings served the earl's secret organization here at Whitehall? Who were they? Chambermaids, no doubt; pages, hostlers, seamstresses, each supplying Pembroke with a thread of information to be woven into his elaborate web. And of these, how many were discovered and done away with, swiftly, secretly, by the king's enemies?

She is expendable.

Pembroke's words, so carelessly spoken, kept hammering at Dirk's brain. He could not remain detached, for he was remembering how Melora's slender body had trembled as she had pressed close against him; how she had clutched at his arm, while she had confided her haunting childhood memory. How tightly she had clung to him that night; as if she were seeing again the head of the traitor impaled on a spike of the bridge, the empty eye-sockets gaping after the sharp-beaked ravens had done their work.

He would not forget how he had comforted her, had held her and stroked her hair and given his word to protect her from danger.

"You've always had a way with women, highborn or low," the earl was saying, and Dirk forced himself to concentrate.

78

"Already you have persuaded Mistress Standish to deceive the king so that she may realize her own ambitions, and help you to get what you want, too. I doubt you'd have much difficulty enlisting her in my service, if the pay were high enough."

The earl paused, his black eyes following the intricate play of light and shadow on the plaster frieze that decorated the wall. A log on the hearth broke in two, and the golden sparks shot upward. The silence stretched between the two men, until Dirk felt the muscles at the sides of his jaws start to ache with tension.

Unable to keep still any longer, he took a drink of wine and spoke with feigned carelessness. "Suppose Melora does agree, my lord? Queen Anne's hardly likely to discuss affairs of state with a lady-in-waiting, a newcomer to court."

Dirk found himself hoping fiercely that he might be right. The less Melora knew about affairs of state, the safer she would be.

Whitehall Palace stretched for nearly half a mile, a maze of galleries, apartments set aside for favored courtiers, carefully tended gardens. Melora, entering the great hall on her first evening at court, drew in her breath sharply, awed by the splendor of her new surroundings. She rested her hand lightly on Dirk's forearm, as he led her forward to present her to King James and Queen Anne.

The hall was already filled with courtiers who were passing the time with flirting, gossiping, and displaying their richest finery. The light from the myriad wax candles and flaring torches accented the splendors of their silks and velvets, taffetas and satins, and brought out the elaborate designs of their gold and silver laces; it touched the gleam in a heavy strand of pearls, an pear-shaped emerald earring, a pattern of sapphires on a sword hilt. The men wore the starched ruffs, pleated breeches, and silk hose that were now the height of fashion; while the ladies were decked out in daringly low-cut gowns and full skirts, draped over stiff canvas farthingales and tightly laced whale-bone stays.

Dirk bowed low before the king and queen, who were seated side by side on a velvet-covered dais. He cast Melora a quick look and she made a deep curtsy, her lilac taffeta skirts billowing out around her. She was sure that the queen's other ladies-in-waiting had been trained in proper court etiquette from early childhood. It would not do for her to betray her own lack of breeding by the slightest trace of awkwardness. She stifled a small sigh of relief as she assured herself that she had executed the complicated maneuver with grace and dignity.

While keeping her head lowered respectfully, she shot a quick glance at the king, from under her long lashes. Seeing him for the first time, she felt a shock of disappointment; for although he wore a magnificent burgundy velvet suit, an ermine-collared mantle, and a heavy gold chain set with rubies and diamonds, he did not look particularly impressive. His beard was thin; his eyes wandered about uneasily. He kept shifting his bony frame and fingering the the chain, playing nervously with the largest of the diamonds.

The queen, although she was short and undeniably plain, held herself with regal poise, and inclined her head slightly.

"Ah, yes—Lady Rosalind Grenville," said the king. "You come from Northumberland. Ashcroft Hall, isn't it?" Melora found it a little difficult to understand his thick Scots accent.

"There's fine hunting up there on the border. No doubt your father's fond of the chase, as I am," he went on.

Her father. Not Edmund Standish, but Sir Nicholas Grenville, master of Ashcroft. "Tell me, what's his favorite sort of game? The stag or the pheasant?"

Caught off-guard, she searched her mind for a suitable answer. She tried to take a deep breath to steady herself, but the whalebone stays pressed into her ribs, and what air she managed to draw in made her giddy; for it was heavy with the mingled scents of musk, lavender, and frangipani.

Then she heard Dirk's voice, calm and reassuring. "The

forests of Ashcroft are filled with tall stags early in autumn, sire. And there will be fine sport with the pheasants and partridges in spring. This time of year, my uncle hunts the boar and the wolf."

King James favored Dirk with a smile of genuine pleasure. "A boar hunt! Your uncle keeps a good kennel?"

"His staghounds are considered the finest in Northumberland, your majesty," Dirk said.

"How we should like to join him in hunting a boar! It's a dangerous game—a true challenge for the hunter!" The king's face lit up briefly. Then he sighed and fingered his jeweled chain again. "Can't get away from court now—affairs of state—the Christmas revels."

"No doubt you will enjoy our Christmas merrymaking, my dear." Queen Anne spoke quietly to Melora, and held out her hand.

"You do our family great honor in choosing me for your service, your majesty." Melora bent her head and touched her lips to the queen's short, blunt fingers, grateful for this timely interruption. She was quite at a loss when it came to talk of hunting. "I shall endeavor to please you in every way."

The carefully planned speech came out smoothly enough. It was not so different from speaking a part upon the stage, Melora told herself firmly.

You boasted of your talent as an actress. Now you must prove your skill.

But even in her most fantastic daydreams, Melora had not imagined making her debut before so splendid an audience. She felt a tightness in her throat as she realized that the courtiers were watching her closely. During her presentation, the hum of their voices had gradually faded. Those who had been clustered about the great hall now moved nearer the royal dais.

Thank heavens for Dirk, standing beside her. She longed to clutch at his arm, but that would not have been correct; instead, she drew strength even from his nearness, from the sight of his tall body next to hers. His close-fitting jacket of tawny velvet, the full sleeves slashed with gold, accented the width of his

81

shoulders. She remembered the hardness of his powerful muscles, when he had held her against him earlier that day, as they had waited for a boat to take them upriver.

"Lady Rosalind will be an ornament to our court," Queen Anne said to him, with a gracious smile.

Before Dirk could acknowledge the queen's compliment, Melora heard a deep, unfamiliar voice. "Your cousin is fair of face, indeed, Master Grenville."

She turned to the speaker, a courtier of medium height but arrogant bearing, decked out in sky-blue taffeta embroidered with silver lace. Although the stranger had complimented the beauty of her face, his pale gray eyes were fixed on the firm thrust of her breasts, beneath her low-cut, purple velvet bodice. Her wide skirt concealed the curves of her hips, but even so, she felt as if he were stripping her naked—and relishing every moment of the inspection.

"Grenville! Will you do me the honor of presenting me to this flower of Northumberland?"

Dirk made the introductions as brief as possible. It was plain to Melora that he had no liking for the honey-tongued nobleman—Basil, Viscount Rokeby, with a few more titles besides—but he could scarcely refuse the request with their majesties and the all the court looking on.

She started slightly at the brazen sounding of trumpets.

"I hope you've brought a keen appetite from Northumberland, Lady Rosalind," said the king.

Her brows went up slightly in bewilderment. Then a pair of great carved doors at the far end of the greathall swung open and she caught a glimpse of servingmen moving about swiftly in the room beyond, carrying heavily laden bowls and platters.

"Yes, indeed, sire," she began. "I—"

But before she could go on, the king rose to his feet and turned from her to Lord Rokeby. "Tonight we dine upon that fine stag you brought down in our last hunt. You have the devil's own skill in the chase."

The pale-eyed viscount inclined his head. "A stroke of luck, no more. I've no doubt you will outdo me in the field tomorrow morning, sire."

Once more, Rokeby turned his avid gaze on Melora. She recognized that look well enough; for it was no different from the lecherous stare that Tobias Abernathy, and countless others—hostlers and farmers, country squires and blacksmiths—had turned upon her, when she had performed at country fairs or in market squares. In spite of the viscount's elaborately curled hair and moustache, his starched ruff, the pearl that hung from his ear, his pleated breeches, and his pointed satin shoes, bedecked with lace roses, she sensed his aggressive masculinity.

He moved closer. "Mistress Grenville, if I might have the pleasure of your company at—"

But Dirk interrupted him. "Perhaps another time, my lord," he said, tucking Melora's hand into the bend of his arm. He drew her aside to make way for their majesties, who were descending from the high dais.

King James, plainly oblivious to Rokeby's disappointment, was rumbling on in his thick Scots accent. "That new falcon you ordered from Spain, the peregrine you boasted about—do you mean to try her in tomorrow's hunt?"

"No, sire," Rokeby said. "She'll need more practice before she is ready to show her skill to best advantage. The finest peregrines tend to be the most skittish. Their training requires great patience." He turned from the king for a moment, and his eyes locked with Melora's. "I find it worth the waiting, however. Once trained, they prove most—satisfying."

Melora went cold all over. She might be unaccustomed to the ways of the court, but surely her instincts did not deceive her. She could have sworn that although Rokeby spoke of a falcon, his look, his words, were meant for her. But even now, the king and queen were moving in the direction of the banquet hall, with Rokeby close by James's side, while the rest of the courtiers made way, then closed in behind them like a glittering, multicolored river.

The tantalizing scents of beef and ham, of venison and partridge, of pastries and hot spiced wine, made her realize that, in spite of her tension, she somehow had worked up a sharp appetite. Perhaps she would never wholly forget the aching hunger that had been her constant companion while she was traveling the roads.

But before she and Dirk had reached the entrance to the banquet hall, he drew her aside and led her out into the nearest corridor. They went down a wide passageway, turned off into a narrower one, and stopped at last before a deep alcove. He looked about quickly, then drew her into the shadowed recess.

She looked up at him anxiously. "What's wrong, Dirk? I think the queen was not disappointed with me. But the king—did I displease him, perhaps?"

"You carried off the presentation well enough," he assured her, pressing her gloved hand lightly. "But you still have much to learn. In future, you must be careful not to allow your feelings to show so plainly."

"If you mean my feelings about Rokeby—"

He drew closer, so that she breathed in the now-familiar scent of him. "He has maneuvered his way into the king's favor."

"You don't like him, either," she protested.

"I neither like nor trust Rokeby. And with good cause. Nevertheless, it would be most unwise for either of us to offend him."

Now thoroughly bewildered, she asked, "Then why didn't you allow him to take me into the banquet hall? Surely, that would have pleased him."

"I know Rokeby. He enjoys a challenge, whether in the hunting field, or in a bedchamber." Dirk told her. "You heard what he said about that precious falcon of his. She's skittish, not easily tamed."

"I'm no hunting bird, to be trained for Rokeby's—satisfaction." Her face burned with resentment. "What would you

84

have me do if Lord Rokeby pursues me in earnest? Should I lie with him, to keep his favor?"

"No, damn it! You're under my protection."

"And if his lordship corners me when you're not near?"

"He takes pride in his skill at seduction. He won't try to rape you."

Dirk pulled her against him. "Forget Rokeby." He brushed her cheek with his lips, and the warmth of his breath stirred the sweet-hot hunger deep inside her. He cupped her face in his hands, his mouth came down on hers. She parted her lips. His tongue was teasing, caressing, sending flickers of heat down the length of her body.

Her legs began to tremble. His arm went around her, supporting her. Then she felt his fingers working deftly, undoing the ribbons of her tightly laced bodice, freeing one of her breasts. His mouth moved from hers, and his lips closed on her taut nipple. She moaned deep in her throat.

He pressed her farther back into the shadows of the alcove. Before she quite realized what was happening, he had lifted her skirt, then the petticoat beneath it. Swiftly, expertly, he dealt with ribbons and hooks that fastened her remaining undergarments. He was caressing her flat belly . . . moving downward to explore the soft dark triangle at the apex of her thighs.

Instinctively, she arched her hips, and pushed against his hand. Only he could ease the aching, burning need that grew until it possessed her. Until her body cried out for release.

Then she heard a door open, farther down the corridor. She caught the sound of laughter, the murmur of conversation. She fought her way back from the hot, swirling darkness, back to sanity.

"Let me go. Now."

"Melora—"

"No! This was not part of our bargain."

He let her go. She swayed and would have fallen, if she had not reached out and clutched at his arm.

Her hands were unsteady, her fingers clumsy. It seemed to

take forever before she finished fastening her undergarments, and smoothing the ruffles and panniers of her skirt.

In silence, he led her back to the banquet hall. She held herself erect, and moved with outward poise; but deep inside, she felt the aching emptiness. Her body still yearned for release.

Even if Dirk kept his promise to protect her from other men, how long would she be able to fight back her own fierce need for him?

Chapter Seven

Lady Felicity Brandon fastened the small diamond-and-sapphire butterfly into Melora's topknot of dark, shining hair, then nodded with satisfaction. "And now the other, here, perhaps? No, a little higher, I think."

Melora, who was seated on the satin-cushioned chair before the dressing table, moved impatiently. She had been perfectly satisfied when her maid had finished arranging her coiffure, but now Felicity insisted on enhancing the effect with a few touches of her own.

"Do hold still, Rosalind. You want to look your best, tonight, of all nights, if only for your cousin's sake. *Sir Dirk Grenville* . . . It has a fine ring to it, don't you agree?"

Although it was scarcely more than a fortnight since Melora had taken her place among Queen Anne's ladies-in-waiting, she had not yet become completely used to her new name. It was even harder for her to remember that when her father was mentioned, the speaker was referring to Sir Nicholas Grenville, master of Ashcroft Hall, and not to Edmund Standish, strolling player. How many more weeks would it be before she could speak easily of Lady Jessamyn as her mother, of Hugh Grenville as her brother?

Sometimes she felt as if she were walking a tightrope over a market square; but the rope that supported her was as fragile as a strand of silk, and it stretched high above a dark abyss. Her slightest misstep might send her tumbling, spinning downward, hurtling to destruction.

She thanked her stars for Felicity, whose bedchamber she shared. Vivacious, self-assured Lady Felicity Brandon had accepted her without question as Dirk's cousin, and had set about training her in the complicated duties that went with her new position at court.

The young ladies who served the queen helped her to choose a new gown each afternoon, along with the satin slippers, scarf, and fan to set it off to perfection. They took turns in presenting the jewel cases, and waiting patiently while her majesty made her selection from among the glittering display of rings, brooches, necklaces, and earrings. Then they hung the discarded gowns back inside the huge carved armoire.

Every evening the whole process was repeated again. Would her majesty prefer the gown with the silver and carnation stripes, or the purple velvet, embroidered with pearls and gold roses?

During the hours when the king was out hunting, and Queen Anne remained in her chambers, the ladies read aloud, or played at cards—whist, hazard, or the new and fashionable one-and-twenty; or at chess. At such times, even as Melora sat listening to the autumn rain pelting against the mullioned windows, and the river wind rattling the branches of the elms and oaks in the gardens below, her thoughts began to stray.

What would have become of her if Dirk had not appeared at the Leaping Stag and claimed her as his cousin? Suppose he had not taken shelter from the storm at Tobias Abernathy's inn.

None of the other patrons would have come forward to keep her from being dragged before the magistrate. It would have been her word against the landlord's. There was no question in her mind as to the verdict.

How could she have borne the filth and brutality of the jail cell, the slash of the whip, the searing pain of the branding iron? Her stomach churned at the thought. And if, by some miracle, both she and her father had survived and been set free, what then?

She flinched, seeing in her mind's eye the shabby caravan buffeted by storms, lurching and swaying along the roads, sinking deep into the mud. There would have been no chance to perform at a fair or outdoor marketplace until next spring.

Instead, she would have been forced to earn a few coppers in a dingy taproom, heavy with the stench of smoking oil lamps and unwashed male bodies. She would have had to smile at the men, even as she avoided their calloused hands clutching at her skirts, fondling her breasts.

How long would it have been before she'd lost her courage, surrendered the last vestiges of pride? Before she'd found herself lying on a dirty pallet, cringing beneath the weight of a fat landlord, a hostler, or a mule-driver?

Dirk had saved her from all that, and she would repay him. She would do everything in her power to keep her part of their bargain.

Already she had proved useful to him. Following his instructions, she had not put herself forward; but when the queen had heard her playing her lute one afternoon, and had asked her to sing, she had obeyed willingly. Afterward, at her majesty's command, she had gone on, choosing only such ballads as were suitable for these regal surroundings.

The queen had smiled her approval, had complimented her on her skill with the lute, the purity of her voice. "And your songs! They are charming—and new to me. Wherever did you learn them all?"

Hastily Melora had invented a "Welsh musician" who had taken shelter at Ashcroft. "My father gave him board and lodging for a winter, so that he might teach me to play and sing."

At first, a few of the other young ladies had scarcely managed to conceal their annoyance at the queen's praise of this newcomer to court. But most had enjoyed the new ballads, and had

89

asked for more. Gradually they had followed Felicity's lead, and had tried to make Melora feel welcome at Whitehall.

But she knew that she would never feel really at ease in the midst of these pampered young ladies. She was not one of them, and never could be.

Now, as she sat before the marquetry dressing table, and gazed into the gilt-framed mirror, she wondered what would happen if she were to betray herself. Her punishment would be swift, and much too awful to contemplate.

"Now, wasn't I right about the sapphires?" Felicity's voice dispelled her rising anxiety.

"They are dazzling," she agreed. She leaned forward and studied her reflection once more. Her thick, shining hair had been combed into the most fashionable new coiffure, with a center part, a high-piled, intricate topknot, small ringlets at her temples, and a mass of full, round curls artfully arranged to fall over her shoulders and down her back.

At Felicity's insistence, the maid had plucked Melora's brows, had added a touch of rouge to her lips and cheeks, and had pasted a tiny black satin beauty patch in the shape of a crescent at one corner of her mouth.

"Sapphires are most becoming to you," Felicity was saying. "Or amethysts, to deepen the color of your eyes. It won't be long before you have so many fine jewels of your own that you'll be hard put to choose among them," her friend assured her. "Any one of those gentlemen who have been casting languishing looks at you would be eager to deck you with jewels, if only you'd offer them a little encouragement. And as for your dashing cousin, he will surely wish to show his gratitude for the honor the king is about to bestow on him."

"I have nothing to do with that. Dirk's being given his title because of his father's devotion to the cause of Mary of Scotland."

"Come, now—there's no need to play the little innocent. Surely you can see that it would scarcely do for such a close

90

relative of one of the queen's ladies to be addressed as plain 'Master' Grenville."

Felicity's hazel eyes sparkled. "You know, my dear, you're the envy of her majesty's other ladies."

"Because the queen has been kind enough to praise my singing?"

"Your singing's got nothing to do with it—nor your skill with the lute."

"Then what can they find to envy about me?"

"You're not that naive, surely. You must have noticed how Lady Millicent waggles her bottom, exactly like a bitch in heat, each time she brushes against your cousin in the great hall, or in one of the corridors. And as for Lady Alyson, she never fails to show him her ankles when he partners her in the dancing. I warrant she'd like to show him much more." Felicity's small, even teeth flashed in a teasing grin. "But now that you're here at court, they'll have no chance with him."

"Why, I—Dirk cares nothing for me—not in the way you mean."

"Don't expect me to believe that." Felicity leaned closer so that Melora was enveloped in the pungent scent of her frangipani perfume. "It's said he wields his sword with masterful skill. Tell me, is he equally adept with his—other weapon?"

Although Melora had heard such bawdy talk often enough among the girls who performed at country fairs and taverns, she had never expected one of the queen's ladies to speak this way. "Dirk's my cousin, he's fond of me, and I am devoted to him. But as for what you're suggesting—"

"You may save such maidenly airs for the queen," Felicity interrupted. She gave Melora a wink. "He lived with you and your family at Ashcroft—wasn't that what you told us?"

"Yes—yes, certainly. After his mother was left a widow, and stripped of her property, my father could do no less than to invite her and Dirk to make Ashcroft their home."

Melora was on her guard now; for she knew she must take care not to make a slip. She sent up a silent prayer that she had not forgotten even the most trivial detail about Ashcroft, and Dirk's early years there. If only he had not been in such haste to bring her to court; if he had spent a few more days preparing her for this demanding role.

"No doubt the two of you went exploring in the woods together," Felicity was saying. She laughed softly, suggestively. "All those fine spring afternoons, when you and Dirk went rolling around in the grass. Or searching for plovers' eggs under the tall hedgerows. And when the weather turned cool, you discovered that a hayloft makes a soft, sweet-smelling bed."

"You do let your imagination run away with you." She tried to sound casual. "Dirk and I never—" She had to stop short, for her heart was beating unsteadily. If she had not caught herself, she might have blurted out the truth: that she and Dirk had never laid eyes on one another until a month ago.

"I was six years old—scarcely out of the nursery—when Dirk sailed for the New World."

Felicity was silent for a moment, obviously disappointed at being cheated out of a choice bit of gossip. "But when he returned, surely he came back to Northumberland for a visit."

Melora shook her head. "When his ship anchored at Plymouth Harbor, he found another, bound for the Continent. There he took up arms as a mercenary in the service of one foreign prince, then another. It was only a little over a month ago that he appeared at Ashcroft, and told my father that I'd been chosen to wait upon the queen."

Eager to distract her friend from troubling her with further questions, she deftly changed the subject. "You rarely speak of your own home, Felicity. Do you never miss your parents?"

"Hardly. My father's years older than my mother, a scholar who rarely takes his eyes from his books. He has been translating the works of Cicero—or Horace—one of those Romans—for years now. He was kind enough to me, I suppose—when he remembered that he had a daughter."

"And what about your mother?"

"Dear Mama was far too busy with her own pleasures to concern herself with me. She turned me over to the care of the nursery maids. Later, when my father insisted I must learn to read and write, and pick up a smattering of French and Latin, she hired a creaky old tutor." Felicity gave a smile that did not quite reach her eyes. "But she couldn't keep me hidden in the schoolroom forever. I blossomed early, and when visitors began to praise my looks, and speak of my marriage prospects, she didn't like it. I suppose she feared her admirers would start comparing us . . . to her disadvantage."

"She was jealous of you? Her own daughter?"

Felicity nodded. "So she shipped me off to my Uncle Quentin's estate in Sussex." Her lips curved in a reminiscing smile. "My uncle pretended to be a real tyrant. When I misbehaved, he'd summon me to his chamber, and give me a few strokes across my bare bottom with a switch. Afterward, he was overcome with remorse. He took me on his knees and comforted me—in his own special way."

Melora grasped Felicity's meaning, and went hot with embarrassment.

"Then Mark came home," Felicity went on. "Uncle Quentin's younger brother."

She grinned. "Mark completed my education. He'd just returned from a tour of the Continent, and was more than willing to instruct me in all the little refinements he'd learned at the court of King Louis—and at the Venetian bawdyhouses. He said the whores of Venice were the most skilled in their trade of all the doxies in Europe."

Melora bent her head, so that her thick, dark curls shielded her face. She fumbled with the lacing of her bodice. "I do believe you're trying to shock me."

"Why ever should you be shocked? It was all perfectly respectable."

"Respectable?" Melora stared at her in utter bewilderment.

"Certainly. I was still a maid when I arrived at Whitehall last year."

93

"But how could you—how was that possible?"

Felicity ran the tip of her tongue over her lips. "Melora, you do have much to learn. A girl may take her pleasure in all sorts of delicious ways, and still keep her maidenhead."

Melora rose abruptly, smoothed the folds of her blue taffeta skirt, picked up her fan, and started for the door. Felicity had to quicken her pace to keep up, but even as they went out into the corridor, her friend went on: "What a pity first cousins cannot marry. You and *Sir* Dirk Grenville would make a striking couple."

But Dirk's not my cousin. He would be free to wed me if he wanted me for his wife.

And now, against all reason, a host of sensuous images swept through Melora's mind. Suppose—just suppose—it had not been Dirk's ambition that had drawn them together. Suppose they had been equals, betrothed since childhood. Suppose they had danced together at a dozen balls at Ashcroft, ridden out side by side on hunting parties. Suppose he had fallen in love with her . . . She let herself surrender to the fantasy.

She and Dirk together, as they had been that night in the chamber of Pembroke's manor. But suppose it had been their own bridal chamber. The bed would have been hung with garlands, the room scented with musk and bowls of fragrant waters.

The bridesmaids and groomsmen, having settled the two of them in bed, and offered them the bridal posset of hot wine and spices, would be gone at last. There would have been no need to hold him off.

Would she have turned wanton, shameless? Helped him slide her nightdress down over her breasts, her thighs? Reached up and drawn him to her . . . her bare arms clinging, her thighs parting to receive the first searing thrust of possession?

A surge of liquid fire rippled through her veins as she allowed herself to surrender to her illusion. Her nipples peaked, and began to tingle under the tightly fitting bodice of her gown, at the memory of Dirk's caressing fingers; the hot, wet suckling of his lips at her breast . . .

Felicity's tinkling laugh brought her back once more. "You're blushing! Why, I do believe you're almost as inexperienced as you claim to be."

She gave Melora's arm a friendly little squeeze. "Never fear—I shall tell you all you need to know to please your bridegroom, when the time comes. But only if you promise that I may be your bridesmaid."

"Even if Dirk were not my first cousin and—if I loved him—the way you mean—" Her words came rushing forth, shrill, unbidden, too loud in the quiet corridor. "It could never happen. Never."

Startled by the fierce pain that shot through her, she reminded herself that she had plans of her own, and they did not include marriage. As soon as Dirk told her that she was free to leave the court, she would bring her father to London. She would help him find a titled patron, establish a new troupe. Somehow, they would make a place for Osric and Caleb; yes, and Bronwen, too. They had proved their loyalty, and they would be suitably rewarded. Dirk's generous payment for her services would make all that possible.

Melora realized that Felicity was staring at her with open curiosity, and she spoke quickly. "My cousin has plans of his own. He is determined to get together a fleet, fill his ships with men and women who wish to leave England and settle in the New World.

"Is he, indeed!" Felicity raised her carefully plucked brows in surprise. "I'd have thought he'd had enough of roving."

"You know little about him. This time he is determined to get a grant and establish a colony in the name of England and King James. And he's not coming back here, ever."

"He really wants to live the rest of his days in a wilderness, among wild beasts and naked, painted savages?"

Felicity shook her head. "Men do take the strangest notions." Then she shrugged. "If he means to go junketing off across the sea, then you must make the most of the time you have together."

She linked her arm with Melora's. "Just you wait until the Christmas revels are in full swing," she went on. "All the court rules are forgotten then, what with the wine and the mummery. And the Lord of Misrule in charge. Other will be seeking their own pleasure, and there are so many empty chambers far from the banquet hall, with deep carpets and soft velvet cushions."

"Do stop your nonsense!"

She spoke aloud, but the reprimand was for herself, not for her friend. New visions, conjured up by Felicity's words, threatened to set fire to Melora's imagination once more. No! She must not give way to such dangerous folly—not if she was to keep her wits about her.

But Felicity would not be silenced. "I can't imagine any girl not itching for a tumble in bed with Dirk Grenville." She searched Melora's face. "But maybe there's another gentleman you fancy more. Could it be Lord Rokeby, perhaps?"

"Rokeby!" Melora could scarcely repress a shudder of revulsion.

"You needn't sound so shocked. You danced with him three times at last night's ball."

"I couldn't keep refusing him without being downright rude. But that's as far as he'll get with me, you may be sure."

"I've heard it said that Rokeby has some curious ways of taking his pleasures. Although I know of at least one lady who shares his tastes. Jocelyn Fairfax—the one they call 'Lady Jade.' But she's been his mistress for a year or more. And she's hardly in the first bloom of youth. Perhaps Rokeby's tiring of her and is looking about for an untouched young girl."

Melora's eyes flashed amethyst sparks. "To the devil with Rokeby—and his women. I'll never be one of them."

Her fingers closed around the carved ivory sticks of her fan, and she quickened her pace along the corridor, so that Felicity could scarcely keep up with her.

* * *

Melora's pulse speeded up at the blare of trumpets, the roll of kettledrums. Her eyes rested briefly on the plum-colored satin cloaks of the musicians, on the fluttering gold banners that decorated their instruments. Then, inevitably, her gaze moved to Dirk. Her lips parted in awe as she watched the king touch Dirk's wide shoulders with the flat of his ceremonial sword.

"Arise, Sir Dirk Grenville."

Already she had proved her usefulness. She had won the queen's favor, and no doubt her majesty had used her influence with the king to help win Dirk his title.

Dirk rose, bowed to the king, and moved backward, step by step. Only when he had taken the requisite number of paces demanded by rigid court protocol did he turn away from the throne; and now she realized that he was making his way through the crowd directly toward her.

If it was true that the other ladies envied her, it was not to be wondered at, for Dirk Grenville—*Sir* Dirk Grenville—was an impressive figure, his powerful shoulders strained against his close-fitting doublet of dark-brown velvet; his long, muscular thighs were sheathed in tight black hose; a heavy jewel-studded belt accented his lean waist. He held his head high, and moved with the lithe, easy stride of a forest cat.

But before he reached her side, he was intercepted by the Earl of Pembroke. Although Dirk had introduced the earl to her shortly after her arrival at court, she had not exchanged more than a few words with him. Now she felt the first stirring of uneasiness, as she realized that both men were looking over at her; even at this distance, she sensed a certain tension between them.

Then Dirk and Pembroke came to join her. Dirk's jaw was set, the skin drawn taut across his cheekbones, and she caught a look of wariness in his gold-flecked eyes.

The earl gave her a brief smile, an elegant bow. "This is a

97

most auspicious evening for the Grenvilles, don't you agree, my lady?"

He glanced about as if in surprise. "I should have thought Sir Nicholas and his lady would have come down from Ashcroft for tonight's ceremony."

Although Pembroke's last remark seemed casual enough, he watched her so intently that she flinched under his probing gaze. She hoped he wasn't personally acquainted with Sir Nicholas Grenville, or Lady Jessamyn.

"My mother's health has been indifferent lately," she said. "And the journey from Northumberland is not an easy one this time of year. The state of the roads is quite deplorable."

"And your brother? I trust young Jeremy's not also in delicate health."

Why in heaven's name was he watching her that way? There was no lust in his deep-set black eyes, only a hard, unwavering curiosity.

Perhaps he recognized her blue taffeta gown. Yes, that must be it. "Dirk was anxious to return to court with me, before the winter weather set in. He would not even wait long enough for Mama to provide me with a suitable wardrobe."

She gave the earl a demure smile. "So if you think you've seen this gown before, you're quite right. When we stopped to rest at Netherwood, Dirk assured me that you would not mind if I borrowed it."

"Your cousin was quite right, Lady Rosalind. And the gown is most becoming."

She relaxed slightly, but her relief was short-lived. "We were speaking of young Jeremy," he persisted.

"My brother's name is Hugh. Hugh Arthur Sanford Grenville."

"Your pardon, my lady. But I'm sure I've heard of a certain Jeremy Grenville. A young lad, about your brother's age."

She glanced at Dirk beseechingly, but he offered her no help.

Jeremy Grenville. Who the devil was Jeremy Grenville? And why should the earl take such a close interest in her family? As if preparing to dive into an icy lake, she braced herself, took a quick breath.

"The young man you're thinking of may be a member of the Cornwall branch of our family."

"But you're not sure, is that it?"

She fought back an impulse to strike him with her fan, to turn on her heel and leave the great hall.

"I've never met any of my Cornwall relations," she said evenly. "My father seldom leaves Northumberland."

"And why might that be?"

If only she knew more of the ways of the gentry. "He doesn't choose to entrust the running of Ashcroft to his hired subordinates. He prefers to deal with the needs of our tenants himself. What leisure he can find, he devotes to hunting."

Before Pembroke could come up with another question, she shifted her ground. "Are you fond of hunting, my lord?"

"That depends on the quarry." His voice had an edge to it. "But once I do take up the chase, I never slacken until I have run my prey to earth."

His onyx eyes held hers in a level gaze. She forced back the rising surge of panic inside, but it took all her willpower to keep up an appearance of poise under such scrutiny. Thank goodness Felicity had insisted that she wear a touch of rouge; no doubt it helped to conceal her pallor.

She breathed a heartfelt sigh of relief as she realized that the king had signaled to the musicians to start up the music for the first dance.

The earl bowed before her. "May I have the honor, my lady?"

"I—I fear I've not yet mastered the steps of the volante," she said quickly. "But later, if there's a sarabande, I should be only too pleased to partner you, sir."

Pembroke accepted her excuse with a gracious smile, and strode off in the direction of the banquet hall. Melora realized that her legs were trembling under the heavy folds of her skirt. "Find us a place to sit down."

"As you wish." He led her to a high-backed seat wide enough for two, cushioned in velvet and set apart in a flower-decked niche near one of the windows. She sank down, grateful.

"The earl suspects me. I'm sure he does."

Dirk did not answer. His eyes were fixed on the lavish arrangement of hothouse roses and lilies.

"You heard how he questioned me—as if I were a—" Her throat tightened "—a prisoner on a rack in the Tower."

Why didn't Dirk say something, anything, to ease her fear?

"Pembroke doesn't question every newcomer to court so closely, does he?" she persisted.

"Probably not."

"Then he does doubt I'm your cousin. I must have made some slip, given myself away, somehow—"

"The earl knows exactly who you are," Dirk cut in. "He's known all about you ever since the night you arrived at White-hall."

"But I tried so hard—really, I did. She put a hand on his arm. "Don't be angry with me."

"I can scarcely blame you, sweeting, since I told him who you are." He gave her a reassuring smile. "Don't worry, he won't betray us."

But in spite of the smile, she still sensed an air of tension about him. If he was so sure he could trust Pembroke, what did he have to fear?"

"All you have to do is to go on playing your part, as you have so far."

She was not appeased by his soothing words. "Dirk, what's wrong?"

"Nothing that need concern you—yet. Or ever, if I can help it."

There was a tight-reined anger in him, and although she could not guess the cause, she felt a rising apprehension. All at once, Bronwen's words echoed in her mind. *You go to a royal hall where danger holds court . . . deception coiled in the shadows . . . your eyes*

100

. . . dazzled by the light of a thousand candles . . . watch the darkness beyond . . .

"Dirk, you have your title," she said. "Surely, the king will soon give you the ships, the land grant. Can't I leave now?"

"Give up your fine clothes, your soft bed? The best of food and wine? I should think you would wish to luxuriate in these surroundings as long as you can."

"Yes, you would think that!" She had been cautious so long, had chosen her words with such care. Now a rising strain broke down her control. "I don't expect you to understand. You care for no one but yourself. But I'm not like that—I wouldn't wish to be."

"Guard your tongue. This isn't the time or place for such vaporings—"

But she would not be silenced. "I lie awake nights, thinking of my father. He was delirious, burning with fever, when I left him. Suppose he—" She could not bring herself to voice her deepest fear. "And my friends, what of them?"

"Keep your voice down!" His fingers closed over hers in a painful grip. "I'll find a way to get word of your father, and his motley crew."

"Can you? Would you? If I could be sure that Papa is getting well, that Bronwen and Osric—"

"And Caleb and the bear. Let's not forget Old Bruin."

Perhaps he was capable of understanding her concern, after all. "Osric can read and write. If you could find someone to carry a letter from him."

"I've said I'd arrange it. If you'll do me a service in return."

She might have known that Dirk never offered a favor without expecting payment.

"What kind of service?"

His answer took her by complete surprise. "No doubt the queen's ladies spend much of their time gossiping."

"They do little else, but why should—"

"I suppose you've made a few friends among them."

"There's Felicity Brandon."

101

"She'll do. Encourage her to confide in you."

"Felicity needs no encouragement. Shall I write down all her chitchat?"

"That's the last thing I would want. You have a good memory."

"But why should you want to know—"

"That needn't concern you."

"As you wish, my lord. Let me see. Felicity thinks it's too bad we can't wed, because of our being so closely related." She flushed to the roots of her hair, remembering Felicity's advice, that she should make the most of her time with Dirk. Her talk of the Christmas revels, of leading him to a deserted chamber where no one would intrude on their lovemaking . . .

"But there's Lady Millicent. She's quite taken with you, Felicity tells me. And Lady Alyson is, too."

"That's of no interest to me."

"Then what is it you do want to know?"

"Find out about the preparations for the twelve days of Christmas. Whitehall will be swarming with visitors. Frenchmen, Italians—and Spaniards. And if one of the queen's ladies should arrange a secret meeting with some foreign dignitary— particularly a Spaniard—or a member of his entourage, find out all you can about him."

She stared at him in disbelief. "Can this be the same Dirk Grenville who assured me he had no interest in court intrigues? That he wanted to leave Whitehall—to sail from England—"

"Guard your tongue." His voice, soft but urgent, silenced her. She looked up and saw that Lord Rokeby stood before them.

"Forgive me for interrupting what seemed to be a most absorbing conversation."

Dirk rose to his feet and gave his hand to Melora, who stood up quickly. "We were speaking of the Christmas festivities, my lord," Melora said with a forced smile.

"Then this is a most opportune moment to join you, if I

may," Rokeby said. "Her majesty has been praising your musical skills, Lady Rosalind."

"The queen is most gracious," Dirk said, his icy stare fixed on Rokeby. "Now, if you will excuse us—"

But Rokeby was not to be put off so easily. "King James has suggested that I create a masque for the holiday entertainment. We will have professional assistance, naturally. Master Inigo Jones is to design the setting—castles, woodland bowers, perhaps an artificial lake—and he will also contrive the most impressive lighting effects. And I shall devise the words and music. His majesty wants the production to be more magnificent than any yet seen in court."

"No doubt he'll have what he wishes," Dirk said carelessly. He took Melora's hand and tucked in into the crook of his arm. "We were about to join the dancing, Lord Rokeby."

"A moment more, if you please. His majesty is set upon Lady Rosalind taking part in the masque. He wants your talented young cousin to assist me in choosing a suitable theme from classical mythology. Gods and goddesses, nymphs and fauns and satyrs. She and I are to work closely, writing the verses for the ballads. What's more, my lady, you will take a leading role in the production."

"I couldn't possibly—"

"Have no fear. I will help you to prepare for your performance."

"You flatter me, Lord Rokeby. But I believe that her majesty has exaggerated my small talent. I am most obliged to his majesty for his suggestion, but I fear I must refuse."

"If you were not new to court, my lady, you would understand that this was no mere suggestion."

"Are you saying that the king commands me to take part in this mummery?"

"Perhaps that is putting it too strongly," Rokeby said. "But it would be advisable to comply with his majesty's request. Don't you agree, Lord Grenville?"

Melora looked up at Dirk. He had to find a way to get her

103

out of this impossible situation. The thought of working closely with Rokeby was distasteful to her.

"Lady Rosalind has never been away from home before. It's natural for her to feel unsure of her ability, reluctant to perform before their majesties, and the whole court."

"Then I am to tell the king that she refuses this honor?"

"On the contrary," Dirk said. "Once she gets used to the idea, she will do her best to please her audience."

Before Melora could protest, she felt the pressure of Dirk's fingers on her arm. "Think of your father, cousin Rosalind. You must not refuse, for his sake."

Her own father, not Sir Nicholas Grenville. This was Dirk's way of reminding her of their bargain.

She set her jaw, took a steadying breath. "You may tell his majesty that I will be pleased to assist you in in preparing the Christmas masque, Lord Rokeby."

Chapter Eight

"Perhaps you don't understand the elaborate preparations that go into staging a court masque," said Rokeby. Melora had danced twice with the viscount; and now, when she had told him she was too fatigued for a third dance, he had remained at her side.

She looked about the great hall, hoping to catch a glimpse of Dirk. Since that evening, over a week ago, when he had received his title, she had not seen him. Having forced her to agree to take part in the masque, he had disappeared, leaving her to deal with Rokeby on her own.

"Ought we not consult with Master Inigo Jones about costumes and scenery?" she asked. With Master Jones present, surely Rokeby would not force himself on her.

"We'll have no need of Master Jones until we choose the subject for the masque," said Rokeby.

"You did mention one of the classical myths, my lord."

"But which one? Since you are to take the leading role, you must help me decide."

It was already after midnight, and many of the ladies had retired, Felicity among them. But Rokeby was making it impossible for Melora get away.

Why had Dirk disappeared when she needed him? He had promised to protect her; yet he had led Rokeby to believe that she would enjoy appearing in the masque, once she had gotten over her shyness. And now, when she needed him most, he was nowhere to be found.

Was this Dirk's way of challenging her to handle Rokeby on her own? She kept a forced smile on her lips, but resentment seethed within her. Perhaps he wanted her to be alone with Rokeby, to use her feminine wiles to gather court gossip.

Maybe Dirk had arrived here late tonight, and she had missed him in the crowd. She glanced quickly around the hall, but he was nowhere in sight.

The great hall swam before her eyes in a kaleidoscope of brilliant colors, and the noise of the revelers assaulted her ears until she felt giddy. Servants in the royal livery moved among the crowd, putting fresh wax candles into the gold and silver candelabra, pouring rose water into porcelain bowls, sprinkling dried herbs into the corners.

She started at a shout of triumph from one of the men seated at a nearby card table. Another called for a fresh deck, while the remaining players loudly demanded a dozen more bottles of Malaga.

From a wide, cushioned settle in a garlanded alcove came a high-pitched squeal of protest. Melora turned and saw a plump blonde in canary-colored brocade lying across the knees of an amorous gentleman. His face was flushed, his eyes hot with lust. He had pushed the girl's skirt and petticoat high above her knees, and now he thrust his hand underneath. But she was no longer protesting his advances. Indifferent to the crowd that milled about them, she spread her silk-sheathed legs apart.

She wriggled her bottom against his breeches. Her rouged lips parted, her half-naked breasts rose and fell with the urgency of her need. Then, as if desperate for release, she reached out and fumbled at the lacing of his satin codpiece.

Melora went crimson and turned away, only to meet Rokeby's gaze. He, too, had been watching the pair in the alcove. He clasped Melora's arm. "Let us find more private quarters."

"It's late—I wish to retire."

106

"I won't keep you from your bed much longer," he said, sliding his arm around her waist. "We must begin sometime, my lady—and tonight's as good as any."

"Lord Rokeby!"

"The masque, Lady Rosalind. I was speaking of the masque. We must decide which ancient legend would please his majesty best." His avid, pale gray eyes moved over her slowly. "And reveal your—talents—to greatest advantage."

His eyes caressed the lush swell of her breasts. Her bodice was cut fashionably low, so that the lace only just covered the rosy peaks. She flinched from his gaze, for it was as if she already felt his fingers toying with her nipples. Revulsion churned inside her.

"We might use the legend of Cupid and Psyche. You would make a charming Psyche." His voice was soft, insinuating. "I should like to see your hair piled atop your head, in the Grecian mode, bound by a wreath of blossoms . . . your neck and shoulders bare, a narrow sash about your waist . . ."

He tightened his arm around her waist and his free hand stroked the curve of her neck, the satiny whiteness of her shoulder. Unable to control herself another moment, she jerked free from his encircling arm.

But her movement only seemed to stir him more deeply. "How young you are . . . young and untouched. You might be better suited to the role of Artemis, goddess of the moon—the divine huntress worshipped by mortal men. But only from afar."

"It's late, my lord. I wish to leave now."

As if he had not heard, he went on, his tone almost hypnotic. "Artemis, virgin goddess, untouched by god or man . . ."

"My lord, I—"

"Yet even *she* felt the divine fire. She yielded her glorious silver body to the mortal Endymion."

She had to get away, and quickly. Her eyes were fixed longingly on the nearest flower-hung archway leading to the corridor.

"Artemis, queen of night. You shall wear a robe of blue and silver. No farthingale, no petticoats to conceal your soft thighs, your lovely legs. I've no doubt that your hidden parts are as alluring as the rest of you."

How much longer could she stand the probing eyes, the soft, suggestive voice? "I must leave now, my lord. I'm not used to keeping late hours."

Without even a formal "Goodnight," Melora turned and fled from the great hall, through the archway. She plunged into the labyrinth of corridors, where the torches burned low in their sconces. Concealed by shadows, she hurried up a flight of stairs, then another, and on to her bedchamber.

Her head ached, her knees were unsteady, not from dancing, or the noise of the revelers. She was exhausted by the effort of leading Rokeby on, of tantalizing him, while refusing to yield to him.

She thought of that evening in the taproom of the Leaping Stag. At least she'd been able to fight off Tobias Abernathy with one well-aimed blow from a tankard. Then she reminded herself that she would have paid a terrible price for her impulsive action, except for Dirk.

It was only because of Dirk's intervention that she had escaped jail—she and her father and the rest of the troupe. Because of Dirk, she had found sanctuary in Whitehall Palace, with her body clothed in silks and velvets and her hunger satisfied with the finest delicacies; and sheltered from the oncoming winter in her warm, perfumed chamber.

But for how long? How many more evenings would she be able to hold Rokeby at a distance, while flattering his outrageous vanity; how much longer could she keep him hot to possess her, then leave him unsatisfied? Sooner or later, she would have to get to work with him, planning the masque. Then he would have a perfect excuse to spend hours alone with her.

She could not deal with that problem tonight. Now she only

longed for the refuge of her canopied bed, her thick down coverlet, and the welcome oblivion of sleep.

But when she opened the chamber door, she felt a pang of dismay; Felicity had waited up for her. Prudence, the flaxen-haired young girl who served them, was here, too, her round cheeks rosy with excitement.

Before Melora had time to close the door, Felicity had already started speaking. "Look at this—a footman brought it in half an hour ago—what kept you so long?" Melora stared at the handsome trunk at the foot of her bed. It was made of black leather and trimmed with polished mahogany wood and shining brass.

"I ordered no trunk," she said. "There's been some mistake."

Felicity pointed to the engraved "R. G." on the brass plate. "None of the queen's other ladies has those initials. Do open it."

Melora shook her head in bewilderment, but made no move to comply. Felicity pushed past her.

"Then let me." She opened the lid, stared inside, and cried, "Look at this!" She clasped her hands and gave an envious sigh. "I wish someone would surprise me with such fine gifts. Prudence, come and help me unpack."

The maid hurried over, lifted out a cloak of heavy purple velvet, and placed it across Melora's bed. "Oh, my lady! Just look—fit for her majesty, it is." She turned the cloak over and Melora saw that it was lined from neck to hem with the thick, dark sable; the hood was trimmed with a deep ruff of the same rich fur.

"And a dress to go with it." The maid smoothed the soft folds of the wide skirt, then laid the dress down beside the cloak.

"I have a perfectly good riding habit," Melora said.

But not like this one. This particular shade of blue-violet had been carefully chosen to accent the color of her eyes. The skirt and the full sleeves were lavishly trimmed with the same midnight sable as the cloak.

"I told you that you'd soon be showered with gifts," Felicity said, her face aglow with vicarious pleasure. "I'll wager Lord Rokeby sent these." She handed Melora a cream-colored parchment.

Not Rokeby. She'd take no gifts from him.

"If you don't open that note, I will," Felicity said.

Melora broke the wax seal, opened the parchment, read the enclosed note, then gave a brief sigh of relief.

"It's from Dirk," she said. "He says that the king wants me to join the royal hunt tomorrow morning."

Why had he sent her a new riding outfit, when she might have worn the same one she had borrowed from Pembroke's house? Dirk never acted without some carefully planned purpose. But right now, she felt only relief that it was he, not Rokeby, who had sent the gift.

"It was thoughtful of my cousin," she said. Even as she spoke, there was a knock at the door. Prudence hurried to take another letter from a man decked out in a silver breastplate, red velvet doublet, and short cloak. He bowed. "For Lady Rosalind Grenville," he said.

As he departed, Melora caught a glimpse of the king's arms, embroidered in red and gold on the back of the cloak. Her eyes slid over the few lines of the formal invitation. Then her thoughts returned to Dirk.

If he'd been here at the palace during the week following the ceremony of knighthood, why had he not once attended the festivities in the great hall, or tried to arrange a meeting with her elsewhere? Was he to attend tomorrow's hunt? He had not said so in his note, but her spirits soared with anticipation.

"Your star's on the rise!" Felicity's eyes glowed with pleasure. "You've just come down from Northumberland, and already your cousin's been knighted. The king's chosen you to help arrange the Christmas masque—and play the leading role. And now, an invitation to the royal hunt. Only two other ladies are going—Alyson Waring and Jade Fairfax. But they've both been at court ever so long. Lady Jade can't bear to let Rokeby out of her sight."

Rokeby was to be one of the hunting party. She might have guessed. He had boasted to the king of his magnificent new falcon.

"As for Alyson, she was bred to the saddle—never misses a hunt if she can help it—"

As Felicity rattled on, she was stroking the thick, glossy fur that lined the cloak. She lifted a corner of the garment and inhaled the faint, heady scent.

"And look here, my lady," Prudence said. She lifted some smaller boxes from the trunk.

"Open them, girl," Felicity ordered.

The largest held a pair of boots, crafted of the finest cordovan leather; the next, a riding crop with a silver stock, ornately engraved by a master's hand. "And there's a pair of gauntlets, too." She drew out a pair of doeskin gloves, sewn with seed pearls.

"Jade Fairfax will be positively green with envy." Felicity laughed softly, obviously pleased by the thought.

"If so, her complexion will match her eyes," said Melora. "Such a curious, pale shade of green, they are. No doubt that's why she's called Lady Jade."

"Jade's also another name for a common harlot," Felicity reminded her. "Or were you shielded from such vulgar words, in Ashcroft Hall?"

Not at Ashcroft Hall; Melora had never even stepped through its gates. But she had heard many a serving wench called a jade. A drab. A doxy, or kinchin mort. She, too, had been reviled by country squires, by hostlers and carters, and by Tobias Abernathy, when she had recoiled in disgust from their questing hands and loose, hot mouths.

She forced such unwelcome memories to the depths of her mind. "Put these away in the press, please," she said to Prudence. The girl completed the task with quick efficiency, then helped Melora change from her ballgown to her nightdress, took the bodkins from her hair, and brushed the dark waves until they gleamed.

Later, with the candles out and both girls in their beds, Felicity was still going on about tomorrow's hunt, about Dirk's fine gifts, and Lady Jade's envy. "She's had other lovers besides Rokeby—a score of them. And not only courtiers, but stable lads who happened to take her fancy. One night she was seen in the stables, her petticoats pulled up to her waist.

"There she was, on her knees, with her legs spread and her bare bottom raised and the hostler was covering her, like a stallion with a mare—"

"Felicity! That's enough."

"Still determined to cling to your maiden modesty?"

"I'm determined to get at least a few hours' sleep," Melora retorted. "Since his majesty has done me the honor of inviting me to the royal hunt, I don't want to disgrace myself when we ride out by falling behind the others."

But long after Felicity had dropped off to sleep, she lay wide-eyed, staring into the darkness.

Would Dirk be at the hunt? If he did ride with the king tomorrow, she would have a chance to thank him for his handsome gifts. She shifted restlessly and pulled the satin coverlet up over her shoulders.

Dirk had to come to the hunt—he had to.

But why should it matter so much? Surely there would be plenty of other occasions to tell him how much she liked the new riding outfit. Why must it be tomorrow?

Because of Rokeby, that was it. Dirk had promised to protect her, if the viscount grew too urgent in his advances.

She closed her eyes, but sleep would not come; for the hard core of honesty inside her would not allow her to accept such half-truths.

She ached to see Dirk again. Even if he did not touch her, but only rode beside her, she needed that much. The thought of being with him again sent a hot current stirring, moving

112

through her body. Under her silk shift, her skin began to tingle, as if brushed by the wings of a flight of butterflies.

All right then, she told herself. Dirk was handsome, virile, passionate. An adventurer, a man of daring. Plenty of other court ladies found him attractive. They flaunted their charms shamelessly before him, hoping for a night's assignation, or a few weeks of stolen pleasure.

But she had come to court with him for her own reasons, and those did not include a night in his bed, or a season as his mistress. She was his partner in a risky enterprise. If she wavered, if she allowed herself to give in to her emotions, however briefly, the danger would be that much greater.

If the banked fires of her womanhood were stirring within her, there was no shame in that. Such feelings were natural enough.

Women had their needs, just as men did. Bronwen had told her so. "And if the stallion don't chase after the mare, she must come seeking him in his pasture," the old Welshwoman had said.

But what if her need for Dirk was more than a simple physical urge? What if she were falling in love with him?

There were those like Lady Jade, like Felicity—and countless others, no doubt—who could lie with a man, share in his pleasure, reach fulfillment along with him, and yet remain free. But even now she sensed with an instinct that went bone-deep that she was not one of these. She never could be. She was too much like her own mother. If she were to give herself to Dirk, she would have to follow him wherever he went.

But he would not want that. He would not permit it. His eyes were fixed on the sea, and those untamed lands that lay beyond.

And she was committed to her own vision of the future: a new beginning for her father, here in London. A fine theater, a powerful patron, the most talented troupe of players they could assemble.

The Christmas festivities would pass, the winter would be

over. Dirk would sail away, without a regret or a backward glance.

And maybe later—oh, much later—she would be free to fall in love.

Melora lifted her skirts and hurried down the corridor, her velvet cloak streaming out behind her. From the courtyard beneath the tall, narrow windows she caught the first high-pitched silvery notes of a hunting horn, and the shrill barking of hounds, carried on the early morning air.

She stopped short as Queen Anne emerged from her own suite. She curtsied. "Good day, your majesty."

Queen Anne inclined her head slightly. "Felicity told me of your plans, my dear. No doubt you are looking forward to your first hunting party at Whitehall."

"I would have asked your leave to attend," she said. "But as you had already retired when I received the invitation last night, I asked Lady Felicity to carry my message." The royal protocol decreed that no lady-in-waiting might leave the palace grounds without the queen's permission; Melora had already learned that much.

"Lady Felicity told me of your plans, even as you were putting on your new finery. I did not know you enjoyed the pleasures of the chase," she went on.

"I don't—what I mean is—"

Melora was foundering, and the queen intervened with practised skill. "But then, you've been here so short a time. I fear I have not come to know you as well as I should like."

And pray heaven, you never will.

"I'm not particularly experienced at hunting," Melora said. "My mother preferred that I should occupy myself with my music and needlework."

She had caught herself before she had admitted that she had never gone hunting, not even once. The pleasures of the chase were only for the nobility, or the prosperous country squires. A

114

farmer might kill a fox or a weasel that raided his henhouse; a shepherd's dogs were trained to drive off a wolf; but lowborn folk were forbidden to hunt for sport.

When her father's troupe had fallen on hard times, and Osric had snared a rabbit, the loyal little man had known well enough the risk he was taking. Poaching was an offense punishable by flogging or even hanging, if the local magistrate should choose to inflict the full penalty of the law.

How many more times would she be able to sidestep such a pitfall before she betrayed herself? Melora wondered. Right now, she could imagine what a fleeing deer must feel, as the yelping hounds drew near: the frantic heartbeat; the struggle for breath; the search for a hiding place. And then, the terrible certainty of death.

How many nights she had lain awake in her canopied bed, going over the events of the day before, reviewing each word she had spoken, her least important gesture. How often she had wondered if the queen, or a lady-in-waiting, or even her own maid, had suspected that Lady Rosalind Grenville was not what she pretended to be.

"You have our leave to go now, my dear," the queen was saying. "It would be unfair to deprive the gentlemen of seeing you in such a becoming cloak and gown."

Before she could acknowledge the compliment, she saw that her majesty was looking past her. "Our young Lady Grenville looks most bewitching this morning, does she not?"

Melora wheeled about and found herself face to face with Lady Jade Fairfax.

"She does, your majesty." But there was no trace of warmth in Lady Fairfax's pale green eyes. Her silver-blond hair was pulled back and twisted into an intricate chignon. A few paces behind her stood her pageboy, holding a hooded falcon.

She gave Melora a tight little smile. "I am particularly looking forward to today's hunt. Do you prefer the peregrine, Lady Rosalind? Or are you content to fly a pretty little merlin?"

Luckily, Lady Jade did not wait for her reply. "A merlin or

goshawk will be of little use today," she went on smoothly. "We hunt the crane. And only a peregrine has the strength and speed to bring down such quarry. Don't you agree?"

"Lady Rosalind was trained in domestic skills," the queen said.

"Was she indeed? Supervising the making of preserves, the distilling of cordials, the sorting of linens, no doubt."

Queen Anne turned a long, steady look on Lady Jade. "A young lady who is to marry one day, and oversee her husband's home, has need of such training. No matter how many servants she may have to wait upon her, it is her duty to keep the household running smoothly. And to pass her skills on to her own daughters."

The dart found its mark. Lady Jade curtsied, then withdrew as quickly as etiquette would allow. The queen waited until Lady Jade disappeared down the stairway.

She placed a hand on Melora's arm. "Wait a moment, my dear. I think it my duty to warn you that you may have made an enemy—one whose resentment is not to be taken lightly."

"Lady Jade is jealous because Lord Rokeby has sought out my company?" Melora was too unnerved to choose her words with her usual care. "She need not lose any sleep over that. I have no liking for the viscount."

"Neither do I."

Melora was startled by the queen's frankness. She spoke as if Melora was a confidante of long standing, rather than a newcomer to court.

"I would not have praised your musical talent so highly, if I'd realized that his majesty would single you out to assist Lord Rokeby with the masque."

"I've had no experience devising a masque or performing in one. Surely any of your other ladies would be far better suited."

"None of them has your melodious voice. And you play the lute as skillfully as some hired musicians who earn their living by their talents here at Whitehall."

Melora's uneasiness over Rokeby gave way to another,

greater fear. Suppose the queen were to suspect that she had earned her living with her lute and her singing? She chided herself for falling prey to such farfetched imaginings.

Why should her majesty suspect that the daughter of Sir Nicholas Grenville had learned her skills not from a Welsh master, but from a series of wandering performers at fairs and in taprooms along the backroads of the realm?

"I can understand why you don't like being thrown together with Rokeby." The queen's eyes were shadowed. "His majesty is too ready to place his trust in those who least deserve it."

Melora tensed, sensing an unexpected opportunity to supply Dirk with the information he wanted. If only she could draw the queen out, encourage her to speak of the affairs of state.

"Perhaps his majesty sees certain qualities in Lord Rokeby that are hidden from others," she ventured.

"It is possible." But the queen spoke without conviction.

"His majesty also favors the Earl of Pembroke, I believe." Melora was feeling her way with caution. "Is he to be trusted, do you think?"

The queen's plain features relaxed, and her lips curved in a smile. "I would trust Pembroke with my life, and his majesty's, too. Indeed, we've had to place our safety in the earl's keeping before. He did not fail us then, and should the need arise again—" The queen broke off abruptly. Her eyes looked past Melora, as if they were fixed on some disturbing vision of the future.

Melora took a step nearer. She must forget her scruples, if she was to obey Dirk's orders.

But now the hunting horns sounded again from the courtyard below, and the hounds set up a frenzied barking. "It's high time you were on your way," the queen said. "Even if you don't care for hunting, a ride on a fine, bright day like this should do you good."

There would be other chances to speak with the queen,

Melora consoled herself. She had gathered a little information, and if only Dirk were waiting down there in the courtyard, perhaps she would find an opportunity to pass it on to him this morning.

Chapter Nine

The autumn sunlight gilded the red brick palace walls, and when Melora emerged into the courtyard, a crisp, cool breeze tossed the heavy folds of her cloak so that it flared out behind her. Her heart lifted as she caught sight of Dirk, mounted on his black stallion. A hooded falcon perched on his gloved right hand. She called out to him. He turned his horse, cantered to her side, and swept off his plumed hat.

As his eyes moved over her, he smiled with satisfaction. "Your riding costume's most becoming, cousin Rosalind." He gestured to a stableboy who held the reins of a chestnut mare. The lad hurried forward and helped Melora up into the saddle.

The rest of the hunting party was already mounted. Although the king clutched at his horse's reins and gripped the beast tightly with his thighs, he was having some difficulty controlling the spirited mount.

Melora remembered the hostler who had ridiculed the king's clumsy horsemanship. Although Dirk had reproved the hostler for speaking out so freely, the man had been right; James certainly was not at ease in the saddle.

Melora glanced about at the rest of the party. Rokeby had already positioned himself as closely as possible to the king, while Lady Jade remained a few paces behind, her falcon on her wrist. Lady Alyson sat erect in the saddle, with the confidence of a born horsewoman. She smiled at Melora and said, "Fine weather for your first hunt."

A sturdy, heavy-shouldered man in the brown woolen doublet and breeches of an upper servant handed Rokeby his bird. The peregrine closed her talons about the viscount's gauntleted fist, flapped her broad wings, and gave a few shrill, high-pitched cries.

The falconer looked up and spoke softly to the viscount. With the barking of the hounds, the whinnying and stamping of the horses, Melora could not catch all of the man's words, but she heard enough to realize that he was uneasy about the condition of the hawk. "My lord, if you will take my advice—at least another week of training—she's still off her feed—the long journey from Spain—"

But Rokeby silenced the falconer with a hard stare. "You've had nearly a month to prepare Doña Esmeralda," he said. "That should have been long enough, Master Lovell. If a falconer's skilled in his trade."

The man flushed and lapsed into silence.

"I think you should heed Lovell's advice, my lord," Lady Alyson said. "My father once had a hawk from Granada, and his falconer had the devil's own time training her. Nervous, overbred, she was."

But Melora was no longer interested in the talk of falcons. Dirk was here beside her, and that was all that mattered. Her misgivings of the night before were swept away. Had it had been a week since she'd seen him last? It seemed far longer.

She told herself that for this one day she would forget all about court intrigue, about the coming winter, the elaborate Yuletide festivities, the difficulties she would no doubt encounter in planning the masque with Rokeby. She would not allow herself to think of the day when Dirk would leave court, sail off to the New World, and be lost to her forever.

Today she would ride beside him in the autumn sunlight. She would fill her eyes with the sight of him, so that his tanned face, with its angular cheekbones and jutting chin, the curve of his

120

mouth, the line of his jaw, would be engraved in her memory.

Her spirits plunged when Lady Jade cantered over to them. "Your cousin has no bird of her own, I see. Surely there is still time to find one for her. A little merlin, or goshawk. Either one should be suitable for bringing down a few larks."

"Lady Rosalind's had little experience at hunting," Dirk said.

"Ah, yes, now I remember. Your little cousin prefers the fascinating duties of the stillroom, the pantry, and the linen cupboard." She gave Melora a supercilious smile. "I wonder why she chose to ride out with us today."

"Lady Rosalind's here at our invitation, madam." The king's Highland burr silenced her. "Rokeby suggested that she might enjoy the ride, after being confined indoors since she arrived at Whitehall."

He turned to Melora with a smile. "I hear you've been reluctant to start planning the Christmas masque. But there's no need for such shyness, my lady. Her majesty speaks highly of your talents, and I promise that you'll find a most appreciative audience here at court."

"She and Rokeby will have little time for planning a masque, during the speed of chase," Jade Fairfax said. "Even supposing Lady Rosalind is able to keep up with the rest of us."

This time it was Rokeby who silenced her. He jerked his head in the direction of a freshly painted cart laden with hampers and boxes. "After Doña Esmeralda's brought down her quarry, we'll stop at the old abbey to enjoy our repast. Lady Rosalind and I will have all the time we need, to share a bottle of fine Canary or Rhenish, and talk over the details of the entertainment."

The king nodded with satisfaction. "We shall look forward to your masque with particular interest," he said. Then he raised his hand; the horns sounded high and shrill on the clear air, and the party was off. Across the courtyard they went, and into a wooded stretch, where branches, still thick with leaves of russet and gold, shaded their path.

Melora tried not to think about the prospect of sharing her midday meal with Rokeby. Seeking distraction, she fixed her eyes on the handsome greyhounds, who were straining at the leash. Even the strongest of the handlers were having some difficulty in controlling the powerful animals.

Turning to Dirk, she asked, "Since the falcons will do the hunting, what need is there for hounds?"

"These are no ordinary hounds," he assured her. "They are raised with the hawks and share their food. They may be needed to reach a struggling crane and keep it from injuring a falcon."

"But I'd have thought a crane would be no match for a falcon. Since a hunting falcon's bred for strength and speed, and trained by men like Master Lovell—"

"These falcons are costly birds. Their owners don't wish to take the slightest chance of losing even a single one." He paused, a frown drawing his brow together. "As for Rokeby, in his place I would have taken the falconer's advice about Doña Esmeralda. I'm told the bird went off her feed after the long trip from Granada. That's not uncommon. But she should have been given a chance to regain her full strength. And to settle into her new surroundings."

Melora's eyes widened with distress. During the time she had traveled the roads with Bronwen, spending the nights in remote woodlands and lonely moors, the old Welshwoman had often spoken of her own beliefs: of the oneness of all living creatures, birds and animals, plants and trees. It was an ancient, half-forgotten lore, but one that had struck a responsive cord in Melora.

"If the crane manages to escape Rokeby's bird, it will still be torn to pieces by the dogs, is that it?" she asked.

Dirk nodded. "That's how it's done."

"It doesn't seem right to me. And as for using hawks to hunt larks, I'm glad I won't be called upon to try." She shook her head. "I don't believe I shall ever come to enjoy such cruel sport."

122

She spoke softly, so that only Dirk could hear hear.

"You dislike the thought of a lark pitting her strength again a hawk's." He threw her a teasing smile. "Yet I seem to remember a small songbird who almost split the skull of a certain landlord. Even the gentlest creature will fight, if provoked."

Melora glared at him, then spurred her mount forward, but Dirk overtook her easily. "I gather you've been keeping Rokeby at a distance," he said. His smile had disappeared. "Don't carry such delaying tactics too far."

The joy she had felt in being with Dirk again began to ebb away. She tried to sound indifferent, but she could not quite manage it. "What about today? Am I to have my midday meal with him?"

"It might be a good idea."

Resentment surged up inside her. He had chosen this new riding habit carefully, to emphasize the deep violet-blue of her eyes; to set off the whiteness of her skin; to call attention to the curves of her body. Now she was to flaunt herself for Rokeby's pleasure.

The viscount might fondle her, and make suggestive remarks, as he had last night; and it would not arouse Dirk's jealousy. He would stand by, an impassive spectator, and watch her dine with the viscount, share a bottle of wine, flirt with him.

And he would not mind at all.

Why should he mind? What was she to him, what had she ever been but a useful tool? A means toward an end. Hot, angry words shaped themselves in her mind. She pressed her lips together, and gripped the handle of her riding crop so tightly that, even through her glove, she felt the silver engraving cutting into her hand. It took every bit of willpower she possessed to keep her from berating him before these courtiers, before the king himself.

The hunting party moved forward at a gallop now, and she spurred her horse. In spite of her lack of experience in riding, she had no difficulty in keeping up with the rest. The swift motion, the wind against her burning face, gave some outlet for the pent-up tension she could express in no other way.

They sighted the first crane an hour later, above a marsh shielded by elms and cedars, overgrown with rushes and broad-leafed vines. The crane rose from the water and went soaring overhead; dipping, wheeling, riding the currents of the cool morning air. It moved with a dancer's grace, thought Melora, and she found herself smiling appreciatively.

"With your majesty's permission, my bird will take the first kill." Rokeby's words shattered her euphoric mood.

The king nodded his assent. "You have spoken so highly of the prowess of your Doña Esmeralda. Now let us see what she can do."

Rokeby drew the plumed hood from the falcon's head. She was, indeed, a handsome creature, Melora thought. But deadly, too, with her hooked beak and powerful taloned feet. Doña Esmeralda ruffled her feathers, glared about her with round yellow eyes, then gave a piercing cry.

"I trust she'll live up to your praise, Rokeby," said the king. Do you intend to have her wait on the crane, or ring it?"

"She'll ring the crane, sire, and bring it down with single pass."

But Master Lovell rode forward, hesitated a moment, then said, "My lord, it would be better if Doña Esmeralda were to wait upon her prey. To try the ringing maneuver would be unwise. The peregrine's not yet ready for—"

"Hold your tongue, man." Rokeby shot the falconer a black look. "I've made my decision."

"Rokeby, wait," Dirk said. "Take heed of Master Lovell. Your peregrine's been caged and carried from Spain, passed from hand to hand during her journey. Surely there'll be time enough to let her show off her skill another day."

"I've no need of my falconer's advice. Or yours, my lord. Perhaps you doubt your own skill at handling your bird. Or is it her common lineage that makes you fear she won't prove the equal of Doña Esmeralda?"

Melora reminded herself that it was the bird Rokeby was speaking of. Yet his look, his tone, made her feel he was disparaging Dirk's lineage, and perhaps reminding him that he had received his own title only a week ago.

She could feel the tension that flared between the two men; it was as real, as deadly, as a bolt of lightning. Dirk carried no sword, but she caught the flash of the dagger's jeweled handle, thrust into his belt.

Dirk stroked his falcon's gleaming back with an easy, soothing motion. "My bird's of good English stock," he said. "She suits me well."

"Enough, my lords!" The king interrupted impatiently. "More of your talking, and the crane will be out of sight."

Rokeby loosened his peregrine. Melora caught her breath, awed by the swiftness of the bird's ascent. The crane caught sight of its pursuer. It was already flying higher, climbing far above the red-gold of the autumn woods, spiraling upward. Higher still, it went. Melora shaded her eyes with a gloved hand.

"That is called 'ringing,'" Dirk told her. "The crane's using all its evasive maneuvers. It won't be taken easily."

Now the peregrine was in full pursuit. Melora's lips parted and her breathing quickened as she watched Doña Emeralda's upward gyrations. This was a duel to the death, and although there was terror in it, there was a primitive beauty, too.

"The falcon must get above the crane," Dirk explained. "Then she'll stoop and strike. It's a demanding maneuver, but perhaps she can bring it off."

"Damnation!" Lady Jade's cry of dismay rang out across the clearing. "Not yet! She's not high enough!"

Bewildered by Jade's outburst, Melora watched the peregrine wheel about, then sheer off to the left. The crane dived downward, and was lost to view. A moment later, the falcon disappeared. From deep in marsh came the frenzied shrieking of the two birds, the beating of their wings.

The creak of wheels heralded the arrival of the painted cart that carried the provisions for the midday meal, but the spectators paid it no heed. All eyes were fixed on the tall rushes and tangled vines that concealed the peregrine and the crane, now locked in their death struggle.

A handler called to Rokeby. "Shall we loose the hounds, my lord?"

"No, damn you—"

"You must, Rokeby," said a red-faced, heavy-set huntsman "Else you'll surely lose that valuable bird."

Rokeby glared at the other man. "Not yet, I say!"

"Loose the hounds!" The king's voice rang out, and the handlers obeyed instantly. The greyhounds plunged into the undergrowth, their long, lean bodies moving with power and grace.

The hunters, Dirk and Melora along with the others, went galloping after the hounds. Melora averted her eyes, but not quickly enough to avoid a glimpse of the slaughter. The dogs had driven the crane away from the falcon. Now they were tearing it to pieces. Melora choked and pressed her hand to her mouth. But no one else in the party appeared to have the least concern over the fate of the crane.

Master Lovell leaped from his sturdy mount, plunged into the water, and made straight for the falcon. He lifted the injured bird in his arms, cradled her against his chest. Her wings beat feebly against his woolen doublet, staining it with her blood. His hands moved swiftly over her battered body.

"Left wing's broken, my lord. Her leg's badly mangled. Yet with time and care, perhaps I can save her life."

"Save her? To what purpose?"

"She fought bravely, my lord. Please, let me try to—"

"Give her to me." Rokeby's voice shook with fury. Or was it chagrin, that all his boasting had come to this?

126

"I beg you, my lord. If you'll permit me to carry her back and tend her—"

"You wretched idiot! You've already failed in your duties."

Melora felt a surge of revulsion for Rokeby. His words were cruel and unjust. Master Lovell had tried to persuade the viscount not to fly his bird today. Instead, Rokeby had insisted on trying her out in the more difficult maneuver. Now he was shifting blame to the falconer.

She might know little of hunting, but her father had taught her the rules of common decency. A man, highborn or low, must take responsibility for his actions.

"Give me the bird."

But Lovell held the falcon close to his chest a moment longer. He stroked the torn feathers and spoke in a low voice, as if to a wounded child. Then, slowly, with infinite gentleness, he handed the bird up to Rokeby.

The viscount drew his dagger from his belt, and with one swift movement, he slit the falcon's throat. He struck with such force that the head was severed. It went spinning off, and fell to the ground. He flung the battered body after it.

"Most unfortunate," said the king. "The bird was probably beyond saving. She surely would not have been able to hunt again." He sighed and shook his head.

Then he dismissed the matter, and turned to Dirk. "Your bird's had some experience in the field, Grenville," he said. "Set her against the next crane."

"As you wish, your majesty."

"She's one of our own English birds, you said?"

"Bred in the borderlands, sire."

A smile touched the king's mouth. "The border." He nodded with satisfaction. "And she had at least one fine Scottish bird in her bloodline, I've no doubt. Perhaps we need not look to foreign lands for our hunting hawks."

He raised his hand, gesturing the party forward. "Let's seek the next quarry."

"A moment, sire, if you please." Rokeby spoke respectfully,

but his voice betrayed him. He had been humiliated before the king. His boasting of the falcon's skill had proved hollow.

He looked about, and his cold gaze lit on Master Lovell. "You—come here."

The falconer approached with a steady stride, then stood looking up, awaiting his master's pleasure.

Rokeby swung back his arm, and slashed Lovell's face with his riding crop. Blood streamed from the deep welt on his forehead.

"Doña Esmeralda was not to blame for what happened, my lord." Lovell's voice was even, his fists were tightly clenched.

"You think I don't know that?" Rokeby leaned toward him. "The fault was yours, Lovell."

He motioned to a pair of sturdy dog handlers. "Take this man to the oak there."

"I tried to keep you from flying your bird today, Lord Rokeby."

"You tried to cover your own lack of skill. Your damned incompetence cost me a fine hawk. For that, you will pay."

The handlers led Lovell to the oak. Rokeby dismounted and strode over to the cart. "Hand me a length of stout rope," he said to the driver. Then the viscount jerked the horse whip from its holder. Melora drew her breath in sharply. In spite of the chill in the air, she started to perspire under her velvet dress.

Rokeby strode to the oak, tossed the rope to the handlers. "Take off his doublet, and bind him to the tree." The handlers hesitated a moment, then did as they were told.

Rokeby seized the collar of Lovell's shirt and ripped the garment in two, exposing his broad back. Melora looked away. She caught a glimpse of Lady Jade's face; her pale green eyes were avid, her lips parted in a look of fierce anticipation.

"No! It is unjust!" Melora was shocked at the sound of her own voice, ringing out across the clearing.

The king looked mildly surprised. "The hawk was Rokeby's," he told her calmly. "The man is his servant. It is his right to inflict punishment as he sees fit."

Although she kept her eyes averted, she heard the whip whistle through the air, heard the crack of leather on bare flesh. She set her jaw and drew a deep breath, fighting off the nausea that churned inside her. Again Rokeby struck, and this time Lovell cried out.

Unable to bear the sickening spectacle any longer, she wheeled her horse around and galloped out of the clearing. She did not know where she was going; she did not care. She only knew that she had to distance herself from the others.

She took the first path she could find. The mare's hooves pounded the hardened earth. A low-hanging branch slapped across her cheek, but she was scarcely conscious of the stinging sensation.

A flock of cawing rooks swooped across the path. Her startled mare reared and plunged. She clung to the pommel and managed to stay in the saddle. Then she heard the sound of hoofbeats close behind her.

Dirk overtook her, seized her reins, and got the mare under control. She saw that he had left his falcon behind, before setting out after her. Perhaps he'd been concerned for her safety, but right now, she could feel no trace of gratitude. "Let go of my reins," she said, and tried to pull them out of his grasp.

"You'll stay right here until you've gotten hold of yourself. Then you'll rejoin the hunt."

"I won't! I'm going back to the palace."

"You still have much to learn about proper manners. No one rides off helter-skelter as you did without taking formal leave of his majesty. Besides," he added with a slight smile, "you were going the wrong way. This path leads to the abbey."

She glanced about and realized that she had lost her bearings completely.

"The abbey's not far. Come, I'll show you."

He dismounted, reached up, and lifted her from her saddle. He held her against him for a moment, and she caught the scent of leather and linen, and of the man himself. He set her down, fastened their horses to a nearby tree, and led the way through a grove of elms, around a turn in the path. "There it is," he said.

Only three sides of the abbey were still standing. He took her arm and she followed him into the shelter of the moss-covered gray stone walls. A few jagged pieces of glass remained in the windows; they glowed deep amber, green, and purple where the sun struck them.

Melora was still shivering. He tossed his plumed hat aside, then drew her into his arms, and held her against him.

"Easy, sweeting. I'm here. It's all right now."

"How can you say that? Poor Master Lovell— Sweet Jesu, couldn't you at least have tried to stop Rokeby?"

"You heard what his majesty said. Lovell is Rokeby's servant."

"And that makes it right for him to punish the man so brutally for something that was not his fault? Is that the code among you highborn gentlemen?"

Dirk slackened his grasp abruptly. "Most gentlemen leave such punishment to a baliff," he said. "Or, if they are on their own land, the duty is relegated to their estate agent."

"Then you admit Rokeby acted out of sheer malice."

"Certainly I do. He'd boasted of his falcon, and when he was humiliated in front of the king—the whole party—he needed a scapegoat."

"If you believe that, you should have spoken out." Her voice shook with indignation.

"Melora, be reasonable." He drew her against him once more.

"Let me go! I want no comfort from you." She tried to pull free, but he kept his arm tightly about her. "How could you sit by and allow Rokeby to punish an innocent man?"

"You spoke out," he reminded her. "And what good did it do? I hope you realize that the king was unusually forbearing with you. That's because you're a lady, young and unfamiliar with the ways of the court."

He went on stroking her back, his hand moving from her shoulders down along her spine to her waist. His touch stirred

130

her senses. A shower of sparks flared up inside her and went spiraling through her body.

But she would not yield to the urging of her senses. "You feared the king would not show forbearance to you, is that it?" she challenged him. "Were you afraid you might fall out of favor with his majesty?"

She caught the flicker of anger in his eyes. Or was it some other emotion, one she did not wish to recognize? Had she wounded him with her accusation? Was it important to him that she should respect him? But there was no time for such considerations, not now. She could not stem the torrent of her words.

"Lady Jade took a kind of—of unholy pleasure from watching the flogging. I think, in some twisted way, she was aroused by Rokeby's cruelty. Maybe you, too, are stirred by the sight of—"

"Hold your tongue." He did not raise his voice, but she flinched under his icy anger. "I'd have thought you knew me better."

"I don't know you at all—I don't want to—not now. I want to get away."

"From me?"

"From you and Rokeby and all of your highborn friends."

"Rokeby's no friend of mine."

She tilted back her head and her eyes searched his. "But you dare not offend him. You may need his influence to help you get your ships, your land grant."

"That's how favors are won at court."

"So I've begun to learn. You don't care what you must do, what you force me to do—"

"I haven't forced you to do a damn thing you weren't willing to do. Have I?"

She paused, her breasts rising and falling quickly, her face flushed. He grasped her shoulders hard. "Have I?"

And when she did not answer, he shook her until her hood fell back and the bodkins slid from her hair. The dark waves

131

tumbled down around her face. She pushed them back impatiently.

How could she deny the truth of what he said? She had come with him willingly. She had deceived Rokeby, Felicity—the king and queen—into believing she was his cousin. Only a few hours ago, she had tried to gain the queen's trust so that she could trick her into revealing confidential information.

"You came to court, and you'll stay here until you've fulfilled your part of our bargain. Not because you think I'd use force, but because you stand to gain by it."

"I can't, not now. Since I saw you last week, everything's changing. Rokeby's always at my side. He won't leave me alone. He wants me."

He ran his eyes over her, a hot light kindling in their depths. "What man wouldn't want you?" He pulled her against him, but this time he was not trying to comfort her. His body pressed against hers, bending her backward. She could feel the hard muscles of his thighs against her legs. He lowered his head, his face poised above hers, so that the heat of his breath seared her cheek.

She tried to turn away, to twist her body out of his arms. But she managed only to free one hand. Filled with helpless rage, she drew back her arm. He caught her wrist, then slowly drew off her glove. He raised her hand to his lips, palm upward, and his tongue flicked lightly over the bare skin. She was caught up in a rising tide of passion.

He released her hand, and now his mouth covered hers. This was no gentle kiss. She was shaken to the depths of her being by the fierce hunger, the leashed violence she felt in him.

Her own hunger surged up, sweet and hot and stronger than anger, and her lips parted. She did not resist the first exploring thrust of his tongue. She welcomed the sweet invasion. His mouth claimed hers, probing the smoothness within.

When he raised his face, it was only so that he might look down at her, his eyes searching hers. "Melora."

And it was good, so good, so wonderfully reassuring to hear

the sound of her own name. For this brief time, she could let go. She could drop her guard, put aside all caution.

She was completely aware of his driving need for her. His male urge to enter her dark, hidden softness, to possess her and take satisfaction from their joining. But as he kept his gaze locked with hers, she saw far more. She was stunned by all that was reflected in the depths of his gold-flecked eyes. She had never known such a look from him before—tender, protective, adoring.

She reached up and her hands caressed his shoulders. But it was not enough. Her remaining glove, his doublet, his shirt, all were barriers, to be stripped away. She ached to know the feel of his bare skin beneath her fingers.

He was drawing her down, and she did not try to stop him. She lay back against his arm. He unhooked her cloak, and it fell to the leaf-strewn stones of the floor and he was spreading it out. She was helping him. And now she was stretched out on the thick, soft fur.

He opened the buttons of her bodice slowly, carefully, one by one. From time to time, he stopped to kiss her brow, her cheek, her lips, the little hollow at the base of her throat.

She stripped away her remaining glove, and now she could thrust her fingers into his hair, stroke the back of his neck. She slid her hands under his shirt and felt the heat of his heavily muscled back, the rise and fall of his breathing.

Not enough. It was still not enough. She needed to know the whole length of his unclothed body against her own.

He shifted and now he was above her, straddling her hips. With one hand he raised her skirt, her petticoat. She arched her body and felt the hardness of his manhood against her.

She gave a cry, but before she could draw back, he took her hand and brought it to the source of his need. He moved her hand, teaching her the motion, but she needed little teaching. She knew, with a knowing that was a part of her blood and bone, that always had been.

Abruptly he drew away from her. She cried out again, but

this time it was a cry of protest, a wordless expression of her wanting.

Then she, too, heard the pounding of hooves, the voices carried on the autumn breeze. She bit down hard on her lower lip, and sought to regain her self-control. The hunting party was heading this way.

She remembered someone saying something about taking the midday meal in the ruins of the abbey . . . but even now, she could not move quickly enough. Dirk had to help her to sit up, then raise her to her feet.

He smiled down at her, and his eyes held a promise she could not fail to understand. "Not yet, Melora," he said.

Chapter Ten

Not yet, Melora.

She could not forget the words Dirk had spoken in the ruined abbey, or the warmth in his dark, gold-flecked eyes. But her mood of joyous anticipation had been rudely shattered by the pounding of hoofbeats, heralding the approach of the others. Before the king and the rest of the party had appeared, she had rearranged her hair and buttoned her bodice. With unsteady hands, she had brushed away a few dry leaves and twigs that had clung to her skirt.

Ignoring her inner turmoil, she had assumed an appearance of composure as she'd left Dirk and joined the others. The supply cart arrived, followed by another, larger wagon carrying a table and chairs. Servants scurried about unpacking hampers, taking out baked hams, beef pasties, and potted pigeons; they arranged the platters, and filled the drinking flagons with Malaga, Rhenish, and Burgundy. It was plain that the violence the others had witnessed—the slaughter of Rokeby's falcon, the flogging of Master Lovell—had not taken away their appetites.

Although Melora found the sight of Rokeby, the sound of his voice, more hateful than ever, she told herself that she could not allow her emotions to override her good sense. She decided that since she would have to begin working on the masque with him, and soon, it would be better to do so here and now.

At least they were not alone; surely, in the presence of the

135

king and courtiers, he would be forced to rein in his amorous impulses.

"Artemis and her shepherd lover," James said, stroking his beard. "A fine idea, Rokeby. Our Lady Rosalind is well suited to the role of the chaste young moon goddess."

The others began offering their own ideas for the masque. The rest of the queen's ladies might appear as wood nymphs, said Lady Alyson. There should be a lake, or a stream, and water sprites, one of the gentlemen suggested.

The king nodded his approval. "An excellent notion. We may count on Master Inigo Jones to provide whatever effects are called for," he said with calm assurance.

Only Jade Fairfax maintained a tight-lipped silence. Since Melora was to have the leading role, she would not content herself with a lesser one.

Later, when they had returned to the palace courtyard, and Dirk had lifted Melora from her horse, she drew him aside.

"What of Master Lovell?" she asked.

"He's been carried back to his quarters." Dirk's lips tightened. "He's a sturdy fellow. It will take time, but he'll recover."

"He should have a physician's care, surely."

"He is Rokeby's servant," Dirk reminded her.

"And you really think the viscount will see that he's properly looked after?"

"Right now, Rokeby's too preoccupied with planning the masque to spare a thought for Lovell. If it will make you feel better, I'll go down to the falconers' quarters later this evening," he promised. "There's a skilled Moorish physician here at the palace. I'll see that Lovell gets whatever care he needs. I give you my word on it."

"If you knew how I loathe working with Rokeby." She kept her voice low, but it shook with revulsion. "I'll never look at him again without remembering his cruelty to—"

"You must learn to conceal your feelings," he reminded her. "I've warned you before. Don't force me to keep reminding you."

Melora stiffened at his rebuke. "The queen dislikes him, too, and she doesn't make a secret of it. She told me only this morning that she—"

"Careful," he warned. But he looked down at her, his eyes alert. He took her arm and led her to the topiary garden at the far end of the courtyard. With the approach of evening, a chill wind blew from the river; the branches of the hedges swayed and trembled with a rustling sound.

"Now tell me, what did the queen say?"

She looked up at him, startled by the intensity in his voice.

"She said his majesty often acts on impulse in choosing his favorites. That he sometimes puts his trust in those who least deserve it."

"What else?"

"She believes he's right to trust Pembroke."

"Go on." He moved closer, his eyes searching her face, as if intent on getting the smallest fragment of information.

"She said—Dirk, do stop staring at me that way. I can't remember it all."

"You must try. It could be important."

She searched her memory. "Her majesty said she would trust Pembroke with her own life, and the king's."

"Go on."

"She said that once before, they placed their safety in Pembroke's hands, and that he did not fail them."

"Can you recall anything more?"

"I'm not sure. She did not say it in so many words, but I thought she sounded uneasy. As if she feared that she and the king might need Pembroke's help again. Dirk, what does it all mean? Do you know?"

But he ignored her question.

"What else did she say of Rokeby? Did she hint that he might be plotting against the king?"

His eyes locked with hers, as if he could drag the information out of her with the force of his will.

She shook her head. "I think she realized she had already

said more than she had intended. Then we heard the hunting horns. She told me to go down and join the others. I think—" She hesitated, but his hard, watchful look urged her on.

"She has been kind to me, Dirk. Ever since I arrived at the palace, she's done what she could to make me feel comfortable."

"You've won her favor, as I hoped you would," he interrupted.

He turned his head briefly, and looked out across the garden to the river. But although he watched the crimson sunset, the high-piled purple clouds, he was not distracted. "The queen likes and trusts you."

"I believe so. She warned me that I had made a dangerous enemy of Lady Jade."

He nodded, with a brief, tight-lipped smile. "Excellent."

"I don't see why you should be pleased that Jade Fairfax dislikes me."

"To hell with Jade Fairfax! But if the queen cares enough about you to warn you against her, it means you are already in a most advantageous position. Now you must do all you can to get even closer to her majesty. To win her confidence completely."

"So that I can try to catch her off-guard?" She stared up at him with indignation. "I'm to trick her into telling me more than she intends?"

"You're quick-witted, you have a charming air of innocence. You'll manage well enough."

He glanced back at the windswept courtyard. Most of the others had already gone back inside the palace, where blazing fires and hot wine possets awaited them.

"Come along, now." He took her arm and led her away from the garden. There was no trace of tenderness in his manner. It was not easy for her to remember that only a few hours ago he had kissed her, had drawn her down beside him, had caressed her with passion and tenderness.

All through the hours of the night, she tossed restlessly, as she

138

tried to recapture the memory of his glance, the deep tone of his voice, when he had said, "Not yet, Melora."

"There is a tradesman outside, my lady—a mercer with a chest full of silks and velvets and fine brocades." Prudence's eyes were aglow. "He says they are the latest designs from France and Italy."

Melora had been playing her lute, singing a few lines of verse, pausing from time to time to make notations on a sheet of paper beside her. She looked up from her work with a puzzled frown. "There must be some mistake. I sent for no merchant," she said.

"Perhaps Lord Rokeby did, my lady. So you might choose the materials for masque. All those splendid costumes—" The maid took a vicarious delight in the preparations for the lavish spectacle.

Melora put down her lute, pushed the paper aside, and set the quill pen in its gilt stand. "Show the man in."

The king had insisted that no expense should be spared, to make the new masque as lavish and impressive as possible. Master Inigo Jones had already been sent for to supervise the design and construction of the scenery, and to offer his suggestions for the costumes.

As the first week of December drew near, the plans had taken shape. Rokeby was busy composing the music for the principal ballads, and Melora was at work on the lyrics. Since the day of the hunt, she disliked Rokeby more than ever, but she nonetheless found herself caught up in the preparations for the masque.

She discovered that the viscount had not only an extensive knowledge of classical mythology, but also a genuine gift for music. As long as she concentrated on their joint endeavor, it was possible for her to set aside her personal feelings. She would prove herself worthy of the king's confidence in her abilities.

The prospect of making her first appearance before so sophisticated an audience was a little frightening; but it offered a challenge, too. When her confidence wavered, she reminded herself that she was Edmund Standish's daughter. Her mother had been a talented actress back in her native France. She was determined to do credit to her family heritage.

She heard Prudence saying, "Lady Grenville will see you now."

Perhaps Rokeby had taken the liberty of sending for the silk merchant without consulting her. No matter. She must make sure that her costume, and the costumes of the other performers, would enhance the production.

The mercer bowed his way into the chamber, and gestured to his apprentice, who set down the chest, then drew out a roll of tawny amber silk. He unrolled it, then passed it to his master, who held it up so that she might get the full effect of the splendid fabric. "This silk arrived from Paris only a week ago, my lady," said the mercer, a short, plump man. "You can see it is of the finest workmanship." He ran his fingers lightly over the soft folds.

Melora nodded appreciatively. "It's quite lovely, but not the right color for Artemis. Blue or pale mauve would be more suitable."

The mercer nodded. "Quite so, my lady. And I have it in those shades as well." He paused and his eyes met hers. "The ship carrying the merchandise arrived in one of the northern ports. It was carried to London all the way from Northumberland."

She drew in her breath, and her lips parted. The mercer had not mentioned Northumberland by chance—she was sure of it. But she must not allow her swift rush of excitement to drown her caution.

"You may go, Prudence," she said quickly. Then, seeing the girl's look of disappointment, she added: "See if you can find Lady Alyson. I believe the amber silk would be perfect for her costume, but I should like her opinion."

As soon as the maid had departed, she turned to the mercer.

"My home's in Northumberland." It was a seemingly casual remark, but the man responded instantly.

"Indeed, my lady?" He turned to his apprentice. "Take the chest closer to the fire, and find the blue and violet silks. And the embroidered ribbons." No sooner had the boy turned to his task than the mercer reached into his pocket and handed her a small, folded sheet of paper. Although she longed to read it at once, she could not take even so small a risk. Reluctantly she slipped the paper into her patchbox.

Although it took all the self-control she could muster, somehow she managed to control her impatience, while the mercer went on showing her more silks, velvets, and brocades, and lengths of ribbon. She settled on a length of lavender silk for her own costume. "And the dark blue ribbon for the sash is to be embroidered with silver crescents," she told him.

Prudence returned with Alyson, Felicity, and the other ladies-in-waiting, who had been chosen to play the wood nymphs. It wasn't easy for her to wait while they exclaimed over the silks and velvets, and tried to decided among the amber silk, the leaf green, the cinnamon.

"Green doesn't suit me at all," Felicity said. "It makes me look positively sallow."

"Not a deep shade of green," said Millicent.

"I should prefer the amber or the cinnamon for my costume. Or perhaps a tawny brown," Alyson said.

Melora, her lips set in a forced smile, tried to keep her attention fixed on their lengthy discussion. What jewels should they wear? What sorts of fans and slippers would be best?

"A wood nymph would wear sandals," said Felicity, who was proud of her small feet and trim ankles. "And I don't believe she would carry a fan at all. Would she, Rosalind?"

Melora started slightly, as she realized that Felicity was speaking to her. Although she had finally become accustomed to her assumed name, at the moment her thoughts were fixed on the letter tucked inside her patchbox.

"Perhaps the fan might be overlaid with rows of small gold

141

and amber leaves," she said hastily. She turned to the mercer. "Do you think you could have eight such fans made up for us?"

"Most certainly, my lady. I import goods from every part of Europe. No doubt my warehouses already hold whatever you may need. And if it pleases you, I would be happy to recommend a skilled cobbler to come and take the measurements for the sandals. Gold for the wood nymphs, and silver for you, my lady."

At last the mercer took his leave, followed by his apprentice. But the ladies were still engrossed in their talk, and when Melora could bear the waiting no longer, she slipped the patch-box into her pocket, and picked up her lute. She was already moving toward the door.

"I was interrupted by the mercer before I could finish going over one of my ballads." It was the first excuse she could think of. But she had no intention of practicing any of the ballads.

Instead, she hurried down the corridor, and out onto a balcony. She closed the doors behind her, set down the lute, then took out the letter. As her eyes moved over Osric's neatly written message, she gave a deep sigh of relief.

He began by offering his thanks to Lady Rosalind for sending such a generous sum toward their board and lodging. Now that Master Standish, although still weak, had recovered from his fever, they were preparing to leave the Leaping Stag. They would move on to a larger, more comfortable inn, run by a respectable widow. The Rose and Thistle was located near a town called Kilwarren, some ten miles west of Abernathy's establishment.

Osric's letter was a masterpiece of discretion. If it had fallen into the wrong hands, there was not the slightest implication that "Lady Rosalind" had any personal connection with the troupe.

He closed by saying that she was a most kind lady to remember the humble players who had offered her a few hours of entertainment at her father's home, last summer. He made no mention of Dirk, so that anyone reading the letter would have assumed that the pouch of coins had come from "Lady Rosalind."

"May we offer our heartfelt thanks for your kind patronage?" Tears stung Melora's eyelids as she read the last line. She put the letter into the bodice of her gown. Even as the chill wind from the river drove her inside again, she felt an inner glow. Dirk had done more than fulfill his promise to get word to her from her father. He had sent more money, enough to get Papa and the others away from the odious Abernathy.

She started back to her chamber. If only Felicity and the others had returned to the queen's apartments, she might have an hour or two of privacy before it was time to prepare for tonight's festivities in the great hall.

She had promised to meet with Rokeby tomorrow, to devise another ballad for the masque. But for now, she would put the viscount out of her mind. So far, although he had devoured her with his looks, had brushed his hand against her breast or the curve of her hip, whenever he got the chance, he had gone no farther.

She had the queen to thank for that. Her majesty had proved steadfast in her responsibility, determined to protect the youngest of her ladies.

More than once, just as he was becoming too insistent in his advances, the queen would walk in, as if by chance. She seated herself, and took out a piece of embroidery. She said little, as though reluctant to interrupt the work on the masque, but she remained there, a watchful presence. At other times, she was accompanied by a few of her ladies, who busied themselves helping her untangle her skeins of brightly colored silk and arrange them in her work basket.

Even when the queen's other duties kept her away, Felicity, Alyson, Millicent, or one of the others had a way of coming in and seating herself in a corner. Since they were to perform in the masque, it was perfectly natural that they would take a lively interest. But Melora suspected that they were there at the queen's orders.

Master Inigo Jones, a slender, bearded man, was a frequent visitor to the palace, accompanied by his apprentices. He consulted with Rokeby about the scenic effects and the placement of the candles and torches that would help to create the illusion of the forest grove where the goddess Artemis was to appear and give herself to Endymion, her mortal lover.

Master Jones had done the sketches of the stairway, which would be half-concealed from the audience by a drift of clouds. Down the stairway the moon goddess would descend.

"You will find it perfectly steady, my lady," Master Jones assured Melora. "You have no fear of heights, I hope."

"None at all," she said with a smile.

"Good. Then we'll have no need of a railing to detract from the effect. You are to move slowly, to give the illusion that you are descending from the evening sky."

As long as Master Jones and his apprentices were bustling about the chamber, Melora felt at ease. The apprentices were occupied with finding storage space for the movable stairway, the muslin clouds stretched on frames, the backdrops with their painted trees and shrubs.

Rokeby could raise no possible objection to the presence of Master Jones; the talented craftsman had supervised most of the court masques since King James had come to the throne.

They had yet another visitor, one who arrived at unexpected times, to watch the progress of the masque. Lady Jade's dislike of Melora grew steadily; her unrelenting jealousy drove her to walk in on them whenever she could find a plausible excuse.

Had Rokeby received her invitation to the small private supper in her chambers that evening? Servants could be so careless in delivering messages.

Had he forgotten that they were to go riding that afternoon? She would wait until he had finished his tiresome duties.

Jade kept up the pretense that Rokeby was devoting so much time to the masque only because the king had commanded it. Under other circumstances Melora might have felt some sympathy for the older woman. But she would never forget the look

144

of perverse enjoyment in Jade's eyes as she had watched Master Lovell's punishment.

Early in December, the Yuletide visitors began arriving from all corners of the realm: from Sussex they came, and Devon, and from King James's native Scotland. There were foreign visitors, too. Each night Melora met perfumed noblemen from the court of King Louis of France and dignified ambassadors from Madrid. She danced with a Russian grand-duke, a Hungarian count, a Danish prince who was related to Queen Anne. All flocked to Whitehall to enjoy the lavish hospitality of England's new king. They brought with them their wives, mistresses, servants, musicians, and jesters. Fortunately the red brick palace, with its countless apartments, was large enough to accommodate all of them.

Other entertainers, who traveled on their own, came seeking shelter from the winter cold; food left over from the nightly banquets; warm fires; and an occasional handful of coins, tossed by a courtier.

Once within the precincts of the palace, they managed to find shelter in the outbuildings or the courtyards. Melora, seeing them here, thought wistfully of Osric, Bronwen, and Caleb. The hardships they had shared, as well as their occasional small triumphs, had bound her to them. She even found herself missing Old Bruin, the great, shaggy bear.

With every passing evening the feasting grew more impressive. The king had ordered oversized gold and silver platters, especially made to hold the gigantic carp and eel pies; the whole roasted boars; the peacocks, cooked and then skillfully reconstructed, from their colorful combs to their magnificent tails, before being served at the banquet tables.

Long before midnight, many of the gentlemen had already drained two or three bottles of wine. Now they were eager to sample the hospitality of the court ladies, who were decked out in their newest gowns, their most dazzling jewels.

The queen's ladies-in-waiting were captivated by the foreign visitors. Felicity, who had been carrying on a flirtation with a young courtier from Sussex, now turned her attention to a dashing Frenchman.

"The Duc de Beauvilliers knows all the newest dances from Versailles," she told Melora. "He moves with such exquisite skill." She gave a soft little laugh. "It's been my experience that a gentleman who dances with such grace performs equally well in other circumstances."

She touched Melora's arm lightly with her fan. "But perhaps even now, after all these weeks at court, you don't yet understand . . ."

"I understand well enough," Melora said. But how could Felicity drift so casually from one liaison to the next? Perhaps she had been initiated into the physical side of love too early, thought Melora; perhaps those experiences had shut off her capacity for deeper feelings.

Melora, wearing a gown of turquoise silk trimmed with silver lace, entered the great hall. A pearl necklace and matching teardrop pearl earrings set off the whiteness of her skin and her shining ebony hair. Dirk had sent the jewels only this afternoon. She told herself that it had been a practical gesture. It would not do for his "cousin" to appear in public without some jewels of her own, when all the other ladies flaunted their glittering ornaments.

She paused for a moment to look about her. Would she ever become accustomed to the blaze of the candles, the hothouse flowers, the tapestry hangings? Tonight garlands of holly, ivy, and evergreens festooned the walls. It was not yet time to bring in the Yule log, but already she felt a rising anticipation as the holidays drew closer.

As she made her way across the hall, she saw that a game was in progress. Octavia Sutton, one of the queen's ladies, had been blindfolded with a silk handkerchief, then spun around until she swayed giddily. After she had regained her balance, she began moving through the laughing, jostling crowd.

She stopped before a Spanish gentleman and put her hand on his arm. Then she reached up and traced the man's features. "I think perhaps—alas, I'm not quite sure yet."

"Not sure, indeed!" Melora heard Alyson say to the young man beside her. "She's lain with the Marquis de Carvajal nearly every night since he arrived here. She never returns to her own chamber until dawn."

"Perhaps she should touch him elsewhere," said Alyson's partner. "No doubt she would recognize him quickly enough, if she were to take hold of his—" Alyson's shrieks of laughter drowned out the rest.

Melora was rapidly losing the last of her illusions about the ways of the nobility. A starving, ragged trollop who sold herself for a farthing could be arrested, whipped, and branded. But a court lady who pleasured herself in the beds of a dozen different gentlemen need not suffer any such penalty.

Felicity had told her of a lady-in-waiting who had been made pregnant by the handsome, dashing young Buckingham. "She married another gentleman, who knew all about it. But he was burdened with gambling debts, you see, and the bride's family offered a huge dowry." Felicity had laughed heartily. "The baby arrived six months after the wedding, and a lusty full-time boy he was. Buckingham stood godfather to the child."

And what was the difference between the wretched harlot, her back cross-hatched with whip scars, and the lady of whom Felicity had spoken? A high-sounding title was useful, Melora thought; but it was the bride's fortune that had protected her from punishment. Yes, she was learning the ways of the gentry.

Now Lady Octavia was giving the gentleman a long, lingering kiss. She hesitated only a moment longer, then called out, "The Marquis de Carvajal." He removed her blindfold and put it in his pocket.

"How clever of you, my lady," he said, with a touch of irony in his deep voice. He bent and whispered something in her ear.

147

She looked up from under her lowered lids, and tapped him sharply with her fan. Then they disappeared into the crowd.

"It's your turn, Rosalind." Before she could protest, Felicity placed a handkerchief over her eyes, spun her around several times, and gave her a little push forward. Melora blinked rapidly, then realized that she was able to see through the gossamer-thin silk and lace blindfold.

So much the better. She would seek a gentleman she knew, call out his name, and pretend to be surprised when she discovered she was right. She peered through the blindfold, and caught sight of young Ambrose Corbett. He was a shy young man who would claim his kiss and a dance, and be well pleased.

She started toward him, veering from side to side, so as not to spoil the game. But before she could reach Ambrose, another man stepped directly into her path. Squinting through her blindfold, she saw Rokeby. His feet, in their satin slippers, were planted firmly apart; his arms were outstretched.

She repressed a shiver of revulsion. Bad enough to have to work with him on the masque. She certainly did not want to submit to his kiss, or dance with him.

Then, from somewhere in the crowd, Dirk appeared, and swiftly moved between her and Rokeby. Startled but relieved, she went through the motions of the game, tracing the width of his forehead, his high, angular cheekbones, running her fingers along his jaw.

"Now, let me think." She took his hand in hers, and touched his fingers, one by one. "Here's a signet ring . . . but what is the design?" She slid off her silk glove. "A lion, perhaps? Or is it a fox? Perhaps if the gentleman would remove his glove . . ."

She ran her finger over the ring. From the circle of courtiers that surrounded them, she heard the buzz of voices, the laughter.

"My father wears a signet like this one." she said. "You are—Dirk."

He took off her blindfold, and bending his head, he brushed his lips over hers. "It took you long enough, my sweet cousin."

"Now, for your forfeit. You shall be my partner in the next dance."

The king signaled to the musicians, who struck up a lively volante. Dirk led her through the first measures. She caught a glimpse of Rokeby, his body taut with anger, his eyes glinting with frightening intensity.

Other couples joined in the dance, moving through each elaborate figure; until the moment when the gentlemen were to grasp their partners about the waist and raise them high in the air. There was a flurry of taffeta and brocade skirts, a glimpse of silk-sheathed legs.

Melora gave a stifled cry. Rokeby was moving toward her and Dirk with a purposeful stride. Surely the viscount would not be so rash as to create a scene here. Yet his face had gone white, except for the two spots of color that burned high on his cheeks. His eyes were narrowed to slits, like those of an angry cat.

The other gentlemen had set their partners down and were moving into the next figure of the volante. But Dirk held Melora high for a moment more. Then, before her feet could touch the floor, he slid his arm beneath her knees. Holding her tightly against his chest, he started from the great hall.

It was a breach of court etiquette, no doubt; but she had seen gentlemen taking far greater liberties tonight. She glanced over at the king. His majesty threw back his head and laughed loudly. The courtiers closest to him began to laugh, also; the rest joined in.

Melora put a hand on Dirk's shoulder and he carried her out of the hall. He strode the length of the corridor and kept going. She looked up at his face, now illuminated, now plunged into darkness by the fitful light of the torches on either side of the long passageway. He turned one corner, then another, and now he was carrying her up a long flight of stairs.

When they reached the top, he set her down, took her hand, and led the way through another maze of corridors. Then he stopped, opened a heavy door, and led her into a lavishly furnished suite.

An antechamber with a frescoed ceiling opened onto another, larger chamber beyond. She caught a glimpse of a bed with heavy brocade curtains.

"Whose quarters are these?" she asked.

"They're mine. Pembroke arranged that I should stay here at the palace for as long as I wished." He locked the door and returned to her side.

"Dirk, I don't understand. You said you needed to keep Rokeby's favor, but now—did you see his face as you carried me out of the hall?"

"Would you rather I'd left you with him?"

She shook her head. "No—but if Rokeby should turn against you—"

He cupped her chin in his hand. "Put Rokeby from your thoughts. Forget him, and Lady Jade. All of them. For now there's only the two of us."

His words, his look, sent tiny flames moving through her. He drew the pearl-tipped bodkins from her hair and laid them aside. Then he ran his fingers through her hair, smoothing it back from her forehead, loosing it to fall over her shoulders in thick blue-black waves.

"No more waiting." His lips brushed hers. "This night belongs to us, Melora."

But for all the caresses they had shared before, she still was hesitant, uncertain. Was she prepared to give herself to Dirk completely? She longed to yield to the sweet invasion he promised; but she feared the ultimate surrender.

Instinctive caution made her wary. Even as he drew her closer, she could not cast aside her thoughts of the future. What of all the nights to come? How would it be for her, after she knew what it was to be possessed by him . . . after he had sailed away never to return?

Yet even as her mind gave its warning, her hands were caressing his hair, his strong, corded neck, and his wide shoulders. She wanted him, hungered for him with all her being.

His fingers dealt quickly, expertly, with the buttons of her

150

gown. He slid the bodice from her shoulders, down over her breasts. The silk made a faint whispering sound as it fell around her in a pool of turquoise and silver.

He stripped away her embroidered, lace-trimmed undergarments, pausing from time to time to feather kisses along her throat and shoulders. Even when she stood before him clad only in her transparent linen shift, her silk stockings, and high-heeled satin slippers, her pearl necklace and earrings glowing in the candlelight, he made no move to possess her.

She raised her face, and his mouth sought hers. She parted her lips to invite his questing tongue. She pressed herself to him, caught up in the urgency of her mounting desire.

If the time they shared must be so brief, why not take what joyous fulfillment he offered her tonight?

Her tongue moved, touching his, withdrawing, then touching yet again. When he raised his mouth from hers, she made a wordless sound of protest. He swept her up in his arms and carried her into the bedchamber.

Chapter Eleven

Dirk moved the heavy folds of the bed curtain aside and set her down on the silk coverlet. He stood for a moment watching the candlelight play over the curve of her throat, the swell of her breasts. It was useless to try to deceive himself any longer. He had wanted her since he'd first caught sight of her in the ravine beside the North Road, since he'd heard her plaintive song carried to him on the night wind.

Her sweet, clear voice, the swift, graceful movements of her body, had stirred him; but he had been unwilling to admit his feelings, even to himself. He had fought hard against his growing desire for her.

His thoughts had been fixed on his one overriding purpose: his determination to return to court as quickly as possible, to keep the king's favor by whatever means he could contrive. His preoccupation had kept him from thinking of Melora as anything more than a useful pawn in the complicated game he was playing.

On the night of their first meeting, he had told himself that he had no desire to make love with this dark-haired, violet-eyed stranger who'd entertained the patrons of the taproom with her bawdy verses, yet who fought like a tigress when cornered; who carried herself like a highbred lady, but bargained with the hard-won skill of strolling player, desperate for a meal and a night's lodging.

What the devil had come over him since their first meeting? How had he allowed himself to fall under her spell? Looking down at the white oval of her face, framed by her black hair, and her fathomless amethyst eyes, he thought perhaps she was a sorceress, after all. Surely she had bewitched him.

Her sheer silken shift clung to her pointed nipples, her narrow waist, the swell of her hip. Leaning closer, he caught a glimpse of the dark triangle that concealed her untouched womanhood.

He made himself look away, even as he felt the aching need that stirred in his loins. His fingers closed around the bedpost with a grip so hard that the carved surface bit into his palm.

But it was useless to try to hold back any longer. He reached out and slipped his hand beneath her head, raising her slightly, then opened the clasp of the pearl necklace. The pearls were still warm from contact with her skin, and he held them for a moment, rolling them against his fingers.

He dropped the necklace on the small table next to the bed, stroked her sweet-scented hair, then brushed aside the ebony waves and removed her earrings.

When he started to take off his clothes, she looked away quickly. She had told him the truth, after all. The realization was deeply moving to him. During those years of traveling the roads, she had not given herself to any man. And even here at court, where she had been admired and sought after since her first appearance in the great hall, she had held herself inviolate.

Even while he was stirred by his conviction of her innocence, it caused him to hesitate. As he tossed aside his doublet and shirt, as his eyes took in every curve and hollow of her slender body, he warned himself that he would have to rein in the driving urgency of his need.

He would move slowly, until he was sure she was ready for him, until she shared his need for complete fulfillment. Nothing in his experience with women had prepared him for this. He had known the free-and-easy tavern wenches who had satisfied his physical hunger during his years as a mercenary; he had lain with the copper-skinned girls of the Indies. And the court ladies, bored with their husbands' routine lovemaking, had sought diversion in his arms.

But never before had he bedded a virgin.

Now, in spite of the fierce aching in his loins, the hunger that threatened to overwhelm him, he knew he must hold back until she was fully aroused and ready to give herself freely.

"Don't turn away from me, Melora." His voice was soft and husky.

Slowly, half-reluctantly, she made herself look at him. She drew in her breath, and he saw her breasts rise, the pointed nipples pushing against the silk of her shift. Her eyes widened as they moved from his face to his chest. Her gaze swept downward, and she tensed. Hot color flooded her face. Even though the lower half of his body was still clothed in his tightly fitted breeches, he was powerless to control the proof of his passion. He must not frighten her. He must use all his skill to prepare her for what lay ahead.

But now it was his turn to be startled, for with one swift motion she reached out and took his hand. She drew him down and he found himself seated on the edge of the bed. Her action had been simple, direct. Yet he felt the slight tremor in her fingers, and saw that her violet eyes were shadowed with a lingering fear.

"Easy, sweeting," he said, keeping his voice low, soothing. "Nothing's going to happen until you're ready. I want so much to pleasure you."

He leaned forward and put an arm on either side of her, his hands resting on the pillow; but he was careful not to touch her. "You've nothing to fear from me, Melora."

"It isn't you I fear." Her lips curved in a tremulous smile. "It's— How can I make you understand?"

"No need to try, sweeting," he said. "It's perfectly natural. You've never been with a man before. You don't know what to expect."

"But I do!" His throat tightened at the conviction in her voice. "I know all about it—Bronwen explained how—"

"You know nothing, love. There's so much that cannot be taught with words. Let me teach you . . . my way."

He slid his arm beneath her shoulders and raised her to him. His tongue traced her lips, outlining their delicate contours. With no further urging from him, she parted her lips, and his tongue darted into the moist smoothness. Then he felt a jolt of surprise, of pleasure, as her tongue moved to meet his.

Her arms twined around his neck and she yielded herself up to his long, searching kiss. The touch of her breasts against his chest sent a molten heat moving through him. His hands dropped to her shoulders, and slowly, carefully, he drew her shift down around her waist.

He held her closer, and she gasped with surprise, then pure pleasure as her nipples hardened. She brushed them against the crisp, curling hair of his chest. The friction sent a swift current of melting heat coursing through her.

He kissed the hollow at the base of her throat, the spot where her neck joined her shoulder. He nipped lightly, flicked his tongue over her satin skin.

Although her body was bared to the waist, he left the lower part of her shift in place. He cupped her breasts in his hands, then stroked her nipples over his lips. He drew one of her nipples into his mouth, and suckled at it. Then he turned his attention to the other. As his lips tugged gently at the nipple, it grew hard and hot.

She gave a shameless, wordless sound of protest as he drew away. Then she saw that he was raising himself only to slide her slippers from her feet. His hand returned, moved higher. He drew off one of her garters.

He rolled down her silk stocking, let it fall to the floor. The other stocking followed. But this time, his fingers moved still more slowly. With his fingertips, he traced swirling patterns along the soft, sensitive skin of her inner thigh.

She lay still, looking up at him. She watched as he unfastened his belt, as he drew off his tight breeches, kicked off his shoes. Half-fearful, half-fascinated, she let her eyes move downward.

She had not expected—had not imagined— How was it possible that she would be able to take the first thrust of that huge, iron-hard arousal into herself?

He dropped down beside her again, put his arm around her, and lifted her onto his thighs. She felt the hardness of his arousal against the rounds of her bottom.

Once before, he had held her like this. But this time, it would be different. This time, there would be no drawing back . . .

He raised her just enough to draw her shift off completely. He stroked her thighs. She parted her legs and his touch moved upward and higher still to that hidden place, where his fingers came to rest. She made a small sound of protest. For a moment he paused, to allow her to get used to the new sensation.

Then he took the hard, moist bud between his fingers and teased it, played with it, tugged at it, until his touch sent tiny tongues of fire racing from the moist, hot center of her being and upward, outward, through every part of her body. She began to move, rubbing her buttocks against his hardness.

He groaned softly. "Hold still, sweeting," he said, his voice unsteady. "You don't know what that's doing to me."

She did not know, but she could guess. She slanted a quick look up at him, then moved once more, slowly, enticingly.

He lifted her from his thighs, pushed her gently down on the bed, rolled her over on her side. He stretched out beside her, drawing her against him, so that for the first time, she knew the full length of his bare body, molded against hers.

He raised one of her legs and placed it over his thigh, so that she was open to his touch. His hand moved to the wet-hot satin flesh. Slowly, gently, he stroked every crease and fold of her womanhood.

She pressed her hard bud against his hand, seeking release from the mounting pressure inside her, a release only he could give her.

156

He moved her over onto her back and kneeled between her legs. "Dirk—not yet—"

But even as she protested, she sensed that he could delay no longer. She gasped at the first hard, burning thrust of possession. But she held onto him with all her strength, sensing that the fulfillment she sought lay beyond this instant of searing pain.

He was deep inside her now, filling her completely. He remained still, and she knew he was giving her time to get used to the sensation of their joining. Her hands began to move instinctively, from his shoulders down along his back. Her fingers pressed into the flesh at the base of his spine.

Slowly, gradually, the pain began to ebb away. Her fingers caressed him tentatively at first, then with growing assurance. Her hips arched upward, drew back. She was pushing herself against him again with ever-growing urgency.

And now he was moving, too, slow and easy, thrusting deep, deeper, as if seeking the center of her being. Drawing back, then thrusting again. The rhythm of his movements quickened and she was moving more quickly, too, matching her pace to his.

For an instant, they clung together, suspended over a gulf of darkness. Then they were rising together, caught up in a dark whirlwind. Her hands held him tighter, and they were spinning upward. And again upward. Moving in ever-tightening circles. Moving toward that instant of explosive sensation, of joining. Of sharing the ecstasy of fulfillment.

"Melora."

He lay beside her, his body curved around hers, her head resting against his chest. His hand came up to stroke the damp, tangled masses of her hair.

"Melora—my sweet Melora—"

She gloried in hearing him speak her name in that deep, husky tone. The sound of it gave her back her identity. Yet even now she knew that she was not the same as before.

Not Rosalind. She never had been Rosalind. But now she

was no longer the same girl who had lain down with him in his bed.

She was not the same, and never could be again. From now on, she would always be a part of him. They were joined together, not only by their shared fulfillment, but by the very essence of their beings. They were two, yet one, and nothing could separate them ever again.

But even now, she felt him drawing away from her. She reached out and laid her arm across his chest, to hold him back.

He raised himself on one elbow. "The candle's burning down," he said softly.

"I don't care." Her voice was drowsy with contentment.

"But I do. I want to see you. I want to see your face." His finger stroked the delicate cleft of her chin. "This—" He ran his hand along the line of her jaw. "And this—" His hand stroked her shoulder. "And this—" He touched her breast, cupping it in his hand. "All of you."

Something in his voice, his look, sent the first faint quiver of uneasiness moving through her. It was as if he was trying to memorize each contour of her face, each curve and hollow of her body, so that he would not forget.

But why should he feel such a need? She stiffened and her breathing grew faster. Small, icy tendrils of fear ran along her spine.

"What is it, sweeting? You don't feel guilt for what we did, surely? Or regret?"

"How could I? It was good. So good. Better than I ever imagined it would be. If only—"

She hesitated, and for the first time, she envied Felicity, who could take her pleasure lightly, and move on unscathed to find another love. Felicity and all those others like her who gave themselves with no thought for the future, who could disguise their feelings with words, who could play with words as if they were brightly colored spheres tossed by a juggler.

Such easy loving, such skilled deception, were not for her.

Not where Dirk was concerned. He searched her face anxiously. "Something is wrong. Tell me, Melora. What is it?"

She did not look away, and she spoke from the depths of her being. "You were looking at me, touching me, as if you were trying to be sure you would remember me afterward."

"Afterward?"

"After you leave me."

"But we have the rest of the night ahead," he said. "And all the other long nights of winter."

"And in spring? What then?" A warning voice sounded deep in her mind.

Don't ask questions. Not unless you're sure you want the answers.

"The king is capricious. You've been here at court long enough to know that." He spoke with forced lightness, but his eyes did not meet hers.

"The king! What has he to do with it? Why should his whims concern us now?"

He cupped her chin in his hand. "You weren't asking about now, sweeting. You were asking about spring." His lips curved in a hard, mirthless smile. "Maybe you'd better ask your witch woman, Bronwen. Tell her to cast her rune stones and read your future there."

"My future? I want to know about our future *together*." Her throat tightened. "And I need no rune stones to tell me of that." Her eyelids burned, but she did not cry. "I think maybe you are telling me."

"Melora, don't. It's foolish to brood over the future, to spoil what we have now."

He kept hold of her chin and his mouth sought hers. But she would not part her lips for him. His tongue teased her lips and traced their contours as he tried to gain entry to the softness within. She turned her face away. With a sigh, he released her.

"You told me of your own plans for the future," he reminded her. "Surely you haven't forgotten. You are going to help find a wealthy patron to lend his support to your father's new company. The best players in London, and a fine new theater."

Even as he spoke, he drew the silken comforter up over her. She wondered if he was afraid to look at her. Did he fear that the lure of her body might stir his senses, might tempt him into making promises he could not keep?

"I've not forgotten." She grasped his arm, and her eyes held his. "But that won't part us. Don't you see? Once my father has established himself again, he won't need me. There will be time for us then."

His face hardened, and his eyes were looking beyond her, beyond the confines of the chamber. What was he seeing now? She knew; and knowing, she was gripped by a terrible, aching emptiness.

He was seeing the green, untouched vastness of the lands beyond the sea. Copper-colored, half-naked men and women decked out in ornaments of gold. Brilliant flowers, birds, and animals unknown here in England. It was an alien world, one that held no place for her.

But she could not surrender her hopes willingly and let him leave her. "Dirk, listen to me. You said you cared nothing for life here at court." She spoke with swift urgency. "And I've no wish to remain at Whitehall a moment longer than I have to. I can't simply walk away, I know that. I must get through the Yuletide festivities, perform in the masque. But afterward, there'll be nothing to keep me here."

"Are you so sure?" His voice was calm, reasonable, like that of a schoolmaster trying to teach a difficult lesson to a stubborn pupil. "You've already won the queen's trust. The king has honored you. He's singled you out to play the leading role in the masque. If you keep in their good graces, there is no limit to the rewards you might reap."

Disappointment clutched at her and she opened her lips to speak, but he did not give her the chance. "What girl would not make the most of such opportunities, and be grateful for what was offered her? Especially if—"

"If she was only the daughter of an failed actor," she interrupted. Hurt began to give way to anger. "If she'd learned the

160

hard way what it meant to tramp the roads, to play and sing in taverns. To be ogled and pawed by any man with the price of a tankard of ale."

He stiffened and drew back as if she had slapped him. But he did not answer.

"That's what you were going to say, isn't it? At least be honest with me. You owe me that much."

He swung his long, muscular legs over the side of the bed. He paused, and she thought he would try to reassure her. Instead, he started to put his clothes back on.

"I didn't think of what I owed you. We wanted each other. We made love to each other and it was good for both of us. It can be again." He turned away, reached for his belt, and buckled it around his lean waist.

"You were speaking of my future." Somehow, she managed to keep her voice steady. "My prospects here at court. What would you advise me to do, once you've sailed away? Shall I take some young nobleman into my bed? I wouldn't expect an offer of marriage."

"Melora, be still!"

But she ignored his interruption. "No English nobleman, no matter how I pleased him, would marry without making inquiries into my background. How long do you think it would take for him to find out the truth?"

"I never suggested you find a husband."

"No, you didn't. You want me for your mistress, until it's time for you to leave. How soon do you think that will be?"

"How can I know that?" He put a hand on her shoulder, but she jerked away. "It depends on the king."

"That's right, isn't it? And the king is easily swayed."

She was taunting him now. But at least she would not give way to tears. She would not cling to him; she would not beg him not to leave her. Let him believe she was as hard, as unfeeling, as he.

"Maybe you were rash in dealing with Rokeby as you did

161

tonight. Perhaps you won't get your precious land grant at all, now that you've offended one of the king's favorites."

"Rokeby won't be a royal favorite much longer."

She stared at him, caught off-guard his words. "And why not?"

He moved closer to her, but did not try to touch her again. Instead, he gave her a curiously impersonal look, as if he was trying to come to a decision. The silence stretched between them until it became unbearable. "Why not?" she repeated.

"Be quiet and hear me out." His calm, reasonable tone, his lack of emotion, only drove her to greater anger.

"Why should I?" He was clever with words, but there was nothing he could say to soothe her outraged pride, the pain that held her fast. To make her forget how easily he would leave her, when the time came.

With one swift motion, she flung back the coverlet. She was on her feet, and reaching for her shift. Her hands shook violently, but somehow she managed to pull the flimsy garment over her head.

She found her shoes and stockings and put them on. Even in her blind rage, she realized that she could not go running along the corridor half-naked.

But where was her dress? She must find her dress. Somehow she gathered her whirling thoughts. She had left it in the antechamber. She started for the door.

"Melora, wait!"

Her hand darted out. She scooped up the necklace and earrings from the bedside table and flung them. They landed at his feet.

She got as far as the outer room, but he caught up with her in two strides. He pinned her against the wall, and stood so close that her senses reeled with the familiar scent of him, the heat of his breath against her face.

"You will not leave until I'm ready to let you go." She writhed in his grasp until the strength drained out of her. Her body began to shake, and she had to set her jaw to keep her teeth from chattering.

Unable to resist, she let him lead her to a chair beside the fireplace. She watched as he stirred the embers, until the flames flared up and the sparks glowed. But although she could feel the heat, it did not stop her shaking. Dazed, she sat and watched as he pulled on his shirt, then seated himself opposite her.

He poured a glass of wine from the decanter on the table and handed it to her. Her hands shook so that he had to reach over and help her raise the glass to her lips. She swallowed, and gradually the wine began to take effect.

"You asked why Rokeby's days as the king's favorite might be numbered. I did not wish to speak of it, but now I must."

She stared at him. The intensity in his voice was oddly disquieting. "Why are you speaking to me of Rokeby at such a time? What makes you think I could possibly care about that odious man?"

"You will listen to me," he went on, with calm determination. "And give yourself time to think carefully about what I say. After that, you are free to do exactly as you wish."

Free. She fought the urge to give way to tears. For she knew that after what had happened between them tonight, she might go from the palace, from London; she might put the width of the kingdom between them; but she would never be free again.

Chapter Twelve

"Finish your wine," Dirk said. She obeyed automatically, and she began to feel more in control, but she still shivered from time to time. Dirk got a robe of dark brown wool from his armoire and placed it around her shoulders, then seated himself opposite her again.

Although the robe was much too large for her, she drew it close around her and caught his familiar male scent in the heavy folds. It was the same scent that she had inhaled, that had stirred her senses when she had lain in his arms, had pressed her face against his shoulder. She had held nothing back, had given herself completely.

She warned herself that she must forget, but how could she stop the swiftly rising tide of memories? Desperately, she cast about, seeking escape. "About Rokeby," she began. "You were starting to tell me—"

He interrupted her with an impatient gesture. "Finish your wine first. We can talk of him afterward."

He must sense the depth of her misery, she thought. He was trying to give her what comfort her could. Did that mean she might have been mistaken about him?

Her fingers tightened about the stem of her goblet. She took another sip of the sweet, warming liquid. She would not, dared not allow herself to feel the slightest hope that he might love her.

"You said Rokeby might not be one of the king's favorites

much longer." She kept her voice even, impersonal. "What makes you think so?"

He leaned toward her. "I have reason to believe Rokeby's a traitor."

A moment passed before she could take in the full implication of his words. King James, already living in constant dread that those around him might be plotting against him, would deal mercilessly with a traitor. Guy Fawkes and his followers had met a swift and horrible punishment. Even the great Sir Walter Raleigh, condemned on the flimsiest evidence, now lay imprisoned in the Tower.

"I loathe Rokeby as much as you do," she said. "But can you really believe he means to try to overthrow the king?"

"And why not? Have you forgotten what you told me when we were returning from the hunt? You said Queen Anne distrusts Rokeby, that she believes his majesty is wrong to place his confidence in the man."

"I've not forgotten. But that's not the same as saying that he is plotting to take his majesty's life. I should think Rokeby already has wealth and power enough to satisfy him—and every prospect of getting more. So even if he were to succeed in this scheme—whatever it may be—what would he have to gain?"

"More than you might suppose, Melora."

"Surely you're not suggesting that Rokeby means to overthrow the king in order to try to gather enough support to rule in his place? The people would never accept him. He's neither a Tudor nor a Stuart—he has no possible claim to the throne."

"Not directly, no," he agreed. "And though he has an unlimited lust for power, he's no fool. He knows he could never hope to win the support of the common people."

"Then why should he—"

Dirk ignored her interruption. "There is someone who could produce a valid claim to the throne. A stronger claim than King James's, if it comes to that."

"Queen Anne?"

He shook his head. "If Rokeby strikes, he will use no half measures. He will dispose of the queen, and of young Prince Henry, and Prince Charles, and the little Princess Elizabeth, too."

"Then this claimant you spoke of—who is he?"

"She. Lady Arabella Stuart."

"Arabella Stuart." The name was familiar to her. She was silent for a moment as she tried to follow his line of reasoning. "Yes, the people might accept her. Both she and King James are descended from Margaret, sister to Henry the Eighth."

"And there are those who believe Arabella Stuart has a stronger claim to the throne, if only because she was born in England." The more she considered the idea, the more plausible it sounded to her. "Queen Elizabeth named James as her successor."

"There's always been some uncertainty about that," he reminded her.

"But they say that Lady Arabella is content to live in seclusion in the country. That she's shy and retiring, and hasn't even been to court since the coronation. Why would she allow Rokeby to drag her into such a dangerous enterprise?"

Dirk shrugged, and a faint smile touched his lips. "Perhaps to escape the rule of her guardian. Old Bess Hardwick—Lady Shrewsbury—is a real tyrant. Or perhaps there is a spark of ambition behind Lady Arabella's quiet facade, who knows? She is a Tudor, after all."

"You really think she might be swayed by Rokeby?"

"He can be most persuasive when he chooses. And some women find him desirable."

"Lady Jade, for one," she agreed. "But all this is only speculation. You still haven't told me why you're sure Rokeby is prepared to risk such a dangerous undertaking."

He regarded her with a long, speculative look, as if he were trying to come to a decision about her. She moved uneasily under his hard scrutiny. Gradually, she became aware of the small sounds around them. The cracking of a log in the fireplace . . . the night wind rattling the narrow windows . . . the eerie cry of a hunting owl . . . She set down her goblet and pressed her hands together tightly. The silence stretched between them until she began to find it unbearable.

"You can't give me an answer, can you?" she demanded.

"Yes, I can," he said with conviction. Swiftly he reached out and gripped both her hands her in his. This time, she did not try to withdraw from his touch, for there was nothing sensual about it. "But before I do, I must have your promise that you will not repeat what I tell you. Not to anyone."

Startled, confused, she heard herself saying, "I promise."

"Swear it."

Never had she heard him speak that way, or seen such intensity in his eyes.

"I swear it."

He appeared satisfied. "This is not the time or place to discuss affairs of state, I know that. But we have reason to believe that Rokeby means to strike before we expected. We must get proof as soon as possible."

His grip tightened so that she winced, but the pain seemed unimportant. "We?" She repeated.

"Lord Pembroke and the others. The men and women who serve him."

She felt a pang of fear, not for herself, but for him. "Dirk! Are you one of them?"

"I'm not a member of his organization, if that's what you mean. But I have given him certain useful information from time to time. It is important to me that James should remain on the throne."

"At least until you have your land grant and ships." Her lips curved in a faint, ironic smile. "I might have known that whatever you do, it's only to serve your own private ambition."

"Not entirely."

"You really expect me to believe that you would give up your plans so that you might thwart Rokeby?"

"I'd give them up—if I were forced to choose."

"How noble of you, how selfless." She did not even try to keep the mockery from her voice.

"Believe what you choose about me. I've neither the time nor the inclination to try to change your mind."

"If you're so pressed for time, why are you keeping me here, discussing these affairs of state?" she demanded.

"Because you may soon find yourself involved in them. Pembroke has need of your services. He wants to enlist you in his organization as soon as possible."

Her eyes widened and she stared at him, not sure she had heard right. "My services?"

"The earl has watched you closely since your first night at court. He is much impressed by your swift progress, and, shall we say, your acting skills. You've managed to convince the king and queen, the other ladies-in-waiting, even Rokeby, that you are my cousin."

"Sweet Jesu! Pembroke knows I'm not!"

"Certainly. He's known from the beginning."

"But—"

He interrupted calmly. "Don't worry, sweeting. Pembroke's the last one who would betray you. Can't you see that you can only be of any real use to him in your role as Lady Rosalind?"

"To the devil with Pembroke! You had no right to tell him who I really am. How much more did you tell him?"

"Everything he needed to know." He spoke without a trace of guilt. "Who your father is, how and where I happened to meet you." He paused, and a corner of his mouth lifted. "I also warned him of your most serious failing."

"And what might that be?" She tried to jerk her hands from his grasp, but his fingers tightened, and he held her fast.

"I told him that you sometimes allow your emotions to get the better of you."

"As I did tonight." Shattered pride, a sense of betrayal, and an unbearable feeling of loss mingled within her. Then all her other feelings were swallowed up in a rush of overpowering

168

anger. She longed to strike out at him, to wipe away that look of calm self-possession.

Gradually, she fought her way back to sanity. Somehow, she even managed to keep her voice steady. "I think I am beginning to understand now."

She gave a brief, self-mocking laugh. "I thought it was such a gallant gesture when you lifted me and carried me out of the great hall." She was speaking more quickly now. "You didn't get me away from Rokeby to protect me from his advances, did you?"

Without waiting for an answer, she hurried on. "You thought you could persuade me to serve Pembroke. That's why you made love to me, and no doubt you enjoyed it."

"Melora!"

"Oh, I don't doubt you pleasured yourself in the process."

"If you can calm down long enough to let me——"

"It's true I lacked the skills of more experienced ladies like Felicity—or Jade Fairfax—but perhaps you took a special satisfaction in being the first with me."

"No! That's not true. You can't possibly think that."

But she would not allow herself to be trapped by her feelings for him, not again. "Never mind what I think." She wrenched her hands free and gripped the arms of her chair.

"I gave you my word to say nothing of Pembroke's organization," she went on. "And I will keep that promise. But if you suppose that I'm about to spy for him, to risk my life for his cause, you're mistaken. I'll see you in hell first—and Pembroke with you!"

"You are in no condition to decide yet." He spoke with infuriating self-assurance. "Right now, you had better finish dressing and return to your own chamber. Get a few hours of sleep. Tomorrow, when you've calmed down and had time to consider what's at stake here, perhaps you'll change your mind."

"I know what's at stake for me. Rokeby's possessed by his ambition, his lust for power. You said so yourself. And he's a

169

violent man, pitiless and totally without scruple. If he would have the king killed—the queen and the young princes—he surely wouldn't hesitate to rid himself of a nobody like me. I'm sure he has his informants, too."

Terror shot through her at the thought of Rokeby's capacity for cruelty. "If he had reason to suspect me—and if it's really true that he's plotting against the throne—"

"He is. I've no doubt of it. But we must have solid proof."

"Then you must find it however you can—without any help from me." She sprang to her feet. Stooping, she retrieved her silk gown. She put it on and tried to fasten it, but her fingers were suddenly stiff and clumsy.

Then he was beside her. "Let me help."

She struck his hand away. "Don't touch me."

"As you wish." He stood by, watching her as she managed to fasten her bodice and smooth her skirt. She twisted her hair into a knot at the back of her head, and used the bodkins to hold it in place.

"Your pearls," he said. He held them out to her. "You forgot to take them."

Her voice was icy. "Keep them. If some other girl's not so quick to be swept away by your charm, you may offer them to her as a bribe—to enlist her in Pembroke's service."

"The pearls are yours. No one else will ever wear them. If you believe nothing else, believe that much."

She hesitated, then retrieved the necklace and earrings. "I will keep them. No doubt I can get a good price for them, before I leave London for Northumberland."

He grasped her shoulders and stood looking down at her with hard-eyed determination. "You're not leaving Whitehall yet."

"Oh, but I am. No doubt it will prove a bit awkward to tell the king that your cousin will not be performing in his splendid masque after all. That she is unable to remain at court to serve the queen any longer. But you have a way with words. I'm sure you'll find some suitable explanation for my unexpected departure."

"I'm not going to let you leave, until it suits my purpose."

"And how do you mean to stop me?"

"You are my cousin, remember. I have a certain family responsibility toward you. I could say that you have been taken ill quite suddenly—that you are delirious with fever. Then I could have you placed under lock and key, here in my own chambers, with Pembroke's personal physician to attend you."

"But you'd have no reason to keep me your prisoner, not for long," she told him. "Because I'd be no use to you, unless I were free to come and go as I pleased. Locked up here, I would be in no position to gather whatever information Pembroke wants, would I?"

"You are willing at least to consider joining his organization, then?"

"No, I am not. We had a bargain, you and I. I was to come to court, to play the part of Lady Rosalind. I've done that much. As for Pembroke, you'll have to go to him and tell him to find another of the queen's ladies to help him in his schemes. Tell him you'll even be willing to lie with her, if that will help to persuade her."

For a moment, she thought he might strike her. Instead, he only stood looking down at her, his lips clamped together tightly, the muscles standing out along his jawline. Then he turned, crossed the room, opened a cupboard. He took out a leather pouch and came back to confront her again.

"I'll make a suitable excuse to the king and queen. As for your journey back to Northumberland, this should allow you to travel in comfort."

He thrust the pouch into her hand. "For services rendered, Mistress Standish," he said softly. She flinched at his words, and the mocking look that accompanied them. Was he speaking only of her services as lady-in-waiting?

Or was he telling her that he had included extra payment for the pleasure of lying with her tonight?

"Sleep well, sweeting." He started for the door, then paused. "You should get what rest you can, before you set out on your journey tomorrow."

Before she could speak, he turned on his heel and strode from the antechamber. The door closed behind him, and she stood unmoving, the leather pouch clutched in her hand.

Now there was no longer any need to hold back the tears that welled up in her eyes. She stumbled back into the bedchamber and flung herself down across the rumpled silk coverlet. Her body shook with the violence of her sobbing.

She pressed her face into the pillow where she had lain with her head close to his. Here she had made love with him, had felt the weight of his body on hers, the movement of his fingers, exploring, caressing every part of her. The first fierce thrust of possession, the spiraling passion, and the wonder of fulfillment.

And she had been innocent enough to believe that their lovemaking had joined them together, had made them one for all time. She drew in her breath, bit down hard on her lower lip, and choked back her tears. Gradually, her weeping gave way to a numb sense of loss.

She pushed her hair back from her face, and rolled over onto her side, and her hand brushed against the necklace she had flung down carelessly. She raised herself on one arm, scooped up the string of pearls and the earrings. She would never wear them again.

Maybe she should have left them lying at Dirk's feet. She could put them on the bedside table, for him to find when he returned. No! She would not be controlled by her emotions this time. Dirk had told Pembroke that she was inclined to let her feelings overpower her common sense. She would not let that happen again.

With a shock, she realized how she had changed. He had changed her. From now on, she would be as hard, as coldly realistic as he was.

And why not? She had not only her own future to consider, but her father's, too. She brushed the back of her hand across

172

her eyes, then looked about, seeking the leather pouch. *For services rendered, Mistress Standish . . .*

There it lay at the foot of the bed, where she had dropped it. She reached down and grasped the tightly-knotted strings. Then, crouching on the coverlet, she opened it.

The light from the candle stub caught the glitter of the gold coins. She hefted the pouch, and even without counting, knew that Dirk had been generous indeed, especially since she had not kept her part of the bargain.

She had promised to stay at court through the winter, to wait until he gave her permission to leave. But that had been before—

No! She could not let herself think about their lovemaking, not now. The memories would only start her weeping again, and her tears would change nothing.

She must be practical, to make her plans, step by step, and carry them out without looking back. Very well, then.

She must arrange for her journey back to Northumberland. Maybe Felicity could provide her with the name of a reliable jeweler. After she had sold the pearls, she would add the payment to the hoard of coins Dirk had given her.

If she could persuade Dirk to pay her fare back to Northumberland, so much the better. She would have a little extra money when she arrived at the inn where her father was now living.

Osric had given her the name of the inn. The Rose and Thistle, that was it. Ten miles from Abernathy's Leaping Stag. She would set out on her journey as quickly as possible, for travel would be slow and difficult, now that winter had begun.

No matter. Before too long, she would be back with her father. How good it would be to see him again! And her friends, too.

With the money she would bring them, they would all be welcome guests at the inn for the rest of the winter. The coins in her pouch would buy ample time for her father to make a complete recovery. Good, nourishing food would help to restore his strength. A warm fire, a soft bed with thick woolen blankets, would help to ensure that he would not be stricken with the ague again.

And now she had the means with which to reward the three who had remained so loyal. There would be a new cloak for Bronwen, who could pass the evenings embroidering her mystic symbols on the garment, a gaily colored suit and cap for Osric, and a good leather jerkin for Caleb. And enough honey to satisfy even Old Bruin's insatiable appetite.

In spring, they would return to London.

Would Dirk have left England by then? It did not matter. She would not let it matter. She would not play the lovesick little fool, looking about the crowds, seeking a glimpse of him.

She would occupy herself in planning a new beginning for her father and herself. First, they would need to find a wealthy, titled patron with an enthusiasm for the theater. No actor-manager could organize his company and be licensed to perform on the London stage without the backing of a nobleman who would lend the prestige of his name to the troupe.

All at once she stiffened, brought up short by a new and devastating thought.

If she remained at her father's side, once they returned to London, if she went about with him, helping him to seek his new patron, she would run the risk of being recognized.

She had met so many noblemen since her arrival at Whitehall. She had danced with them, flirted with them, then fended off their attempts to take her to bed. Sooner or later, one of them would see her and remember Lady Rosalind Grenville, who had disappeared so abruptly from court.

Suppose Rokeby were to recognize her? Or Lady Jade? She dared not take such a risk.

Could her father establish his company without her help? It would not be easy, but no doubt he could manage it. Yet even if he succeeded, what then? He could not introduce her as his daughter. It would be risky for her to be seen in his company.

Her heart sank at the prospect of remaining in hiding in some obscure lodgings, for—how long?

She had never really resigned herself to accepting the law that kept her from performing on the public stage. But now, she would not be able to take part in setting up the new company, or helping to find the proper site for her father's theater. She would not even be able to attend the first performance given by his new company.

Her spirits plunged still lower as she realized that she would never be sure of going about on the most ordinary errand without taking a chance of being recognized. Was she to hide behind the shuttered windows of a house in some obscure part of the city?

Perhaps it would be safer to leave England, at least for a time. She could cross the channel to France, her mother's birthplace. She had spoken French fluently in her childhood, and the language would soon come back to her.

She hefted the pouch of coins once more. Yes, Dirk had been generous, under the circumstances. But after a winter in Northumberland, the return journey to London, the rent on a house, however modest it might be, a handsome new wardrobe for her father, who could not afford to look shabby when he set about finding a wealthy patron—how much would be left after all that?

It was expensive to live decently in London; and it was necessary for an actor-manager to make a good impression in order to get ahead.

She set down the pouch and pressed her fingertips to her temples. She was exhausted, her eyelids heavy, her whole body crying out for sleep. She closed her eyes, but she could not quiet her racing thoughts.

Her father, back in London, with a company of players, a theater of his own . . . and all the while she would be living in Paris, in a respectable lodging house. How could she bear the empty days, the nights when the memory of Dirk would surely return to torment her?

Her eyes flew open and she sat bolt upright. There was another course of action open to her, if she had the courage to take it.

Pembroke.

The Earl of Pembroke wanted her to join his organization, to help collect proof of Rokeby's treachery. It would be dangerous, far more dangerous than posing as Dirk's cousin and serving as lady-in-waiting. But because of the greater hazard, she would be in a position to demand a far greater reward.

The earl was immensely wealthy. If she served him well, there was no telling how high a price he would be willing to pay. Surely enough so that she and her father would be able to travel to France. In France, a woman could appear on the stage. She could rise as high as her talents would carry her.

Her father had performed in France. His command of the language was still excellent. He could establish his new company in Paris, and she could appear in his productions. It would take money, a great deal of money, to make the right kind of start. Pembroke would provide her with as much as she needed, for she would drive a hard bargain.

She rose from the bed, smoothed the folds of her gown, and picked up the leather pouch. She wrapped the necklace and earrings in her handkerchief, then stuffed them inside, on top of the coins.

She paused for a moment, unable to keep from remembering how she had lain here with Dirk's arms around her. Had he made love with her only to persuade her to enter Pembroke's service? Or was it possible that he loved her in his own way?

Resolutely she turned and went into the antechamber, then left Dirk's rooms, closing the door behind her. She made her way down the corridor, still tormented by her doubts. She tried to convince herself that, whatever he might have felt for her, it had not been strong enough to turn him aside from his own purpose.

He had said that if he were forced to choose between helping Pembroke to thwart the plot against the king and pursuing his own ambition, he would put his duty to the king first. But there would be no need for him to make such a choice, for if Rokeby was condemned for treason, Dirk's efforts on the king's behalf would be richly rewarded. King James would give him all the land he wanted, a fleet of ships, and perhaps another, even higher title. He would sail from England with the thanks of his sovereign.

He would leave England for the New World, while she crossed the Channel to France, to follow her own path. At last, after all the years when it had seemed only a hopeless dream, she would know the wonderful reality. She would perform as a member of her father's company. She would be famous, applauded, sought after. More important, she would have the opportunity to develop her talents to the fullest.

She had reached the door of her chamber, and she paused, bewildered. Why did the promise of such triumph leave her unsatisfied? That was easily answered: she was still exhausted by all that had happened tonight.

She opened the door as quietly as she could. Dirk had told her to sleep, to give herself time to think over his offer. Would he be surprised when she told him that she had changed her mind, that she would remain at court through the winter?

She would meet with Pembroke and they would strike a bargain. She dared not let herself think of what might happen after that. Whatever the dangers, she was prepared to accept them.

She swayed slightly, then realized that her legs were unsteady. Her head still ached and her eyes burned from weeping. Too exhausted to undress, she unbuttoned her bodice, loosened the lacing of her gown, then dropped down across the bed to sleep.

Chapter Thirteen

When Melora awoke the next morning, the pale winter light was slanting through the window. She sat up in bed and saw that Felicity, who was already wearing her morning gown, stood at the dressing table, observing her with open curiosity. "I should have gone to the queen's chambers an hour ago—but I had to wait until you awoke.

"Why—you slept in your gown," she went on. "And you never even sent for Prudence to brush your hair."

"I was too tired to bother."

Felicity gave a tinkling little laugh. "No doubt you were."

Ignoring the words and the look that went with them, Melora sat up and swung her legs over the side of the bed.

"I suppose you can imagine the stir you and Dirk created last night," she went on. "The way he swept you up in his arms and carried you off—no one could speak of anything else during the banquet. As for Rokeby—"

But Melora had no wish to hear about Rokeby. Quickly she turned away, went to the commode, and filled the china basin with water. Her eyelids were probably still swollen. She splashed the cool water on her face, hoping to repair the ravages before Felicity noticed.

"Rokeby was positively livid with anger," her friend rattled on. "I swear he would have gone after Dirk—but just then, the trumpets sounded and Lady Jade came up and said something to him. He escorted her into the banquet hall." Her grin held a touch of malice. "I suppose Jade hopes to win Rokeby back, now that you and Dirk—"

But Melora did not want to talk about Dirk, or answer her friend's questions about what had happened last night. She pulled on the bell cord to summon Prudence.

"You'd best go to wait upon the queen," she said. "Make some excuse for my tardiness. I will come to her chambers as soon as I'm dressed."

"But Melora—you haven't told me—"

"I can't." Something in her face silenced even the usually irrepressible Felicity.

"As you please," she said, and flounced out of their bed-chamber, almost colliding with Prudence.

But before Melora went to take up her duties in the queen's chamber, she sent a brief message to Dirk. She wrote that she had thought over his proposal and was prepared to consider it.

She could not face him this morning. She needed more time to get her unruly emotions under control.

The following day, she and Dirk traveled downriver together. He called to the boatman, who drew his craft up to the nearest stairs.

As she started to alight, he took her hand to help her. Even now, his touch stirred her more than she wished to admit. They had come here together on a matter of business, she told herself firmly. She must not allow herself to be distracted.

The lodgekeeper opened the tall iron gates, bowed, and ushered them inside. He did not ask Dirk to identify himself. No doubt he was a familiar visitor to Pembroke's London town-house, she thought.

Dirk took her arm and she realized that she could not let down her guard agianst her own turbulent emotions, not even for a moment. In silence, she walked beside him up the wide flagstone path that led to the tall mansion, set about with ancient elms. The wind tugged at her purple velvet cloak and whipped a stray lock of hair against her cheek, but she was oblivious to the chill weather.

Netherwood, and this townhouse, too—how many more great houses did Pembroke own, she wondered? One thing, at least, was certain: if he had need of her services, he could well afford to meet whatever terms she cared to set.

During the short river journey from Whitehall, Dirk had said little; he had appeared to be lost in his thoughts, and she had sensed that they were not pleasant. His expression had been grim, and he had fixed his gaze on the swirling gray waters.

She quickened her step to keep up with him, and she wondered at his brooding silence. He should be pleased that he had succeeded in getting her to consider entering the earl's service.

She drew her cloak more closely around her, for the afternoon was gray and cold, and the raw wind drove thick, lowering clouds across the sky above the river. In summer, no doubt, the earl's garden would be a blaze of glorious color, she thought; but now, in early December, the carefully pruned shrubs and leafless elms had a forlorn look.

A liveried manservant, responding to Dirk's knock, admitted them and ushered them into a large, paneled chamber where Pembroke awaited them. He was seated before the fire, stroking a handsome Persian cat. It was difficult for her to believe that the tall, lean nobleman, lounging at his ease, attired in a close-fitting black velvet doublet with a broad collar of Venetian lace, and fashionably wide breeches, could have any more serious concerns than tonight's banquet at Whitehall.

But he rose swiftly as they entered, and set the cat down on a tassled brocade cushion. As he greeted her and ordered the servant to bring refreshments, his ebony eyes were fixed on her face. Even after she was seated before the marble fireplace, she was aware of the earl's close scrutiny.

As soon as the servant had gone, Pembroke wasted no time in getting to the heart of the matter. "Grenville has told me that you are prepared to enter my service."

"Perhaps I will, my lord. If your terms are satisfactory." She took a sip of wine, then set down her goblet. "There is still much I need to know before I can commit myself.

"You will be told only what is absolutely necessary, Mistress Standish." His thin lips curved in a brief, mirthless smile. "You will be safer that way."

"And so will you, my lord—if I should be caught and interrogated." She tried to ignore the chill that rippled through her as she mentioned the mere possibility. If she was to make a new life for herself and her father, she must not waver in her course.

"I see that I was not mistaken in my opinion of you. Certainly you will need to be daring, if you are to be of use to me. But you will have to know when to be cautious, too. I want in my service no reckless fools who allow themselves to be swept away by our cause, so that they forget to give thought for their safety."

"Believe me, my lord, however I may feel about the importance of your cause, I put a far higher value on my own survival," she told him.

He nodded with satisfaction. "I believe you'll serve me well, Mistress Standish. Now, no doubt you wish to know exactly what sort of information I seek. And how you may best go about finding it."

"We will get to that," she said. She would not allow herself to be intimidated by the earl, no matter how important a personage he might be. If she did not have daring enough to bargain with him, she could not hope to match wits with Rokeby.

"First, we must agree on a suitable payment for my services."

Dirk gave her a brief, startled glance. Was he remembering the desperate girl in the taproom, with her torn skirt and ragged shawl, she wondered? Or maybe he had seen the change in her, since she had lain in his arms, warm and willing—

Don't think about that, not now.

"I mean to serve you as well as I can, my lord," she went on coolly. "But after I have done what you wish, I have plans for

181

my own future. And I will need a substantial sum of money to carry them out."

Dirk shifted uneasily in his chair, but he did not interrupt her. He seemed content to listen, while she and the earl bargained over how much she would receive. When they had agreed on a sum that was satisfactory to both, Pembroke went on to explain what he expected of her.

"So far, you've spent a good deal of time in Rokeby's company, working on the Christmas masque," he said. "But you have met him in one of the chambers in Whitehall. And rarely without others present—the queen, Master Inigo Jones. Lady Jade Fairfax."

Pembroke had been watching her closely indeed, she thought. Or had she also been under surveillance by others in his pay, ever since her arrival at the palace?

She tried to ignore the thought, for it made her uneasy.

"From now on, you must contrive to be alone with him, Mistress Standish."

She was about to say that it would be easy enough get Rokeby to accompany her to a deserted chamber in the palace. Wasn't that exactly what he had wanted all this time? But a warning sounded in her mind.

"I have made no secret of my dislike for Rokeby," she said. "He may become suspicious of the abrupt change in my feelings toward him."

"I have confidence in you. If you play on his vanity, and use your feminine wiles to best advantage, you'll manage well enough." He gave her a brief smile. "Surely no mere male has to advise you how to go about that."

The smile vanished as quickly as it had appeared. "Once you are alone with him, you will begin to speak about your feelings toward the king."

She looked at him, bewildered. "What feelings should I have, but those of any loyal subject? His majesty has treated me well enough." She paused and searched her memory. "During the

182

falcon hunt, he even went so far as to overlook what he considered my shocking breach of manners."

The earl's dark eyes narrowed slightly. "Did he, indeed? Grenville didn't tell me anything about that."

"No doubt he thought it was unimportant."

"Nothing is unimportant when it comes to your dealings with his majesty," Pembroke said. "Suppose you tell me now."

"Rokeby's prize falcon—a most valuable bird brought from Spain—was maimed by a crane. It was Rokeby's fault. Doña Esmeralda—the falcon—was not yet in fit condition to be set against the crane. But he had boasted to the king of the falcon's prowess, and rather than admit he had been mistaken, he blamed the loss on his falconer. He struck Master Lovell with his riding crop and—" She closed her eyes for a moment, as if to blot out the memory of the whole ugly scene. "I cried out in protest. But it did no good." Even now she felt a hot resentment against the viscount for his cruelty.

"We were speaking of the king," Pembroke reminded her.

"His majesty told me that Rokeby had the right to deal with his servants as he pleased. But he excused me for protesting in such an unseemly manner, because I was still unfamiliar with the ways of the court."

Pembroke nodded. "That was considerate of him, I agree."

"But it didn't spare Master Lovell an undeserved flogging," Melora interrupted.

"Rokeby's done far worse in his time," Pembroke said. "As for his majesty, he proved himself well disposed to you, in his way. And he chose you, over the other court ladies, to help prepare the masque. You are to play the role of—the moon goddess, Artemis."

Melora was deeply impressed once more by the scope of the earl's information. But she was disquieted, too. Was nothing about her a secret from him? "No doubt you can even describe the costume I am to wear."

"I admit I can't," he said, with the hint of a smile. "If I thought it might be of any real importance, I would make it my

183

business to find out." He paused and his eyes held hers. "I do know that the mercer who visited you at the palace brought you something besides his silks and trimmings."

She turned on Dirk with a reproachful look. "Was there any need to speak of Osric's letter?" she demanded.

"I already knew all about your devotion to your father," Pembroke interrupted. "He was seriously ill, and you agreed to impersonate Lady Rosalind so that you might save him from the pillory and a cell in the town jail."

And how much more did the earl know about her now? Her cheeks burned and she looked away. Had Dirk provided him with the details of their lovemaking? Or her foolish hope that he would give up his plan to leave England, so that he might remain with her? Surely he would not have humiliated her that way.

She forced herself to set aside such useless speculations, and to listen to what the earl was saying.

"So the king has treated you well, and Rokeby knows it. That may make it more difficult for you to convince him that you have cause to dislike his majesty. You will have to proceed cautiously."

Melora nodded. "I'll manage it somehow. But to what purpose?"

"If Rokeby can be persuaded to believe that you have a grudge against the king, he may confide his plans. He may even try to draw you into his treasonous scheme."

"You ask too much, my lord! It had not occurred to me that you would expect me to pretend to conspire with Rokeby while serving you."

"That's because you're new at this game," the earl conceded. "But I think you will be quick to learn the rules."

Melora went icy cold inside as she remembered what Dirk had said: Rokeby would not be content with taking the king's life; the queen, the young princes, the princess—all must be killed to clear a path to the throne. Only then would the viscount have a chance to put Lady Arabella Stuart in the king's place.

She could easily guess what his next step would be: he would lose no opportunity of gaining control over the new queen, and making her his pawn.

Her confidence gave way to uncertainty. How could she hope to match wits with a man as clever and ruthless as Rokeby? Already she was beginning to feel that she was far beyond her depths.

"You will begin by disparaging his majesty in small ways," Pembroke was saying. "It shouldn't prove too difficult. He's never won the love of the people, nor their respect."

"And yet you are determined to protect him," she interrupted. "Why, my lord?"

"That's no concern of yours. Be quiet, and hear me out. You will criticize the king's extravagance. His coarse accent, his clumsy manners. His uncertain temper. His tendency to vacillate on important matters of state. Feel your way cautiously, and take your cue from the viscount's response."

All at once, she remembered Bronwen's warning of the dangers that lay in wait for her at the palace. Surely the old Welshwoman could not have foreseen any of this when she had cast her rune stones in the stable, back at the Leaping Stag. Or was it somehow possible that she had? Did Bronwen really have the power to foretell the future?

If so, was there still a chance for her to retreat, before she found herself completely enmeshed, unable to draw back?

"You are having second thoughts, aren't you, Mistress Standish?" the earl asked.

She looked away, unable to meet his steady gaze.

"You would be a fool indeed if you did not realize the risk you will be taking. It's too bad I cannot offer you more time to make up your mind. But as Grenville has no doubt told you, we have no time to spare. I must have your answer before you walk out of here today."

185

"And if I should refuse your proposal," she said slowly, "would you allow me to leave?"

The earl laughed softly. "My dear young lady, are you suggesting that I would dispatch you with my own hands to ensure your silence?"

"You would not have to," she said. "I'm sure you have others you employ to do such work for you."

The earl did not deny it. Instead, he turned to Dirk. "You told me that Mistress Standish swore to say nothing of the organization, whether or not she agreed to join us. Do you believe she'll honor her oath?"

"I know she will," Dirk said.

"You're sure you have not allowed your estimate of the young lady's character to become clouded by your feelings toward her?"

"You do him an injustice, my lord," Melora said. "He believes emotion to be an unfortunate weakness." She gave Dirk a brief, cold look. "Isn't that so?"

But she could not bait him into losing his self-control. "You won't back out, Melora," he said. "Think of the reward you'd forfeit. Now, suppose you listen to the rest of what our host has to say."

Again, he had judged her aright. She had too much at stake to refuse Pembroke now. She must consider not only her father's future, but her own. The ambition that had possessed her all these years now was within reach—if she had the courage to grasp it.

The earl seemed willing to accept Dirk's judgment, for now he went on with his instructions. "When you speak with Rokeby in private, you must find fault with the queen, too. Devise some reason why you dislike her. I'll leave that to you."

"I'll try," she said. The queen had befriended her, but perhaps Rokeby would not know that. It was a risk she would have to take. "Is that all, my lord?"

"Hardly, Mistress Standish. If any of these foreigners who have come to court for the Christmas revels should seem particularly friendly with Rokeby, find out who they are. Do what you must to pick up any scraps of conversation, however unimportant they may seem. Grenville says you have a good memory."

"I don't understand. Why should Rokeby turn to foreign noblemen for help in his conspiracy?"

"You will have enough to do, without concerning yourself with matters outside your sphere," he rebuked her. "Now, as for the ladies-in-waiting, here you may be of great service. Some of them are light-minded, bent only on pleasure. Lady Felicity is involved with one of the nobles from France, isn't she?"

"She is my friend. We share the same bedchamber," Melora protested. "Light-minded though she may be, I would not harm her."

"Have I asked you to?" Without waiting for an answer, he went on. "It's her French admirer who concerns me. We are at peace with France—for the present. But that could change. Find out all you can about the duke's opinion of his majesty. And as for Lady Octavia Sutton, she spends her nights in the bed of the Marquis de Carvajal."

"I scarcely see how that could pose a threat to his majesty."

"Any of these nobles could be persuaded to support Rokeby for a price. Find out which ones gamble beyond their means— how deep in debt they may be. Such information will be of use to me. That's all you need to know. I will want a report from you at least three times a week—more often, if necessary."

"The queen gives her ladies some measure of freedom, but you surely must know that she doesn't permit us to leave the palace whenever we choose. What possible excuses could I give her for going off on my own?"

"You are not to come here again, either with Grenville, or alone," he said. "I will provide you with a suitable messenger. Probably more than one."

"There is no need," Dirk interrupted. "I have a better idea.

Melora has three loyal friends who could be brought to court at once. And none of them would be suspect."

"No! Not Osric or—either of the others," she pleaded.

But Pembroke turned to Dirk. "Osric's the juggler, isn't he? And the other two . . . a Welsh soothsayer, and a bear leader."

Dear heaven! How much more did the earl know of her past?

"With so many traveling mummers at Whitehall for the Yuletide season, three more would attract no particular notice," Dirk went on.

"True enough," Pembroke agreed. "But why would the dwarf and the others be of any special value?"

"Because, though your own messengers might prove loyal, you can't be absolutely sure. A lady's maid, a mercer's apprentice, a court musician—any one of them could be in Rokeby's pay, as well as in yours."

"It's happened before," Pembroke admitted. "I will do all I can to ensure Mistress Standish's safety, but I cannot promise that there will not be some danger to her."

"Her three friends would not betray her," Dirk insisted. "Isn't that true, Melora?"

"Yes—certainly—"

Was Dirk really concerned for her? He was willing to have her serve Pembroke, yet now he spoke of a way to reduce the risks she would have to take.

Very well, then—maybe he would not wish to see her come to harm. Maybe he even felt a certain responsibility for her. What did that mean?

When he had brought her to court, he had promised to protect her, had given her his word. The word of a Grenville. It was not his concern for her, but his own pride in his family honor that compelled him to keep his word, insofar as that was possible.

"Osric's special skills should make him ideal as a messenger," he went on. "He's agile enough to earn his way as a juggler and acrobat, and small enough to conceal himself where an ordinary man could not. As for the other two, that witch woman

Bronwen has a way with words. I'll warrant she's able to talk her way out of many a tight place. And the bear leader—"

"I don't want any of them involved in this," Melora protested.

"Your concern for your friends does you credit," Pembroke said. "But I'm inclined to agree with Grenville. We will have them sent for at once. I will speak to them, as I have to you. Then they can make their own decisions."

"And if they refuse, they will be allowed to return to Northumberland?" she asked.

"If that's what they want to do. Or if they choose to remain and not take service with me, they will be in an excellent position to make the most of their skills, and reap a greater reward from the guests at court than they could hope to gain if they stayed up north all winter."

Melora hesitated as she weighed his words. With her friends close by, she would feel a measure of reassurance.

"You have not found me ungenerous," he said. "I will pay your friends fair wages, should they serve as my messengers. Does that satisfy you?"

Again she wavered, torn by indecision. Then she nodded. "I suppose so."

She half-rose from her chair, but the earl gestured her to remain seated. "We've not quite finished," he said. "So far, you and Rokeby have been together in the palace, and on the day of the falcon hunt—always surrounded by others. But he, too, has a townhouse on the Strand. You will persuade him to invite you there."

Before he could say more, Dirk was on his feet. "That's not necessary, is it?"

The earl's black brows shot up. "You know better, surely. He's not likely to meet with his fellow conspirators in Whitehall, if he can avoid it. But in his own house, that's a different matter. Once our Mistress Standish has spent the evening there with him, she can make an excuse to stay as late as possible. She is to keep watch, to take note of who comes to his house by way of the river. To search his papers."

"Exactly how far do you wish her to go to get your information?" Dirk's voice was tight with anger.

"That's for the lady to decide."

Dirk remained standing for a moment longer. The muscles of his shoulders and arms strained at his doublet. His mouth thinned into a tight line. Then he brought himself under control with an obvious effort, and resumed his seat.

She was stirred in spite of herself by Dirk's unexpected outburst. Surely he did not care if she bartered her body in exchange for information. Or did he? She searched his face, but it was now impassive.

Pembroke got to his feet. "I believe we've finished," he said. He reached for the bell cord. "If I have anything more to tell you, I will send word by Grenville."

The interview was at an end. The liveried servant came and led them out.

On the boat trip back to the palace, Dirk was silent once more; but he looked at Melora uneasily. She was not the girl he had carried to his chamber a few nights before . . . who had reached out to him and drawn him down to her, and given herself freely, passionately.

There had been a change in her, and it troubled him more than he cared to admit. She had bargained with Pembroke with the cool skill and determination of a hardened adventuress.

But how deep did the change go? Was there nothing left of the vulnerable girl he had known? Perhaps it would be better if she had become as hard as she seemed. For otherwise, how could she hope to be a match for Rokeby?

He tried to reassure himself that she would be able to cope. From their first meeting, she had proved herself clever enough: able to think quickly, to assume a role without advance warning, and carry it off convincingly. And with her father and her friends depending on her, she was not likely to take any un-necessary risks.

Rokeby would not suspect she was in Pembroke's service. No doubt the viscount was conceited enough to believe that she had become attracted to him. He might even suppose that she had held him at arm's length this long only because of her virginal reticence.

But surely she would not go so far as to lie with the bastard. He was possessed by a killing rage at the thought of her pliant white body, naked in Rokeby's embrace. Not Melora . . . not his Melora . . .

But she was not his. She might have been, if he had told her of his feelings. He fixed his eyes on the mist-shrouded bank of the river, and on the familiar shape of the palace ahead.

How far was she prepared to go with Rokeby to get the necessary information? She was no longer inexperienced. He flinched from the thought that he was responsible for that. And he had humiliated her when he had turned from her that night.

He had always been so sure of himself in his dealings with women. Most of them had meant no more to him than a necessary physical release: a few had charmed him, or intrigued him for a little longer. But he had not loved one of them. Love was a word for moonstruck fools, or balladmakers.

He turned and looked at Melora, her face framed by the hood of her cloak. Her cheeks were damp with the mist; tiny droplets clung to her black hair, her thick, curving lashes. All his instincts urged him to draw her into his arms, to tell her that even now, it was not too late for her to break her promise to Pembroke. He would take the blame for her change of mind. Then he would take her away from court, to some distant haven. Perhaps even across the sea, to the islands of the Caribbees. He would abandon his dream of a fleet and a colony of his own.

He wanted to cry out that she belonged to him, only to him. That he would strangle Rokeby with his bare hands before he allowed her to give herself to him.

191

Then he battled his way back to cold reality. He was not free to follow his instincts, for too much was at stake here: not only his own long-held ambition, but the safety of the throne, of England.

Besides, he doubted that she would ever trust him completely again. There was nothing he could do to change that. But he swore to do all in his power to keep her safe as she embarked on this perilous undertaking.

She, too, remained silent until they stood at the entrance to one of the palace courtyards. "Dirk, wait a moment."

Inside the courtyard, a larger than usual crowd was milling about: liveried servants, hostlers, carters and itinerant peddlars. A skinny girl was performing somersaults, and the men shouted lewd encouragement every time her ragged skirts flew up to reveal her bare legs.

She put her hand on his arm, her eyes troubled. "You should not have asked Pembroke to send for Osric and the others," she said. "Perhaps it's not too late to stop him."

"I did it for your protection," he reminded her.

"You expect me to believe that?" She gave him a look of withering contempt.

"Believe what you choose," he said. Then he gripped her shoulders and pulled her against him with one swift movement. His arms went around her, and he bent his head to taste the sweet honey of her mouth.

For the briefest instant, he thought he felt the first flickering warmth of her response. Then a cart went rumbling through the gate and he caught the resinous scent of new-cut branches. "Out of the way," the driver shouted. "You and your lady should find a better place for such dalliance."

She stiffened in his arms and turned her face away. "Rokeby is expecting me," she said.

"To hell with Rokeby," he said, but her cold stare silenced him.

"The earl would not wish me to offend him by keeping him waiting."

The Publishers of Zebra Books Make This Special Offer to Zebra Romance Readers...

AFTER YOU HAVE READ THIS BOOK WE'D LIKE TO SEND YOU 4 MORE FOR *FREE* AN $18.00 VALUE

NO OBLIGATION!

MORE PASSION AND ADVENTURE AWAIT... YOUR TRIP TO A BIG ADVENTUROUS WORLD BEGINS WHEN YOU ACCEPT YOUR FIRST 4 NOVELS ABSOLUTELY *FREE* (AN $18.00 VALUE)

Accept your Free gift and start to experience more of the passion and adventure you like in a historical romance novel. Each Zebra novel is filled with proud men, spirited women and tempestuous love that you'll remember long after you turn the last page.

Zebra Historical Romances are the finest novels of their kind. They are written by authors who really know how to weave tales of romance and adventure in the historical settings you love. You'll feel like you've actually gone back in time with the thrilling stories that each Zebra novel offers.

GET YOUR FREE GIFT WITH THE START OF YOUR HOME SUBSCRIPTION

Our readers tell us that these books sell out very fast in book stores and often they miss the newest titles. So Zebra has made arrangements for you to receive the four newest novels published each month.

You'll be guaranteed that you'll never miss a title, and home delivery is so convenient. And to show you just how easy it is to get Zebra Historical Romances, we'll send you your first 4 books absolutely FREE! Our gift to you just for trying our home subscription service.

BIG SAVINGS AND FREE HOME DELIVERY

Each month, you'll receive the four newest titles as soon as they are published. You'll probably receive them even before the bookstores do. What's more, you may preview these exciting novels free for 10 days. If you like them as much as we think you will, just pay the low preferred subscriber's price of just $3.75 each. *You'll save $3.00 each month off the publisher's price.* AND, your savings are even greater because there are never any shipping, handling or other hidden charges—FREE Home Delivery. Of course you can return any shipment within 10 days for full credit, no questions asked. There is no minimum number of books you must buy.

4 FREE BOOKS

TO GET YOUR 4 FREE BOOKS WORTH $18.00 — MAIL IN THE FREE BOOK CERTIFICATE TODAY

Fill in the Free Book Certificate below, and we'll send your FREE BOOKS to you as soon as we receive it.

If the certificate is missing below, write to: Zebra Home Subscription Service, Inc., P.O. Box 5214, 120 Brighton Road, Clifton, New Jersey 07015-5214.

ZEBRA HOME SUBSCRIPTION
SERVICE, INC.
120 BRIGHTON ROAD
P.O. Box 5214
CLIFTON, NEW JERSEY 07015-5214

"Melora, wait—I won't touch you again. I only want to speak with you a moment longer."

She shook her head. "Master Inigo Jones is to be here, to try out the new scenery," she went on. "After that, I must do what I can to be alone with Rokeby. That is one of my duties, isn't it?"

Without giving him a chance to reply, she lifted her skirt and darted into the crowd, her purple cloak billowing out behind her.

Chapter Fourteen

In a bare, dusty cubbyhole, at a safe distance from the great hall and the royal apartments, Melora welcomed her friends to Whitehall. She had not realized how much she had missed them until now. Although she still felt misgivings about the wisdom of bringing them here on such a dangerous errand, it was good to see them again. "To think you came all the way from Northumberland—however did you make the journey so quickly?" she asked.

Osric grinned. "The North Road was as rough as ever—the rain's already started freezing over in the ruts. And the narrower roads are no better than cart tracks, most of them. But this time we traveled in a fine, sturdy coach, with outriders and a change of horses every night." A smile lit his thin face. "The earl did well by us."

"And we ate as well as any fat-bellied squire," Caleb said with satisfaction. "Beef and pigeon pie, a whole pig with apples, a fat roasted goose. And plenty of ale to wash it down with."

"You and Old Bruin are two of a kind," Osric teased the burly bear leader. "Do you and that great, lumbering beast never think of anything but your victuals?"

"It takes a lot more to fill up my insides than it does yours, little man," he retorted.

Melora's eyes misted and her throat tightened as she remembered how often they had gone hungry during their wanderings together. She thought of the nights when they had stopped to cook a meager meal over a roadside fire. Caleb had restrained his voracious appetite so that the others might have their share; and Osric had risked the pillory and the lash to poach a rabbit or a woodcock from a nobleman's land so that she and her father would not starve.

"You'll all eat well from now on," she assured them.

"As your father's doing," Osric said, with a chuckle. "The widow Frobisher—she owns the Rose and Thistle—has taken a great fancy to Master Edmund. She prepares all manner of delicacies to tempt his appetite."

"You said in your letter that he was recovering." She glanced at him anxiously. "You didn't say that only to set my mind at ease, did you?"

"You may take my word, mistress. The master's fever is long gone, and he doesn't cough nearly as often as he did. But it will take time until he is strong enough to travel the roads again."

She promised herself that if only she could serve Pembroke well, her father would never have to travel the roads again. But it was too soon to share her plans for the future with her friends; she would wait until she held Pembroke's gold in her hands. Then, if they chose, they could accompany her and her father to France. No doubt he would find a place for them in his new company; they could perform before the curtain rose, to put the audience into a merry mood.

"Now, as for your lodgings," she began.

"You need not trouble yourself about that, mistress," said Caleb. "Osric and I have already found ourselves a sturdy shed, close to the west gate of the palace. Old Bruin's chained up there now." He motioned to the dwarf. "Time we were getting busy," he said. "We'll look for a few boards to nail over the cracks and a heap of clean straw to bed down on, and we'll do well enough." He started for the door, with Osric scampering at his heels. "We'll be ready to carry your messages as soon as you give us the word."

"You are sure you wish to work for the earl?" she asked, her eyes shadowed with concern. "If not, you'll still be free to stay and perform at the holiday festivities."

Osric shook his head. "You will be better served by us than by strangers."

"I'm certain of that. But you must not underrate the danger," she told him.

"And aren't we used to running risks, tramping the roads?" the little man reminded her, with a rueful smile. "This time, at least, we'll be well paid."

Before she could raise any further objections, he and Caleb took themselves off, leaving her with Bronwen.

"And what of you?" Melora asked the old woman. "We must find you a place to sleep."

"Why, I'll bed down with the others in the shed, mistress."

"You'll do no such thing," Melora protested. "There are no end of unused chambers, larger than this one." She glanced about the narrow little cubbyhole, with rows of sturdy shelves lining three sides. "Probably it was once used to store linens or provisions," she added.

Bronwen had already set down her small, battered wooden trunk on one of the shelves. It held her bags of herbs—trefoil, woodruff, valerian, and yarrow—her rune stones and the pack of cards with their curious pictures, and all the other tools of her arcane trade.

"This suits me well enough. It is far better than those creaky old wagons we used to travel in. Or have you already forgotten the nights when the rain came pouring through the canvas, and the wind whistled through every crack?"

"I've not forgotten. But now that you are here, I would be only too willing to make up a pallet in my own chamber. It's only that Felicity—one of the queen's ladies—shares it with me. She is as curious as a monkey, and would ask no end of questions. And how she loves to gossip."

Bronwen shook her head. "It would never do. No one must even suspect that we know each other. The earl made a great point of that."

196

Melora cast about in her mind for some way to reward Bronwen for her loyalty. "You must have new garments, at least. Your shoes are worn through. You shall have another pair. And a good woolen gown, and a new cloak."

But Bronwen drew her faded cloak around her as if she feared Melora would snatch it away. "That's a daft notion," she protested. "This is no ordinary cloak, as I've told you many times." She stroked the shabby garment. The symbols embroidered on the sides and hem were sadly tarnished from years of hard wear, but they had special meaning for her.

"I've already bespoken a new cloak from the mercer—gray, like this one," Melora told her. "And skeins of gold and silver thread. You will be able to copy those designs."

"Designs, indeed!" The Welshwoman bridled at the word. She whipped off the cloak and spread it before Melora; the light from a stubby candle set on a nearby shelf flickered over the intricate patterns.

"See this?" She pointed a skinny finger at the pentagram, the five-pointed star with a circle around it. "The Druid's Foot, they call it back in my native land. "Or sometimes the Goblin's Claw. And here, the sword of Calleich—"

"You can embroider them all on the new cloak, can't you?"

"It will take time," Bronwen shrugged her bony shoulders. "But I suppose I'll have plenty of that, idling about here, like some fine lady."

"You won't be idling," Melora reminded her. "You will have to make the journey from here to Pembroke's house in all sorts of weather."

"A swift ride along the river in a boat, what's that? I've made longer journeys through rain and snow. And for far smaller reward." She wrapped the cloak around her again. "But what of you? Let me have a closer look."

She took the candle from the shelf, held it up, and peered at Melora with eyes that looked startlingly young and alert in contrast with her deeply lined face and white hair.

"A fine court lady you've become, in your sweet-smelling

197

silks and laces." She moved closer, then nodded slowly. "Ah, it's as I thought when I first saw you."

Melora shifted uneasily under the searching gaze.

"You are no longer a maid." She spoke with calm certainty, but without the slightest hint of reproach. "The tall young lord who brought you to London, he has taught you what it is to be a woman."

Melora knew from long experience that denial would be useless. "He taught me—much," she admitted.

"And the teaching was not without pain," Bronwen said.

"I was prepared for that. You explained to me back last summer—"

The old woman's hard, bony fingers closed on her wrist. "Not bodily hurt. That is swift and sharp, but quickly forgotten. I speak of a deeper pain." She shook her head and sighed. "A wound to the heart."

"Whatever wound he dealt me, I've already recovered."

"Don't try to cozen me, mistress. You love the young lord, with his gold-touched eyes and his fine, strong limbs."

Melora glared at the old woman in helpless frustration. "He was right—you *are* a witch!"

"Witch, indeed! Say, rather, that I am a Wiccan. A follower of the Old Religion, taught in the old ways, like my mother and her mother before her." She gave a short, dry laugh. "*Witch* is a word spoken by those who look but do not see, who walk the earth but know nothing of its wonders. Poor fools who fear what they do not understand."

"Have it as you wish," Melora said hastily. "But I must warn you, Bronwen: be cautious here within these walls. His majesty is one of your—" She hesitated. "Your frightened fools. He has been writing a book, condemning your craft and those who practice it. Should the king suspect that you follow the Old Religion, even Pembroke would not be able to protect you from his wrath.

"And how should a humble old woman like me draw the notice of the king?"

Bronwen was right. King James, surrounded as he was by his courtiers, and with a procession of highborn guests arriving at the palace every day, was most unlikely to be aware of her existence.

In the shed he shared with Caleb and Old Bruin, Osric whirled and capered so that Melora could get the full effect of the yellow-and-green doublet and purple hose. He tossed his head, and the bells on his close-fitting cap of blue and red made a merry tinkling sound. Unlike Bronwen, the dwarf had been delighted with his bright new outfit.

Caleb, although less demonstrative, grinned and smoothed the new leather jerkin that encased his massive chest. "A fine piece of workmanship," he said. "My thanks, mistress."

"And I've not forgotten Old Bruin," she said, taking a pot of honey from her bundle.

"If you overfeed him, he'll soon be too fat and lazy to dance," Osric said. "Like his master."

"I leave the jigging and capering to you," Caleb retorted. He ran his hand over the bear's heavy coat. "Look at that. As fine and glossy as the king's own robes."

She nodded absently, for her thoughts were fixed on a more pressing reason for her visit. "I've a message for the earl," she said.

Osric spoke up eagerly. "Caleb went last time—it's my turn again, mistress."

He listened intently to each word she spoke, then repeated them without a mistake. She gave him a shilling to pay the boatman, and watched him leave the shed.

Caleb was already opening the honeypot for Old Bruin. As the bear dropped down on all fours to enjoy his treat, his master rubbed his furry head.

She could never quite get used to the ease with which Caleb handled the great, lumbering beast. She knew that he could

199

have felled the strongest man with a with a single swipe of his huge paw.

"Finest bear in the realm, he is." Caleb spoke with pride. "But it wasn't me that trained him to dance," he said. "His first master taught him the skill. I never did find out who the fellow was, or how he and Bruin came to be separated."

Although she had heard the tale many times, Caleb enjoyed telling it, and she did not interrupt him.

"I'd been serving as a gunner in her majesty's fleet, and I was fed up with the sea. Takin' orders from a lot of stiff-necked officers who treated us like scum. An' a rope's end across our backs if we didn't move fast enough to suit 'em.

"Back ashore I was, not knowin' what to do next, when I found the beast, torn and bleedin', in an alley back of a Southwark tavern. A mob of worthless idlers had set their dogs on him. He fought off the pack bravely. Even when they threw pepper in his eyes to blind him he stood his ground.

"I drove them bastards off. Cracked a few of their heads with my staff, I did. Then I sewed up the beast's wounds with my own hands, and cared for him. And one day, when he was healed, he got himself up on his hind legs and started dancing about, as nimble as you please.

"Right then and there, I saw the hand of Providence. I'd found myself an honest trade. I decided I might as well make the most of it."

She smiled at the sight of the bear with his nose buried in the honeypot. Yes, it was good to have her friends around her again, even Old Bruin.

It was growing late, and soon it would be time to dress for evening. She did not wish to give Felicity any cause for suspicion about her unexplained absences from their chamber. She took leave of Caleb, and went out into the winter dusk.

Moving quickly, she kept close to the wall, her thoughts on Osric and the message he carried. Pembroke had been right when he had advised her to listen to the ladies' careless, sometimes malicious gossip. So far she had gleaned several promising pieces of information and sent them along to the earl.

Only this morning, as they were getting ready to wait upon the queen, Felicity had provided her with a particularly interesting tidbit.

"Lady Octavia spent last night with her Spanish marquis. She boasts that he's going to remain here at court after the holidays, and only because he can't bear to be parted from her. But I doubt that's the real reason."

"What is, then?" Melora asked.

"He petitioned King Philip to make him governor of Valencia. But the king gave the post to his own nephew, instead. Or was it his cousin?"

"And why would that make the marquis decide to stay in England? Surely he doesn't expect King James to give him a post at Whitehall, or in one of our English counties?"

Felicity shrugged her plump shoulders, and leaned closer to the mirror, to study her reflection. Then she set a patch in place next to her eyebrow. "Do you think it looks better here, or at the corner of my mouth?" she asked.

"It is most becoming right where it is," Melora said. "But you were speaking of Octavia's marquis."

"The marquis is a proud, sort, like all these Spanish grandees. He feels that Philip's refusal dishonored him and his fine family."

"I still don't see—"

"Octavia's father is one of the wealthiest men in England. Carvajal may be persuaded to marry the silly fool—if the dowry is generous enough."

"And would her father wish to see his daughter married to a Spaniard?" In spite of the uneasy peace between the two nations, the memory of the Armada and the old conflicts still lingered.

"Better than seeing her sent home in disgrace, with a big belly and no husband at all."

For the rest of that morning, while Melora had sat with her

head bent over her needlework, she had brooded over Felicity's words. The Marquis de Carvajal. A malcontent, a foreign nobleman who felt his own king had used him unfairly . . . It might mean nothing. Nevertheless, she would send the information to the earl as quickly as possible, and let him judge its value.

She quickened her steps as the fog rolled in from the Thames, obscuring her view. When she reached the west gate, she decided to avoid the crowded courtyard, and took a shortcut through one of the palace gardens, instead. She hoped Felicity would be too absorbed in her own plans for the evening to ask questions.

She started down the lime walk. The wind blew the fallen leaves around her feet, and set the branches of the trees creaking and swaying overhead. Then she caught the sound of footsteps behind her.

Whirling around, she caught her breath. It was Dirk, looming up before her like some apparition.

She had not spoken with him since their visit to Pembroke's house. Now she felt a swift pang of uneasiness. She did not want to be alone with him.

"Have you been following me?" she demanded.

"And if I have?"

"I'm already late—I must go back inside—Felicity will be asking questions—" If only she did not find it so difficult to breathe, when he stood close to her like this.

He caught her arm. "Surely you can spare a moment. I must talk to you."

"Do you have some new instructions for me from Pembroke?" Without giving him a chance to reply, she went on quickly. "If so, you might have chosen a more opportune moment to pass them on to me."

"This has nothing to do with Pembroke." His grip tightened, and he drew her closer. "Don't pretend there's no more between us than our shared allegiance to his cause."

"The only cause I serve is my own," she told him. "I've been promised a rich reward, and I mean to earn it."

"And what then?"

"I have plans for the future."

"So you've said. What are these plans? Surely I've a right to know that much."

"You have no rights at all, where I'm concerned."

She dared not let herself be moved by his nearness, or the sound of his voice. "If Pembroke's displeased because I've not yet visited Lord Rokeby at his house, you may tell him I'm only waiting for a suitable opportunity."

"You are not to go to Rokeby's house," Dirk said. "There is no need. I won't have you offering yourself to that damned lecherous bastard."

"You've no right to tell me what I may or may not do, Dirk Grenville!"

But even as she spoke, a part of her longed to have him refute her words, once and for all. If only he would say that she belonged to him, that he would keep her with him always. That her future would be one with his, and nothing and no one could ever separate them.

Or he need not speak at all. He need only cover her mouth with his and claim her with his kisses. Until she forgot all about Pembroke's schemes, Rokeby's treachery . . . forgot even her dream of going off to France—

But he did not speak and he did not try to kiss her.

She tilted her head back and searched his face. "It was you who persuaded me to enter Pembroke's service. With such great affairs of state in the balance, what does it matter if I spend the night with Rokeby?"

And when he remained silent, desperation drove her to goad him. "You're the only man I've ever had—so far. Maybe you fear that once I've lain with Rokeby, I'll find him a better lover than you were. Or maybe I'll discover that one man is like another in the dark."

She heard the harsh intake of his breath. He pushed her away, then drew back his arm. She braced herself, expecting

203

him to strike her. Even in the half-light of the garden, she could see the violent trembling of his body.

But he did not touch her again. And when he spoke, his voice was hard with contempt. "Do what you will to earn the earl's gold," he said. "I'll not try to stop you." He turned away, leaving her alone in the windswept garden.

Wax candles shed their light along the polished surface of the long mahogany table and glittered over the silver and crystal. Melora, wearing a gown of white silk trimmed with insets of delicate black lace, sat opposite Rokeby. The dining chamber of his house on the Strand was as richly decorated as the palace banquet hall.

She glanced at her host, and tried to quell her fears. Had she been wise to come here? Yet what better way to get the information Pembroke wanted?

If Dirk had given her proof of his love, she might have waited. She might have tried to get what information she could in other, safer ways.

Even as she made polite, aimless conversation with the viscount, her thoughts lingered on her brief meeting with Dirk the night before. It was his face she saw, his voice she heard, cold and indifferent. His voice, saying, "Do what you will to earn the earl's gold."

"Is the marchpane not to your liking, my lady?"

Rokeby's voice brought her back to the present. "It's excellent, my lord," she said.

"But you've scarcely touched it," he said.

"I must confess, my fears have taken away my appetite." She seized on the first excuse that came to mind. "Now that the night of the masque is so close, it makes me most uneasy to think of performing for the king and queen."

"You will enchant them, as you have me." She tried to ignore the gleam in his pale eyes.

"Perhaps if I had a little more practice. Do you keep a musician here, who might play for me?"

"I will accompany you on the harpsicord," Rokeby said. "It will be my pleasure."

In the library, Melora took her place at the top of the spiraling iron steps used to reach for books on the highest shelves. Her silk skirt swayed about her. She reminded herself not to rest her hand on the stair railing; the staircase Jones had designed, covered with shimmering cloth of silver, would have no such convenience.

Rokeby played the introduction to the plaintive ballad. She held her head high, drew a deep breath.

Long hours have I pined alone,
Waiting for my love . . .

She went through the verse, in which the virgin goddess revealed her forbidden passion for the handsome young shepherd, Endymion. Then, swaying gracefully, she began her slow descent.

When she reached the bottom of the steps, he got to his feet and crossed the room. "If you perform half so well for the court, you will charm your audience." He took her hand. "As you have me."

She forced a smile, and kept it in place, even as his fingers caressed her palm.

"It's too bad we don't have Master Jones's lighting effects to enhance the scene properly," he said. The place where the clouds obscure the rays of the moon, while Artemis yields to her lover. A masterly touch."

He had already put out the candles on either side of the harpsicord. Now he moved swiftly to the nearby table and extinguished the remaining candles, plunging that end of the room into darkness. "Now, my fair Artemis, shall we go on and play out the rest of the scene?"

She understood well enough, and it sent a chill coursing through her.

The rest of the scene.

On the night of the performance, the members of the audience would have to imagine the moon goddess bending to the embrace of Endymion, yielding up her virginity to her mortal lover. A daring notion, but still within the bounds of propriety.

But here, with Rokeby . . . She tried to retreat, but the iron steps were at her back, and he stood pressing his body against hers.

"Loose your hair for me, Artemis," he said, his voice soft and caressing. "Let it fall about your face." His hand came out and his fingers ran lightly over her skin. "And over your shoulders . . ." He pressed his mouth greedily against the curve of her shoulder, then moved it to the swell of her breast.

She tried to draw back, but he thrust his fingers into her hair. The scattering bodkins made a tinkling sound against the polished wood of the floor.

"No, my lord—"

His hands moved impatiently, tugging the dark waves free from the looped ribbons that bound them. His voice was hoarse, his breath hot against her face. "Let me—let me—"

He pressed his mouth to her nipple. She felt his teeth through the silk of her gown, like the teeth of a ravening animal, biting, tugging . . . She gagged at the overpowering scent of musky perfume and sweat.

She never should have come here—no matter what Pembroke had said—she never should—

She was so engulfed by panic that it was a moment before she heard the sound, a knocking at the library door.

He raised his face. "Go away!" he called out.

"My lord."

"Away, damn you!"

"But you have visitors, my lord."

The voice was deferential, yet insistent. He stepped back, swaying slightly, then went to the door.

"They said their business was most urgent—I dared not send them away—"

206

"Guard your tongue, you wretched fool!" He stepped outside.

He paused only for a moment. "I was not expecting callers tonight," he told Melora. "I will come back as quickly as I can."

She stood in the darkened room, her nails digging into her palms. She could not go through with this. She did not care about Pembroke or the promised reward, not now. No matter what she stood to gain, she could not go through with it.

But perhaps there was another way to make the most of her visit here tonight. No ordinary visitors would have diverted Rokeby from his purpose.

She moved cautiously toward the door and opened it a few inches. Thank goodness he had blown out the candles. There would be no telltale light to catch his attention.

"—it could not wait, I tell you."

She knew that voice. It was Ambrose Corbett who spoke, the shy young son of an Essex squire. He was an amiable young man who admired her but had never quite gotten up the courage to try to make love to her.

What had she heard about him? Only that he was the younger son, who would have no claim to his father's property. But no—that wasn't all—there was something more. If only she could remember.

"The king's hound is hot on the scent." Another, deeper voice. ". . . This afternoon . . . a serving man . . . going through my papers—"

Her hand flew to her lips as she caught a glimpse of Lady Octavia's lover, the tall, arrogant Marquis de Carvajal. She did not recognize the third visitor.

Rokeby glanced over his shoulder in the direction of the library, and she stepped back, pressing herself against the wall. He led his three guests away. Her heart seemed to stop, then began hammering against her ribs with such violence that she feared she might faint.

She dared not try to follow them, for she did not know her

way around the house; but she had learned a great deal already. Pembroke would be well pleased.

She could not be sure how much time had passed before the men emerged once more. Then she realized with a shock that although their visit had interrupted Rokeby in his purpose, he would return to her. So far he had not used force, for he prided himself on his skill as a practiced seducer.

But she knew that whatever she might gain by yielding to him, she could not do it. She would have to get out of the house, and quickly.

The visitors were preparing to leave. She forced herself to move forward on unsteady legs. One step, another. She must keep moving down the long hall that seemed to go on forever.

"Lady Rosalind!"

"Please—Master Corbett—don't go yet—" There was no need for playacting, not now. The desperation in her voice was real.

Ambrose Corbett stared at her in the light of the flaring sconces that flanked the wide front door.

Her fingers tightened on his sleeve. "His lordship and I were—rehearsing the masque."

A slight, cynical smile touched Carvajal's full, sensuous mouth. But she ignored him, and the third visitor, a thin, pockmarked man.

"I had not realized the lateness of the hour," she went on. "I must ask you to escort me back to Whitehall, Master Corbett."

"I should be honored to be of service," he said. Ignoring Rokeby's hard stare, the young man motioned to the servant who hovered nearby. "Bring the lady's cloak at once."

She kept close beside him, for she feared that Rokeby might try to detain her by force. Even when they were outside and heading toward the river, she did not relinquish her grasp.

A small boat lay moored at the foot of the slippery stone stairs leading down from Rokeby's landing. There was no hired boatman, but the pockmarked man sat down on the front plank, took up the oars, and began to row with swift, steady strokes.

During the journey, the Marquis de Carvajal sat in brooding silence, his heavy cloak wrapped around him; Corbett and Melora shared the opposite seat. She let herself rest against him.

"I came to Lord Rokeby's house while it was still light," she said. "But these winter afternoons are so short, are they not? Before I realized it, the sun had set. I wanted to go back to the palace. But his lordship invited me to dine with him and I—I did not know how to refuse without offending him."

The breeze from the river tugged at a lock of her hair, and she pushed it under the hood of her cloak. "I am so thankful you arrived when you did, Master Corbett—Ambrose." She looked up at him with undisguised gratitude.

"You must be more discreet in future, my lady."

"I fear I am not yet experienced in the ways of the court."

Corbett's arm went around her shoulders in a protective gesture. She wished that she did not have to include his name in her report to Pembroke. She could only hope that the young man was not yet too deeply involved in Rokeby's schemes.

Chapter Fifteen

Bronwen opened the small pouch and cast the rune stones out upon the floor. "It's as I told you, mistress. The night of the winter solstice . . . it will mean danger for you."

Although the old woman's words filled her with a sense of foreboding, Melora forced a smile and tried to make light of them.

"For the love of heaven! I've enough to worry about without your dismal croaking. Tomorrow night I'll be performing in the great hall, with the eyes of their majesties and all the court upon me."

"You've said the queen favors you. Speak to her; make some excuse. Tell her you cannot perform tomorrow night. Let one of the other ladies take your place."

"Impossible! No one else knows my songs. Besides, Master Inigo Jones and his apprentices have been working on the sets all afternoon. The candles—dozens of them—are being set in place. The backdrop's nearly finished. And the stairway—even now, they're covering it with yards of the finest cloth of silver."

"A pox upon your Master Jones and his candles and silver stairway. My stones speak to me. They warn of peril—I see a beast rending its prey with fang and claw—and blood . . ."

Only Melora's deep affection for the old woman forced her to keep her temper under control. Sweet Jesu, didn't she already have enough to stretch her nerves to the breaking point?

Even now, the seamstress was waiting in her chamber to put the finishing touches on her costume. None of the other ladies had been permitted to see what she would be wearing, not even Felicity.

"You must whet their curiosity," Rokeby had insisted. "Let no one see you in your costume until you step out onto the stage."

Since the evening she had fled from his townhouse on the Strand, escorted by Ambrose Corbett, the viscount's behavior toward her had been polite but distant. It was as if he had dismissed all memory of his failed attempt to make love to her.

She tried to convince herself that he had given up and had turned his attentions back to Lady Jade, who had never ceased to pursue him. For the past few nights, he had chosen Jade for his partner in all the dances; he had escorted her into the banqueting hall and talked and laughed with her as if there had never been any estrangement between them.

And after all, Lady Jade was still a striking woman, with her tall, well-formed figure, her silver-gilt hair, and those pale green eyes. Heads turned each time she entered the great hall dressed in a new and costly gown, designed in the latest fashion and enhanced by the magnificent jewels that glittered at her throat, at her ears, and in her elaborate coiffure. Queen Anne herself was not more splendidly arrayed.

But although Rokeby's renewed attentions to Lady Jade should have calmed Melora's fears, she could not throw off her misgivings completely. Even in the short time she had spent at court, she had come to know the viscount too well to hope that he would forgive her for frustrating him. Her refusal to surrender to him had been a blow to his pride; worse yet, Ambrose Corbett and the Marquis de Carvajal had been present to see his humiliation.

She turned her attention back to Bronwen, who was still bending over the scattered stones, tracing the symbols engraved on their surfaces. "Hear me, mistress," Bronwen said. "If you must go through with this folly in spite of my warnings, there may still be a chance to escape disaster."

"But all this time you've been saying that the night of the winter solstice brings evil."

"It is a time of darkness. But it is followed by the rebirth of light," Bronwen went on. "It is the longest night of the year. The night when the wolf and the adder hold sway over the earth. But once it is past, and the wheel of the year turns back toward the sun—" She broke off abruptly.

"What is it? What do you see?" In spite of herself, Melora was caught up in the hypnotic spell cast by the old woman's chanting voice.

"Lord Rokeby, with his eyes like pale gray stones, and his soft, bejeweled hands. Cruel, he is, and clever. He will harm you if he can, mistress."

"I need no soothsayer to tell me that," Melora said. Nevertheless, she felt an icy fear flicking at her nerves.

"And not you alone. His powers are far-reaching. Others, too, may perish at his command. Many others—even to the highest in the land—even to the throne—"

"Be still, for the love of heaven! You and the others are only messengers. I won't have you risking your lives by meddling in matters that do not concern you."

"I do not meddle," Bronwen said calmly. "I only speak what my rune stones tell me."

Melora's hand shot out, scattering the stones across the floor. "I'll hear no more of your spells and omens! No one believes in them except simple-minded country wives and kitchen maids!"

"You believe, mistress," Bronwen picked up the stones, one by one, and dropped them into her pouch. "Yes, and your tall, bold lover with his gold-touched eyes—he believes, too."

"That proves how little you know. Dirk Grenville believes only in himself. He makes a mockery of your foolish spells and charms."

She broke off, then looked away, seized by a wave of remorse. She was deeply fond of Bronwen. Only her overstrained nerves had caused her to lash out with such scornful words. But even before she could apologize, she heard the old woman's soft laughter.

"He believes only in himself, does he? He mocks my words?" Her eyes sparkled in her wrinkled face. "I've not forgotten that morning in the stable of the Leaping Stag. What was it he said? Ah, yes—that a man shapes his own fortunes, if he is willing to take risks. He spoke bravely enough—until I told him what errand had brought him to Northumberland."

The memories of that morning came flooding back, catching Melora unawares. "I told him of the wedding of his young kinswoman," Bronwen went on, "and how her marriage had thwarted those fine plans of his. He tried to brazen it out, but he was shaken by my words."

Melora longed to say that Bronwen had made a lucky guess. But how was that possible, when she could not have known anything about Dirk, or his purpose in coming to Northumberland to fetch his cousin? And he, for all his pretended scorn, had been shaken.

Bronwen smiled ruefully. "A most headstrong young man, that one. You will not tame him easily, and as for making a life with him, it will take all your devotion, and your own strong will to pit against his."

"I've no wish to tame him. And if you think for one moment that I would wed such a—a—selfish blackguard, you're not nearly as wise as you pretend."

"Yet he is the one for you, mistress."

Melora rose swiftly, and smoothed her skirts, brushing the dust from the velvet folds.

"And where are you off to in such haste?"

"My seamstress is to make the final fitting on my costume. I've already kept her waiting too long."

Then, without giving Bronwen time to launch into another warning, Melora slipped out into the corridor, and headed for her bedchamber.

The seamstress and her assistants had placed the costume

across the bed, and now stood ready with shears and needle and thread; but although they worked diligently, snipping and basting, they were not yet finished when Dirk's message arrived.

His note, more of a command than a request, told her to meet him in his chambers after tonight's banquet. Melora's first impulse was to send back a curt refusal. Better yet, she would not reply at all. Let him fret and stew until he realized that he could not summon her whenever it pleased him, as if she were a servingmaid.

But he might have some word for her from Pembroke; if so, she dared not ignore his message. It was all she could do to stand still while the seamstress finished arranging the sheath of thin silk over Melora's breasts and hips.

"A most daring costume, if I may say so. But one that suits you well, my lady," she said.

"Pembroke is pleased with your work."

Dirk, who had been pacing the floor of his antechamber, awaiting her arrival, now paused before the wide fireplace. "You have done even better than he expected."

She tried not to look toward the door leading to his bed-chamber. In spite of all her sensible resolutions, she could not help but remember the night he had taken her inside and carried her to the canopied bed. Was he remembering, too? Or perhaps some other woman had shared his bed since then . . .

"You had no need to summon me here, only to tell me that Pembroke is pleased with me," she snapped.

"There's more," he said. "The earl already suspected that Carvajal was one of Rokeby's followers, but you have helped to confirm it. Now he wants you to try to win the confidence of Lady Octavia, and find out as much as you can about the Spaniard. As for young Ambrose Corbett, you can take full credit for that particular discovery."

She felt a swift pang of remorse. "Ambrose was kind to me.

He helped me to get away from Rokeby's house, and I repaid his kindness by betraying him to Pembroke. I can take no pride in that."

Dirk caught her by the shoulders, and she felt the tension in his grasp. His eyes searched hers, and she read the unspoken question in their depths.

"I did not lie with Rokeby."

Dirk's look of relief moved her more deeply than she wanted to admit. "Melora—sweeting—"

There was no mistaking the emotion behind his words. His fingers began moving gently, caressingly; and she did not want to draw away from the warmth of his touch. He did care, no matter how he might try to deny it. She longed to bury her face against his chest, to put her arms around him. To cling to him with all her strength, and beg him never to let her go.

Instead, she spoke with feigned calm. "Perhaps it may be possible to spare Ambrose from punishment, once the plot against the king has been exposed. Ambrose may be foolish and headstrong, but I still can't understand why he came to be involved in such treachery."

"I believe I can."

"Was he so embittered because as a younger son, he cannot inherit his father's estate?"

When he did not answer, she hurried on. "But there are hundreds of wellborn young men in the same position. They take service in the army, and win fame that way. Or if they are of a more peaceful bent, there is the diplomatic service, the law, the church."

"But others, like that rash young fool, are reckless enough to get themselves involved with traitors like Rokeby."

"Then he joined forces with the viscount only to gain wealth and power?"

"I think, in Corbett's case, there may be another motive as well," Dirk said.

He drew her down beside him on the cushioned settle before the fire, then put his arm around her. She rested her head against his shoulder. "Young Ambrose had a sister who was here at court a few years ago."

Felicity had once made some vague, slighting reference to Ambrose Corbett's sister; but at the time, Melora had been too preoccupied to pay her any heed.

"Lord Beresford, a favorite of the king, seduced the girl, got her with child, then refused to marry her. Her dowry was not large enough to satisfy him, you see. Squire Corbett came to court and tried to persuade the king to force Beresford to marry her. But his majesty refused to intervene. He believed that Beresford could do better than to wed a squire's daughter."

"And the girl? What became of her?"

"Her father arranged another marriage, with a doddering old tyrant who'd already buried two wives. But the night before the wedding, the girl killed herself."

Melora's heart constricted with pity. "A word from the king would have made all the difference," she said. "I think he acted badly—shamefully!"

"He sometimes does," Dirk agreed.

"He is no judge of men; Queen Anne has said as much. He chooses and discards his favorites as lightly as he changes those fine satin doublets. And though he is far more extravagant than Elizabeth was, he lacks her wisdom."

"I don't deny it."

She drew away and stared at him, her eyes wide with bewilderment. "And yet you choose to serve him."

"I do. And what's more, I would risk my life, if need be, to keep him on the throne."

"But in heaven's name, why?"

"It is not James the man I would serve, but what he stands for." She started to speak, but he went on quickly. "Hear me out, Melora, and try to understand. His majesty has all the faults you spoke of, and others as well. But he is more than an ordinary man. He is the lawful successor to Elizabeth, chosen by her to rule England."

216

"But he's not the powerful ruler she was. Some say he never will be."

"Perhaps not. And the common people may not feel any great admiration for him. To the English, he will always be a Scotsman first—an outsider.

"But they do feel a stubborn kind of loyalty to what he represents. He is a force for stability who holds England together by his very presence on the throne. And will do so as long as he lives. More than that, he has two legitimate sons to carry on the Stuart line."

Melora, who had never concerned herself with matters of state, now kept her eyes fixed on his face as she concentrated all her attention on his words.

"And if Arabella Stuart were to rule in his place—" she ventured.

"Arabella Stuart, Rokeby's pawn? If she were set upon the throne, then you would see a civil war that would rend England in two. Papist against Puritan. Northumberland against Cornwall. Noblemen gathering their followers and riding off to battle. Thousands of helpless common people drawn into the conflict. And perhaps even worse to follow."

She was caught up in an icy tide of foreboding that grew with every word he spoke. She shuddered and pressed closer to him. "What could be possibly be worse than that?"

"An attack from Spain," he told her. "When Elizabeth ruled, we were able to drive off the might of the Spaniards.

"She had her greatest captains then, to smash the Armada. But now those men—Frobisher, Drake, Hawkins—all are gone."

Melora spoke slowly. "And if England were weakened and in chaos, controlled by men like Rokeby, whose only loyalty is to himself, you think he might sell his own country out to Spain."

"Can you doubt it?" His face hardened, the tanned skin stretched over his angular cheekbones. "Even now, he conspires with Spanish nobles like Carvajal."

Then, seeing her stricken look, he put his hand over hers. "It won't happen, Melora. It must not be allowed to happen."

He sat in brooding silence, her head resting against his shoulder. Then he leaned over and brushed his lips across her cheek. "You understand why Rokeby must not succeed—however great the cost of stopping him."

She could not answer; there was no need.

He gave her a rueful smile. "Now, be off with you, to your bedchamber."

She looked at him in shocked disbelief. "Do you think, after what you have told me, I could possibly sleep—"

"You must, sweeting. A goddess should not look pale and shaken, as you do now."

"A goddess," she repeated automatically. "The masque. I'd forgotten."

"Forgotten your first appearance on the stage?" He was teasing her now, but she did not mind, for she knew he was trying to comfort her.

"All the court is buzzing with anticipation, waiting to see your performance tomorrow night."

"Tomorrow night." She gave him an anxious glance. "But that is the night of the winter solstice. Bronwen cast her rune stones for me, and she says—"

"What does she say, your witch woman?" He drew her close and she told him of her talk with Bronwen, only that afternoon.

"She believes it, Dirk."

"She's an old woman who wishes to make herself important by frightening others with her foolish maunderings."

Melora gave him a shaky smile. "She frightened you. That day in the stable, when she told you why you had left the court to come to Northumberland, and how your cousin's marriage had spoiled your plans—"

"I admit, I can't explain that. And, yes, it did give me a moment's uneasiness. But if these soothsayers speak enough nonsense, now and then they are bound to make a lucky guess."

He drew her to her feet and then he was holding her tightly, as if to shield her with his own strength. Her breasts were crushed against the hardness of his chest. Her hands reached up and pressed against his wide shoulders. "You have nothing to fear from all her legion of spirits and hobgoblins," he said. "I'll be there tomorrow night to see that no harm comes to you."

His mouth covered hers, and his tongue traced the shape of her lips. The reassuring warmth that spread through her swiftly changed to another, more urgent sensation. Fierce and hot it rose within her, the need for him to carry her off to his bed, to strip away her gown, to make love with her.

But she heard his voice, harsh with his own leashed desire. "Be off with you—while I am still able to let you go."

The great hall was fragrant with the heady scent of dried herbs, evergreen boughs, and pomanders. Masses of holly and ivy festooned the walls. On a velvet-covered platform, musicians in scarlet and gold played lively tunes, while acrobats and jugglers performed to keep the audience entertained while they waited for the masque to begin.

The stage had been set up at the far end of the great hall, and when the heavy curtains were drawn aside, the audience sat spellbound, their eyes fixed on the painted trees, streams, and mossy rocks of a forest glade. Master Inigo Jones had indeed outdone himself in creating the setting for tonight's performance.

The fair-haired young man chosen to play the role of Endymion paused to gaze at the rim of the silver disc still close to the horizon. To the music of a rustic flute, he sang of his adoration for the goddess. Then he sank to the ground, overcome by sleep.

And now came the music of the flageolet, the harpsicord, and the violins, heralding the entrance of the wood nymphs in their robes of leaf green, yellow, and russet silks. They moved into the measures of a slow, sensuous dance. As the tempo quickened, their sandaled feet moved more swiftly, their skirts flaring out around them, their heads thrown back and their faces flushed.

Rokeby, seated at the king's side, felt a surge of pride. This was his creation, the product of his genius. No doubt much of it would be wasted on James, that uncouth Scottish lout; but there were those in the audience who would understand and appreciate all that had gone into the production.

And for him, the masque had a special meaning. It would serve as a fit setting for the loveliness of Lady Rosalind. She had played her own private charade long enough, had tempted him, had tormented him with her lush beauty; and then she had resorted to that clever ruse to escape before he could possess her.

After the first pangs of frustration had passed, he had decided that now he understood her better. She enjoyed the pleasure of the chase, of watching men run after her, court her. No doubt she had played the same game with that arrogant cousin of hers, with young Ambrose Corbett, and who could say how many others.

But he was no adoring young fool to be led on and then thwarted by a capricious girl. She would discover that, and sooner than she supposed. He would break her pride, bring her to her knees before him. He would teach her the refinements of erotic pleasure. No other man would be able to arouse her, then satisfy her as he would . . .

A hush fell over the audience and Rokeby looked up. Melora was poised at the top of the stairs, slender and bewitching. She had cast convention aside to create the role of the goddess, and she captivated her audience completely.

Until now, no matter what part a girl might play in a court masque, her gown was in the current style, with stiff farthingale and tightly laced busk. But the girl who stood at the top of the silvery path from moon to earth was garbed as Artemis might have been. The sheer silk clung to her pointed breasts with their rosy nipples; it sheathed her narrow waist, her flat belly, and the delicate swell of her hips. The skirt fell to her silver-sandaled feet, but was slit up the sides so that, with her every step, her long legs and tapering thighs were revealed.

"Shocking!" a woman's voice whispered.

"How could the queen have permitted such a shameless display?" asked another.

"Perhaps even she did not know—"

But if the women in the audience were outraged, or pretended to be, every male who watched the slow, regal descent of the goddess was caught up in her spell.

> *Long hours have I pined alone,*
> *Waiting for my love . . .*

For Dirk, it brought back the memory of that first evening when he had stopped above the firelit ravine, held motionless by a song carried on the wind. By the sight of a dark-haired, violet-eyed girl in a ragged skirt and shawl . . .

> *To know his touch, to taste his lips,*
> *To cast away the trappings of my power . . .*
> *For this would I risk the wrath of mighty Zeus,*
> *And vengeance of Hera, his queen . . .*

Melora, he thought; Melora, my love. She was no goddess, but warm and mortal. Did she know how much he had wanted to take her last night, to carry her to his bed, to make love with her? Tonight, when the masque was over and the crowd had gone, he would tell her he loved her.

And one day he would find a way for them to be together. In the meantime, he would protect her as best he could. He would not let her out of his sight.

The audience leaned forward in their gilt and velvet chairs, and watched as the first of the clouds, suspended on their thin silver cords, slowly drifted over the face of the moon.

Artemis unfastened the clasp at the shoulder of her silver overdress, letting it slide from her body. Clad only in her sheath of lavender silk, she sank to her knees with one slow, sensuous movement. Endymion reached up and drew her down beside him.

Another, larger cloud covered the moon, and the stage was plunged into darkness. The audience, each in his own imagination, was free to shape an endless procession of erotic visions.

The moon appeared once more, and Artemis began her closing ballad: a plaintive lament, as she discovered that her Endymion, although not struck dead by vengeful Hera, was fated to sleep through all eternity. A song of sadness and farewell. Night after night, she would watch over him from above, and kiss him with her silvery light, but she would never know his embrace again.

The masque was over, and the hall rang with the applause of the audience. Melora felt a glow of pride. If only her father could have been out there in the audience, her triumph would have been complete.

Her handmaids gathered around her, to drape her once more in the silver overdress. She bowed low, first in the direction of the royal dais, then to the whole audience. The young man who had played the role of the shepherd rose from the artificial greensward and took her hand. The woodland nymphs clustered around them and received their share of applause. Melora caught a glimpse of Felicity's face, smiling and flushed with triumph.

Then, before she had time to retire and change from her costume to a suitable ballgown, the king, beaming with pleasure, motioned her to the dais.

"Our congratulations, Lady Rosalind," he said, his thick Scottish burr even more pronounced than usual; he had been drinking freely during the performance.

"And you, Rokeby—we are well pleased with you. A fine spectacle." He grinned with vicarious pride and puffed out his narrow chest.

"You have great talent, my dear," Queen Anne said, with a gentle smile.

Now that the performance was over and the excitement that had carried her along had started to ebb away, she was beginning to feel drained, and a little shaky. She longed to withdraw to the privacy of her chamber, but before she could ask permission, Rokeby leaned toward the king.

"I am most gratified, sire. If we have pleased you with our humble efforts, we can ask no greater reward. But even I must admit that the ending of the masque was a shade melancholy. Why not have a lively dance, to raise our spirits?"

"The very thing!" The king clapped him on the back.

"If I might suggest the *Kerause* . . . a Danish dance in honor of our queen."

"Most fitting!" His majesty grinned, then turned and signaled to the musicians. "The *Kerause*," he shouted. "And all must join in."

Then he descended from the dais and took his place, with the queen behind him, her hands resting on his waist.

Melora had never heard of the Danish dance. She watched as the courtiers hurried out to the center of the hall, where they formed a line in single file, each placing his hands on the waist of the dancer in front of him.

To her dazed eyes, it looked like a great snake, multicolored and glittering. The kettle drums were pounding to a wild rhythm, the horns blared. Her senses reeled at the sound. She must find a chance to slip away to her chamber.

The line was moving now, the men shouting, the ladies squealing with rising excitement. An orgiastic dance, she thought, quite different from the stately sarabande or the pavane.

She would not have thought the Danes would have favored such a barbaric display. Perhaps it had been handed down from the distant past, when they had been a race of fierce sea raiders.

She started for the door, but before she quite knew how it happened, she was pulled into the line of dancers, her waist grasped tightly by the man behind her. "No—I don't wish to—"

She tried to free herself, but the man's hands held her in a steely grip. Either he had not heard her, or he had chosen to ignore her protest. Against her will, she found herself pushed and dragged along, as the line moved swiftly out of the great hall and into the torchlit corridor.

Chapter Sixteen

The dancers wove their way through the wide corridors, and Melora was forced to move along with them. Her legs felt unsteady, but the man who had seized her and pulled her into the dance kept a tight grip on her waist, so that she had no choice but to keep going.

She turned her head, and although she caught only a brief glimpse of his face in the glare of the torchlight, she saw that he was no courtier, flown with wine and carried away by the festive spirit of the evening. She gasped and her heart speeded up with panic; for she realized it was not the first time she had seen that pockmarked face, framed by its mop of lank, oily hair.

She cried out in dismay as she recognized the man who had come to Rokeby's house, along with Ambrose Corbett and the Marquis de Carvajal. Terror coursed through her veins in icy ripples.

"Let go of me!"

But he ignored her plea, and his thin, wiry arms swiftly encircled her ribs like bands of steel, crushing the air from her lungs. Moved by desperation, she somehow managed to cry out again.

"Somebody, help me!"

But her voice was drowned out by the uproarious shouts and shrill laughter of the revelers. The musicians, who had accompanied the dancers out of the great hall, played their drums and horns even more loudly than before.

With a swift movement, Melora's captor pulled her out of the weaving line. Frantic with fear, she kicked at his leg, but her foot, in its fragile silver sandal, inflicted no real damage. Twisting around, she clawed at his cheek, leaving a row of bright crimson streaks where her nails had made contact with his skin.

"Damn she-cat!" He lifted her off her feet and threw her over his shoulder. She hung her head, and sparks of light flickered before her dazed eyes. There was a sound in her ears, like the roaring of a storm-lashed sea. The sound grew and swelled until it blotted out the music and the drunken cries of revelers.

The pockmarked man was carrying her away from the main corridor, and into the shadows of a narrow, deserted passage. She pounded her fists against his shoulders, but he ignored her blows and kept on going.

She was starting to sink into a pool of swirling darkness when he halted at last. A door swung open and she heard another man's voice saying, "Set her down over there and leave us."

The pockmarked man dropped Melora on a low divan piled with soft cushions. She lay there, limp and shivering, as the man left and the heavy door slammed shut behind him.

She blinked rapidly. The swirling darkness was beginning to clear now. Looking up, she saw Rokeby bending over her, holding a porcelain cup to her lips.

"Drink this, my dear." She caught the inviting scent of hot spiced wine. Too dazed to resist, she swallowed, choked, and then felt the warmth of the fragrant liquid spreading through her.

"Forgive me for using such unconventional means to bring you here," Rokeby said. His lips curved in a faint smile. "I feared that if I asked you to come with me, you would have refused."

She raised herself on one arm, pushed her tangled hair away from her eyes, and looked about, but she had no idea where she

226

was. There were so many little-used passageways in the palace, and so many unoccupied rooms.

But this was no dusty cupboard, like Bronwen's. It was small but exquisitely furnished in an Oriental style. Examining her surroundings more closely, she saw no high-backed chairs or settles of sturdy oak, but only cushioned divans like the one on which she lay. The fragile lacquered table, which stood close by, held porcelain cups and a steaming wine bowl painted with brightly colored birds and flowers. The firelight flickered over a tall coromandel screen, incised with figures of elephants, peacocks, and tigers.

She tried to rise, but a wave of dizziness forced her to fall back against the heap of silk and velvet cushions. She could only lie there and watch helplessly as Rokeby walked to the door. She caught her breath sharply as he locked the door and pocketed the key.

Then he returned and seated himself on the divan close beside her. His gray eyes moved over her face, then down to her breasts. Even with the silvery overdress covering her silk gown, she felt naked and completely vulnerable. She wanted to push him away, but she would be foolish to waste her energy in a useless struggle.

She must play for time. Surely, when the dance was over, someone would notice that she was missing from the great hall. When she did not appear at the banquet, his majesty would send servants to search for her.

In the meantime, she was on her own. She lowered her lids and looked up at Rokeby from under her dark, curving lashes. "The wine's excellent, my lord," she said softly. "May I have a little more?"

"Certainly, my dear. You are my guest."

She fought back the urge to remind the viscount that a guest was not carried off by main force to join her host, or locked in with him. He held the steaming cup to her lips again. She drank only enough to restore her strength, for she would need to keep her wits about her until help came.

When he began stroking her arm, she could not keep back a slight shiver of distaste.

He caught her reaction, and smiled. "Are you afraid of me?" he asked.

"No, my lord. It's only that I am a little tired. And I fear I may have caught a chill. Do stir up the fire." She gave him an appealing glance. *Play for time.*

He rose and went to the fireplace with its ornately carved mantelpiece. He thrust a poker into the embers and she saw the flames leap up in a crimson blaze.

She looked longingly at the poker. It would make a good weapon. She lowered her eyes before he could catch the direction of her gaze.

He returned and dropped down on the divan, then stretched out beside her. She caught the smell of the musky perfumed oil he used on his elaborately curled hair, and it was all she could do to keep from gagging.

"You've led me a merry chase so far, Lady Rosalind." His hand curved lightly around her shoulder. "At first, I put your reluctance down to virginal modesty. You are still a maiden, aren't you?"

"Such an unseemly question." But she forced herself to smile and flutter her lashes even as she protested.

He had called her Lady Rosalind, and she drew what reassurance she could from that. At least he did not know she was an impostor. It was not likely he had found out that she was in Pembroke's service, either. If he had, she might be lying at the bottom of the river, instead of here on the divan.

He moved closer so that his satin-sheathed leg rested against her thigh. She spoke quickly, to distract him. "I've been hoping to speak to you alone, my lord. I wanted to explain about the night I left your house so suddenly."

"Do go on."

"It was not because I found your—your advances distasteful."

"Really? Then why didn't you remain in the library until I

228

returned?" His full lips curved in a sensuous smile. Her insides churned. "I assure you, I would have made the waiting worth your while, my lady."

She searched for some explanation that would satisfy his immense vanity. "I was afraid, I admit it. But not of you."

Before he could speak, she went on hastily. "Lady Jade has been your mistress for ever so long, and everyone says she—she is devoted to you. The queen herself warned me—"

"The queen? What the devil does she have to do with it?"

"Her majesty said that if I aroused Lady Jade's jealousy, she could be a dangerous enemy."

His fingers moved from her shoulder and cupped her breast. "My timid little Rosalind. You think I could not protect you from a shrewish trollop like Jade Fairfax?"

"How could I be sure?" She gave him an appealing smile and tried to ignore his questing fingers.

"I suppose you couldn't." His eyes hardened abruptly. "Any more than I can be sure that you are speaking the truth, even now," he said.

"My lord—I would not dare try to deceive a man of your— vast experience."

He moved closer. "Let us find out."

He unclasped her silver overdress, then drew the bodice of her silk gown lower, baring her breasts completely. Bending his head, he flicked at her nipple with his tongue. Her body went rigid, but although it took all her self-control, she did not try to pull away.

Even when he put his other hand through the slit of her skirt and ran his soft-skinned palm along her thigh, she remained immobile. She set her teeth and closed her eyes tightly. He touched her dark curly triangle, and then his fingers began to probe the smooth, moist crevice of her womanhood. The intimacy sickened her. She couldn't stand much more. Try as she might, she was losing control.

He rolled over and rested his weight on her. She flinched

when she felt the bulge of his shaft, stiff and hard against her belly. She couldn't let him—she couldn't!

Her instincts took over. Drawing back her arm, she struck him a stinging blow across the face. He caught her wrist and twisted it behind her. Pain shot all the way to her shoulder.

"I was right about you." Even in her agony, she caught the triumph in his voice. "You are no modest little country mouse. You're one of those females who wants a man to take her by force."

Holding her down with weight of his body, he rubbed his hard arousal against her. "I'm ready to oblige you." Still gripping her wrist, he closed the fingers of his other hand on her nipple. They bit into the sensitive peak like steel pincers. Darts of fire slashed through her whole body. Her cry of pain echoed through the chamber.

"Not yet, my dear. We've just begun." He kept his eyes fastened on hers, and now he was speaking softly, telling her exactly what he was going to do to her, how and where he would invade her body. And what he would force her to do in return, to satisfy his perverted lust. Her insides lurched and she thought she would retch.

With a strength born of desperation, she bucked and twisted, but her frenzied efforts only made him laugh softly. She screamed as loudly as she could.

"Mistress Melora!"

Was she imagining she heard a voice calling her name? No, it was real enough. She recognized Caleb's hoarse bellow, coming from outside the door, and she went weak with relief.

Rokeby's hand slid away from her breast. He lifted his weight only slightly, but enough to let her twist free. Although she was still dazed with pain, she managed to get to her feet. She stumbled toward the door.

"Caleb! I'm in here—help me!"

The brass doorknob turned, the door rattled on its hinges, but to no avail.

"It's locked! He's locked me in!"

The bear leader's powerful weight struck against the door, but still it did not give way. Her senses reeled. She kept her eyes fixed on the door. "Caleb!" Then she heard a metallic object pounding against the lock.

Rokeby seized her around the waist and flung her aside. She hit the floor with jarring force, but she did not lose consciousness.

"Caleb!"

Another blow. And another. The wood splintered and the door swung wide. Caleb stood there, legs planted apart. He was clutching a metal sconce he had torn from the wall. Rokeby drew his jeweled dagger, but Caleb knocked it from the viscount's hand with his own improvised weapon.

The viscount lunged for the poker, to ward off the burly intruder. Melora cried out a warning. "Guard yourself, Caleb!"

Caleb dodged aside with impressive agility for a man of his size. From somewhere behind him came the clanking noise of a chain being dragged along the floor.

Then Rokeby started violently. He heard a ferocious snarl that could have come from no human throat. His pale eyes widened in disbelief as a great, shaggy beast came lumbering forward on his hind legs, his yellow fangs bared. To Rokeby, the bear must have seemed like a creature out of a nightmare.

The terrified viscount thrust the poker into the fire, then struck out at Bruin. Melora caught the acrid smell of burnt fur. Bruin, maddened with pain, howled and lashed out with his huge forepaw.

Rokeby cried out, then staggered back, blood pouring from his shoulder, staining his satin doublet. He fell to the floor, writhed, then lay motionless. Caleb seized the chain and dragged the beast away.

"Did that foppish bastard harm you, mistress?"

She shook her head, steadied herself for a moment, clutching at the door frame.

"She's here, Lord Grenville!" Caleb called out.

Melora caught sight of Dirk, rounding the corner of the

231

corridor, dagger in hand. She ran to him, and he caught her in his arms. He held her against him.

"You're safe now," she heard him saying. "Melora, it's all right."

"I tried to play for time—but then he—he was going to—"

"Hush, now. He won't harm you. No one will harm you."

She gave herself up to the comfort of his embrace, his soft, reassuring voice. She buried her face against his chest, and slid her arms around his neck.

Then she felt his body stiffen. He was pushing her away. But why? A moment later, she understood.

From the far end of the corridor, she caught the gleam of torchlight flickering over the length of a heavy pike.

"What the devil's going on here?" One of the palace guards was advancing swiftly, with his weapon at the ready. He shouted over his shoulder. "This way, all of you! Make haste!"

More guards came swarming into view. Servants and courtiers crowded behind them, jostling one another.

Dirk thrust her into Caleb's huge arms. "I'll deal with the guards. You get her out of here."

Caleb lifted her and carried her off, with Bruin trotting at his heels. They plunged into a narrow passageway. He stopped for a moment at the top of a long flight of stairs.

From the distance, she heard Dirk rapping out orders. "You, there! Carry Lord Rokeby to his chamber! And you, go find the royal physician!"

Melora let her head drop forward against the bear leader's massive shoulder. Still holding onto him as tightly as she could, she let herself be carried down the stairs, through an endless maze of hallways, and then out into the courtyard.

A blast of icy air enveloped her, and a flurry of snowflakes came drifting through the darkness. Her silk gown was quickly soaked through, so that it clung to her body. But it didn't matter. She was safe, for now.

* * *

She crouched on a straw pallet. "We'd best wait here 'til Lord Grenville comes," said Caleb. They had taken refuge in the shed near the west gate of the palace.

Caleb fastened Bruin's chain to the wall, then stripped off his leather jerkin and wrapped it around her. "Lord Grenville saw that pockmarked whoreson pull you into the dance. He tried to follow—we both did. But by the time we'd got through the crowd, you'd disappeared. We split up an' went searching for you. Then I heard you hollerin'."

He broke off at the sound of booted footsteps approaching the shed. He opened the door a crack and peered into the darkness. A flurry of white flakes came swirling in before Dirk could shut the door behind him.

"Rokeby—is he alive?" Melora asked.

"He was unconscious and bleeding badly when they carried him to his chamber, but the king's physician says he's likely to live."

"More's the pity," Caleb muttered. "I should've let Bruin tear him apart."

Dirk silenced him with a gesture. "You and Melora must get away from Whitehall at once."

"But why?" she protested. "Surely, when I tell the king that Rokeby tried to rape me, Caleb won't be blamed for helping me."

"It's not the king I'm concerned about." She looked at him, uncomprehending, and he went on quickly. "You called out for Caleb. Rokeby heard you. Once he regains consciousness, he'll started wondering how Lady Rosalind Grenville happened to know a traveling bear leader by name. And why the bear leader risked his neck to rescue you."

"And then he'll discover that I've been serving Pembroke," she said.

"It's possible. One thing's sure—we can't risk his finding out."

"You want me to get her back to Northumberland, sir?" Caleb asked.

"Not until I've talked with Pembroke. We'll have to take this one step at a time."

"What about Southwark?" Caleb suggested. "I could take her there."

"It might be best, for now," Dirk agreed.

"Her'n me will go across the river an' take cover there. Plenty of places in Bankside where no one'll find us."

Melora knew about Southwark, from the days when she and her father had lived in London. She remembered that it lay outside the jurisdiction of the city, and, among its other uses, it served as a sanctuary for those fleeing the law. The Bankside district was a conglomeration of crowded streets and alleys, many of them lined with disreputable taverns and brothels, bear gardens and cockpits. It also provided cheap lodgings for strolling players, musicians, and other entertainers down on their luck.

Dirk was silent as he considered the plan carefully. "Once you've gone into hiding, how am I to get word to you?"

Caleb grinned. "Tell Osric we've gone to ground in Ram's Alley. He'll carry your messages."

"Ram's Alley! That's no place for Melora."

"I'll guard her well, my lord. No harm will come to her."

"You've certainly proved your ability to do that." Dirk clapped the burly man on the shoulder. "I'll stay here with Melora. You go and find a boat," he said.

The bear leader went hurrying out, slamming the door behind him. Dirk helped Melora to her feet and held her close.

"The winter solstice. Bronwen warned me, and I mocked her."

"She'll not mind, so long as you're safe."

He buried his face in the blackness of her hair. Its familiar fragrance stirred his senses. "There was so much I meant say to you tonight. But now, all I can do is to send you away into hiding."

"But you'll come for me, when it's safe?"

"You know I will. Melora, sweeting."

She gave herself up to his embrace, to the warmth of his kisses on her eyes, her cheeks, her mouth. Then slowly, reluctantly, they drew apart.

Caleb opened the door. It was snowing more heavily now and the wind was growing fiercer. "I've borrowed a boat."

"Stole it, you mean," said Dirk, with a faint smile.

"It'll be better if I do the rowing myself. That way, there'll be no boatman to go jabbering about how he took a bear leader and his beast and a dark-haired lady to Southwark."

Dirk nodded. "Come along, then." He drew the heavy leather jerkin more closely about Melora, and they made their way down to the landing, with the bear padding along after them.

While Caleb led the beast down to the boat, Melora slid her arms around Dirk's neck and looked up at him anxiously. "By morning, Felicity will report that I'm missing and the queen will want to know my whereabouts. What then?"

"I'm supposed to be your cousin, remember? I'll say you received word from Northumberland. Some family crisis—an illness or accident. Trust me."

"But what if something goes wrong? What if—"

His lips, hard with urgency, cut off the rest of her words. She clung to him, and drew reassurance from his embrace. All too soon, he disengaged himself from her arms. "I'll come for you as soon as it's safe."

Then Caleb was leading her down the slippery steps and helping her into the boat. He covered her with a length of canvas. Bruin's chain was secured to one of the oarlocks. The beast raised his head, caught Melora's scent, then placed his head on his paws and lay quietly.

She huddled close to the bear for warmth, but kept her face turned up, toward the landing. Dirk raised his arm in a gesture of farewell. Tears mingled with the melting flakes on her lashes. She blinked them away, and kept watching until the boat rounded a bend in the windswept river, and his tall figure was lost from sight.

Chapter Seventeen

Rokeby opened his eyes, raised his head from the pillows, and looked about him in momentary confusion. Where the devil was he, and what was causing his right arm and shoulder to ache so damnably? He pushed aside the coverlet and saw that he was wearing one of his own linen nightshirts. But he was not lying in his own bed; of that he was certain. Yet those bed curtains of pale green brocade, embroidered with silver; that dressing table across the room; the velvet and gilt chairs, the Turkish carpet—all were familiar to him.

Lady Jade came sweeping into the room, her hair falling in loose waves about her shoulders. She was wearing a black lace robe and high-heeled satin slippers with jeweled buckles. As she approached the bed, Rokeby began to remember, but only in bits and pieces.

The night of the masque. Lady Rosalind screaming, as she fought him off. Someone pounding at the door—a splintering of wood. And a monster with fangs and claws, springing at him, knocking him to the floor.

"Why was I taken to your chambers, instead of my own?" he demanded.

"I had them bring you here so that I might look after you," Jade said. She hovered over him, rearranged the coverlet, and patted the pillows. "Basil, my love, I have been with you all this time."

She seated herself on a chair beside the bed. "But perhaps you're still not quite yourself." Her green eyes narrowed. "That arrogant fool of a physician has kept you drugged with his nostrums." She gestured toward the bedside table, with its collection of bottles and jars.

"That fool, as you call him, may well have saved my life," he muttered. For the past few days, he had drifted in and out of consciousness; but during his more lucid moments, he had managed to piece together some of the events that had taken place after the masque.

But there were still many details that eluded him. Rosalind had called out a name, a man's name. What was it? He could not remember yet, but sooner or later he would.

Jade drew her chair closer to the bed, took his hand in hers, and began stroking it. "Such a dreadful accident," she said. "And no one was able to explain how it came about. Tell me, now, what really did happen?"

"That is no one's concern but my own." He spoke brusquely, and threw her a look meant to discourage further questions. But Lady Jade was not easily daunted.

"Basil, my love, when I realize how close I came to losing you! Oh, my dear, I could never have borne it."

Rokeby knew his mistress too well to be wholly convinced by her protestations of devotion. True, she had lusted for him with an insatiable craving; and he had rarely failed to satisfy her in bed. But he did not believe there was much real capacity for feminine softness in her nature.

"Had I been killed, you soon would have found another lover to console you."

She pressed a hand to the lush curves of her bosom. "How can you speak so cruelly? Surely you know that no other man could take your place."

She leaned toward him, her silver-gilt hair brushing his cheek. He breathed in the heavy, sensuous fragrance of her jasmine perfume and did not try to draw away. Her words offered a soothing balm to his outraged vanity. After having

237

been repulsed by the capricious young Lady Rosalind, he needed a woman's flattery, whether it was completely sincere or not.

"I've heard so many fantastic tales about what happened to you that dreadful night. Some say you were attacked by a lion that had escaped from the menagerie in the Tower. Others insist it was a wolf. How ridiculous! As if such creatures stalked the corridors of Whitehall."

As soon as he had begun to regain his senses, he had decided to keep the facts—what little he knew of them—to himself. He certainly was not about to admit that he had tried to rape Rosalind Grenville. Yet perhaps it might be wise to offer Jade some sort of explanation, if only to satisfy her curiosity.

"A doltish bear leader must have wandered into the palace during the festivities. Somehow he lost control of the beast. It pounced on me out of the darkness and savaged me. That's all I remember."

"But his majesty ordered a thorough search—yet the guards have not found a trace of any such person. Or of any bear, either."

"That is hardly surprising, since the palace was swarming with all sorts of rogues and vagabonds."

"There are those who claim that Dirk Grenville found you, torn and bleeding, and saved your life."

His lips tightened. "No doubt that swaggering adventurer would try to take the credit for helping me in order to win the king's gratitude. But I assure you, it was the palace guards who drove off the beast."

"I might have guessed as much," Jade said. "The Grenvilles are a thoroughly unprincipled lot. They're possessed by ambition, too. Not only Dirk, but that flighty cousin of his." She smoothed the coverlet once more. "The girl's surely the most addlebrained creature who ever came to court."

In spite of the gnawing pain in his shoulder, he was distracted by Jade's remarks about Rosalind.

"Dirk Grenville's bent on making a favorable reputation for

238

himself," he said. "The upstart never misses an opportunity to ingratiate himself with his majesty. But as for Lady Rosalind, why should you call her flighty or addlebrained?"

"Why, the whole court's abuzz with her doings. The black-haired little minx made a shameless display, showing herself off half-naked in the masque." She paused for breath, then hurried on. "And as if that were not enough, off she went from White-hall the very same night. She did not even have sufficient breeding to take leave of the queen. Or his majesty, either."

"Rosalind has left court?" He raised himself higher on the pillows. His teeth sank into his lip as he tried to hold back a cry of pain. The throbbing in his shoulder was getting worse by the minute.

"You've not heard? But how could you, with the king's physician keeping all visitors from your side? He even insisted that I should sleep on the couch in the next room."

"We were speaking of Rosalind Grenville," he reminded her, restraining his impatience with difficulty.

"She disappeared from the palace right after the masque."

A confusing memory tugged at a corner of his mind. Rosa-lind had called out for help that night. She had called to some-one by name. Then the pain was stabbing at his shoulder with such intensity that the memory was swept into oblivion.

"You're not saying the girl was kidnapped, are you?"

Jade shook her head. "Nothing like that. She told her cousin she was going back home to Ashcroft."

She paused to heighten the dramatic effect of her news.

"Surely she must have offered some excuse for leaving," he persisted.

"Only that she had received a letter from her father a few hours before she was to appear in the masque. It seems her brother had taken a fall while he was out hunting. He was not expected to live. And nothing would do but that she run off to be with him in his last hours."

Had Rosalind's brother been injured in a riding accident? Or was it he himself who had frightened her into running away?

239

The little trollop had certainly been asking for such treatment. But even if she had gotten more than she'd bargained for, that would not explain her headlong flight from the palace. He felt some relief that at least she had left without complaining to the queen. The attempted rape of a lady-in-waiting was no trivial matter, even when the accused was one of the king's favorites.

"Surely if she had been so badly shaken by the news of her brother's mishap, she would not have gone through with her performance," he said.

"According to Dirk Grenville, she felt a sense of obligation to their majesties."

But Jade's explanation did not satisfy Rokeby. He shifted himself in a vain attempt to ease his pain. There was more to Rosalind's abrupt disappearance than her concern for her brother; he was sure of it.

"She did not even confide her plan to Felicity Brandon, who shares her bedchamber."

"Perhaps there was no time," he said. He had ordered that pockmarked hireling Oliver Babcock to carry her off during the dance and bring her to him. And even so, the skittish little bitch had managed to frustrate him. If ever he got the chance, he would make her pay dearly for that.

"Felicity says that the Grenville wench left all her clothes behind," Jade went on.

"That's ridiculous," he interrupted. "Addled or not, Rosalind would not have gone off into a snowstorm, and journeyed all the way to Northumberland, wearing only that flimsy silk robe from the masque."

"But that's exactly what she did. She left behind a fur-lined cloak, all her dresses, her leather boots. Even a new trunk, a gift from her cousin."

"And what of Dirk Grenville? One would suppose he'd have felt obligated to escort her on her journey home."

"She went alone, I tell you. And he is still here at court."

Rokeby groaned. The pain was becoming unbearable. "You must have another dose of poppy syrup," Jade said.

Although he did not want to dull his senses, he would not be able to think clearly much longer anyway; not with the burning pain that tore at his shoulder and spiraled down the length of his arm.

Jade held the spoon to his lips. He swallowed the bitter draught, then sank back against the pillows. Perspiration beaded his forehead.

"I shall sit with you until you fall asleep," she said. She stroked his face with a lacy handkerchief, her touch light and soothing; but he was indifferent to her attentions.

He tried in vain to make some sense of what Jade had told him. Lady Rosalind had gone from court without packing a trunk or changing to suitable garments for the journey north. "Did anyone question her maid?" His voice was blurred, his eyelids heavy.

"The girl—she's called Prudence, I think—swears Lady Rosalind told her nothing about her plans."

Strange, indeed. The maid must be questioned again. He would see to that. He let himself sink into a drugged sleep. He would have to wait . . . make his own inquiries . . . and soon . . .

"But you've got to come to the fair, Melora," said young Tom Warrick. "And Caleb, too." The slender boy pulled his knitted cap down over his blond hair, then tucked his lute under his arm. He was not the only one of the lodgers who was getting ready to venture out into the icy streets this morning.

Melora shook her head, and remained seated at the scarred and battered oak table in the low-ceilinged kitchen of Mother Speedwell's lodginghouse. The snow had stopped falling last night, but the window was so thick with frost that it was impossible to get even a glimpse of Ram's Alley.

She and Caleb had found it easy enough to make themselves at home here; for most of Mother Speedwell's lodgers were traveling performers—musicians, jugglers, rope dancers, and puppeteers. The landlady also rented rooms to a few debtors who had sought sanctuary outside the jurisdiction of the city.

"Come along," Tom urged her. "You're sure to earn a fat purse of coins, if you sing your ballads for the crowd half so well as you've done for us here."

"The boy's right," said Mother Speedwell, a stout, gray-haired woman in a dingy ruffled cap. "You and Caleb aren't likely to get such a chance again soon."

Melora shifted uneasily, her eyes fixed on her plate. Dirk had warned her to remain in hiding, and she must follow his instructions; yet the last thing she wanted to do was to arouse the suspicion of her landlady or the other lodgers. She smoothed the fringe of her shawl and searched for a convincing reason why she should not attend the fair.

The day after she and Caleb had arrived in Southwark, he had gotten rid of the lavender silk robe and silver sandals she had worn for the masque. Then, leaving her in their room with a blanket wrapped around her, he had gone to a nearby stall and bought her a second-hand gown of plain, serviceable blue wool, along with a shawl, a heavy cloak, and a pair of sturdy shoes.

He had also spent a few farthings on some bits of finery: an imitation tortoiseshell comb for her hair, a length of cheap satin ribbon, a necklace of brightly colored glass beads. She had been touched by his efforts to cheer her with his small gifts.

Caleb told the landlady that Melora was his niece, and a fine ballad singer who had traveled the roads with him the summer before. "As soon as the snow's melted, we'll be on our way again," he said.

In the days that followed, the other lodgers had persuaded her to sing, and her performance had been much admired, especially by Tom, who had accompanied her on his lute. She had left her own cherished lute behind in her flight from the palace.

Now he paused at the door leading to the alley and said, "If you change your mind, you'll find me somewhere along the riverbank." Then he and the others were gone, leaving her with only Mother Speedwell and her huge ginger cat for company.

"Sounds strange, don't it?" the woman remarked. "Imagine havin' a fair in London this time of year. But what with the river frozen solid, everyone's making a holiday of it."

She threw Melora a searching glance. "Why don't you and Caleb get yourselves down to Bankside with the rest of them? There's plenty of coppers bein' tossed about, I warrant. No reason you two shouldn't get your share."

"I'll have to wait until he gets back from the cookshop," Melora said. She rose and started for the hall. "Meanwhile, I'll go up to our room and look for a few bits of finery to catch the eyes of the gentry."

"You'll do well enough as you are, my girl." The woman's small, sharp eyes moved over her. "Nice round tits and a trim pair of ankles you got there."

Melora escaped Mother Speedwell's scrutiny and breathed a sigh of relief as she climbed the three flights to the room she shared with Caleb. Since he needed heartier rations than the oat cakes and porridge the landlady provided for their morning meal, he had gone across the alley for a pork pie.

He had been gone for over an hour, but she told herself there was no need for concern. Caleb knew his way around Southwark, and he could take care of himself. Perhaps he had run into a chance acquaintance and stopped to share a pot of ale.

She seated herself near the small, frosty window, and as always, her thoughts went back to Dirk. What had happened to him, after she had fled Whitehall on the night of the winter solstice? Had he been able to come up with a believable excuse to explain her sudden absence from court?

During the past week, through the long nights when Caleb lay snoring on the other side of the tattered length of cloth he had hung across the room, she lay wide-eyed on her lumpy pallet. Even when she dropped off to sleep, she was tormented by a succession of grotesque nightmares.

In one of these, Lord Rokeby was pursuing her through a

243

maze of torchlit corridors, his laughter echoing ever louder as he gained on her. In another, he was following her up an endless silver stairway, higher and higher, while the steps writhed and twisted beneath her sandaled feet, and finally crumbled. She tried to scream as she started to fall down into a black pit, but no sound would come. She woke from such dreams with a start, her body rigid, her skin damp with cold perspiration. If only Dirk were beside her, to hold her close and comfort her. She ached for his touch with every fiber of her being.

The days were a little better, for she found distraction in listening to the talk of the other lodgers, watching their impromptu performances, and singing for them. But today, with the lodginghouse nearly deserted, she could not keep from brooding over the future.

She sprang up from her chair when she heard Caleb's heavy footsteps on the stairs. Bruin, who lay curled up in a corner, raised his shaggy head from his huge paws.

"I brought you a nice hot pork pie," Caleb said, stamping the snow off his boots. He set the steaming pie down on the rickety table, but she shook her head.

"I'm not hungry."

"Go on and taste it. I grant you, it ain't much like the fine fare at Whitehall, but it's more fillin' than the slop Mother Speedwell dishes out." Then, in an obvious attempt to distract her from her lethargy, he went on: "Never did see such weather in all my days. The river's froze up solid. There's not a boat movin', and the boatmen are cursin' somethin' fierce, cause they're losin' all their trade."

He broke the steaming pie in two, and pushed half of it over to her. "Just have a bite," he urged. "You hardly touched your oat cakes."

She broke off a piece of the crust, and chewed without tasting. "Mother Speedwell's been asking questions, Caleb. She's wondering why we haven't gone to the fair with the others."

"Meddlesome old cow," he said. "It's none of her business."

"Still, it's natural enough she would want to know why we're staying away, when there's such a crowd down there, ready to pay well for their pleasure. I told her we might go later in the day, but I'm not sure it would be safe—"

She fell silent as she heard the sound of tapping at the door. A familiar voice called, "Open up, before I freeze out here on the landing."

Melora's spirits soared at the sight of Osric, in his multicolored trappings, standing on the threshold. The dwarf came scurrying in, beating his arms across his chest. His long, thin face was drawn, his lips were blue with cold, but he managed a grin all the same. Although she longed for word of Dirk, she controlled her need so that Osric might have a chance to warm himself before the smoky fire in the small hearth.

"You are to meet Lord Grenville at noon, at a Bankside tavern called the Fox and Hound, mistress," he said. "And you'd best wrap up good and snug."

She went weak with relief at Osric's words. Dirk had kept his promise after all—he had sent for her. She was to see him this very day. After all her waiting, she soon would feel his arms around her again. "He's sure it will be safe?" she asked.

"He would not have sent me to fetch you otherwise," Osric said. "There'll be little risk of your being recognized as Lady Rosalind. As far as anyone at court knows, her ladyship's already back home in Northumberland." Quickly he told her Dirk's explanation for her hasty departure.

"The queen believed him?"

"His lordship can be most convincing," Osric told her. "Bronwen and me and Lord Pembroke are the only ones who know you're here in Southwark."

Caleb patted her shoulder. "Have no fear of being noticed, mistress. By this afternoon there'll be as great a crowd at the river as there was for their majesties' coronation."

She brushed back her hair with her fingers; thrust the imitation tortoiseshell combs into her thick, dark hair; then fastened the colored glass beads around her neck. Caleb helped her on with her cloak of dark blue wool.

No doubt she would be safe enough. Who could possibly see any resemblance between her, as she looked now, and the queen's lady-in-waiting?

As Melora and Caleb approached the snow-covered river-bank, they saw a sight that no one, not even the oldest citizens of London, had witnessed before. The fierce cold that gripped the city and the surrounding countryside had turned the Thames to a sheet of glittering ice. Skiffs, rowboats, frigates, and the canopied barges of the nobility all lay motionless in the grip of the frozen river.

The jostling, laughing crowd of common folk—apprentices, maidservants, seamstresses, shopkeepers, and clerks—mingled freely with the gentry. It seemed to Melora as if all London had come out to buy hot veal pasties, chestnuts, pigs' trotters, sweet-meats, Banbury cakes, wine, and ale. Although it was not yet noon, many were already showing the effects of drink as they went reeling and staggering along the narrow passages between the hastily erected booths and tents.

The puppetmaster who lodged at Mother Speedwell's house had set up his brightly painted wood and canvas stage on a high platform; the audience who gathered around it laughed and applauded at the antics of Punch and Judy, Dog Toby, the Hangman, and other familiar characters. Ballad singers, lute players, rope walkers, fire-eaters, all vied for attention.

An itinerant tooth-drawer had set up his tent, with the flap wide open. He stood over a stout woman, one side of her face red and swollen. She clutched at the arms of the chair, while he brandished a huge, clawed lever, called a pelican.

A few of the more daring young ladies in the crowd, clad in velvet and furs, had put on skates with metal runners, recently imported from the lowlands; they went skimming across the ice, laughing and squealing, as they clung to their partners.

Melora kept close to Caleb, grateful for his strong, protective arm about her shoulders. It was no easy task to force themselves through the mob, but the bear leader, with Bruin trotting at his side, managed to clear the way. "There's the Fox and Hound right up ahead," he said. "It looks like a decent enough place. I'll find a likely spot to put Bruin through his paces. Then I'll come back an' wait for you in the taproom."

She heard no more, for now she was running swiftly along the snow-covered bank toward the tall figure who stood waiting for her, his cloak whipping around him in the icy wind.

The hired chamber on the second floor of the inn was clean and spacious; it was furnished with high-backed, cushioned chairs and a wide, curtained bed. Dirk stood close to the fireplace with his arm around Melora while he told her all that had happened since she had fled from Whitehall.

"Rokeby's managed to survive. He's making a slow recovery, though." Dirk's mouth curved in a brief smile. "He's been staying in Lady Jade's chambers at the palace. Now that you're gone, she has him all to herself, and no doubt she means to make the most of it."

Her stomach tightened with revulsion at the memory of Rokeby's heavy scent in her nostrils, of his bejeweled hands exploring her body. She forced her thoughts away, for there were other, more vital matters to be discussed now. "Perhaps it will be a long time before he'll be able to go ahead with his plot against the king."

Dirk shook his head. "Don't try to deceive yourself on that score. As soon as he's up and about again, he'll be meeting with Carvajal and the others."

"And how long am I to remain in hiding?"

"For another few weeks, at least." His arm tightened around her, and his brown eyes were shadowed by misgivings. "Southwark's no place for you, but at least Rokeby can't harm you, so long as you're in hiding there."

247

"Mother Speedwell's house isn't too bad," she comforted him. "And Caleb's always about, to see that I come to no harm."

Her arms went around his neck, and she pressed her face to his shoulder. "Oh, Dirk, I've missed you so."

"We'll be together again, love."

"But when?"

"As soon as I'm sure it's safe." His lips covered hers, warm and seeking. His kiss deepened, and she parted her lips eagerly. Her tongue found his. A swift current of heat flooded through her.

Then slowly he raised his head. "I met with Pembroke the day after you left Whitehall. He said you had already given him enough information to earn your reward ten times over."

If only she could be satisfied with his assurance. But there was more at stake than the payment Pembroke had promised her. "If Rokeby's still set on going through with his scheme, isn't there some way I can be of further use?"

His muscles hardened beneath her touch. "No, damn it! I won't allow you to risk yourself in Pembroke's service again, ever. I forbid it."

His words, fiercely protective, sent her heart soaring.

"There are plenty of others in the earl's organization to do what must be done from here on," he said. "They are watching Rokeby, the Marquis de Carvajal, Ambrose Corbett, and the rest."

He brushed lingering kisses over her brow, her cheek, her throat. "I should never have led you into such danger."

"You didn't force me into Pembroke's service," she reminded him.

"But I didn't stop you, either. I didn't know, even then, how much you'd come to mean to me." The joy that surged up inside her was almost more than she could bear. "That first night, when I carried you upstairs to my chamber at the Leap-

248

ing Stag—you were frightened, and trying so hard to hide it. I think that was when I started to love you."

She was swept away by a glorious sense of fulfillment such as she had never known before. She clung to him for a timeless moment, content to savor his words, to feel his body pressing close to hers, his hands stroking her hair.

Then slowly, reluctantly, she drew away. "And once Rokeby's treachery has been exposed, once the king is safe, what then?"

He did not answer, and she felt a pang of uncertainty.

"Will you ask the king to give you your ships then? Your land in the New World? Will you go sailing away—"

"Not without you." His arms tightened around her so that she could scarcely breathe. "I can't let you go ever again."

"You'll give up your plans, and be content to stay in England?"

He did not answer at once, and she felt herself go cold. She did not want to know, but she had to.

Then he drew away and looked down at her, his eyes holding hers. She saw the tenderness in his face, but she saw the unshakable determination, too.

"No, sweeting," he said. "I can't give up all I've worked for, planned for, so long." Before she could speak, he went on quickly, urgently. "Say you will come with me, Melora. I don't promise you a soft, easy life, or even a safe one. But we'll be together." He searched her face. "Do you love me enough to endure the hardships, to take what risks may lie ahead?"

If only it were that easy for her to make her decision. But what about her father? How could she put aside her her duty to him? And she had her own long-cherished ambition to consider. If she gave up her plans to go to France and make a name for herself on the Paris stage, would she one day regret her decision? Would even Dirk's love be enough to make up for such a sacrifice?

Then his face was close to hers, the passion in his gold-flecked eyes blotting out all else. His lips captured hers, and her doubts,

249

her misgivings, were no longer important. They were together now, and nothing else mattered.

He lifted her and carried her to the bed. He lay her down gently; then, leaning over her, he began to unbutton her bodice, baring her breasts. He pressed his face to the softly rounded globes.

Her nipples hardened. He took one of the rosy peaks between his lips, and the wet heat of his suckling mouth sent currents of desire moving through her.

He drew away, but only long enough to take off his doublet, breeches, and boots. She did not turn her gaze from him as she had that first time they had made love.

His tall, muscular body, touched by the warm, golden firelight, stirred a hot, aching hunger deep inside her. It spread to every part of her. She did not look away, even from his hard masculinity. She felt a warm moisture in her hidden cleft, an emptiness only he could fill—a needing, a wanting . . .

He stretched out beside her on the bed, and her thighs parted. She reached out to draw him to her.

He laughed softly. "You're becoming quite shameless, sweeting," he teased, his voice low and husky.

"Only with you, love."

He feathered kisses over her breasts, down along the smoothness of her belly, to the dark triangle beneath. Startled, she drew back from this unfamiliar way of loving. But his fingers parted her gently, and she yielded willingly. His tongue flicked at the moist bud within her woman's cleft. He took it between his lips, and she gasped with pleasure. She arched her hips and his tongue probed deeper. His hands slid beneath her buttocks, cupping the firm rounds.

Her hands twisted in his thick hair. A pulsating sensation started its insistent throbbing deep inside her loins.

He moved up and positioned himself between her thighs. He knelt above her. She lifted herself to him and gave a low cry as he slid inside her with a long, hard thrust. She gripped his shoulders, and raising her hips, she wrapped her legs around him. He thrust in and out, slowly at first, then faster and faster. She felt her wet sheath tighten around him, and drew him to the deepest part of her being.

He reached his pulsating climax, spilling himself into her. She threw back her head and cried out, then gave herself up the whirling, dizzying sensation of her own fulfillment.

The late afternoon sunlight slanted across the carpet. They lay in each other's arms, savoring each moment of closeness.

"It's growing late," she said, her throat tightening. "Time I was leaving."

He stroked the length of her slender body, his touch lingering on the curve of her shoulder, the softness of her hip.

"As soon as it's safe, I'll send word to you," he promised. "And maybe then, there'll be no need for us to part again."

She watched him get up and put on his clothes. Then she swung her legs over the side of the bed and went to retrieve her underclothes and her blue woolen gown. Slowly, reluctantly, she began to dress.

If only he could take her away with him now. But that would be impossible, and she knew better than to ask.

Weeks, perhaps months, of uncertainty stretched ahead. Somehow, she would have to find the strength to bear their separation.

At the bottom of the stairs, he kissed her once more. "Wait here until I've gone," he said. As she watched him turn and make his way out the back door, she was overwhelmed by a sense of foreboding.

How long would it be until they were together again? She thought of Rokeby, clever and ambitious. He was still a threat to their future, and he would continue to be, until he was exposed to the king as a traitor. She set her jaw and tried to force back her misgivings.

Her body stiffened as she heard the door close behind him. Then she raised her head, and smoothing the folds of her cloak around her, she went into the noisy, crowded taproom to seek out Caleb.

Chapter Eighteen

She found Caleb seated at a narrow wooden table in a corner of the taproom, with a half-eaten joint of roast pork on a trencher before him, and a mug of ale close at hand. He pushed back his chair and started to get to his feet.

"There's no need to leave before you've finished your dinner," she said, as she sat down on the bench beside him. "I'm not in any great hurry to return to Ram's Alley."

"Then you must have a bite to eat, too. There's plenty here for both of us," he said. He moved the trencher toward her, and called out to a serving wench to bring another mug of ale. She tasted the meat, and found it hot and savory.

The patrons of the taproom looked like a fairly respectable lot—merchants and clerks, for the most part; there were a few of the gentry, too. For the time being, the conviviality of the fair had blurred social distinctions. The room was noisy with conversation and laughter, and thick with a cloud of blue smoke from the long-stemmed clay pipes that had become fashionable in the past few years.

Caleb turned and peered at her in the light of the overhead lantern. "What word from the palace?" he asked. "Was Lord Grenville able to smooth matters over with the queen?"

Melora nodded. "Her majesty believed him when he said I was called away unexpectedly to Ashcroft."

"Then you should be safe enough in Southwark, for now."

She nodded, then fell silent. She could not confide her misgivings about her future, not even to Caleb, trusted friend though he was.

Dirk loved her. How often she had longed to hear him say so. Yet now that he had, she was faced with the most difficult decision of her life.

Once Rokeby had been brought to justice, Dirk would be suitably rewarded for his services to the king. He would be given all the ships he wanted, and as much land as he asked for. There would be plenty of adventurous men, ready and willing to join the expedition, to brave the dangers of the unexplored land across the ocean.

She could not ask Dirk to give up his cherished ambition so that he might stay with her in England. As for his accompanying her to France, only to remain in the background while she sought fame as an actress—no, it was unthinkable. His stubborn determination to explore the unknown, that was a part of him; without it, he would not be the man she had come to love.

"Time we were gettin' back to the lodginghouse, mistress." Caleb's deep voice jerked her back to the present.

Together they went to retrieve Bruin, who lay sleeping in a storage shed that was connected to the taproom by a short passageway. When they came out, the last rays of the setting sun stretched in gleaming golden shafts across the frozen surface of the river. With the approach of evening, the wind was growing stronger. She was grateful for the heavy wool dress and cloak Caleb had bought her.

"Will you and Lord Grenville be comin' back to the Fox an' Hound?" the bear leader asked.

"I can't say. He'll send word when it will be safe for us to meet again." Already she missed him. How long before she would feel his arms around her once more, the hot hunger of his mouth, the hard strength of his body molded to hers?

"You should not look so downhearted, mistress," Caleb consoled her. "Soon as the plot against the king has been brought out into the open, and that bastard Rokeby's been given the punishment he deserves, there'll be nothin' to keep you and Lord Grenville apart."

She remained silent, still unable to share her thoughts with Caleb. Sensing her mood, he did not pursue the matter.

"Old Bruin drew a good crowd with his dancin'," he said, glancing at the beast with pride. "There were a few louts would have paid well to bait him with their dogs." He gave a snort of contempt for ignorance of such folk. "I got rid of them in a hurry—I told them Bruin's no ordinary bear. He's the finest dancin' bear in all of London. In all of England, I'll warrant. I won't have him mangled by a pack of scurvy hounds to please the mob."

Although the short winter day was drawing to a close, the crowd showed no signs of leaving the fair. They jostled about the riverbank; and having drunk heartily at the booths of the wine and ale sellers, they were noisier than ever. Vendors of ribbons, cheap jewelry, sweetmeats, and toys had begun lighting torches coated with pitch to illuminate their wares. Whores decked out in shabby finery, emboldened by the darkness, solicited their prospective customers, and drew them into the shadowed aisles between the rows of booths and tents.

"Guess they mean to keep goin' on like this all night," Caleb said. "An' who's to blame them? None of us is likely see the river frozen solid again, not in the next fifty years."

"Caleb! Melora! Wait for me."

Young Tom Warrick emerged from a narrow passage between two rows of booths and fell into step with them, clutching his lute under his arm. She felt a pang of regret at having been forced to leave her own cherished instrument behind in her chamber at the palace.

"Well met, mistress," he said with a smile. "So you and Caleb decided to come down here after all. I trust you had good luck this afternoon."

"Old Bruin and me did well enough," Caleb said.

"And you, Melora?"

"Mistress Melora never fails to please the crowd," Caleb said hastily. Since the boy assumed that Melora had come to the fair to perform, he must not have cause to suspect otherwise.

"And what of you, Tom?" Melora asked. "No doubt your purse is heavy with coins by now."

He looked a trifle crestfallen. "To tell the truth, I might have done better. The din of the drummers and the horn players drowned out my best tunes."

Before she could offer sympathy, his face brightened. "Perhaps if you would sing some of your ballads, while I played for you, we'd make good pickings. Please say you will."

"No!" Melora cried out, without thinking. "I can't possibly—" She broke off as she felt the warning pressure of Caleb's hand on her arm.

"Please say you will," the boy urged. "And afterward, we'll stop an' buy a basket of cakes and sweetmeats, an' a bottle of wine, an' bring them back to Ram's Alley. We'll make a proper feast of it, in Mother Speedwell's kitchen."

"Why not sing a song or two? If only to oblige Master Tom."

Although Caleb spoke casually enough, she quickly caught his meaning. If she went on refusing, Tom might grow suspicious. He might ask himself why an experienced performer would refuse to take advantage of the chance to earn as much as she could. He might innocently speak of her refusal to Mother Speedwell or some of the other lodgers.

She dared not relax her caution, not even for an hour. No one at the lodginghouse must have cause to suspect that she was other than what she claimed to be: Caleb's niece, a traveling singer, holed up in Southwark for the winter. Clad as she was in her dark-blue woolen cloak and thick-soled shoes, she bore no resemblance to the queen's lady-in-waiting. Lady Rosalind Grenville had gone about decked in velvet and furs, her hair elaborately arranged, jewels gleaming at her ears and throat.

"A pretty girl always helps to draw a crowd," Tom persisted. "And you—you're the prettiest one I've ever seen, Melora." He looked at her adoringly, then blushed at his own boldness.

"If it will please you, I'll sing a ballad."

"Or maybe two?" Tom's round blue eyes brightened.

"Perhaps. But no more."

"Look there. That's just the place for us to try our luck." Tom pointed to the stand, where Luke Inchcliff, the skinny, sharp-featured puppeteer from Mother Speedwell's house, had set up his miniature theater. Taking advantage of the interval before the next performance, Inchcliff was lighting a pair of torches, and fixing them securely on either side of the booth.

With Tom leading the way, they approached the puppetmaster. "May we use your platform?" the boy asked. "I'll play, and Melora will sing. There's room enough for her up there beside the theater, and I'll remain below."

"Not so fast, my boy. It was me that set up the booth. And paid for the torches."

"Yet, it will be awhile before you're ready to give your next show," said Tom "In the meantime, our songs will help to gather a bigger crowd."

"The lass has a fine voice, I'll grant you that." He stroked his stubbled jaw. " 'Course, I'll have to charge a bit for the use of my booth. Say, eight farthings."

"That's no better than robbery!" Caleb protested. "Make it three." Tom, Caleb, and the puppeteer haggled awhile longer, then struck a bargain. Caleb lifted Melora up on the high platform. She stood beside the small, brightly painted puppet theater, while Tom remained below.

"Push back your hood," the boy urged.

She hesitated briefly, then complied. The torchlight played over her dark hair, which was drawn back from her forehead by the tortoiseshell combs and fell in loose, gleaming waves around the delicate oval of her face.

"What shall I sing?" she asked Tom.

"Why not that ballad you sang for us last night in Mother Speedwell's kitchen—*Blow Out the Candle.*"

He ran his fingers over the strings of the lute. Melora raised her head. Her lips parted in a warm smile. She began to sing the opening stanza. One after another, the passersby slowed their steps, then stopped to listen. By the time she had started the second stanza, a good-sized crowd had gathered around the platform. Many of them knew the familiar song, but they liked it all the more for that.

They listened with pleasure to the tale of a young country lass who lay with a neighbor's son. Each time he crept into her room, he urged her to "blow the candle out," so that they would not be discovered by her parents.

Although the ballad was bawdy enough to please the crowd, it held a touch of melancholy, too; for the girl's lover, having gotten her with child, ran off and was never seen again. The unhappy girl was left to bear her shame alone.

Several of the more tender-hearted serving wenches and milliners' apprentices who flocked around the platform were moved to tears. The closing stanza gave the familiar warning to girls who might be tempted to go astray.

> *Come, all you fair young maidens,*
> *And a warning take from me.*
> *Don't give your heart to the first lad*
> *That ever you do see.*
> *For all too soon he'll leave you,*
> *Of that I have no doubt,*
> *Then you'll be left to weep alone,*
> *And blow the candle out.*

As the last notes drifted away on the frosty air, Tom went through the crowd with a tin plate and collected the coins.

"Give us another song!" someone called out.

"Another song, girl!"

"And make it a jollier one this time!"

"D'ye know the words to *Rolling in the Dew?*"

To hold the interest of this audience, she knew she must entertain them with the raffish sort of songs they liked best. Tossing her head, she threw them a smile; then, placing her hand on her hip, she launched into her next offering.

Lady Jade Fairfax, wrapped in a cloak of honey-colored velvet, shifted restlessly on the seat of her carriage. She had hoped that a day at the fair would dispel her gloom, but now, as darkness fell over the river, she was more low-spirited than ever. Last night, she had returned from the banquet hall to her bedchamber to find Rokeby getting dressed with the help of one of king's manservants.

When she had questioned him, he had announced his intention of returning to his townhouse that very night.

"You must not think of going out in such weather, when you've not yet recovered from your wounds," she protested.

"My chest did hurt like the very devil, but the pain's nearly gone now. And the wounds did not go deep enough to do any lasting damage to my arm and shoulder. The king's physician has assured me of that." He spoke with calm assurance. "A few hours of practice each day, and I'll soon be able to handle a sword as well as ever."

Rokeby prided himself on his prowess in dueling. One of the finest fencing masters in London had helped him to perfect his skill, and he had proved a formidable opponent to those foolhardy enough to challenge him. He had killed at least four men that she knew of.

"I've been watching over you day and night," she reminded him. "Who is to care for you once you leave here?"

"Your concern is most touching, my lady. But I've more than enough servants in my house to see to my needs."

Her eyes narrowed. "A pretty young maidservant, fresh from the country, perhaps?"

"And if I have, it's no concern of yours." He made her a bow, picked up his cloak, and walked out the door.

If only he had spent a few more nights in her bedchamber, she'd have won him back. As it was, she sat here alone in her carriage and stared out indifferently at the crowd of revelers milling about the fair. Half a dozen courtiers had offered to escort her today, but she had wanted none of them.

She thrust her head out the window and called to her coachman, "Take me back to Whitehall—at once."

"I fear we may have slow going in this crowd, my lady."

"Make what speed you can," she told him.

He cracked his whip over the backs of the black geldings, and the carriage moved a few yards only to jerk to a halt. The two sleek horses pawed the ground, tossed their heads, and shook their jingling harnesses, but could make no further progress.

"What's delaying us now?" she demanded.

"It must be the crowd gathered around that wench who's singing on the platform up ahead, my lady."

Jade tapped her elegantly shod foot against the coach floor. Then she stiffened and her gloved fingers tightened around her silver hand-warmer. She had heard that voice before; she was sure of it. But where?

She stared out the carriage window, her lips parted in disbelief. If she did not know better, she'd have sworn that the singer was Lady Rosalind Grenville. But that was impossible. The flighty little bitch was gone, and with any luck, she would never return to London.

And yet that girl in the blue wool cloak who stood on the platform bore an uncanny resemblance to the Grenville wench. Not only her voice, but the tilt of her chin, the cascade of shining black hair falling about her oval face—

"I wish to get down at once," she called to one of her tall, liveried footmen. He sprang down from the rear of the carriage, opened the door, and helped her to descend. He started to clear a path for her, roughly jostling the crowd to either side, but before they reached the platform, she stopped. "This is close enough."

The torchlight played over the girl's fresh young face. There might be a score of black-haired wenches who sang as well as Lady Rosalind; but how many would look so like Dirk Grenville's cousin? The singer up there on the platform had the same small, square chin, the same high cheekbones, the same way of holding her head. The same poise, the look of good breeding. And her eyes . . . they were deep amethyst, fringed with sooty lashes, and slightly tilted.

Jade's searching gaze swept from the singer down to the young, blond lute player, then came to rest on a burly man holding a bear's chain.

A huge brown bear . . .

Rokeby had spoken of the bear leader who had slipped into the palace on the night of the masque, of the bear that had sprung from the shadows in one of the corridors and attacked him. The same night Rosalind Grenville had gone from Whitehall, leaving all her possessions behind her.

"I've had enough of the fair," she said to the footman. Dutifully he escorted her back to the carriage.

As he helped her inside, the coachman asked, "Do you wish to return to Whitehall now, my lady?"

A slight smile touched her lips. "Not yet. First, you are to drive me to Lord Rokeby's house on the Strand."

Rokeby, clad in a doublet of burgundy satin slashed with silver, was seated at the desk in his library when Jade came into the room. His eyes were fixed on the sheet of parchment before him, and his quill pen moved swiftly.

"Hard at work, I see," said Jade.

He raised his head and caught sight of his unexpected visitor, and his lips tightened with displeasure. Quickly he blotted the parchment, then thrust it into a leather case.

"You should have taken a holiday and come to the Frost Fair with me. You would have found it most intriguing."

"I doubt it," he said. "My steward had orders that I was not to be disturbed. How did you manage to get in here?"

"Naturally, your steward assumed that those orders did not apply to me."

"Did he indeed? He shall have cause to regret it."

Jade seated herself, then smoothed the folds of her velvet skirt around her. "After you have heard what I came for, no doubt you'll overlook his mistake." Her light green eyes sparkled with malice as she told him of her encounter with the ballad singer at the fair an hour earlier.

"You might have contrived a more believable excuse for forcing your way in here." He gave her a cold stare. "Or perhaps your dislike for Lady Rosalind has unhinged your senses."

"My senses are keen enough," she retorted. "It was Rosalind Grenville I saw at the Frost Fair."

He controlled himself with difficulty. "Lady Rosalind's gone off to Northumberland. Wasn't that what you told me?"

"I merely repeated the excuse Dirk Grenville had given the queen," she reminded him. "Now I have proof he was lying."

"Do you really expect me to believe that one of the queen's ladies left Whitehall to go about singing for the rabble at the fairs?"

"I said I saw the wench who *called* herself Lady Rosalind." Her tinkling laughter mocked him. "To think that you could have been cozened by a little adventuress who claimed to be a highborn lady! Really, Basil—if I were to speak of it at court, you would not be able to show your face there again."

"Claimed to be a lady—what the devil are you hinting at now?"

"Only that you may have been taken in by an impostor, my lord."

He stared at her, swallowed, tried to speak, and discovered that he was unable to find the words with which to refute her insinuation.

"You have no real proof that the girl who called herself Rosalind Grenville was what she claimed to be."

For a moment, the floor seemed to shift beneath his feet. Lady Rosalind Grenville—an impostor.

"I would advise you not to make such groundless accusations

to anyone at court," he said. "Otherwise, it's you who'll be forced to prove these baseless charges, or leave Whitehall in disgrace."

"Think a moment, my lord. You never clapped eyes on the girl before she appeared at Whitehall, did you?"

Before he could reply, she went on, "Dirk Grenville received permission to bring his cousin to serve as lady-in-waiting to her majesty. He rode off and arrived a few weeks later with a young girl he introduced as Lady Rosalind. Who knows where he might have found her?"

"Your jealousy has unhinged your wits," he interrupted. "If you are not careful, you may find yourself in Bedlam."

She ignored the interruption. "Was there even one among the ladies-in-waiting who had ever met Grenville's so-called cousin before? Felicity Brandon? Or Alyson Waring? Did Sir Nicholas Grenville or his lady accompany their daughter to London?"

"Her cousin escorted her. Their majesties accepted her as Lady Rosalind Grenville."

"As you did. But she is an impostor, or worse, my lord. And I saw her this very evening, singing at the Frost Fair."

Before she could go on, he was out of his chair. He advanced on her, his voice shaking with repressed fury. "Are you going to leave willingly, madam? Or must I call the servants and have you taken away by force?"

Jade got to her feet with unhurried poise. "No need of that, my lord. I'll take no more of your valuable time. I shall leave you to consider what I've said."

She swept from the room, while Rokeby remained frozen, staring after her. When he was able to move, he made his way to the nearest window. In the moonlight, the trees cast grotesque shapes on the snow-covered lawn sloping down to the river.

Rosalind Grenville, an imposter . . . no, it was too fantastic. Or was there the slightest possibility that Jade, although possessed by jealousy, had somehow managed to hit upon the truth?

He turned from the window and began to pace the library. How much did he, or anyone at Whitehall, actually know of Lady Rosalind?

Dirk Grenville, taking advantage of Pembroke's friendship, had persuaded King James to send for Rosalind, to serve as lady-in-waiting to the queen. The girl's appearance and manners had been impeccable. She had taken her place at court, where she had been noticed and pursued by a host of infatuated men—himself among them. Her musical talent had won praise from Queen Anne. He flinched at the memory of her skilled performance in the masque. She had carried off the leading role with the self-assurance of a professional entertainer.

Rosalind Grenville, an impostor. An impostor or worse, that was what Jade had said. Rokeby made a wordless, strangled sound. An impostor? Or a spy?

Pembroke had many spies at Whitehall: underlings, most of them—kitchen maids, musicians, footmen. But perhaps, driven by the need to gather information from higher sources, the earl had sought out a well-bred young adventuress and had found a place for her in the queen's own chamber.

One by one, the pieces began to fall into place. A wave of weakness swept over him and he sank down on the nearest chair.

The night she had consented to come to his house, after having refused so long. She had seen Ambrose Corbett, the Marquis de Carvajal, and Oliver Babcock come here to meet with him on urgent business. Suppose he was suspected of conspiracy and brought to trial, like Guy Fawkes and his followers? She could be called to testify about that meeting.

He tried to reassure himself. He had won favor with the king, but what did that count for? James was notoriously fickle. His majesty saw conspiracies on every side, and with good reason. He could not trust the loyalty of his subjects, either commoners or nobles.

Rokeby forced his thoughts back to Rosalind. Now he remembered the afternoon he had been called away to consult with Master Inigo Jones, and had returned to his chamber to find her going through his papers. Her excuse had sounded plausible enough at the time. She was looking for one of the ballads he had shown her earlier. He was not so foolish as to keep any of his private papers in the palace; but she had no way of knowing that.

And on the night of the masque, the bear leader had not responded to her call for help by chance. She had known the lout's name.

Caleb, help me.

The bear leader had come seeking her, had rescued her and carried her off. If Jade was to be believed, the girl was still somewhere in London.

He would have her tracked down and brought to him. There were more than enough men in his employ who could handle that assignment. But he would interrogated her himself. He would find out how much she knew of the plot to overthrow the king. Then he would keep her a prisoner here in his house, until he and his fellow conspirators had carried out their plans. Until he had established himself as the most powerful man in the realm.

Dirk Grenville, condemned as a traitor, and imprisoned in the Tower, would not be able to save her. Or even if, by some chance, Grenville managed to escape capture, he would not risk his neck to try to rescue a girl, no matter how desirable she might be.

At the thought of the dark-haired young beauty, Rokeby felt a hot ache in his loins. Whether she was a lady or an impostor, he still lusted after her. And when the time came, he would possess her.

He closed his eyes for a moment, and gave his imagination free rein. He could see the girl who called herself Rosalind Grenville, her pride broken, humble, eager to please him. He allowed himself to revel in his fantasies. There she was in his bedchamber, her body, with its round, rose-peaked breasts, small, firm buttocks, and long supple legs, bared to his touch. She would lie on his bed, her thighs parted invitingly, her arms stretched out to him. Or perhaps crouch at his feet, awaiting his pleasure. She would be more than willing to satisfy his most outrageous desires.

Chapter Nineteen

"Old Bruin'll be losin' his skill, bein' cooped up in here. Time I was puttin' him to work again," Caleb said. He fastened on the bear's chain and set out to make the round of the taverns, leaving Melora behind in their room at the lodginghouse. The cold that had gripped London less than a month before was gone now. Barges and skiffs moved along the Thames again.

With the coming of early spring, a heavy fog lay over the city, reaching thick, gray tentacles through every street and alley. During the past fortnight, Melora had been seized by a growing restlessness. And today, with Caleb gone, it seemed to her that the hours crept by even more slowly than usual.

It was close to sunset when Mother Speedwell knocked at her door. "There's a fine gentleman come callin' for ye." The stout, gray-haired landlady wiped her large, roughened hands on her soiled apron. "He's got his coach waitin' in the alley. 'Twas Inchcliff who brought his message. He says the gentleman's in a rare hurry to see ye."

Dirk. It had to be Dirk. Melora's spirits soared at the prospect of seeing him again, of feeling his arms around her, his mouth on hers. She took her cloak from its peg, threw it over her shoulders, then followed the landlady downstairs.

The low-ceilinged kitchen with its smoke-blackened beams was not as crowded as it had been during winter. Some of the lodgers, encouraged by the milder weather, had already set out on the road. Only Inchcliff and young Tom Warrick were sitting at the table. The moment the puppetmaster caught sight of Melora, he set down his mug of ale.

"Yer caller's coach is waitin' at the end of the alley," he said. Why had Dirk come across the river to Southwark himself instead of sending Osric, as he had before?

She started for the kitchen door, filled with anticipation. Inchcliff sprang to his feet. "It's not safe for a young girl out there in Ram's Alley alone."

"I'll go with Melora," Tom volunteered.

"Much use a stripling like you would be, in case of trouble," the puppeteer scoffed. The boy looked crestfallen.

"It's good of you to offer, Tom—" she began, wanting to sooth his wounded pride. But Inchcliff took hold of her arm and hurried her out the door.

As they stepped into the swirling fog, Melora was grateful for the puppeteer's supporting hand. She could barely see the far end of the alley, and the garbage-littered cobblestones were wet and slippery underfoot. They had almost reached the coach before she caught sight of its dark shape looming up before her, and the faint yellow glimmer of its lanterns.

"Here's the lady, safe and sound," Inchcliff called out. She raised her eyes to the coach door, eager for a glimpse of Dirk's face. She ached for the warmth of his embrace, for the pressure of his lips, hard and insistent, as they parted hers.

The door swung open, and a short, stocky stranger jumped down and caught her around the waist. She stared at him, startled.

"Dirk?" she called. There was no answer from inside the coach.

"Up ye go, my lady." She caught the hint of mockery in the rough, unfamiliar voice, and tried to pull away.

"None o' that, now," the man warned. He lifted her and thrust her into the coach. She lost her balance, stumbled, then fell to her knees. "Inchcliff!" she cried. "Get me out of here!"

But the puppeteer ignored her. "I'll have the rest of my

money," he said to the stocky man, who tossed him a purse, climbed back into the coach, and slammed the door behind him.

She heard Inchcliff call after her from the alley. "A pleasant journey, Melora." The driver cracked his whip and the coach moved into the fog, bearing her away to some unknown destination.

Melora managed to pull herself up on the seat. She pressed her face against the window, drew a deep breath, and screamed with all her strength, "Help me! Someone—help!"

"Stop yer caterwaulin'. Won't do ye no good—not hereabouts!" Her heart sank. The district around Ram's Alley was one of the roughest parts of Southwark. Its narrow streets were lined with brothels and taverns. A girl's cry for help was unlikely to attract attention.

She twisted around on the seat and tried to claw her captor's face. He gave her a slap across her cheek. "Behave yerself, or ye'll get worse."

"Where are you taking me?"

"You'll find out soon enough."

She grabbed for the door handle.

He tore her hand away, then struck her harder than before. "Ye'll not get away from me." He seized her, threw her across his heavy thighs, and held her down, crushing the breath from her body. With his free hand, he shoved a wad of dirty cloth into her mouth. Then he turned her over. As she lay face down, he tied the gag in place with a handkerchief.

She bucked and twisted with a strength born of desperation. Cold sweat sprang out all over her body, so that she felt as if she were sheathed in ice. He jerked her arms behind her back, fastened her wrists together with a length of rough rope, pulling it so tightly that it cut into her flesh. "That'll keep ye from carryin' on anymore." He lifted her from his knees and pushed her into the opposite seat.

The coach went lurching and swaying through the rutted alleys and streets. She raised herself with difficulty, twisted around, and peered out the window. Even through the heavy fog, she recognized the familiar shape of London Bridge up ahead.

Houses and shops lined both sides of the bridge. The coachman was forced to drive slowly because of the press of traffic and the gray blanket of fog. In one last, desperate effort, she lunged sideways, throwing her weight against the door.

It did not give way. Tears of frustration stung her lids and coursed down her cheeks. She fell back on the seat, bruised and aching.

Through the humming noise inside her head, she heard the voice of her captor. "That'll teach ye—" The humming grew louder, then changed to a roar. The man's face was a blur. She felt the dark tide rise around her and sweep her into unconsciousness.

She was lying on her back. Her arms felt as if they had been wrenched from their sockets, but she moved them and realized that they were no longer bound. Her head throbbed and her mouth was dry, evil-tasting. She ran her tongue over her bruised lips, opened her eyes, and looked about her.

The panic she had felt back in the coach was nothing compared with the stark terror that engulfed her now. Rokeby was standing over her, regarding her with a tight-lipped smile.

She raised herself from the wide, cushioned settle, supporting herself on one arm. When she looked around, she immediately recognized the library with its dark-paneled walls and its shelves of leatherbound books. Her captor had brought her to Rokeby's townhouse on the Strand.

"How did you find me?" she asked.

"It was not too difficult. You were seen at the Frost Fair. How foolhardy you were, making a public display of yourself, performing on the platform of Inchcliff's booth. It took some little time for me to have the puppeteer tracked down. But once

270

he was found, he was more than willing to tell me where to find you. He even led you to the coach."

"Have you told his majesty? Does he know I am here in London, not Northumberland? And what of the queen—"

"I'll ask the questions, Lady Rosalind. Or do you prefer to be called Melora?"

Not only had he tracked her to Southwark, he had also found out her real name. How much more did he know about her? She fought against the mounting fear that threatened to overwhelm her.

By now, Caleb must have returned to the lodginghouse and found her missing. He would go out looking for her, scouring the dens of Southwark. How was he to know that she had been carried off across the river to Rokeby's house?

She would have to find a way to escape by herself, as soon as she got the chance. For now, it was all she could do to keep her emotions under tight control.

"I asked if you prefer to be called Melora." Rokeby leaned over her.

"Call me what you please, my lord. It makes no difference to me." She tried to sound unconcerned, even arrogant, for she knew from experience that a woman's fear only served to arouse his lust.

"You admit you're not Lady Rosalind Grenville?"

She sat back on the settle, and turned her face away.

"Look at me when I speak to you." His hand closed on her shoulder in a bruising grip. "You remember how I dealt with my falconer, when he displeased me?"

A shudder moved through her. "I remember."

"Then you know what to expect, if you give me cause for anger."

He would not hesitate to use the lash on a woman, of that she was certain. "There's no need of threats, my lord. I admit I'm not Dirk Grenville's cousin. He found me a few months ago, singing in a taproom. What else do you wish to know?"

271

She had caught him off guard, and she must make the most of her advantage.

"Why did Grenville bring you to Whitehall and introduce you as his cousin?"

"The real Lady Rosalind was no longer available to serve the queen," she said. "It helps to have a relation serving as lady-in-waiting to the queen."

"But you knew the risk you were taking."

"Certainly, my lord."

"Were you so much in love with Grenville that you were willing to do whatever he asked of you?"

"Love is for simpering young ladies who can indulge themselves." She gave him a wry smile. "It's a luxury I can't afford."

She would have to proceed carefully, giving Rokeby as little information as possible. "Grenville paid me to impersonate his cousin, so that I might help him gain advancement at court."

"The king has given him a title. What more does he want? Does he hope to get rich on trade monopolies? The building of lighthouses, the inspection of woolen cloth, the retail sale of wine?"

She shook her head. "He wants a fleet of ships and a land grant. He dreams of establishing a colony in the New World."

"In the islands of the Caribees, perhaps? Or in the forests of the mainland to the north? Still the footloose adventurer, eager to go seeking wealth and power halfway around the world." He raised one eyebrow, and gave her a mocking smile. "And I suppose you are to go with him."

"He would take me along, if I wished it. But I can get all I want without leaving England."

"And what is it you want, Melora?"

"A highborn gentleman who'll keep me in luxury. Or, if I'm clever enough, I might find one who'll marry me. I should like a title, an estate, a townhouse like this one."

"Would you, indeed? Until a few months ago, you made your living entertaining in taprooms. For a common trollop, you aim high." She caught a flicker of admiration in his eyes.

"I am most uncommon, I assure you," she said, with a toss of her head. "And no more of a trollop than any of the queen's other ladies."

"You already have the arrogance of a duchess," Rokeby said. "And the speech and manners to match. How did you come by such advantages?"

So far, she was doing better than she had ever dared hope. Now, if only she could improvise a convincing account of her background, perhaps he would leave off his questioning. "My mother was a shopkeeper's daughter who caught the eye of a wealthy squire," she began. "But she was beautiful, and ambitious."

"And he married her?"

"He was already married." She shrugged. "I was born on the wrong side of the blanket, but my mother and I were given a comfortable cottage on his estate. And I was educated at the manor house, along with his legitimate daughters."

"His wife must have been a most understanding and kind-hearted lady."

"The frozen-faced bitch hated me, and my mother. But my father was absolute master of his house as long as he lived."

"And after he died?"

"The mourning bells were still tolling when she turned us off the estate." Melora sighed. "My mother could not survive the hardships of life on the road. She did not outlive my father by more than a year."

"And Caleb? How long have you known him?"

"We were traveling together when Grenville found me," she said carefully.

"That's not what I asked you."

"If you mean to go on questioning me all night, you might at least offer me a glass of wine. My mouth's dry and evil-tasting from that filthy gag your hireling used to silence me."

He brought her a goblet of Malaga, and she sipped slowly. So far, she had wanted only to fend off his anger by giving him plausible answers. Perhaps if she kept her wits about her, she might also gain information that would prove useful to Pembroke.

"Caleb found me singing at a fair. It's not easy for a young girl traveling alone. So many drunken louts want to—"

"Who can blame them?" His eyes moved to her breasts and lingered there. She went on quickly, hoping to distract him.

"He suggested we should travel together. I have a fine singing voice, as you know, my lord. I helped to attract a crowd."

"And at night you shared a loft or a ditch beside the road. How long was it before he took your maidenhead?"

"Caleb prefers a fat wench with breasts like melons and a backside as broad as a mare's," she said. "He usually managed to find one, hot and willing for a night's sport."

Rokeby gave her a searching look. "I suppose next you'll tell me that you're still a virgin."

"I was, until Dirk Grenville carried me to his bed." It was difficult to speak of such intimacies, but she had to convince him that Dirk meant nothing to her; that she was an opportunist whose services were for sale to the highest bidder.

"No doubt he thought I'd be honored to lie with a fine gentleman."

"And you weren't?"

"I should suppose one man's much like another between the sheets."

"Yet you fought to keep me at arm's length all this time."

"Grenville has a jealous disposition," she improvised. "Like your Lady Jade."

She set down her goblet, and rose from the settle. Rokeby's hand shot out and caught her arm. "I've not finished with you yet."

"Surely I've told you all you could possibly want to know."

"You've told me a great deal." His pale gray eyes held hers. "I don't doubt you're an adventuress." His fingers tightened. "Are you also a spy, Melora?"

With a sinking sensation, she realized she had not succeeded in overcoming his suspicions after all. How far would she have to go to convince him that she was no threat to him?

"I did give Grenville—certain information."

He pushed her back onto the settle and stood over her.

"What sort of information?"

"Only some snippets of idle gossip I gathered from the other ladies-in-waiting."

"And didn't you wonder why Grenville should be interested in such trivial affairs?"

"That was his concern, not mine. So long as he paid me, I did as I was told. Call it spying, if you like. I would be perfectly willing to perform the same service for you."

"What makes you think I have any use for such information as you could bring me?"

"You want power, my lord. And you would stop at nothing to get it."

"I already have power."

"You want more. I think you are a man of limitless ambition." She knew she was treading on dangerous ground, but it would be worth the risk. "If I were allowed to return to court as lady-in-waiting, I could be of use to you, as I was to Grenville."

"Perhaps," he said, regarding her thoughtfully. "I have many informers in court, but a clever girl like you, who has already gained the queen's trust—you might be of special value to me."

"If you can persuade Lady Jade not to betray me, I know I can convince her majesty that I was in Northumberland all this time. That my brother has recovered and I am eager to take up my duties in the palace again."

"Not so fast, Melora." His voice was low and silky. "What of the more intimate services you gave to Grenville?"

She lowered her lashes, drew a deep breath, and held it, as she tried to force a blush to her cheeks.

"Don't play the innocent with me. We know each other too well now. Supposing I were to silence Jade and take you back to the palace myself. Would you lie with me, as you did with Grenville?"

"I'm sure Lady Jade is a most accomplished lover. Or if you seek a younger mistress, no doubt there are any number of girls newly come to court who would be honored to—"

"I want proof of your absolute loyalty. Unless you agree to give yourself to me willingly, I might begin to think you have some lingering affection for Grenville."

He jerked her to her feet and drew her against him. Somehow, she forced herself to remain motionless, while his hands moved down the length of her back. His mouth pressed down on hers with bruising force.

She tried to tell herself that this was only another role she was playing. Slowly, reluctantly, she opened her lips and his tongue thrust into her mouth, hot and seeking. His hands slid down the length of her back. He cupped her buttocks and forced her against him. She felt the hard bulge beneath his satin breeches pressing against her thigh. Revulsion surged through her.

Did he mean to take her here and now? She would not be able to go through with it, no matter how high the stakes.

He raised his lips from hers and released her. She went weak with relief. "I am expecting a visitor tonight," he said. "He should be arriving soon."

His eyes moved over her slowly, lingering on her mouth, her throat, the rounds of her breasts, the curve of her waist. "Later you will have the opportunity to prove that no matter what you may have felt for Grenville, he no longer means anything to you. And I would advise you not to try to deceive me. I've had enough experience with women to know the difference between a passionate lover and a paid trollop who is only going through the motions."

She could not ignore his warning. A chill prickled along her spine. He reached for the bell rope and gave it a tug.

When a liveried footman appeared, he said, "This lady will be remaining for the night. Show her upstairs to the Blue Chamber, and sent one of the maids to wait on her."

Then he turned back to Melora.

"You will have ample time to bathe and put on more suitable attire. Another glass of wine, a short sleep, and I trust you will be prepared to welcome me with more ardor than you've shown so far."

Although she did not know who was coming to visit him tonight, she was sure she could not get out of the house, using the same trick as before. But she would escape, one way or another. Before Rokeby was ready to come to her bed, she would be out of the house and far away.

Chapter Twenty

Melora stepped from the marble tub, which stood in a curtained alcove on one side of the Blue Chamber. The room,
which had taken its name from the magnificent blue velvet bed
curtains and the matching drapes on the two tall windows, bore
the stamp of Rokeby's lavish taste. A tapestry, depicting Venus
and Adonis locked in a passionate embrace and surrounded by
nymphs and fauns, covered an entire wall.

Under other circumstances, Melora might have taken pleasure in her elegant surroundings, but now her thoughts were
fixed on the need to get away as quickly as possible.

The maid helped her into a white silk nightdress trimmed
with broad bands of delicate black lace, a matching silk-and-
lace robe, and a pair of high-heeled satin slippers. Until now,
she had done her work with scarcely a word.

"Is there anything more you require, my lady?"

She could not let the girl leave yet. There might be a chance
of winning her over. "You have served me well, indeed. But I
don't even know your name." She gave the girl a warm smile.

"It is Nancy, my lady," the girl said. Although she could have
been attractive, with her glossy brown hair, even features, and
well-rounded figure, her apathetic expression and subdued
manner made her appear plain, even drab.

"You don't speak like a native of London. Where are you
from?"

"I come from Sussex, my lady." She answered Melora's questions in a dull monotone, and kept her eyes cast down. It would be far easier to plan an escape with Nancy to help her, but so far, she was making little headway.

"You have a family there?"

"Yes, my lady."

"Do you like working here?" Melora persisted.

The maid nodded.

"No doubt Lord Rokeby's a good master."

Nancy kept her eyes lowered, her fingers plucking nervously at her apron. "He—treats us fair enough so long as we do as we're told." She looked toward the door. "If you please, my lady—it is getting late, and I have other chores to see to, downstairs."

It would be useless to delay the girl further, Melora decided. A master like Rokeby would break the spirit of any but the most courageous of servants.

Melora accompanied the maid to the door. "I will be sure to tell his lordship how well you carried out your duties," she said.

She looked into the hall. A liveried footman stood at the head of the front stairs. The closest escape route was cut off. But she would not be defeated so easily.

She turned her head and caught a glimpse of Nancy's retreating figure, moving quickly in the opposite direction. In a house this large, there would have to be a servants' stairway at the rear, leading directly to the kitchen and scullery. It would have helped if she could have persuaded the maid to guide her down and out the back way. She dismissed the notion of trying to get help from any of the staff. Somehow, she would have to manage on her own.

She looked about the chamber with mounting anxiety. Only one door, and that was a few yards from the head of the front stairs, where the footman stood guard. Two tall windows. The bed, with its padded headboard and curtains.

The velvet bed curtains. Surely they would be strong enough to support her weight. Perhaps if she could tear them into strips and knot them together, she could climb down from one of the windows.

She considered the possibility, then dismissed it. She would never be able to tear such heavy material with her bare hands, and she had no scissors or knife.

She opened the chamber door a crack. The footman still stood there. Her insides tightened with fear. If she did not get out soon, Rokeby would have completed his business with his visitor. She had to be gone before then.

She opened one of the two windows and leaned out. The fog had turned to a light, silvery mist. She caught sight of the broad terrace below, and the flight of steps leading down to the garden. Beyond lay the river.

If only she could get down to the terrace. But how?

She dragged over a hassock, stood on it, and leaned out farther. Her eyes moved along the back wall of the house, and came to rest on a small stone balcony. It jutted out from the window of the chamber next to hers.

She caught her breath and hope surged up inside her. A narrow ledge ran the length of the wall, only a few feet below her window.

If she could get across to the other chamber, and from there into the hall, she would run down the servants' stairway and out a back door.

But what if the footman turned and caught sight of her? What if she lost her footing on the narrow ledge, or blundered into a page or scullery maid downstairs? She dared not dwell on possible risks. The moments were ticking by and she had to be gone before Rokeby came upstairs.

Her lips curved in a wry smile. If she really was the calculating adventuress she pretended to be, she would give herself to Rokeby without a qualm. Whatever outrageous demands he might make, she would satisfy them. In her bed, he would forget about Lady Jade. Then she would use her power over him to find out all she could about his plot against the king.

But she couldn't do it. Her love for Dirk was all-consuming.

She belonged to him, and she always would. It did not matter how little time they might have together before he sailed. Even after he was gone, she would have her memories to sustain her through the years to come.

She pulled off her robe, tossed it to the floor, slid her feet from her satin slippers. She ripped the lace bands off the bottom of her nightdress, so that her legs were left bare to the knees.

She put one leg over the sill, then the other. The raw chill of the night enveloped her. Slowly, step by step, she made her way along the ledge, which was wet and slippery from the night mist. She did not look down, but kept her eyes fastened on the balcony of the adjacent chamber. Her heart thudded against her chest. A single misstep, a fall from this height to the terrace below—Icy tremors skittered along her spine. She would not let herself think about it.

One step. Another. And another.

She bit down on her lip to stifle a cry as she felt herself caught and held fast. Carefully, she turned her head and saw that she had snagged her gown on the branch of a thick vine. It grew up along the side of the house, clinging to the brick wall.

Should she try to get across the heavy, shapeless tangle of branches that covered the ledge, blocking her way? Osric, with his acrobat's skills, might manage it. But she remained frozen, her body rigid, afraid to make the attempt.

Yet her only other course would be to retreat along the ledge, back to the chamber from which she had come.

Or perhaps there was another way.

She reached out her hand and tugged on the branch. It might be strong enough to hold her.

If it was, she would have no need to reach the other chamber or to go exploring the unfamiliar passageways of the house until she found a way out. She would climb down the vine, straight to the terrace, and make a dash from there, across the lawn to the river.

She grasped the branch with her other hand. An ominous creaking sound made her stiffen with apprehension. But the branch took her full weight. She reached down with one bare foot and felt with her toes for the branch below.

The night wind molded her damp robe against her, sending a clammy sensation through her body. Her nipples puckered and her legs began to quiver, but she kept moving downward.

"—the perfect opportunity—" At the sound of Rokeby's voice, she stopped, her body rigid. She looked down and saw him coming from the house out onto the terrace, along with another man. A tall man in a dark cloak and high-crowned hat.

"When his majesty sets out on his progress—less than a week." She strained to hear all that Rokeby was saying, but she was still too high above the terrace.

Yet she had already heard enough to know that no matter how great the risk, she had to try to find out more.

"You used your powers of persuasion well." She recognized the voice of the Marquis de Carvajal.

"It took little persuasion. The king's only too eager to show himself off to his subjects."

Melora's fingers tightened on the branch. She forgot her own danger as she strained to catch every word.

King James was preparing to go on a royal progress northward to Scotland. He would stop along the way to receive the homage of the common people, and to offer certain fortunate noblemen the honor of entertaining him at their estates.

"He insisted that I was to accompany him," said Rokeby.

"—hunting trip—an unfortunate accident . . ." That was Carvajal.

Pembroke had expected Rokeby and his fellow-conspirators to strike soon, but had even he thought they would move so quickly?

Melora reached down and set her foot on a lower branch.

"His majesty is such a clumsy rider. He might well break his neck without any assistance from us . . ."

"—we can't leave it to chance . . ."

Melora could scarcely force herself to remain where she was.

She no longer felt any concern for her own safety. She must get every possible scrap of information.

Then, as soon as Rokeby had escorted the marquis to the landing and returned to the house, she would make a run for it. She would persuade a boatman to take her to the palace. If she could not find Dirk there, she would go straight to the queen.

She placed her foot on the branch directly below. It gave way with a sharp, cracking sound, like a pistol shot. She managed to scramble onto another branch and regain her balance. Both men turned and stared up at the back wall of the house.

Rokeby swore, then shouted for the servants. They came running from the open doors out onto the terrace, with torches held high.

Melora flattened herself against the vine, but she was caught in the glare of the torchlight. Rough hands dragged her down and held her, half-naked and too frightened to make a sound.

Melora sat huddled in a chair in the library, her arms crossed across her breasts. Carvajal stared at her in disbelief.

"Madre de Dios! This girl is one of the queen's ladies. Lord Grenville's cousin."

Rokeby gave a harsh laugh. "She's an impostor. A spy."

"You are sure?"

"She admitted as much to me, only a few hours ago."

"Grenville knows of this?"

"It was he who brought her to court and paid her to gather information against us."

Melora flinched under Carvajal's pitiless gaze. "In that case, our course is plain enough," he said. He drew the side of his hand across his throat. "With the river so near, we'll have no difficulty getting rid of the body."

Terror stabbed at her vitals. It was as if she could already feel the sharp edge of a dagger slashing her flesh. She would disappear into the dark waters of the Thames, and no one would know what had become of her.

Dirk would search for her without success. At the thought of him, her fear was mingled with an overpowering sense of loss. She remembered saying goodbye to him at the inn, on the day of the Frost Fair. There had been so much still unsaid between them. How could she have known that she would never see him again?

Rokeby regarded her thoughtfully. "Perhaps you're being too hasty, Carvajal," he said.

"Too hasty? Will you wait until she finds out every last detail of our plan?" His eyes moved over her and she caught the brief flicker of lust. Her nightdress, torn and damp, clung to every curve and hollow of her body. "You cannot allow your desire for this trollop to make you forget what is at stake here. Slit her throat and be done with it."

"I may have a better use for her."

"She's a rare piece, I grant you. I would be tempted to make use of her myself. But under the circumstances——"

"Enough," said Rokeby. He jerked Melora to her feet and grasped her shoulders, holding her immobile.

"Tell me, Melora, how much does Dirk Grenville really mean to you?"

"He was not like any man I'd ever known before. A highborn gentleman, and handsome, too. I suppose I was infatuated with him for a time."

"You were in love with him. I think you still love him, even now."

"No! That's not true!"

"Yet you were trying to escape from me. I find that most unflattering."

Only boldness would save her now. "You are mistaken, my lord. I was growing restless, impatient, waiting for you, when I saw you and the marquis come out onto the terrace."

"Do go on, my dear."

She tried to ignore the mockery in Rokeby's voice.

"It's not the first time Carvajal came here late at night to meet with you. Since you did not send him away, I guessed that you had important business with him."

"And you were determined to find out more. Tell me, where did you plan to sell your information this time?"

"To the highest bidder, naturally."

"Grenville? Or Pembroke?"

"I would have gone straight to her majesty."

"What makes you think she would have believed you?"

"She's never trusted you, my lord. She told me so herself. And for such information as I could have given her tonight, she would have paid me any price I cared to name."

Rokeby gave a brief, harsh laugh. "You're bold enough, I'll give you credit for that. But you are too greedy, my dear. This time you have overreached yourself."

"So it would seem." If only she felt as cool and self-assured as she tried to appear.

"Since you have failed, you must settle for what I have to offer."

Her despair gave way to the first faint stirring of hope. Was it possible, even now, that she had a chance to escape? Drawing on her last ounce of courage, she forced herself to meet his eyes. "How much?"

"I offer the highest reward of all, Melora—your life."

Carvajal made an impatient gesture. "I say, kill the bitch and be done with it."

But Rokeby did not take his eyes off Melora. "You were Grenville's mistress."

"I've never denied it."

"You will be in a perfect position to testify against him when he is brought to trial, and charged with the king's assassination."

Stunned by the full impact of his words, she could not reply at once. Her mouth went dry, and her throat constricted. Rokeby intended to kill the king, and get rid of Dirk, one of his

285

most loyal supporters. How many others did he plan to destroy in his ruthless climb to power?

Melora chose her words carefully. "Even if I agree to do as you wish, who will believe me? The king received Dirk at court, gave him a title—"

"But not the ships he wants and the land grant."

"Only because Dirk hasn't asked for them yet."

"That is where you come in. You will say that Grenville did ask for both, and that the king refused his request. He would not have denounced his majesty openly, but when he was with you, his mistress, in the privacy of your chamber, he swore to get even. You heard him speaking of killing the king, not once, but many times. With your testimony, Grenville's sure to be found guilty."

"I dare not, my lord. To try to deceive a clever man like Sir Edward Coke—"

"The king's chief justice is clever enough, I grant you. It will be up to you to convince him that you are speaking the truth."

He gave her a tight smile. "Of course, the choice is yours. If you love Grenville too much to testify against him, perhaps you won't mind going to the headsman's block with him."

She felt the trap closing around her. Should she refuse outright to agree to Rokeby's demand, she had no doubt that he would go along with Carvajal's plan. In an hour, maybe less, she would be at the bottom of the river.

If ever she needed to draw on her acting skills, this was the moment.

She threw herself on her knees, and looked up at Rokeby beseechingly. "I'll say whatever you wish—I'll tell the court that Dirk was the king's assassin—I'll make them believe me!"

"No doubt you will." He gave her an ironic smile as he raised her to her feet.

She hesitated briefly. "And after the trial—what is to become of me then?"

"I may be persuaded to let you live. But only as long as you do exactly as I command. From this moment on, you will obey me without question."

He led her to the desk at the far end of the library, and pushed her into the chair. "Your first task is to write to Grenville." He shoved a piece of parchment in front of her and put a quill into her hand. She bent her head over the parchment and began to set down the words Rokeby dictated. She tried not to think what Dirk's response would be, when he read her letter.

It was dawn when Rokeby entered the Blue Chamber. Melora, still wearing her torn nightdress, lay on her back on the wide bed, her arms stretched above her head, and fastened to the headboard. She writhed helplessly, trying to turn away, until she saw, by the look in his eyes, that her movements aroused his desire. With an effort, she forced herself to lie perfectly still.

"You will remain here until I return. It may be a matter of days, or even weeks. Nancy will give you your meals and attend to your personal needs."

The young maidservant stood a short distance from the bed, her eyes expressionless. "For the rest of the time, you will be kept tied as you are now. My footmen will be on guard outside your door. Others will watch the grounds and the river landing."

He leaned over her and ran his fingers along her cheek, the curve of her throat, the swell of her breasts. "I know you will be impatient for my return, Melora."

She watched him leave the room, then turned her face away. In a few days, King James would set out on his progress, accompanied by Rokeby and his fellow-conspirators. Unless she could get out of here before they left London, it would be too late to stop them.

* * *

In the small shed outside the palace wall, Dirk stood with booted feet planted apart, a torn, soiled piece of parchment crumpled in his fist. Although Caleb had arrived at Whitehall an hour ago, it had been difficult for the bear leader to persuade a frozen-faced servant to find Lord Grenville and deliver Melora's letter.

Now Dirk smoothed the soiled bit of parchment, and read Melora's words once more, although there was no need. He already knew them by heart.

I am leaving London today. I do not want to be involved in your rash schemes any longer. I should be grateful to you for taking me from the surroundings in which you found me, and showing me a way of life I had never known before. Now I have found another gentleman who can provide well for me. He does not wish to take me across the sea to live among savages in a wilderness. I can have all I ever wanted, here in England. Perhaps I may even persuade him to marry me.

"Who is this gentleman she speaks of? Where did she meet him?"

"I don't know, my lord."

"Did she give you any hint that she was going to leave London?"

"Not a word. I already told ye—"

"Tell me again."

Patiently, Caleb repeated his account of all that had happened since he had last seen Melora. He had left her at the lodginghouse and gone out with Bruin. When he had returned that night, he had found her gone.

He had questioned Inchcliff and Mother Speedwell. Both had insisted that Melora had simply walked out the door and disappeared into the fog. He had wasted no time but had gone straight out again to search for her.

"I never went back upstairs, an' I was out all night, goin' from one tavern to another—I searched the bawdyhouses, too."

Dirk felt his muscles tighten with revulsion. Why had he left Melora in Southwark? Then he reminded himself that she had not been dragged off to any tavern or brothel against her will. She had found herself a fine gentleman, one who would give her the kind of life she craved. One who might marry her.

"I never got back to our chamber at Mother Speedwell's 'til this mornin'. That's when I found Melora's letter," Caleb was saying. "I never learned to read. Inchcliff, the puppetmaster, he read it to me. An' I brought it here as fast as I could."

Dirk crumpled the parchment into a tight ball again, thrust it into his doublet, and began pacing the small shed.

The letter had been written by Melora. But the words did not sound like hers. Yet what did he know of her, even now? *I have found another gentleman.* One of the courtiers who had pursued her at Whitehall? Ambrose Corbett? Or perhaps a foreign nobleman who had visited court during the Christmas season.

"It's not like Melora, going off without telling you," he said.

"I got to speak plain, my lord. She's been cooped up in the lodginghouse since she saw ye at the Frost Fair," Caleb reminded him. "She didn't have no word from you since then."

"She knew that I had other business to attend to. Urgent business."

Pembroke's business. Why couldn't she have understood? Why couldn't she have waited a few days longer?

Because she had not loved him enough to wait. He had been deceiving himself all this time.

He tried to remember every word she had said that afternoon at the Fox and Hound. She had asked him if he was willing to forget his plans to leave England, to stay with her. And he had refused. He had been deluded to believe that in time, he might persuade her to come with him to America.

"I'll go back an' keep on lookin' for her in Southwark," Caleb offered. "I'll take Osric with me this time. A sharp one, he is."

"Spare yourself the trouble." His voice shook with barely controlled rage. "She's left London by now. She and her fine gentleman."

Another man might have been silenced by his anger, but

Caleb was not easily shaken. "I don't claim to know a lot about how women think or what their feelin's are, but I know Melora. She wouldn't have gone off like that, without even sayin' good-bye to me."

"Maybe neither of us knew her as well as we thought," Dirk said, with a tight, self-deprecating smile.

He turned and stalked out of the shed and into the palace courtyard. He forced his way through the milling throng, scarcely aware of the bustle of activity all around him, for his thoughts were far from his present surroundings. For now, he was back on a rainswept stretch of the Great North Road. He heard Melora's voice, carried on the wind, and saw her dark hair blowing about her face, her slender white arms cradling her lute.

He's gone . . . he's gone away,
To stay, a little while . . .

The plaintive words of her ballad returned to mock him. For it was she who had gone away. He would never see her again.

He felt a stab of loss, sharper than any thrust of sword or dagger, a searing pain that grew and grew until it overpowered him.

Melora. His Melora. But no, she had never really been his. She had come into his life by chance. Now she had left him, with nothing more than a brief message of farewell.

"Your pardon, my lord." Grenville stepped aside to avoid colliding with a servant carrying a heavy trunk. Other serving-men hurried back and forth, laden down with heavy ironbound trunks, cases of wine, and baskets of provisions; enough supplies for a small army. Courtiers, pages, musicians, ladies' maids, and hangers-on would be accompanying their majesties on their journey.

It was typical of the king to start out on a progress now, while the nights were still damp and chilly, and the roads up north were knee-deep with mud. Elizabeth would have waited until summer to travel through the countryside; but her successor, anxious to win the approval of his subjects, commoners and nobles alike, was set on leaving at once.

He would stop at estates along the way, where he would be feted by the owners. The royal visit would stretch the resources of even the wealthiest noblemen, for they would be expected to entertain his majesty in lavish style, with dancing, elaborate banquets and hunting parties. They would compete with one another to give him the costliest gifts they could afford.

"I have arranged for you to travel with his majesty," Pembroke had told Dirk. Although he had not welcomed the order, he understood that the king must be closely guarded by men who were not only loyal, but able to protect him by force of arms in case of need.

With the day of the king's departure drawing near, Dirk had planned to send for Melora, to spend the night with her. He would have asked her to wait until the threat to the king's life had been removed and he was free to marry her. He had been so sure he could find a way to persuade her to leave England, to cross the sea with him and share his life in the New World.

What an arrogant, self-deluded fool he had been.

I have found another gentleman . . .

He had never allowed himself to love any woman before. He never would again.

Chapter Twenty-one

Melora, released from her bonds, flexed her fingers and rubbed her bruised wrists to restore the circulation in her hands. Nancy set down the tray of food and eyed her with respect as well as sympathy.

The young lady had borne the indignities of her imprisonment without complaint. She had not pleaded to be released, nor had she given way to hysterics, as another in her position might have done.

Instead, she had lain quietly on the wide bed, sometimes staring up at the blue velvet canopy, or sideways, in the directions of the windows. When she closed her eyes, Nancy could not be sure whether she was asleep. How could she sleep soundly, with her arms pulled up over her head, her wrists tied and attached to heavier ropes fastened to the headboard?

Little by little, Nancy had allowed herself to be drawn into conversation with Melora. She had spoken of her family back in Sussex and had described the one-room cottage that housed her five brothers and two sisters and her parents. She had spoken with particular affection of her mother, who, although overworked, underfed, and exhausted by childbearing, was always ready to help an even less fortunate neighbor.

"Times are hard for folk like us. The land we used to till was taken over by the gentry and made into sheep runs," Nancy had confided. "Oat bread, cheese, and porridge—that's all we have to eat. And never enough of those. And another baby coming along every year. My mother didn't want me to leave home, but she had all she could do to care for the others."

Because Melora had listened with interest, and had expressed genuine concern, Nancy had responded by doing what little she could to ease the young lady's discomfort. She had bathed Melora's face, brushed her hair, and washed her nightdress.

Now Melora sat up in bed, and turned to look at her dinner tray. "There is more here than I can eat," Melora said. "Won't you share it with me?"

The idea of having more than enough to eat was new to Nancy, who cast a wistful glance at the golden-brown roasted duckling, the fine-grained white bread, the syllabub, a rich concoction of heavy cream with sugar and cinnamon.

"I really shouldn't," she said. But she could not take her eyes from the tempting food before her.

To think that Mistress Melora, in spite of her own desperate situation, was able to spare a thought for a housemaid. Nancy had met with precious little kindness from the other servants since she had come to work here, and she was moved by such uncommon thoughtfulness. If only there were more she could do to help the young lady. But she dared not disobey Lord Rokeby's orders. Like the rest of the staff, even Master Dalrymple, the steward, she stood in fear of the master's wrath.

Lady Jade picked up the perfume bottle and threw it. The fragile Venetian glass shattered against the door of her bedchamber. Glittering shards flew in all directions, and the air was heavy with the scent of frangipani.

But her gesture gave her only a momentary release from the rage that seethed inside her. She cursed Rokeby in language that would have startled a seasoned sailor.

Men were ungrateful swine, all of them; but Rokeby was the worst of the lot. She had cared for him day and night after his accident, had showered him with attention, had put up with his

293

endless complaining. The broth was too hot, the posset too cool. None of her servants had been trained to make a bed properly. Once, she had actually been reduced to changing the linens herself.

And as soon as he had been able to get back on his feet, he had left her palace chambers to return his townhouse. He had discouraged her visits to his home, insisting that he had no time to spare for her. He had not even taken her into his confidence, as he once had, but had referred vaguely to "important matters" only he could deal with.

Then, on the evening of the Frost Fair, when she had forced her way into his library to tell him that the girl who called herself Lady Rosalind Grenville was an impostor, he had refused to believe her. He had accused her of jealousy, and said that her resentment of the girl had unhinged her wits.

Although his response had infuriated her, she understood why he had behaved that way. Men were not only ungrateful, they were outrageously conceited. None more so than Rokeby, who prided himself on his understanding of women, his ability to see through their pretenses, his skill in manipulating them as he chose.

How could he bring himself to admit that the clever little slut who called herself Lady Rosalind Grenville had deceived him, that she had encouraged him go chasing after her like a love-struck boy? Had she given herself to him even once, Jade wondered? Or had she kept him at arm's length with her touch-me-not airs, and then gone back to the streets to follow her trade?

He had been taken in by a common street singer who entertained the crowd for a handful of coins. And if a man had an itch in his loins and an extra farthing to spare, no doubt "Lady Rosalind," like all her kind, was willing enough to raise her skirts and pleasure him against a wall in the nearest alley.

Lady Rosalind, indeed!

But sooner or later, Rokeby would have to face the truth. What would he do then? He might try to find the girl and punish her for making a fool of him. Or he might put the whole unfortunate episode out of his mind. It did not matter to Jade, so long as she was sure that she would get him back in her bed.

While she waited, she did not retire to the seclusion of her palace chambers; nor did she retreat to her country estate. Instead, she attended every court ball.

She spent a small fortune on clothes. One night she appeared in a gown with a standing French collar decked with pearls, and a farthingale so wide that all the other couples had to make way for her as she and her partner moved through the measures of the dance. On another night she carried a small, fluffy dog with a diamond collar in one of her hanging Danish sleeves.

She spent long tedious hours in front of her dressing table, having her silver-gilt hair arranged in the most striking coiffures and decorated with towering ostrich plumes.

She danced, played at cards, and flirted shamelessly with half a dozen courtiers, but refused to start an affair with any of them. Instead, she had satisfied her voracious sexual appetite with one of her sturdy young footmen, who soon learned to please her in whatever unusual way she might demand on a particular night. Yet she found herself growing more restless, more uneasy, as she waited for Rokeby to come back to her bed.

Then, a few nights ago, the blow had fallen. The court was astir with the news that Rokeby had persuaded the king to undertake a royal progress out of season.

The ladies, after they had recovered from their surprise at the king's impulsive decision, had gloated over their invitations, then had ordered their trunks brought down. Seamstresses and jewelers swarmed through the corridors. Carriages were refurbished, and coachmen were fitted out in new livery.

Jade had received no invitation.

Unable to play a waiting game any longer, she had confronted Rokeby last night. "This progress was your idea." She kept her voice low, to avoid drawing attention to herself. "You talked the king into it."

"His majesty's easily swayed." He gave a careless shrug. "A

295

visit to his native Scotland, the chance to show himself off before his subjects along the way and try to win their admiration . . . nothing would please him more. As for the ladies, they are only too willing to brave the roads of the north, even in this season. It gives them an excuse to show off their finest furs." He was baiting her deliberately, and she knew it, but she still refused to give vent to her fury.

"I was not invited," she said softly. "You could have arranged for me to be included. You still can."

"My dear Jade, you know court protocol better than that. It is the queen who decides which ladies are to be invited on a royal progress." He gave her a look of feigned sympathy. "Perhaps you should have made a greater effort to win her favor, while you had the chance."

Before she was able to think of a properly scathing reply, he turned and left her without so much as a backward glance.

She had gone to bed alone, dispensing with the services of her obliging footman. For the rest of the night, she had lain awake, seething over Rokeby's outrageous behavior.

To hell with court protocol! He could have used his influence with the king to get her an invitation. Even now, it was not too late.

Although it was almost dawn when Jade drifted off to sleep, she rose early. She did not ring for her maid, but went to her dressing table, lit the candles on either side of the mirror, and studied her reflection more closely than ever before. She winced when she saw the dark smudges under her eyes, the faint lines around her mouth. She patted the flesh beneath her chin with the back of her hand, seeking the slightest trace of slackness.

She chided herself silently. She had never fallen prey to self-doubt, and she must not start now. She had not lost Rokeby, not yet.

She went over his behavior since the night of the Frost Fair. He had avoided her because she knew how he had let himself be taken in by "Lady Rosalind." He had not gone to the king and accused Grenville of having passed off an impostor as his cousin. Otherwise, Grenville would not longer be here at court.

Rokeby had kept silent about the deception because he had not wanted to be laughed at. He did not want her to come along; he had made that plain enough. And she knew why: he was still smarting with chagrin because she had taunted him for falling under the spell of that scheming little trollop.

But surely, when he returned from his journey, he would seek her out. Everything would be as it had been before that black-haired young doxy had come to court.

The thought should have reassured her, but it didn't. If Rokeby had been aroused by "Lady Rosalind's" youthful radiance, might he not meet some other sweet-faced little ninny during his travels with the king? The daughter of a country squire who would respond eagerly to his practiced flattery. A girl who would be carried away at the slightest prospect of a marriage that would whisk her off to the splendors of Whitehall and allow her to move in the highest circle of the court.

Marriage? Rokeby, married! Impossible.

And yet, she had seen more than one libertine who had played the field, and mocked at marriage, only to take a virginal bride to bear him sons.

Stubbornly, Jade sought reassurance. Rokeby might marry. He might get his bride with child and leave her on one of his remote estates while he returned to court alone.

Jade told herself that such an arrangement would please her well enough. So long as he came back to her bed, and all went on as before, who cared about some sad-faced little creature, pining away in Yorkshire or Cornwall?

But suppose he were to marry the daughter of a wealthy nobleman's family, a girl whose glowing young face and slender, lithe body had cast a spell over him? What if the girl, urged on by ambitious parents, insisted upon coming to court?

Was it possible that he might bring the simpering little bitch back here with him?

No! The very thought was intolerable.

Jade's eyes swept over her dressing table, and her fingers

moved among the porcelain patch boxes and glass vials. It would be futile to smash every fragile object before her. She must take more direct action.

She would forget her pride, go to Rokeby's house, and use her most skillful arts to persuade him to get her an invitation. Without making any direct reference to his embarassing blunder, she would let him know, somehow, that she would never speak of Lady Rosalind again.

She rang for her maid, then tapped her foot impatiently. It would take time to conceal the effects of the past night. A light coating of ceruse, made with the finest imported white lead, would hide the dark circles under her eyes; the application of Spanish paper would add a glow of color to her lips and cheeks. She would wear her peach-colored silk gown, with matching cloak and hood. When she arrived at Rokeby's townhouse today, she would look her most alluring.

Melora shifted on the bed in the Blue Chamber. The past few days had been made more bearable by Nancy's company. But during the nights, her courage had wavered. In trying to gather information that might save the king, she had placed Dirk in harm's way.

Within the next day or two, he would ride out with their majesties and the royal party. Rokeby would do away with the king, and the queen as well, and Dirk would be accused of the crime.

One thing she knew: she would never testify against him, no matter what Rokeby might do. At least she had it in her power to thwart the viscount that far. But her refusal, while it would cost her dearly, would not save Dirk's life. Rokeby would find enough other syncophants who would say whatever he wanted them to, for money and power. By summer, Lady Arabella Stuart would sit upon the throne, but it would be Rokeby who ruled England.

And Dirk, tried and convicted, would go to the block. A

shudder of agony moved through her at the unspeakable vision that rose up in her mind. The ravens circling about the head, fixed to a spike atop London Bridge—his eyes, dark brown, flecked with gold— She made a choking sound, then sank her teeth into her lower lip. It must not happen. She would not let it happen.

"My lady, I must protest! Lord Rokeby is not at home. I've already told you—"

"Stand aside at once."

Melora's body jerked violently as she recognized the imperious voice of Lady Jade Fairfax.

Nancy had gone downstairs to get her breakfast tray. She was alone and defenseless against Jade, who had resented her, who had been possessed by jealousy. And who was as ruthless and amoral as Rokeby himself.

Gripped by rising fear, she tugged against the bonds that held her arms. The ropes bit into her wrists, but she scarcely noticed the pain, caught up as she was in a surge of sheer animal terror. *Break free! Run and hide!*

Then, somehow, she was able to impose control on her emotions. Only if she kept calm and drew on her reserve of courage, her quick wits, could she hope to defend herself against the woman who hated her so fiercely.

If Jade went to Lord Rokeby's own bedchamber and found it empty, it was unlikely that she would go on searching until she had covered every guest chamber, linen closet, and pantry in the house. She might leave without ever knowing that Melora was here.

Nancy came hurrying into the chamber, her eyes rounded with dismay. It was plain that the maid, like the steward, who even now was going on with his futile protests, stood in awe of Jade Fairfax. "Her ladyship's in a proper rage," Nancy said softly, setting down the tray. "She forced her way in—the

299

steward couldn't stop her. And when she didn't find his lordship in the library, she came upstairs."

She cast a sympathetic glance at Melora. No doubt she knew enough about Jade's possessive attitude toward Rokeby to guess how the lady might deal with a possible rival.

"I brought the tray up by the back stairs, same as always. She didn't see me come here." The maid scarcely spoke above a whisper. "I won't let her know you're here. And I don't think any of the other servants will, either. A real she-devil, she is, when she's roused. But if we're real quiet, maybe . . ."

Stay quiet. Wait until Jade is convinced that Rokeby really isn't here. Then she'll leave. It'll be safe, for now.

Once again, Dirk's face rose up before her: angular cheekbones, hard jawline. His mouth, sometimes gentle and caressing, sometimes fierce with hunger. His hands, moving over her, stroking, seeking, stirring her as no other man's touch ever would.

Safe for now. Loving Dirk as she did, her own safety meant nothing unless she could save him, too. Stronger than her fear of Jade, stronger than any other emotion, was her feeling for him.

If she had to risk Jade's wrath, her perverse capacity for cruelty, so be it. There was still time to save Dirk. If only she had time to think, to plan. But there was no time. As if she were about to dive into a freezing sea, Melora drew a deep, steadying breath. "I want Lady Fairfax to know I am here," she told Nancy. "Go and ask her to come in."

Nancy stared down at her, looking like a plump, frightened rabbit. "You don't understand—Lady Fairfax and his lordship—"

"I know all about that," Melora said. "Get her to come in. Quickly."

"But you don't know what her ladyship's like when she's in one of her tempers.

"Call her at once."

She spoke with every ounce of determination she could muster. And even as she lay here naked under her nightdress with her hands bound, her tone must have carried a certain authority. Nancy hesitated a moment, then went out into the hall.

"In here, if you please, my lady."

"I knew it! The steward was lying——" Jade took a few steps into the Blue Chamber, then stopped short. Her lips drew back in pure animal rage.

"Where is he?"

"The steward spoke the truth," Melora said quietly. "Lord Rokeby's not at home."

"But he was here. He spent last night with you." She glanced at the bonds that held Melora's wrists, and the fury in her eyes gave way to contempt. "Now that he knows what you are, he isn't treating you like a delicate flower any longer. He is teaching you how to please him. And you're more than willing to satisfy him——any way he asks."

"I've never satisfied him——not in the way you mean."

If she was to best Jade, she must assert herself at once. "You think I'm here like this, of my own free will? If you do, you're a fool, Jade Fairfax."

Jade advanced on her, but she forced herself to go on speaking. "Rokeby had me kidnapped. I'm his prisoner. He's given orders that I'm to be kept here, under guard, until he returns to London."

Until after the king is dead, and Dirk has been charged with the assassination.

"He means to take you with him on the royal progress," Jade said.

"You are mistaken. I've told you——"

"Why should I believe anything you might say? You're a deceitful little trollop——you lied about being Grenville's cousin. You're lying now."

"Why should I bother to lie to you?"

The sheer arrogance of the question caught Jade off-balance. This was the way, the only way to prevail, Melora told herself.

301

"You're trying to save your skin," she said. Her eyes moved to the ropes that bound Melora to the bed.

"We're not alone, Jade," Melora reminded her.

"Surely you don't think that the maid, or any of the other servants, would dare to interfere with me for your sake?"

"If you are fool enough to—to harm me, Rokeby will get the truth out of them as soon as he sets foot in the house again. They'll tell him what happened to escape punishment."

Melora paused long enough to allow her words to sink in before she went on. "Rokeby means nothing to me. If you set me free, help me to get out of here, I swear, he won't ever see me again."

Jade gave her a long, searching look that seemed to penetrate to the very core of her being. "Are you trying to tell me you would disappear, go back to whatever gutter Dirk Grenville found you in?"

"He found me singing in a tavern in Northumberland," Melora said evenly. "And you're right, I would not be satisfied to go back to that way of life."

Jade stood looking down at Melora, who sensed that for this split second her fate, and Dirk's, hung in the balance.

"I can't return to Whitehall, now that you and Rokeby know me for what I am," she went on. "I would not be safe anywhere in London any longer."

"But if you mean to advance yourself, where can you start, except in London?"

"I wish to go to France," Melora said. "You saw my performance in the masque. You know I have talent. I could make my fortune in the theaters in Paris, as my mother did. I would be seen by any number of noblemen, all as wealthy and powerful as Rokeby. I might catch the fancy of King Louis himself."

She kept her gaze locked on Jade's. She had the advantage, however briefly; she must not waver for a second.

"You're ambitious enough, I'll give you credit for that." Jade conceded. "But how do you mean to get to get across the

Channel—assuming I were to give you the chance to get out of the house?"

Melora permitted herself a faint smile. "I thought perhaps you might advance my passage money. And a little extra, to help me set myself up in proper style."

Jade gave her a grudging look of admiration. "And why should I agree to any such bargain?"

"Isn't it obvious? You want Rokeby. I want to leave England. Help me to get away, and we'll both gain what we're after."

But Jade was not prepared to give in so easily. "Rokeby will know someone helped you to escape."

"I'm sure between us we can work out some plausible explanation for my disappearance," Melora said.

Jade turned her eyes on Nancy. "I suppose we could make it appear that your maid set you free."

"Oh, no—please. Mistress Melora, don't let her put the blame on me. I couldn't go against his lordship's orders. But I tried to make it as easy on you as I could. Didn't I?"

Melora gave her a reassuring smile. "Don't be afraid, Nancy. Do as I say, and you will be far away from here before Lord Rokeby returns.

The maid gave her a bewildered look. "Where would I go?" she asked.

Melora longed to tell her the truth, but this was neither the time nor the place. "I cannot leave for France without a maid to attend me," she said.

Again she caught an unwilling flicker of admiration in Jade's eyes. "We will begin by untying your wrists," Jade said. She reached into the folds of her cloak and drew out a small jeweled dagger.

"Here, you." She handed the weapon to Nancy. "Cut those ropes."

Although Nancy's hands were unsteady, she obeyed with alacrity. After Melora was free and on her feet, Jade and Melora laid their plans, while the maid listened in silence.

Nancy helped Melora to change back to the woolen dress

and cloak she had been wearing when she had been kidnapped and brought here. Lady Jade left the Blue Chamber and created a diversion by confronting Rokeby's steward, who was hovering at the head of the stairs. While she indulged herself in a fit of temper that held the fearful attention of both the steward and every other servant within hearing distance, Nancy led Melora down the hall in the opposite direction. Together they descended the back stairs and went out by the nearest door.

The carriage stood waiting at the back of the house. The coat of arms emblazoned on the door caught the morning sunlight. Melora and Nancy climbed inside. Moments later, Jade appeared and began giving orders to her coachman. "You are to take me to Whitehall," she said. "This other lady and her maid will be going on to the docks. You will then book passage for them on the first ship bound across the Channel."

Melora sat back on the soft leather seat. Nancy, wide-eyed and silent, kept close beside her. Jade seated herself opposite them. The coachman cracked his whip and the carriage moved around to the front of the house, down the drive, and into stream of other vehicles that crowded the Strand.

When Melora caught sight of the palace, she leaned forward. "I'll have the money now, Lady Fairfax."

Jade's face tightened with resentment, but she reached into her cloak, took out her purse, and handed it over. Melora inclined her head slightly, then opened the purse and counted the coins. "There's enough here to pay our passage to France," she said. "But I will need more, for proper lodgings and a new wardrobe."

"I don't travel about with large sums of money on my person."

"In that case, I'll take those earrings you're wearing. They should bring a tidy sum."

Jade stiffened, and for a moment Melora feared that she had overreached herself. Then Jade slipped the diamonds from her ears and gave them to Melora. "I do believe that if you arrived in France barefooted and wearing only your shift, you would make your fortune."

"It's quite possible," Melora conceded. "But the money I will get when I pawn these earrings will help to smooth my way."

The carriage halted at the entrance to the palace courtyard, and Jade descended, with the assistance of her footman.

Melora watched her disappear into the crowd. Only when the carriage started off again was she able to draw an easy breath.

Nancy allowed herself to speak at last. "I thought she might change her mind, right up until the last minute," she said. "I was that scared—"

"So was I," Melora admitted. "I still am."

"But you're free now, and you have all that money. And the earrings, too." She hesitated, then added timidly, "I've never been anyplace except London. It'll seem queer, living over there in France."

With Jade gone, there was no longer any reason to keep up the pretense. "We're not going to France."

"But where—"

"Only as far as the docks. Then I am coming back to White-hall."

"Oh, but we can't. You promised to get me away—you said—"

"I said I could not leave for France without a maid to attend me."

"But you told Lady Fairfax—"

"I told her what she wanted to hear. Otherwise, I never would have gotten away." She put a reassuring hand on Nancy's arm.

"But I'll get caught for sure. Lady Jade is certain to recognize me—or his lordship will." She gave Melora a look of deep reproach.

"You won't have to see either of them again, not ever. Trust me."

It was mid-morning when the carriage halted at the crowded London docks. The coachman remained in his seat, while the footman got down. Before he could set off in search of a packet boat, Melora opened the carriage door.

"A moment, if you please," she said. The footman paused, recognizing the voice of authority. "I do not intend to wait in this stuffy carriage while you find us passage. Help me down at once."

"It may take some time to find a boat bound for France," the man said.

"All the more reason I should take some light refreshments before I sail," Melora said. She looked about her. "That inn over there looks like a respectable place."

She reached into the purse Jade had given her, and handed him a shilling. Then, with the footman clearing a way through the crowd before them, and followed by a bewildered Nancy, Melora moved across the cobblestones to the inn door, her head held high. None of the passersby who saw her would have guessed at the tumult that seethed inside her.

When she and Nancy were seated in the private parlor, she said, "I'm going back to the palace alone. You will return to Sussex."

She took a few coins from Jade's purse and put them in her pocket, along with the diamond earrings. Then she handed the purse to Nancy. "The rest is for you. It will pay your way back to your home."

"It'll do much more than that," Nancy said, still stunned by her unexpected windfall. "A new cottage, maybe. A cow and some hens and—" She broke off and looked at Melora anxiously.

"Begging your pardon, it won't be safe for you in London, either. You said so yourself."

Safe. Would she ever feel really safe again? "I must return to the palace. I have no choice." Melora rose and put her arm around the maid and kissed her. Then she turned and left the parlor.

Outside, the sunlight was warm on her face. She stood for a moment, looking at the river. She felt a brief stir of envy for Nancy, who would soon be home, and out of danger.

But she could not linger here. She turned and was swallowed up in the jostling crowd. Quickly she headed for the nearest landing, where she could hire a boat to take her back to Whitehall.

Chapter Twenty-two

"You see, she is here, as I said she'd be!" Bronwen scooped up her rune stones, thrust them into their pouch, and rose from the rush-strewn floor of the shed.

Osric and Caleb stared at one another. After having known the old Welshwoman for so long, they should have come to accept her peculiar gifts as a matter of course, but they still stood in awe of her.

"We were just goin' to set out lookin' for you, mistress." A grin split Caleb's broad, weatherbeaten face. "But this mornin', here was Bronwen, tellin' us to wait."

Melora's first impulse, on arriving at Whitehall, had been to go directly to Queen Anne's chambers, to tell her of Rokeby's plan. But caution had warned her to stop at the shed outside the palace wall, and take council with her friends.

Now, as they gathered about her, she was comforted by their warm welcome. "We've been scouring the city since you disappeared," Osric told her.

She hesitated, then told herself that there was no point in avoiding the truth, no matter how painful it might be. "And what of Lord Grenville? Has he been searching for me, too?"

"Well, now, ye see, mistress—" Caleb shuffled his feet and looked down at the floor. "I gave him yer letter. But I tried to tell him there must've been some mistake. You never would've gone traipsin' off like that without a word to any of us. But he wouldn't listen. Out he went with a face like a thundercloud. Ain't none of us seen him since."

Although Caleb had refused to accept the contents of the letter at face value, Dirk had not hesitated to believe she had deserted him for another man. Trust was a part of loving. How long would it take before he came to trust her?

"I was forced to write the letter. I'll explain all that as soon as I see him again. Right now, I must get into the palace and find her majesty."

"You are too late," Osric said. "She has already left."

"They've gone, the lot of 'em," said Caleb. "An' a fine sight they were. All them carriages, with the high-steppin' horses, the brass on the harnesses jinglin'. An' the coachmen an' footmen decked out in their new livery."

A wave of despair washed over her. She had been so sure that their majesties would not set out on their royal progress before tomorrow, accompanied by their courtiers. Lady Jade must have thought so, too; otherwise, she would not have come to the townhouse this morning in search of Rokeby.

"When did they leave?"

"Only a few hours ago," Osric told her. "They're going to the theater first, and afterward they——"

"The theater?" She took heart once more. "Then they'll be returning to the palace before dark."

She would still have an opportunity to speak privately with Queen Anne before she went to find Dirk. She would swallow her pride and try to convince Dirk that Rokeby had forced her to write that damnable letter.

But Bronwen was shaking her head. "Their majesties and the royal party are not coming back here. They mean to go straight on to a banquet, the whole lot of them."

"A banquet? But where——"

"At the Spanish grandee's new house in Stepney."

"You mean the Marquis de Carvajal?"

Bronwen nodded. "Aye, that's the one. Lady Octavia's lover. Her ladyship's had me read the cards or cast the stones for her

309

every day since you left. She wants to be certain her fine suitor will marry her before the year's out. But the foolish creature told me much more than I wished to tell her. They'll not be wed, she and her Spaniard—not ever."

Melora's brow furrowed. Their majesties had gone to the theater. But King James did not make it a practice to attend public playhouses. Why should he, when any company of players in London would consider it an honor to be invited to perform at the palace?

But this time he was making an exception, and she thought she knew the reason: Rokeby had persuaded his majesty to undertake the progress so that he might show himself off before his subjects and try to win their admiration.

What better place to start than at a theater filled with Londoners from every walk of life? Prosperous merchants and their wives, soldiers, sailors, seamstresses, blacksmiths, weavers, carters, and raucous young apprentices, as well as elegant ladies and gentlemen—all were avid theatergoers. Hawkers of apples, nuts, sweetmeats, and ale sold their wares.

Melora had assumed that Rokeby would wait until the royal progress had reached some remote part of the countryside, close to the border, before he ordered the king's assassination. But the viscount, with his devious turn of mind, might decide to strike sooner, for some hidden purpose of his own.

"Does any of you know which playhouse they've gone to?" she demanded.

"It's called the Fortune," said Bronwen.

Quickly Melora searched her memory. The King's Men performed at the Globe; the Queen's, at the Red Bull. The Fortune was the theater that housed the Prince's Men, a company patronized by young Henry, the king's handsome fourteen-year-old son. It lay to the north, outside the city walls, near Golden Lane, in Cripplegate. To get there, she would have to cross most of London, traveling by hired coach through a maze of narrow, crowded streets, then go on for another half-mile, jolting across Finsbury Fields.

"Has Lord Grenville gone with them?" Melora asked. In spite of the urgency of her mission, she could not put Dirk out of her mind.

"Like as not he has," Caleb shook his head. "Ain't none of us seen him since he went stalkin' out of here, like the hounds o' hell were snappin' at his heels—"

Melora cut him short. "Go out and find me a coach, as quickly as you can."

He stared at her in dismay. "You're not goin' off again so soon, mistress?"

"I must," she said, with a look that was meant to discourage further discussion. But Caleb stood his ground.

"You'll not stir without Osric an' me to look after you, mistress."

Even if she could have talked him out of it, she decided not to try; it might be wiser to have him and Osric come along. It would not be easy to get to their majesties once the performance had started. She might have to call upon Caleb's strength and Osric's nimble wits. "Come along, then. I will have need of both of you," she said.

Caleb gave a nod of satisfaction and went out in search of a coach, with Osric at his heels.

She turned to Bronwen. "Aren't you going to cast your rune stones again, and caution me not to go?" She gave the old woman a slanting half-smile.

But there was no trace of humor in the thin, wrinkled face. "When has a young girl in love ever heeded an old woman's counsel? You'll go, no matter what I say. You'll venture wherever you must to get to your lover's arms."

"It's the queen I'm seeking, and his majesty."

Bronwen went on as if Melora had not spoken. "His lordship's a proud one, and quick to anger. He has not yet learned to trust any woman completely, not even you. You must teach him, and it will not be easy. That letter you left for him wounded him sorely, but you will find a way to prove to him that the words were not your own."

311

"Sweet Jesú! You have no need of stones or painted cards any longer to see into the future, do you?"

"Not *your* future, mistress." She put a bony hand under Melora's chin. "It was meant from your first meeting that your path and his should be joined. Now they are one. I told you so on the night of the solstice, remember?"

"I remember." But where might that one path take her and Dirk? To a shining future of love and fulfillment? Or to the shadow of the headsman's ax?

She dared not ask Bronwen, for she feared the answer.

The silk flag that fluttered in the breeze high above the Fortune told all those in sight of the playhouse that there was to be a performance this afternoon. A playbill on the wall proclaimed in bold, ornate lettering: *The Devil's Bride*. It was not a new play, but a perennial favorite, with its melodramatic flourishes, remarkable scenic effects, and morally uplifting ending.

The coach carrying Melora, Osric, and Caleb had made its agonizingly slow progress through the usual tangle of carriages, carts, sedan chairs, and pedestrians, so that at times she had feared the play might be over before they arrived at Golden Lane.

But it was mid-afternoon when they finally alighted from the coach. She would still have time to try to carry off the plan she had hastily contrived with her friends during their ride across the city.

Led by Melora, they found their way backstage. The familiar surroundings took her back to the years when she had accompanied her father to his own playhouse, and helped ease the knot of tension inside her.

She heard the players on the stage declaiming their lines in ringing tones. Other actors, clad in silks, velvets, taffetas, and damasks, were milling about, waiting for their cues; stagehands stood ready to work the machinery that let gods and goddesses down from above, or raised devils and ghosts up through the trapdoors in the floor. A tower of painted canvas, stretched on a wooden frame, stood in one corner.

"Now then, mistress," Caleb asked. "Which of these lads is it to be?"

Melora looked about quickly, and her eyes lighted on a slender, smooth-faced boy clad in a blue gown trimmed with gold lace. He wore an elaborate lace headdress over a wig of long dark hair, and held a beribboned bouquet of bluebells and daisies.

"He must be the one who is to play the devil's bride," she said.

Even while she tried to fix her attention on the dialogue from the stage, she felt a brief stir of pity for the boy. This was to have been a most remarkable opportunity for him: his chance to perform in a leading role, before their majesties and half the court. But if all went as she hoped, he would be snatched away before his moment of triumph.

"It's easy enough for you to keep your composure," the boy was saying to one of the other players, who wore a gown of plum-colored velvet, well padded fore and aft, to create the illusion that he was a stout, matronly lady. "You won't have to make that leap from the top of the tower to the stage below."

But his plaintive words only drew a derisive laugh from his fellow actor. "Cheer up, Ned. Better you should risk a few bruises than be forced to yield your maiden's body to the devil's lewd embraces."

"That'll be enough from both of you," said a tall, bearded man. His deep voice carried an tone of unmistakable authority that silenced the other two. "Remember that your royal patron, Prince Henry, will be watching you, along with their majesties. You will be mindful of the honor, and perform so as to be a credit to the company."

Then he caught sight of Melora and her friends. "No strangers are allowed backstage during the performance."

Melora gave him her most graceful curtsy, her most dazzling

313

smile. "If you please, sir—we do but seek permission to earn a few farthings by entertaining the audience during the intervals. Osric is a most skillful acrobat and juggler, while Caleb—" Since Caleb had not brought Old Bruin with him, she was at a loss to say how he might entertain the audience, but there was no need.

"Be off with you," the bearded man said, with a impatient wave of his hand. "I have no time for such foolery, today of all days."

"Perhaps if we might speak with the stage manager," she began, but he cut her off short.

"You are speaking with him, mistress. I am Hector Tregallen, stage manager of this company, and I am ordering you to leave at once."

The stage manager was an important part of every company, for he carried out all the complicated duties that kept the performance running smoothly. He was in charge of the properties: skulls, tombs, caskets, trees, weapons, caldrons, and a host of others. Besides taking care of technical details, he also had to keep order among the actors, to settle their quarrels and calm their fears. Today, with the royal party having decided, at the last moment, to attend the Fortune, his task was even more demanding than usual.

"Allow me to show you a small demonstration of my skills, good master," said Osric.

"Be off with you!" The stage manager drew back his arm, but the dwarf leaped aside, turned a double somersault, then went scrambling up one of the ropes used to move the elaborate scenery. Holding on with his legs, he drew three glittering balls from his doublet and began juggling them in the air.

Actors and stagehands paused to stare up at him. "Perhaps he could play the bride," said the actor in the plum-colored gown. "He's nimble enough, and it is plain he has no fear of heights."

The boy actor flushed. "Mock me all you please. But you need only come mincing into the banquet hall and seat yourself

314

at the table. You will not be called upon to risk life and limb."

He threw a pleading look at the stage manager. "The tower's a foot too tall at least, Master Tregallen. And during rehearsal it swayed so that I became giddy."

"Stop your accursed whining and bickering at once." The stage manager did not raise his voice, but his implacable stare silenced them both. Then he threw back his head. "You, up there," he called to Osric. "Enough of your antics. Get down."

He strode forward, as if he meant to climb up and drag Osric down himself; but a brightly colored ball came spinning from above. It landed at his feet, so that he had to step aside to keep from tripping over it.

"Down, damn you!"

While the others were engrossed in watching the clash between the dwarf and the stage manager, Caleb reached out, clapped a powerful hand over the mouth of the boy actor in his blue and gold gown, closed the other about his waist, and carried him off.

Osric slid halfway down the rope, then flipped over and hung his head down. "You've seen but the smallest sample of my art. If I might show you more—"

"I'll see the back of you, and quickly. Or I'll have my stage-hands boot you out of here."

"Come along, Osric," said Melora, with feigned disappointment. "And you, too, Caleb." She spoke into the shadows at the edge of the backstage area, to create the illusion that she could still see Caleb. But he and the boy had already disappeared.

She gave a deep sigh, then blinked rapidly, as if she were fighting back tears. Osric leaped down; she took his hand. "Perhaps we will do better in one of the other playhouses," she said. They went off, both doing their best to look crestfallen. But once they were out of the range of the stage manager's sight, they hurried down a short passage lined with doors on either side.

"Over here."

In a storage room near the end of the passage, the hapless

young player crouched, stripped to the waist, wide-eyed and shaking with fear, while Caleb stood over him. He thrust the boy's blue-and-gold bridal gown, headdress, wig, and bouquet into Melora's arms.

"Is he all right?" she asked.

Caleb nodded. He glared down at the quivering player. "Ye won't be harmed—not so long as ye keep quiet 'til we're out of here and well away. Otherwise . . ." He jerked the boy to his feet, then doubled a huge, hamlike fist and shook it menacingly. "One sound out of ye—only one—an' ye'll wish ye'd broken yer scrawny neck leapin' out o' that tower."

He hauled the wretched young actor to his feet, shoved him into the passageway, then dragged him out the back door. He was to keep his captive hidden in one of the thickets of willow and alder trees that dotted Finsbury Fields, until the performance was over.

The first step of Melora's plan had worked better than she had dared hope; but the part that still lay ahead was infinitely more difficult. If Dirk was up in the gallery with the royal party, how was she to draw his attention and get him to come down to her without revealing her identity to anyone else in the audience?

"Hurry, mistress," Osric urged.

She took off her cloak and unhooked her dress. "I'll need help with my costume," she told him.

As she spoke, her heart began to thud against her chest and her legs went weak. It had been years since she had last seen a performance of *The Devil's Bride*. From the lines of dialogue she had managed to catch, she guessed that she had only a few minutes before she must make her entrance.

If her inner turmoil was reflected in her face and bearing, she surely would look the part of the terrified young maiden forced into an unholy bargain to wed Satan.

Although her long-cherished dream of appearing on the London stage was about to come true, it had taken on the qualities of a nightmare. Her experience backstage with her

316

father's company had taught her that dialogue was frequently changed to suit the abilities of a particular performer. No matter, for she could improvise her lines until she found a way to send a private signal to Dirk.

Osric's long, nimble fingers dealt skillfully with the hooks and laces that fastened the elaborate wedding costume. Melora tried to smooth the bridal bouquet, which had been crushed somewhat during the young actor's struggle with Caleb.

"Where's that boy got to?" she heard the stage manager asking. "You, Seth—go and find him, at once."

Melora dared wait no longer. She could not even take the time to put on the dark wig. Instead, she pulled the bodkins from her hair, shook the thick, black waves down over her shoulders, and fastened the headdress in place. She managed to draw the front of the lace veil down so that it covered the upper half of her face.

Lifting her skirts, she hurried back along the passage. The stage manager threw her a black look, but she brushed past him, her face averted, and kept going until she was out on the stage.

The Fortune was a circular structure, with curving tiers of seats rising on three sides, and the stage jutting out into the pit. The brilliant sunlight came streaming in through the open roof.

At the back of the stage was stretched a painted canvas representing the interior of a manor house. On a dais stood a group of musicians with lutes, mandolins, violins, and flutes.

She raised her eyes to the first tier of the gallery, where a royal box had been hastily improvised for the king and queen and the most important members of their party; it was partitioned off with heavy curtains of purple velvet.

The rest of the courtiers filled the remainder of the semicircular tier. The attention of the audience was divided; some watched the progress of the play, while others could scarcely take their eyes from the king and queen and their party.

She had made the right decision, she told herself. If she had dared try a direct approach the king's box, she would surely

317

have been stopped by the phalanx of his guards, armed with their heavy pikes. They would have carried her off before she could get close enough to say a word to their majesties.

If only she could find Dirk, and signal him to come down. But he was only one in a crowd of splendidly-dressed lords and ladies whose brilliant costumes and blazing jewels merged into a blur of color.

"Why look you so sorrowful, my daughter?" She started as a portly actor in a purple doublet and yellow breeches approached her and spoke in sonorous tones.

Although it was plain enough that he waited for her to respond, she could only lower her head and wring her hands in a gesture of pathos. The actor was puzzled by her silence, but he was experienced enough to carry off the awkward situation with skill. He took her hand and led her to the center of the stage.

He bent his face close to her ear. "Alas, Father, my true love is far away . . ." he prompted in a whisper. When she remained silent and immobile, her head drooping still lower, he seized her upper arm in a hard grasp.

"My true love . . ." he repeated the cue with growing impatience. He furrowed his brow and Melora went cold all over. Had the lack of hard, wiry muscle in her upper arm already betrayed her? Then a shaft of sunlight from the opening in the roof touched her face, playing over the delicate jawline, the small chin; it illuminated the high, rounded swell of her breasts.

She heard the harsh intake of the player's breath. He had discovered her deception. Self-possessed though he was, the sight of a female on the public stage had shaken him to the very core of his being. Under his thick makeup, his heavy-jowled face went red, then purple.

But he was determined not to show his agitation to the audience, certainly not with the royal party looking down at the stage. He signaled to the musicians on the dais.

"Let us have a merry tune for my daughter, to lighten her spirits," he improvised.

The baffled musicians, now realizing that something was serious amiss, began a lively country dance. "You will pay dearly for this," the portly actor whispered to her under cover of the music.

She tried to ignore him. She raised her head and scanned the gallery once more. She thought she saw Rokeby, a satin-clad figure, seated close to the king. But where was Dirk? There was no longer any time to try to pick him out of those in the lowest tier. She must take action without delay.

She turned to the musicians and drew a deep breath. "Cease, in heaven's name," she declaimed. "My heart is heavy and thy merriment does but mock my sorrow."

This was a complete departure from the script. She was sure there was not an actor on the stage who did not realize that something was wrong. But did anyone but the portly man beside her know that a woman stood among them, here on the stage?

She turned and walked across to the dais, then stood before the lute player. Before he could sense her intention, she took the instrument from him. With slow, measured steps, she returned to the front of the stage. She cradled the instrument, then struck a few chords.

Somewhere up there in the gallery, Dirk sat watching, listening. He had to be there. He would hear and remember that far-off autumn twilight, and the ravine with its wind-gnarled trees beside the Great North Road.

And what then? If her letter, written under duress, had really destroyed his faith in her, would her song, the intensity of feeling in her voice, be enough to overcome his distrust?

She tilted back her head, heedless of the sunlight that gilded her delicate features: the thrust of her breasts, the curve of her waist. It no longer mattered that her secret was revealed for all the audience to see. Her voice rang out, high and pure.

He's gone . . . he's gone away,
To stay a little while . . .

319

>*But he's coming back to me,*
>*Though he ride a thousand miles . . .*

When she had finished, the audience, from the groundlings in the pit to the courtiers in the gallery, were silent, caught up in the bewitching spell of the ballad. Then they signaled their approval with a ripple of applause that grew until it filled the theater. The actors took heart and went on with the play.

Melora waited for the act to draw to a close, so that she might hurry backstage and see if Dirk was waiting there for her.

She stole a quick sideways glance and caught sight of the manager glaring at her from the wings. He beckoned to one of the actors. The man strolled off the stage in a seemingly casual manner.

After a brief exchange with Tregallen, he came back, heading straight for Melora with a measured, purposeful stride. Before she realized what was about to happen, he lifted her in his arms and carried her backstage.

The audience accepted this unexpected turn in the complicated plot, and leaned forward, eager to discover what would happen next.

As soon as they were backstage, the actor set her down. The stage manager advanced on her, his bearded face dark with anger. "Speak, you abandoned creature. Who put you up to this mischief?"

"No one, I swear it. Only I am responsible. But I had no choice—"

"Don't try to deceive me, or it will be the worse for you. Our company has many rivals. Which of them arranged for you to come here and make a public display of yourself, today of all days?"

She stared at him in dismay. She had cause to know that there was endless rivalry between London's acting companies; a jealous manager would stop at nothing to destroy a more successful troupe of players.

"Answer me. Who sent you here?" He seized her by the

320

shoulders and began to shake her so hard that she thought her neck would snap.

"This has nothing to do—with your company—take your hands off me—"

"If you speak quickly, I may possibly be persuaded to let you go. Otherwise, you will find yourself before a magistrate before this day is over."

He spoke in deadly earnest. She looked about in desperation: still no sign of Dirk. She had made her dangerous gamble, and she had failed. If Dirk had been up in the gallery and had recognized her, the ballad had not moved him. Perhaps it had left him angry with himself for having let down his guard, however briefly; for having allowed himself to fall in love with her.

The manager turned to one of the stagehands. "Bring a coach and order the driver to wait until the performance is over."

"A moment, Master Tregallen." Even before she turned her head, she recognized Rokeby's voice. His tone was pleasant and amiable, but she was not deceived. She wheeled around, poised for flight. "My dear Mistress Standish," he said. "This is an unexpected pleasure."

Chapter Twenty-three

The stage manager looked at Rokeby in consternation. "Your lordship." His legs were unsteady, but he managed a creditable bow. "The wench has committed an affront to public morals. She and her friends will pay dearly for it. I entreat your pardon for this—this outrage."

"You are not to blame," Rokeby reassured him. He sighed and shook his head. "I know this unfortunate young lady well."

"You know her?"

"And her family, too. She is a cause of deep distress to them, as you may well imagine. She appears perfectly normal for months at a time. But she is afflicted with a most unfortunate malady." He tapped his forehead meaningfully.

"He's lying—I'm not a—a lunatic—"

But both men ignored her frantic protest. "Surely she should not be roaming about unguarded," Tregallen said.

"Her parents allowed their natural affection for their daughter to overcome their good sense. She was kept at home, and watched over carefully, but she managed to elude her caretakers. She's possessed by a diabolic cleverness, like so many of her kind."

"May I ask where you mean to take her, my lord?

"Where else but to Bedlam? Even her parents now see the necessity—"

Bedlam. A living hell where poor, demented creatures were

shut away behind thick walls and iron bars; beaten, tormented by their keepers; displayed to visitors who paid to be entertained by their bizarre antics.

Tregallen's concern for his own reputation gave way to a stir of pity. But he could not forget that his future and that of his company were at stake here.

"Their majesties—our patron, Prince Henry—"

"They saw that something had gone amiss, but I doubt they suspect the truth. I must congratulate your players. They are carrying on in the highest traditions of their craft."

His hand closed on Melora's arm. "Have no fear, Master Tregallen. I shall look after the young lady. I leave it to you to see that the performance goes on as planned."

"But how can I carry on, my lord? Without the boy who was to have played the devil's bride—"

Rokeby shifted impatiently. "Find another actor to take his place, without delay."

The stage manager cast his eyes upward, as if in silent prayer. Then he bowed to Rokeby and hurried off to look over the waiting players. Thoroughly absorbed in the task of making last-minute changes, he did not spare another glance at Lord Rokeby or the young lady.

Rokeby placed his arm around Melora's waist and held her against him in a grip of iron. She looked about for Osric, but he was nowhere to be seen; as for Caleb, he was far off in some thicket, standing guard over his unhappy captive.

"Come along, my dear," said Rokeby, his voice still amiable. It would do no good to struggle or cry out. Rokeby had convinced the stage manager that she was a lunatic, and such behavior would only confirm the viscount's words.

Rokeby eased her toward the door leading to the passageway. "I'll see you to a place where you'll be well cared for."

"I'll see you in hell first."

Melora felt a swift surge of relief at the sound of Dirk's voice. He stood barring the way, his booted feet planted apart, his hand resting on the hilt of his sword.

He had heard her song and had understood the depth of feeling beneath the familiar words, the message meant only for him. Her love had reached out to him. It had bridged the gulf of distrust, of misunderstanding, and had drawn him to her side. His dark, gold-flecked eyes held hers. For one brief moment, nothing else mattered.

Then she felt the pressure of Rokeby's hard chest against her back. She writhed and twisted, as she tried to break free, to run to Dirk; but Rokeby's arm tightened about her, bruising her ribs, crushing the breath from her body. Then, out of the corner of her eye, she saw the viscount's beringed hand dart into the folds of his cloak. A ray of light flashed along the blade of his dagger. Then she felt it pressing against her throat.

Dirk, his fingers already wrapped around the hilt of his sword, made no move to draw the weapon from its scabbard. "Let her go."

"Not a chance. She is coming with me."

"I must protest, my lord," the stage manager said. "You told me the lady was afflicted in her mind. That you were here to help her."

Rokeby ignored the man. With Melora firmly in his grasp, he took a step back, then another. He was edging her toward the door leading to the passage.

She dared not cry out or make the slightest move to free herself. Her skirt brushed against the side of the tower, a tall painted cylinder made of heavy canvas and stretched across a wooden frame; it stood mounted on wheels, so that it could be drawn out on the stage for the final act.

The actors who had been milling about backstage, waiting to make their entrances, the scene movers, and the tiremen who helped with the changes of costumes—all of them were stunned by this new and baffling turn of events. They backed away warily, clearing a path to the exit. If even one of them had found the courage to come to Melora's aid, he would not have dared to take the risk, as long as the viscount held the blade at her throat.

She kept her eyes fixed on Dirk's face and tried to find a measure of reassurance there. His love for her had proved stronger than his outraged pride, the hurt he had surely felt when he had read her letter. But had she been reunited with Dirk only to be parted from him again—this time forever?

She heard one of the scene shifters cry out, "Up there! In the tower—"

From the corner of her eye, she caught a glimpse of a small figure leaping down from the painted canvas tower. A glittering ball went spinning, arcing through the air. It found its mark. Rokeby gasped as the ball struck the arm that held the dagger, thudded hard against the point of his elbow.

The viscount gave a gasp of pain. The dagger that lay across Melora's throat wavered, slid downward, and clattered to the floor. She cried out as she felt a stinging sensation along her collarbone. It was a moment before she realized that the blade had slashed her skin.

Osric sprang to her side and kicked the dagger out of Rokeby's reach. Rokeby swore, then swung his arm in a back-handed blow, but Osric ducked and spun away.

Melora broke free from Rokeby's restraining grip and ran toward Dirk. His eyes were fixed on her wound, on the blood that streamed down, soaking through the blue silk bodice. A wordless animal sound came from his throat.

She touched his arm. "It's all right, Dirk—the cut's not deep—"

If he heard her, he gave no sign. His skin was stretched tightly across his high, angular cheekbones. His pupils widened so that his eyes burned with a black, unholy flame. His lips drew back from his teeth. She felt the muscles tighten beneath the sleeve of his close-fitting doublet. And all at once she knew that under the silk and velvet of the courtier's garb lay the untamed savagery of the Grenvilles, lords of the northern border, a law unto themselves for countless generations.

Rokeby had threatened the life of his woman, had wounded her. Rokeby would pay for that.

Osric seized her hand and pulled her aside.

Dirk whipped his sword from its scabbard, his eyes still fixed on Rokeby. Quick and fierce as a tiger, he sprang. The viscount took a step back, his pale gray eyes fixed on the supple steel blade. He tore off his cloak, flung it away, then drew his sword and shifted so that his body was sideways to Dirk's.

Melora had heard of Rokeby's skill as a duelist. She clutched Osric's hand tightly and her heart hammered in her throat as the two men closed in combat.

Dirk's arm shot forward in a full-length reach, but Rokeby parried skillfully. Steel rang on steel.

Dirk lunged again, and again Rokeby parried. The viscount had his back to the stage entrance. Step by step, Dirk was forcing him backward. From the stage came the voices of the actors booming out their lines, oblivious to what was taking place a few yards away.

Thrust and parry, thrust and riposte. Now Dirk was forcing Rokeby out of the wings and onto the stage.

"Call my wayward daughter and say I would speak with—" The portly actor who played the role of the bride's father broke off in the middle of his line.

Dirk lunged again and Rokeby darted to the left, vainly trying to shift direction, but he was too late. Now both combatants moved into full view of the audience.

A murmur of bewilderment went up from groundlings in the pit; it spread upward to the tiers of the gallery. The late-afternoon sunlight poured down from the opening above. A dazzling ray of gold ran along the length of their swords.

One by one, the rest of the actors on the stage fell silent, as if frozen in place by a sorcerer's spell.

Then from the royal box came a ringing shout. "Stop! I command you!" Even before Melora looked up, she recognized the king's heavy Scottish burr.

But if Dirk heard his majesty's command, he ignored it. He was oblivious to everything but his driving need to avenge the injury to his woman.

Osric's restraining hand clutched at Melora's skirt. "No, mistress! You must not—" She tore herself free and ran out onto the stage.

Rokeby thrust his shoulder against a standing iron candle holder. It swayed and went crashing to the floor, catching Dirk off-guard.

Rokeby was swift to follow up his advantage. Melora pressed her hand to her lips to stifle a cry. But Dirk had already regained his balance, and he sprang to the left. His blade struck Rokeby's with stunning force, but the viscount managed to keep hold of his weapon.

The king was on his feet. "Throw down your swords, I say!"

Rokeby, sweat pouring down his face and soaking through his satin doublet, lowered his sword, but Dirk lunged once more. The viscount was forced to parry and go on with the combat. But he was on the defensive now, giving ground, moving backward, toward the painted canvas backdrop stretched across the rear of the stage.

"Seize Grenville at once!" the king ordered his guards.

They came running down from the gallery toward the stage, their booted feet thundering on the wood floor, their pikes at the ready.

Melora lifted her skirt and ran to the front of the stage, where it jutted out into the pit. Heedless of the throbbing wound, the blood soaking her gown, she raised her head and fixed her eyes on the royal box. She knew there was no chance for complicated explanations, not yet.

"Treason!" she cried. And again, "Treason!" Her voice rang out across the crowded pit and up to the highest of the galleries. "Your life's in danger, sire!"

The guards came clambering onto the stage. The distraction caused Rokeby's eyes to waver for an instant. Dirk made one final lunge, and his blade pierced Rokeby's chest with such force that it pinned the viscount to the canvas backdrop behind him. Rokeby hung there for a moment, eyes wide with disbelief, mouth agape. Then he sagged forward and slid to the floor.

From somewhere in the gallery, a woman's anguished shriek rent the air.

"Take Grenville!" the king shouted. "Place him under arrest!"

"And his whore along with him!" It was the shrill, vengeful cry of Lady Jade.

Melora stared up at the royal box in shocked disbelief. Was it possible that the king believed Dirk to be the traitor? More likely, he was too panic-stricken to reason clearly. A phalanx of guards that had remained in the box closed in around him, the queen, and Prince Henry, and cleared their way from the gallery.

She tried to get to Dirk, but the guards moved between them, a solid wall of red and gold, hiding him from her view. Her knees began to give way. One of the guards seized hold of her and caught her before she could fall.

The Tower of London stood tall and somber against the crimson sky. It was sunset when the barge carrying Melora veered slightly, then came to a halt before the Traitor's Gate. From high on the battlements above, she heard the harsh cawing of the ravens. The sound brought back the terrifying vision of a traitor's head, impaled on a spike, on that long-ago afternoon; the torn flesh, the empty sockets where the sharp beaks had done their work. And she, a frightened child, had hidden her face against her father's shoulder.

But her father was far away now. And Dirk, where was he? She had not seen him since the guards had taken her from the stage and carried her out of the playhouse.

Had they brought him here in another boat? When would she see him again? A black wave of foreboding swept over her.

The side of the barge thumped against the stone landing. She tried to rise, but her knees buckled. The guard nearest her helped her to her feet.

"Come, mistress," he said. "Once you are inside, they'll send a woman to look to your wound."

She glanced down and saw that the front of her gown was stiff with dried blood. For the first time since Rokeby's dagger had slashed her flesh, she was aware of the throbbing pain. But it did not seem important, not now. "Lord Grenville—where have they taken him?"

The guard did not reply. He called out a command. The latticed gate set in the low stone arch creaked open, and he half-carried, half-dragged her up the steps, out of the sunlight, and into the shadowed entrance to the Tower.

"Where is Melora?" Dirk demanded. "What have they done with her?" He stopped pacing the floor of his cell and caught Pembroke's arm in an iron grip.

"Your lady's safe enough," Pembroke reassured him. "Calm yourself, Grenville."

"She was wounded. That bastard Rokeby—"

"Her wound is not serious. The gaoler's wife is caring for her." Dirk's hold slackened and the earl drew away, smoothing the sleeve of his black velvet doublet. "She'll come to no harm."

"She should not be here at all. She risked her life to save the king."

"And he will be told of the part she played, at the proper time," Pembroke promised.

"How long is she to remain in the Tower?"

"As to that, I cannot say. But I assure you—"

"I must speak with her."

"You should know that is beyond even my powers," the earl said.

"Then go to his majesty at once. Demand an order for her release."

"His majesty will see no one tonight," Pembroke told him. "He's confused, terrified. All these years he's lived in fear of meeting the same end as his father. And who can blame him?"

He sighed, and there was a trace of pity in his voice. "He believed Rokeby to be one of his most loyal followers. It won't be easy for him to accept that the man was plotting his death."

"But you will place the facts before him."

"When I do, there must be no room for the slightest doubt. I must have complete confessions from the Marquis de Carvajal, Ambrose Corbett, Oliver Babcock, and a dozen more."

"To hell with Carvajal and the rest. I'm only concerned for Melora."

"That's plain enough." The earl's thin lips curved in a fleeting smile. "But my first duty is to protect his majesty."

"Will you go to see her, before you leave the Tower?"

"I already have. The gaoler's wife gave her a sleeping draught." He started for the door. "You've not asked about your own release." He gave a short laugh. "If love can so addle the wits of a man like you, may heaven protect me from the malady."

He rapped on the door with his gloved fist to summon the guard. "You will have your audience with the king as soon as I can arrange it." Then he moved quickly into the torchlit corridor and disappeared from sight.

Chapter Twenty-four

Although it was long past midnight, Whitehall palace was still in turmoil. In the royal stables, cursing, sweating grooms and hostlers were unhitching the teams of sleek horses and leading them back to their stalls; manservants unloaded the mountains of luggage from the coaches; and distracted ladies' maids collided with one another in their efforts to ensure the careful handling of their mistresses' trunks and wig boxes. And all the while, the rumors went flying back and forth, growing more fantastic with each retelling.

"*The Devil's Bride* always was an unlucky play," said a gray-haired servingman. "My sister's boy—he was right there in the pit at the Fortune this afternoon, and he swears he seen a shadow fall across the stage. Then a great horned creature seized Lord Rokeby and made off with him."

"Great horned creature, my arse! 'Twas Grenville did the viscount in."

"Lord Grenville fought like a man possessed, so they say."

"He'll pay dear for killin' the king's favorite, see if he don't."

"But what was the cause of the duel? Do ye think it had anything to do with a plot against the throne?"

"Just because some daft young actor cries treason don't make it so."

A brief, uneasy hush fell over the stable. They eyed one another uneasily. The king's deepest fears had been aroused,

331

and no one was safe from suspicion—from Lord Grenville down to the lowliest groom.

A pert young maid came bustling in. "You there!" she called to one of the hostlers. "Don't unload that coach. My mistress wants only a change of horses. Hitch up another team, the fastest you can find. She means to set forth within the hour."

"An' who might yer mistress be, my dearie?" asked the sturdy young hostler.

"She is Lady Octavia Sutton," the girl answered, tossing her head so that a few auburn curls escaped from under her starched white cap. "And keep a civil tongue in your head. I am not your dearie."

"Lady Sutton's about to go off on the progress all by herself, is she?" he asked, with an impudent grin.

"My lady's plans are no concern of yours. See that her horses are well fed and watered, and be quick about it." The maid flounced out of the stables and headed for the palace.

In truth, she had no more notion of Lady Octavia's destination than did the young hostler. All she knew was that her mistress had been behaving most strangely ever since her return from the playhouse. One moment her ladyship's eyes were aglow, her cheeks flushed with excitement; the next, she lapsed into brooding silence.

The maid, on her ladyship's orders, had retrieved her jewel-case from the coach immediately upon their return from the theater. Lady Octavia had added several of her most valuable pieces, including the famous Sutton necklace, of gold scallop shells encrusted with diamonds, with a huge star sapphire at the center.

"What a pity the royal progress must be postponed," said Felicity Brandon. She had changed her brocaded gown for her nightdress and robe, and now sat resting against the velvet-covered headboard of her bed, with her legs tucked under her.

Since the royal party was to have proceeded from the play-

332

house to dine and spend the night at the newly leased mansion of the Marquis de Carvajal, no preparations had been made for dinner in the banquet hall of the palace. But Felicity had sent down to the kitchens for an ample repast, and two of the other ladies had come to her chamber to share the feast.

"I doubt the king means to make the journey at all." Lady Millicent de Vere reached for a honeycake sprinkled with walnuts.

"He has shut himself away in his private chambers with guards at every door," said Lady Alyson Waring.

"I've heard that Queen Anne means to flee to Scotland with the young princes and the princess, as soon as his majesty gives the word," Felicity said.

"And risk being captured by rebels along the way?" Millicent interrupted.

"Rebels? There has been no word of a full-scale rebellion, has there?" Alyson's voice was a trifle unsteady.

"One of the king's own guards told my maid that all the palace gates have already been barred," said Millicent.

"Surely his majesty's not expecting a mob to attack Whitehall?" Even the irrepressible Felicity felt a twinge of uneasiness at the thought, for the London mob was a force to be reckoned with.

The queen's ladies were too deeply engrossed in their speculations to notice Octavia Sutton, who had been hurrying along the corridor clutching a large parcel. The few words she had overheard about the barring of the gates had brought her to an abrupt halt.

She hovered outside Felicity's chamber door filled with mounting apprehension. She had to get out of the palace grounds tonight.

"And that's not all," said Millicent. "I've heard that troops are being dispatched to every seaport."

The parcel fell from Octavia's hands. She was unable to stifle her cry of dismay.

"Octavia, what are you doing out there?" Alyson called to her. "Come and join us."

"No—I can't stop—not now—" She bent to retrieve the package and went on down the corridor, her heavy cloak billowing around her.

The three of them stared after her. "Where do you suppose she is off to in such haste at this time of night?"

"Perhaps she is bound for Carvajal's house."

"But if the gates are locked—"

"She's so hot for her dashing marquis, she would pull bars down with her bare hands and fight her way through a whole troop of guards to get to his bed." Felicity giggled. "Carvajal must have a bigger one than his majesty's favorite stallion."

But they wasted no more time speculating on Octavia's infatuation with the Spanish nobleman. There were more important matters to be discussed.

"Has either of you seen Jade Fairfax since she left the playhouse?" asked Alyson.

Felicity shook her head. "I haven't. She made a shocking spectacle of herself—screeching out like a fishwife." Her hazel eyes narrowed. "And what did she mean about 'Grenville's whore'?"

"Jade was too overcome with Rokeby's death to know what she was saying." Millicent reached for another cake.

Alyson's brow furrowed in a puzzled frown. "It was no whore, but the boy actor who was seized by the guards. And he called out a warning to the king. Why do you suppose—"

"He may have lost his nerve at the last moment. Perhaps he was hoping to save his own neck."

"Or *her* own neck."

"Felicity, whatever do you mean?" asked Millicent.

"I'm not sure . . ." said Felicity. "It seemed to me that the 'devil's bride' bore a most striking resemblance to Lady Rosalind."

"She is away in Northumberland, and besides—"

"I've been wondering about that. Why would she run off

without a word to any of us? She left her new trunk behind. And her gowns are still hanging there in the armoire."

"Wherever she may have been all these weeks, she surely would not have returned to make a display of herself on the stage of the Fortune playhouse," Millicent protested. "She is a Grenville."

"And yet, there was something familiar about the actor who sang that tender ballad. You both remember Rosalind's performance in the masque. Her voice, the way she held her head . . ." Felicity leaned forward and the others moved closer.

Millicent's eyes widened in shocked disbelief. "Lady Rosalind Grenville, on the public stage? Don't be absurd."

Octavia tried to ignore the pressure of her heavy whalebone stays as she quickened her steps, rounded a corner, and descended a flight of stairs, bound for the courtyard. Her thoughts had been in a whirl ever since her brief meeting with her beloved Pedro that afternoon.

Even as the guards had been clearing a path through the noisy crowd outside the playhouse and helping the royal party get back to their waiting coaches, he had drawn her aside, gripped her shoulders, and spoken to her in an urgent undertone.

She was still bewildered by all he had said. Until now, although he had spoken to her in flowery words of his deep passion for her, and had taken her to his bed and set her senses aflame with his expert lovemaking, he had always found excuses to put off the visit to her father's estate, to make a formal request for her hand. He had hinted at important affairs of state that kept him in London.

"But have no fear. You will be my bride when the time is right. Meanwhile, you must trust me, Octavia, my beloved."

Then, at the most unlikely moment, right after the shocking death of his close associate Lord Rokeby, he had declared his wish to marry her at once.

A swift carriage ride through the spring night, a secret meeting, and then . . . How daring and romantic.

But there had been nothing romantic in Pedro's voice. He had sounded harsh and demanding. His black eyes had bored into hers with desperate urgency. And why had he made such a point of insisting that she must bring her jewels, all of them?

"You are to say nothing of this to anyone."

"But I must take leave of the queen."

His eyes flashed with barely controlled anger. "You cannot trouble her with such trivial matters at a time like this." She tried to draw away, but his hands tightened on her shoulders. "If you love me, you must trust me." He spoke more softly. "Octavia, *mi vida.*"

Pedro, her gallant Spanish lover. She did trust him. Certainly she did, and yet . . .

Octavia gave a violent start and shrank back, as a bent figure wrapped in a gold-embroidered cloak stepped out of the shadows.

"Why, what's amiss, my lady? And where are you bound in such haste?" She recognized the voice of the Welsh soothsayer, Bronwen, and felt somewhat reassured.

The old woman possessed the secret wisdom of her Celtic ancestors, the power to see into the future. Surely now, of all times, Octavia was in need of such wisdom to guide her.

Nothing happened by chance, of that Bronwen had always been certain. She had come upon Lady Octavia in the palace corridor tonight because the fates had willed it. But now it was necessary for her to take a hand, to use her powers to help free her beloved Melora from the Tower.

In her small, shadowy chamber, lit only by a pair of candles, Bronwen sat facing Octavia. The queen's lady-in-waiting kept her eyes fixed on the brightly painted cards on the table between them.

Bronwen tapped one of the cards with her finger, sighed

deeply, and shook her head. Octavia's heart leaped into her throat. "Alas, my lady," the Welshwoman said. She paused, as if reluctant to go on.

Octavia stared at the card. The colors seemed to glow with an unearthly light. "That picture—it frightens me. What does it mean?"

"You are sure you wish to know?"

"Tell me! I shall reward you well, I promise."

"This card represents the Lovers."

"But the man and woman are chained together," Octavia said, her voice shrill with mounting terror. "And that figure that hovers above them—it's horrible. Those horns—and the wings of a great bat—"

"He is called Arawan, my lady."

"A demon?"

"The Spirit of Retribution. You and your lover are threatened with great peril."

A shudder moved through Octavia's body. "Is there no escape?"

"Only if the chain that binds you to your lover is severed, and quickly."

"I will not give him up—I cannot!"

"The marquis is doomed, my lady. But perhaps . . ." She paused so that her words might have greater effect. "Perhaps you may yet have a chance . . ."

"But I love him with all my heart. I can't live without him. And only today, I have given him my word—"

Bronwen's thin body tensed under the folds of her cloak. This was what she had been hoping for. She must not fail Melora.

"And what is it he asks of you, my lady?"

Octavia hesitated. "I am to tell no one. He made a great point of that."

"You asked for my help. Unless you confide in me, you make it impossible for me to save you." She started to gather the cards together.

"No, wait!"

337

The girl's instinct for self-preservation warred with her devotion to her lover. "He told me to return here, to gather all my jewels and come to him."

"You are to meet at his great new house in Stepney, no doubt."

Octavia shook her head.

The candlelight flickered over the old woman's wrinkled face. She kept her voice low, but Octavia was caught up in its spell. "Where are you to meet him? Speak quickly, my lady. As you value your life."

"I am to travel by coach to Plymouth, and meet him at an inn near the harbor."

"And what then?"

"A ship will await us there, a Spanish galleon. As soon as we set sail, we are to be married by the captain."

"Alas, my lady. The marquis will never marry you. I knew it from the beginning."

"Why did you not tell me so before?"

"You were not yet ready to believe me."

"I—don't believe you now." But her voice faltered.

"Then you are lost, my lady." Bronwen spoke with chilling certainty. "May the Great Mother have pity on you."

Although the room had no window, Octavia felt a sudden, icy wind sweep across her face. The candle flames bent before the frigid blast. And above the unearthly keening of the wind, she heard the beat of giant, leathery wings. Bat's wings, like those of the creature in the picture before her.

She could hold out no longer. "I'll do as you say. Only, save me!"

Bronwen fixed her eyes on Octavia in a hypnotic stare. "You must save yourself."

"But how?"

The soothsayer drew out another card. "Look, my lady—see how a woman closes the mouth of a lion with her bare hands? It is a symbol of strength. You already have the strength to

338

break the chains that bind you to your false lover, if you will but use it."

Before Octavia had a chance to reconsider, Bronwen swept the cards into a stack and thrust them into her cloak, then rose to her feet. "Come, follow me."

"But where are you taking me?"

Bronwen's bony hand grasped Octavia's arm with surprising strength. "To speak with the earl of Pembroke," she said.

As Melora lay asleep on the hard, narrow bed in her cell, her lips curved in a smile. In her dream, she stood in the depths of a forest, surrounded by great trees ablaze with leaves of russet and gold. Exotic birds such as she had never seen before soared across the sky. Emerald green moss, soft as velvet, covered the clearing where she stood.

Someone was calling her name. She turned and saw Dirk a short distance away. He was reaching out his hands to her.

"This is our new world, sweeting," he was saying. "Come and share it with me." Her feet no longer touching the ground. She drifted toward him, filled with joyous anticipation. A moment more, and she would feel the hard strength of his body pressing against hers, his arms holding her close. He would draw her down on that mossy bed, and she would lie beside him . . .

But unseen hands were clutching at her skirts, holding her fast. A heavy mist, cold and damp, swirled about her. She could still hear Dirk's voice calling to her . . . but she could no longer see him. She struggled against the invisible force that gripped her.

When the mist began to lift, she saw that the forest glade had disappeared. Instead, there was a flight of twisting iron steps before her. She could not see what was at the top, but she started to climb. The steps writhed like a giant serpent under her feet. She clung to the railing, seized by a terrible foreboding.

And now she saw the wooden platform, the headsman's

339

block. She heard the impatient murmur of the crowd. Dirk was already up there, his back toward her. She tried to call out to him, but no sound came from her lips.

He was kneeling before the block, his neck bent, his head resting on the indentation in the wood. In the leaden sky overhead, ravens wheeled and swooped, their harsh cries filling the air.

The executioner stepped forward, a masked figure clad in a jerkin and breeches of black leather . . . he turned and looked down at her. Through the slits in his mask, she saw Rokeby's pale gray eyes, filled with unholy triumph . . .

A scream tore itself from her throat. Her whole body was rigid. Somehow, she fought off the clinging mist of the dream, and now she was sitting upright, fighting for breath, her heart lurching against her chest. Her cotton nightdress clung to her body, now soaked with icy sweat.

The gaoler's wife, who had tended her wound, had brought her the nightdress to replace the bloodstained costume she had still been wearing when she'd been brought to the Tower. The woman had given her hot broth for her dinner, and later, a sleeping draught. She had even left a candle on the wooden table beside the bed.

Melora realized that she was being treated with special consideration, but the thought did little to comfort her. Others before her had also been well cared for here in the Tower—until the hour they had been led to the block.

Anne Boleyn and Catherine Howard, two of King Henry's wives, had gone to their deaths proclaiming their innocence. And young Lady Jane Gray, queen of England for nine days, surely had been guilty of no crime.

Dirk and I risked our lives to save the king.

They would have a chance to defend themselves when they were brought to trial. But Dirk had killed Rokeby, the king's favorite. And she had come to Whitehall under false pretenses, to serve the queen. Even if Pembroke spoke out in their defense, would the king be convinced that they were innocent?

It was useless to lie awake, tormented by such thoughts. The candle guttered low. The pale light of dawn filtered in through the small window.

Perhaps it might be possible to get another dose of the sleeping draught. She remembered the nightmare that had struck terror to the core of her being. Better to remain awake than risk another like it.

Rising, she thrust her feet into her slippers and wrapped the woolen blanket around her to ward off the chill that pervaded the stone cell. She went to the window and stood looking down at the river. She caught sight of the white sails as they billowed out with the dawn wind. A large ship, moving swiftly on the silvery curve of the water. Where was it bound? she wondered.

She remembered Dirk's face, when he had spoken of the fleet of ships that would to carry him and his passengers across the sea, to build a settlement in a new land. She pressed her face against the barred window.

The gaoler's wife had told her that Dirk was here in the Tower. In spite of Melora's questioning, she had not said anything more; no doubt she had been forbidden to do so.

Was Dirk standing at his cell window, even now, watching the white-sailed ship making its way downriver, heading for the open sea?

In the days that followed, an endless procession of couriers came and went from the Pembroke's private apartment in the palace. The earl had issued terse orders, received information; his scribes were kept busy, and the pile of papers on his desk grew higher.

Lady Octavia, already terrified by Bronwen's prophecies, had broken down completely under Pembroke's icy, disconcerting stare, his warning of the consequences to her should she refuse to obey his orders.

She had been dispatched to Plymouth by coach to keep her meeting with Carvajal, with a troop of soldiers riding close

341

behind. One of Pembroke's most experienced agents had accompanied her and had concealed himself to overhear every word of the encounter between Octavia and her marquis.

Angered by his lady's late arrival, the gallant lover had dropped his courtly manners and had berated her, neglecting to choose his words carefully.

"Another hour and the ship would have sailed without us." He had snatched the jewel case from her hands.

"But Pedro, there will be other ships. Why the need for such haste?"

He ignored her question. "You English are fools, all of you. If Rokeby had listened to me, instead of sparing the life of that wretched girl—"

At a signal from Pembroke's agent, the soldiers came swarming into the room, placed Carvajal in chains, and brought him back to confront not only Pembroke, but Oliver Babcock as well.

It had not been necessary to wring the truth from Babcock by the use of torture. A brief visit to the vast underground chamber in the Tower, a glimpse of the rack, the thumbscrews, and the "scavenger's daughter," had terrified the pockmarked, lank-haired man into confessing his involvement in the plot.

When Carvajal and Babcock were brought face to face in Pembroke's chamber, each proved eager to fasten the greater blame on the other, while both insisted that they had been Rokeby's pawns. Pembroke had interrupted from time to time, to gather additional details. The scribes had scratched away busily, and the stack of papers grew higher yet.

After he had finished with Carvajal and Babcock, a procession of others were brought before him. The puppetmaster from Mother Speedwell's lodginghouse in Southwark admitted that one of Rokeby's minions had paid him to help in Melora's kidnapping; the steward of Rokeby's townhouse had testified that Melora had been held there against her will. "The Marquis was for doing away with her. But his lordship said he had a better use for the girl."

342

* * *

Lady Jade Fairfax, who looked as if she had aged a full five years in the few days since Rokeby's death, insisted she knew nothing of the conspiracy.

No amount of questioning would shake her icy composure. "If there was a conspiracy against the king, then you would do better to question Dirk Grenville and his trollop. She's not his cousin."

"I have known that from the day of her arrival," Pembroke said calmly. He stroked the black Persian cat that lay curled in his lap.

"Yet you did not warn the queen that there was a spy among her ladies?"

"I had my reasons. Melora Standish has indeed been a spy—in my service."

Jade's pale green eyes flashed defiance. "Then perhaps it is you who should be answering questions instead of asking them."

Pembroke leaned forward so quickly that the cat leaped from his lap and stalked indignantly to its velvet-cushioned basket.

"Do go on," he challenged her. "I believe you were about to accuse me of plotting against his majesty."

"I did not say that." She fell silent, her hands gripping the arms of her chair.

"You would do well to give careful thought to the shift of power here at court, my lady. You were losing your hold on Rokeby long before his death. Now, without his influence to support you, your position is not an enviable one."

Jade's shoulders sagged slightly. Her face, under the carefully applied mask of white lead powder, the touches of rouge, looked haggard and drawn.

"I am inclined to believe that Rokeby did not take you into his confidence when he plotted against the king," said Pembroke. "You have only to answer a few simple questions, to

343

confirm what I have already learned from others. Then you will be free to leave Whitehall."

"You cannot force me to leave the court!"

"I have no intention of using force. But you know his majesty's suspicious nature. I may have some difficulty convincing him that you were not involved in Rokeby's conspiracy." He paused, and allowed her to consider the unspoken threat behind his words, before following up his advantage.

"I'm told that you have a magnificent estate in Devon. No doubt you'll find the country air, the peaceful surroundings, most beneficial." He gave her a long, pitiless stare. "The hectic pace of life here at court can prove trying for a lady who is no longer young."

With an effort of will, she held herself erect, but the blow had struck home.

"What is it you want to know?" she asked, her voice expressionless.

Jade's carriage rolled through the palace gate, for what she knew would be the last time. A wagon followed, laden with her possessions. She stared out at the carefully tended gardens with their clipped hedges and leaping fountains. The couples strolling in the spring twilight were too engrossed in their own affairs to spare her a glance.

She sought to console herself. There would be other men for her: the tall young footman, always eager to please her in bed; the lusty country squires who would compete for her favors.

But somehow the prospect failed to raise her spirits. Whitehall had been her whole world. It was the center of intrigue, of power. To be banished to the country was to be buried alive.

That same evening, Pembroke sent for Bronwen.

"One day you must tell me how you managed to frighten Lady Octavia into betraying Carvajal."

344

"The girl had already begun to doubt her lover's intentions. Otherwise, she would not have sought my help. I only used the tools of my craft to play upon her fears."

She dismissed Octavia with a shrug of her shoulders. "Now, what of my mistress? She has done the king a great service."

"And she will be suitably rewarded. She wants to see her father back in London, so Grenville has told me. With a new company of players and a theater of his own."

"That would please her well," Bronwen said, with a smile. "I remember Edmund Standish. He was a most gifted performer in his time."

"He could be again, my lord—if he could find a powerful patron."

"I think that can be arranged," said Pembroke. "But what of Melora herself? She is a most extraordinary young lady. Will she be content to remain in London, to bask in the reflected glory of her father's accomplishments?"

"Melora does not seek contentment. She was never made for the easy, placid way, my lord." The old woman's eyes looked past him, as if at a vision he could not share. "If she chooses to follow her lover afar, she will face hardship and danger, but she will touch such heights as few women ever know."

Chapter Twenty-five

The soft spring breeze ruffled the surface of the river, and brought the scents of new grass and budding trees across the water. Dirk watched the tall, menacing shape of the Tower disappear in the distance. Pembroke's private barge caught the swift current and glided on its way toward Whitehall.

"The Marquis de Carvajal has confessed his guilt," said Pembroke. "King James would have preferred to send him to the block, but for the risk of provoking further hostilities with Spain. But Babcock was not so fortunate. I have no doubt as to the outcome of his trial. As for young Ambrose Corbett, the best he can hope for is to be shipped off to the Indies and a life of penal servitude."

"To hell with Carvajal and the rest of them!" Dirk interrupted, his voice harsh with barely controlled tension. "What's to become of Melora?"

"You need not fear for her." The earl gave Dirk a reassuring smile. "She was set free this morning."

"If she came to any harm while she was in the Tower, her gaoler will answer to me."

"She was well cared for. I saw to that. I wish I might have spared her the whole distressing experience, but I could not countermand his majesty's orders.

"It took time for me to gather a mountain of irrefutable proof against Rokeby and the others, so that you and she might be cleared of the slightest suspicion. Even so, it came as a most painful shock to the king to discover that his trust in the viscount nearly cost him his life."

Dirk had to admit to himself that the earl had acted with his usual good sense, waiting until he had been able to confront the king with a solid body of evidence. Nevertheless, the thought of Melora, still recovering from her wound, alone and frightened in her Tower cell, filled him with cold anger.

"As for yourself," Pembroke went on, "the king has promised to grant you an audience this afternoon. You are in an excellent position to ask what you will."

Only a few months ago, Dirk would have been elated by Pembroke's words. Now he found that his concern for Melora overshadowed all else, even the certainty that his long-cherished ambition was about to be fulfilled.

"I admit I had some doubts about taking Melora into my service, young and inexperienced as she was," Pembroke said. "But she performed better than I could have hoped. If she is willing, I'm sure I can make use of her again."

Dirk turned on the earl, his muscles taut with anger. "The devil you will!"

"She would be in no immediate danger, I assure you," Pembroke told him. "I believe his majesty's safe enough for the present. But there will be others in future reckless enough to try to overthrow the Stuart throne."

"I don't doubt it. But you'll have to find someone else to replace Melora in your service."

"That won't be as easy as you might suppose. She has already proved herself. She is quick-witted and resourceful—"

"I'll not have her risk her life again!"

"Don't you think that's for the lady to decide?"

Before Dirk could reply, Pembroke went on calmly, "She is a most impressive young lady. Even when Rokeby had her taken by force from her lodgings in Southwark and brought to his townhouse, she managed to keep her wits about her."

His thin lips curved in one of his rare smiles. "It's a pity, indeed, that she cannot appear on the London stage. She played the role of the calculating adventuress to the hilt, for Rokeby's benefit. And she ferreted out the most essential details of the plan to do away with his majesty."

"She nearly got herself killed in the process." Dirk's eyes glinted dangerously.

"It was you who brought her to me, Grenville," the earl reminded him. "You convinced me how valuable she would be if I took her into my service."

Dirk flinched inwardly. He had used all his powers of persuasion to get the earl to employ her. He had been well aware of the danger she would face; but he had put his own driving ambition before her safety. Remembering, he felt a deep contempt for himself.

But he had been different then. Selfish, possessed only by the need to gain his own ends, no matter what the cost to anyone else.

Melora had changed all that. She had changed him. And so gradually that he had scarcely been aware of what was happening.

He stared out at the sun-dappled river, and the fine mansions along the Strand; but his thoughts had gone back to their first meeting. That autumn night at the Leaping Stag, he had seen only her resemblance to his cousin; he had brought her to London as a means of gaining all he wanted most.

Had he been so thoroughly corrupted by the endless intrigues of life at court that he had begun to regard others only as pawns, to be used, then cast aside when they had served his purpose?

No, he thought, with painful honesty. His cynicism had taken root long before he had come to Whitehall. His harsh, bitter childhood had left him with little capacity for love or trust.

Even now he felt a surge of resentment at the memory of the grim years after his father had died, fighting in the lost cause of Mary, Queen of Scots.

True, his uncle had felt an obligation to offer shelter to him and his widowed mother. But Nicholas Grenville had never ceased to remind her of her husband's disastrous mistake in choosing the wrong side. Mean-spirited and vindictive, Uncle Nicholas had taken out his resentment on the frail young widow and her child in countless ways.

"Traitor's brat." That was what his uncle had called him. And Aunt Jessamyn had never ceased to bemoan the fact that their whole family had fallen from favor with Queen Elizabeth because of his father's impulsive action. "We've always been loyal to her majesty, yet now we dare not show ourselves at court. And how our poor Rosalind's ever to find a suitable husband, I cannot imagine."

Dirk's mother had not dared to protest. Her own family had abandoned her; she had been forced to accept the grudging charity doled out to her by Nicholas and Jessamyn for her son's sake, if not her own.

But Dirk, who had inherited his father's bold, impulsive nature, had fought back; and had been punished harshly for his childish acts of rebellion. Although the punishments had not broken his spirit, they had gradually changed him. He had learned to survive through more indirect means.

Although not of a scholarly bent, he had made the most of his hours with the tutor his uncle had reluctantly hired to provide him with the rudiments of learning.

He had ingratiated himself with the kitchen staff, so that he might cajole an occasional choice dainty with which to tempt his mother's languid appetite. But gradually, in spite of his efforts, she had drifted into apathy. Her spirit broken, she had moved about Ashcroft like a lost soul. When she died, only her son had mourned her passing.

The day after his mother's burial, he had turned his back on Ashcroft. He had traveled to Plymouth, walking when he had to, begging rides from carters when he could, and had taken ship with Sir Francis Drake.

He had felt no passion for the seafaring life. At the time, he had wanted to put as much distance as possible between himself and his relatives. Moreover, even at that early age, he had realized that as long as Elizabeth reigned, the son of a man who had espoused Mary's cause had no chance to advance himself in England.

But with his first glimpse of the New World, the sun-drenched islands of the Indies, and the untamed southern coast of the mainland, he had seen a promising future for himself, far from his native country.

During the voyage, he had grown to manhood, tall and lean, with whipcord muscles and the swift reflexes of a jungle cat. One of Drake's officers, an expert swordsman, had trained him in the use of the rapier, and he had proved a most apt pupil.

Returning from the voyage, he had used his skill as a swordman, selling his services to one or another of the constantly warring European rulers.

Between campaigns, there had been women, plenty of them. Camp followers, tavern maids, officers' wives. He had taken what they'd offered so freely, and had left them behind without a trace of regret.

As soon as King James had ascended to the English throne, Dirk had returned to his native land and gained a place at Whitehall. He had contrived to win Pembroke's friendship and had maneuvered his way upward.

And then, quite by chance, he had found Melora. He had studied her face, her movements, her speech with a calculating eye. She would serve his purpose as well, perhaps better, than his cousin Rosalind.

When had his feelings for Melora begun to change?

He glanced over at Pembroke, seated beside him beneath the gold-fringed canopy emblazoned with the earl's coat of arms. He was remembering their first interview, on his return to Whitehall.

"She is expendable," the earl had said of Melora. And Dirk had been startled by the violent, though unspoken protest that had stirred within him.

But even so, he had allowed her to enter the earl's service. He had tried to tell himself that she would be well rewarded for the risks she would run.

Even now, he could not bring himself to question Pembroke about the letter Melora had written. Instead, he asked, "I thought Melora would be safe with Caleb in Southwark. How did Rokeby find out where she was hiding?"

"It was Jade Fairfax who saw her. She was entertaining the crowd at the Frost Fair with her songs. I'll wager that Jade lost no time in getting word to Rokeby. He had Melora tracked down and brought to his house, bound and gagged."

The image conjured up by Pembroke's words sent a stab of revulsion through Dirk. What degradation, what brutality had Melora been subjected to, as the viscount's prisoner?

"Did Rokeby—" But he could not bring himself to finished the question. He tried not to think of Melora's slender white body, despoiled by Rokeby's touch. Swiftly, he pushed the flood of unsettling images to the back of his mind.

"Caleb brought me a letter," he said. "It gave me reason to believe Melora had left Southwark of her own free will."

"Rokeby forced her to write it so that you would not come seeking her."

But he should have gone searching for her all the same, he told himself. Why was it that Caleb had given her the benefit of the doubt, while he, who claimed to love her, had been so quick to believe that she'd betrayed him? That she'd walked out of his life without so much as a backward glance, and had entered into a self-seeking relationship with another man?

The answer came to him with a painful clarity that shook him to the depths of his being. Even then, he had not yet understood the meaning of love; he had not learned that without unquestioning trust, there could be no real love between a man and woman.

But Melora had always known. After she had managed to escape from Rokeby's house, and had made her way to the Fortune, she had gone out there on the stage and had sung her ballad, because she had trusted him. She had believed that the

351

memory of the haunting melody, its plaintive words, would call him to her side.

Suppose he had not reached her in time. Rokeby would have dragged her off to the living hell of Bedlam, where no one would ever have thought of seeking her.

He realized that Pembroke was speaking to him, and he forced himself to listen. ". . . and it was Jade who helped her to escape," the earl was saying.

Dirk stared at him in disbelief. "Why would Jade want to help Melora?"

"Not out of kindness, I assure you. She wanted to rid herself of a younger rival for Rokeby's affections. Much good it did her."

The barge rounded a curve in the river and moved toward the palace landing.

"Who but Melora would have seized the chance to call her warning to his majesty from the stage of the playhouse? She is a most resourceful young lady," said Pembroke.

"You need not remind me," Dirk said. In spite of his inner turmoil, a brief smile touched his lips. Against all odds, Melora had realized her long-held dream; she had made her appearance upon the public stage in London. A brief appearance, but a memorable one.

"Now the king has been forced to admit that Rokeby betrayed him, that you and Melora helped to save his life, you have your opportunity to ask for the land grant and ships." He gave Dirk a dubious look. "Supposing you're still set on leaving England to live among the savages in that wilderness across the sea."

"There are plenty of perfumed, satin-clad savages at White-hall."

Pembroke shook his head, baffled by Dirk's obstinacy. He pointed in the direction of the sprawling red brick palace looming before them. "Here is the source of power. His majesty is lavish with his favors. Now that he is in your debt, you could make your fortune at court."

"By flattering his majesty, and catering to his whims? By scheming and jostling others aside, to remain in favor? That's not for me—not any longer."

The prow of the barge bumped against the landing. Courtiers, lured out of doors by the unseasonably mild weather, strolled about, decked in their spring finery. Dirk and Pembroke left the barge and climbed the steps of the landing.

"You said that Melora, too, would be suitably rewarded," Dirk said. "Has she told you what she wants?"

Pembroke shook his head. "You did when you persuaded me to take her into my service, remember? You said that she wants her father to have a new theater here in London, and a patron to lend support. Bronwen told me much the same, when I spoke with her less than a week ago."

They entered the palace courtyard. "I would be pleased to offer my patronage to Edmund Standish. And provide him with a handsome playhouse, outside the city's jurisdiction."

Dirk drew in his breath, startled by Pembroke's casual remark. How could he have allowed himself to forget Melora's unwavering devotion to her father?

"You had best get yourself suitably attired for your audience with the king," Pembroke was saying. "Unless I'm mistaken, he will give you everything you could ask for."

"Not quite," Dirk said quietly. He caught the earl's puzzled glance, but chose to ignore it.

Even a royal decree could not force Melora to abandon her her father. She had been willing to take whatever risks were necessary to enable him to return to his former position as one of the leading actor-managers in London. With her unswerving loyalty, she would not leave him so long as she felt he needed her.

Melora had put on a gown of lilac taffeta with a close-fitting bodice and a standing lace collar; she had chosen it from those she had left behind on her flight from the palace. She paused for a moment on the threshold of the queen's chamber. Then, drawing a deep breath, she came inside. Felicity dropped the skeins of embroidery silk she had been sorting and gave a cry of surprise. The other ladies stared at Melora, then at one another. They began to whisper among themselves.

Queen Anne silenced them with an imperious gesture. "I wish to speak with——" She hesitated for a second, uncertain of how to refer to Melora, now that she knew her real identity. "——with this young lady in private," she finished.

She dismissed the rest of her ladies with a wave of her hand. Although they longed to remain and satisfy their curiosity, they rose reluctantly, and left the chamber.

Queen Anne motioned to Melora to come forward. "I have not yet told my ladies of your deception." Her voice was stern. "What have you to say for yourself, Mistress Standish?"

Melora stood before the queen, her eyes downcast.

"You have committed a grave offense, pretending to be Lord Grenville's cousin. Tell me, did you act willingly in this rash scheme? Or did Grenville have some hold over you, to force you to do his bidding?"

"I came of my own free will, your majesty. I agreed to help him carry out his plan because——" But no, she would not make any excuses for her conduct. She spoke with quiet dignity. "I can only throw myself upon your mercy, and ask your pardon."

"We would be ungrateful, indeed, to withhold it. Pembroke has told me a great deal about your service to the Crown."

She took Melora's hand in hers; and now she spoke not as the queen of England, but as a woman. "To think of what would have happened to my husband, my children, had it not been for your courage, your steadfast loyalty. We owe you more than we can hope to repay, Mistress Standish."

"Thank you, your majesty."

"We will talk of this at greater length another time. For the present, I will detain you no longer," said the queen. Her eyes softened and an understanding smile touched her lips. "I believe there is someone else here in Whitehall you wish to see."

Melora's face grew warm. "Your majesty, I— Where is he?"
"Lord Grenville is waiting for you in his chambers."

Melora stood still in the doorway, her heart beating rapidly, her eyes fixed on Dirk. The sunlight streamed in through the window, gilding the hard planes and angles of his tanned face, the breadth of his powerful shoulders and chest.

Then she lifted her skirts, ran across the room, and flung herself into his outstretched arms. She could not speak. She could only cling to him with all her strength, drawing reassurance from his embrace.

She felt his mouth, warm and seeking, as he kissed her forehead, her cheek, the pulse point at her throat. Eagerly she parted her lips to receive his questing tongue. Caught up in the swift current of desire, she met his tongue with her own.

He raised his head at last and stood looking down at her, as if he were seeking to convince himself that she really was here with him. His hands were unsteady as he began to undo the hooks of her bodice.

She saw that his dark, gold-flecked eyes were filled with self-reproach as he fixed his gaze on the raised scar that ran along her collarbone. He touched it lightly with the tips of his fingers.

"It's nearly healed," she assured him. "It wasn't deep."

She remembered the startling change that had come over him as her blood had begun streaming from beneath the blade of Rokeby's dagger and down the front of her borrowed costume. The sight had stripped away Dirk's courtly manners to reveal the unbridled ferocity beneath the polished surface. In a single moment he had become the untamed warrior, the primitive male fighting to protect his woman.

Even now, his voice shook with anger. "If the cut had been a few inches higher—"

She reached up and stroked his cheek. "But it wasn't. And

you were there when I needed you most; that's all that matters. You saved me from Rokeby."

But Dirk could not shake off his lingering guilt. He should have believed in her, in spite of that damned letter. He should have gone out seeking her along with Caleb and Osric, and called on Pembroke's organization to help in the search.

The unwelcome visions he had pushed to the back of his mind now surfaced again and could no longer be ignored. He did not want to know the truth. But he had to.

"Pembroke told me how you were held prisoner in Rokeby's house." He hesitated, then cupped her face in his hands. "He said that Carvajal wanted you killed at once. But Rokeby refused." He felt as if an iron chain were tightening about his throat, but he forced himself to go on. "He said he had a—better use for you." He drew a harsh, uneven breath. "Melora, did that bastard—did he harm you?"

She understood at once, and her eyes, wide and candid, held his in a long, steady look. She spoke with unflinching directness. "He did not rape me."

The tension eased within him as the evil visions melted away. At least she had been spared that degrading ordeal.

"Rokeby intended to keep me prisoner until he returned from the progress. The king would have been killed by then. And you were to be accused of his murder."

He stared at her in stunned disbelief. "What possible reason would I have to seek his majesty's death?"

"That's where I would have been useful. I was to testify that you had been harboring a bitter grudge against the king." Quickly she explained the details of the viscount's plan. "At the time, I had no choice but to pretend to go along with his scheme. And to write that letter, as he dictated it to me."

"But I had a choice," Dirk said. "I should have known you better than to believe what you wrote. If I had gone out and found you sooner—"

"Perhaps it is as well you didn't." She managed a shaky smile.

356

He stared down at her with a baffled expression.

"I was climbing down the back wall of Rokeby's house, trying to get out by way of the terrace, when I overheard him talking with Carvajal of the plan to kill King James on the royal progress. I'd have learned even more, if only that vine had not given way—"

"Good God! You might have broken your neck!"

"But I didn't," she soothed him. Her lips lifted in a smile. "I think even Pembroke would have to admit I served him well."

Dirk's eyes sparked with a hard metallic glint. "So well that he wants you to remain in his service."

"Does he, indeed? It's a most flattering offer." She paused for an instant, pretending to consider the prospect. "Perhaps I might be persuaded to accept."

He caught hold of her shoulders. "You'll do no such thing."

"Indeed, my lord?" she teased him. "And why not?"

"Because I forbid it."

He pulled her against him until their bodies were melded together, then bent his head and pressed his face against the swell of her breast. "I forbid it . . ." But now his voice was husky, caressing.

She felt a hot surge of longing, a mighty tide that grew ever stronger, until it overwhelmed her, sweeping away all memory of the past, all thought of the future.

He undid the remaining hooks of her bodice, down to the waist, and pushed aside the top of her sheer linen shift. He cupped her bared breast, stroked the nipple with his thumb. Her response came swiftly. He felt the rosy peak harden beneath his touch. He drew it into his mouth and suckled avidly.

She gave a stifled moan and clung to him, her hands pressing against the muscles of his back. A swift, hot tingling coursed through her body and down along her thighs. The smooth, hidden folds of her womanhood were laved with warm moisture.

Trembling with the urgency of her need, she drew away and slid off her gown. It fell to the floor with a rustling sound. Her farthingale, and the rest of her elaborate undergarments, joined the heap of taffeta and lace; now she stood before him clad only in her shift and silk stockings with their jeweled, lace-trimmed garters, her high-heeled slippers.

Quickly, she took the bodkins from her carefully arranged hair so that it fell in a gleaming curtain around her face and over her shoulders. The thick, midnight-black waves brushed his face as he caught her up in his arms and carried her to his bedchamber.

He set her down on the wide bed. Swiftly he stripped off his own garments. Her eyes lingered on his muscled chest, then moved to his lean belly and narrow hips. She did not avert her gaze from the hard length of his shaft.

He was more than ready to possess her at once. He fought back the urge to bury himself deep inside her, to find release from the searing ache in his loins. After their long separation, he wanted to make their loving as completely fulfilling for her as for himself.

Slowly, he drew off her shift, removed her slippers, then rolled down her stockings, stroking the length of her legs. He stretched himself beside her on the bed. His fingers started a trail of fire flickering over the soft flesh of her breasts, her flat, satin-skinned belly. He moved himself downward to press his burning face against her thighs, and caught the sweet-hot woman scent of her, the fragrance that was her own.

"Open to me, sweeting." His voice was low, urgent.

She parted her thighs. He touched his tongue to her firm bud, felt it harden and peak as he flicked at it. Sliding his hands under the rounds of her buttocks, he raised her closer, and his tongue thrust into her.

His hands moved from beneath her buttocks. Lifting her long legs, he placed them over his shoulders. She raised her hips, urging his questing tongue to go deeper, ever deeper.

He felt the first rhythmic pulsations spreading from her turgid bud up into her hot satin sheath. Faster and faster came the throbbing. She arched herself up with a wordless cry.

Rock-hard though he was, and aching to fulfill his own need, he still held back. He raised his face and saw her head thrown back, the curve of her slender white neck. Saw the ecstasy in her eyes. A rapture so intense, so all-consuming, that the sight of it filled him with a surge of delight. Never had he realized that he might take such pleasure in her climax, while delaying his own powerful need for release.

She lay back on the bed, her eyes half-closed, her breasts rising and falling evenly. "Come and lie beside me, love." Her voice was soft, husky with passion.

He lifted himself and moved upward until he was stretched out next to her. She ran her hands over his chest, his hard, muscle-ridged belly. Her questing fingers went on caressing him until she touched his hot shaft.

He caught his breath. How much longer could he wait to slake his own overpowering need?

But she did not want him to hold back. She reached out her arms and drew him down to her. He knelt between her thighs. She stroked his back, from his shoulders to the base of his spine. Her fingers splayed out over his buttocks. She pressed her heated mound against him.

He entered her with one long thrust, then lay still, filling her completely, his hardness pulsating against the sides of her wet sheath.

She began to move her hips. He drew back, then thrust into her again. Slowly at first, then faster and faster. She quickened her own pace to match his, and they went whirling upward together, spinning higher, ever higher. Joining, melding, sharing the timeless peak of fulfillment.

She lay cradled in his arms, savoring the sweet contentment that filled her whole being. A soft breeze came through the half-open window, fragrant with the scent of spring. Raising her head, she saw that the sunlit afternoon had given way to the violet shadows of twilight.

The palace gardens soon would be deserted, as the courtiers went streaming inside to prepare for the evening's revelry. In the chambers of the queen's ladies, Felicity, Millicent, and the others would be donning their new finery, fastening on their jewels, and pasting their satin beauty patches in place. And all the time, their tongues would be wagging busily, as they speculated on the surprise of Melora's unexpected reappearance.

"No doubt there's to be a splendid banquet tonight," she said.

"No doubt," he agreed. He gave her a lazy half-smile. "And an equally splendid ball. Or perhaps a boating party, with a shower of fireworks over the river."

"Do you think the king will attend?"

"I'm sure he will. He has put aside his fears, for the time being. He'll be wanting to get back to his customary pleasures."

Reluctantly, she allowed herself to be drawn back from their brief, enchanted interlude to the demands of reality. "You've already seen the king?"

Dirk nodded. "He granted me an audience earlier this afternoon."

Tension stirred within her. "Your ships, your land grant? I suppose you will have them now."

"He was most generous. He has promised me twenty vessels of my own choosing, and a stretch of territory on the mainland of America. From the southern coastline on into the great forests and the mountains beyond. And I'll have no difficulty finding plenty of prospective colonists eager to sail with me."

"Your new world," she said softly.

Our new world, sweeting.

Although he longed to speak the words aloud, he drew on his willpower and forced himself to remain silent.

Pembroke had said he would be willing to offer his patronage to Melora's father. If Edmund Standish was still set on coming to London and starting over again, she would be forced to make a choice. Would she feel duty-bound to remain and help her father to rebuild his career?

This time, Dirk told himself, he would not be driven by his own need. He would not try to manipulate her into sailing with him, even if he could. She must be allowed to decide for herself.

He looked down at her, his gaze lingering on the delicate contours of her face, the soft flush on her cheeks. Her black hair was tangled, her skin still warm and damp in the aftermath of their loving. To lose her—to be parted from her forever—the thought filled him with a sense of desolation such as he had never known before.

Chapter Twenty-six

The gilded coach, emblazoned with the crest of the earl of Pembroke, rattled over the cobblestoned street leading to the wharf. At an order from Melora, the coachman drew the team to a stop; the liveried footman sprang down to help her descend.

The warm breeze was heavy with the mingled scents of cinnamon and cloves, tar and hemp. Sailors stopped their work to stare at the dark-haired young lady in her blue silk gown and cloak. One of them grinned and said, "There's a trim little craft if ever I saw one. Wouldn't mind climbin' aboard 'er."

"Mind yer tongue, ye batherin' fool," warned a big, sun-burned boatswain. "That there's Lord Grenville's lady."

A swift hush fell over the seamen and they stepped back to make way for Melora, who moved past them, heading for the end of the wharf. Dirk, wearing a wide-sleeved linen shirt and close-fitting black breeches, was overseeing the loading of his flagship, a sleek vessel with towering masts, freshly painted hull, and gilded trim. Completely absorbed in his work, he had not yet noticed Melora.

She paused to watch him and she felt the familiar catch at her throat, the surging warmth that suffused her body at the sight of him. Her eyes moved over him, taking in the sun-streaked brown hair, stirred by the river breeze, the movements of his powerful muscles under the thin fabric of his shirt. Coming nearer, she caught the look of intense concentration in his gold-flecked eyes as he watched the ceaseless activity of the longshoremen who were hauling crates and barrels of supplies up the gangplank and stowing them in the hold.

Since the day the king had given him his land grant, Dirk had worked ceaselessly, rising at the first light of dawn, going down to the waterfront, possessed by his eagerness to complete the preparations for the voyage as quickly as possible. Although he spent as many of his nights as possible with Melora, he was often late, so that her carefully planned suppers grew cold while she waited for him.

But she had never reproached him, for she wanted to make the most of their time together, to stroll with him under the budding trees in the fragrant darkness of the spring evening before going upstairs to her bedchamber. His lovemaking, passionate yet tender, swept aside all her misgivings about their future.

She had taken up residence at the earl's house on the Strand only few days after her release from the Tower. At first, Dirk had regarded her move from Whitehall with suspicion.

"If Pembroke thinks he can persuade you to remain in his service by offering you his hospitality, he's much mistaken." Dirk's eyes had glinted dangerously.

"I've already told the earl I am finished with all that," Melora had soothed him. "He's invited me into his home to spare me the embarrassment of being stared at and gossiped about at court."

The earl had set aside for her use a spacious, luxuriously furnished chamber overlooking his garden. Since he was spending most of his time at his Whitehall apartment now, or at his nearby manor, Netherwood, she was assured of her privacy.

"He's provided quarters for Bronwen, too," she had told Dirk. "As for Osric and Caleb, they're lodging in Southwark. But already they're talking of going out on the road again, now that the warm weather's returned."

Melora tried not to pay attention to the signs of the coming summer: the pale green leaves on the oaks and elms, the primroses and violets in the gardens along the Strand. She did not want to think about the passage of the days.

But the arrangements for Dirk's sailing were moving forward with relentless speed and efficiency. Weeks ago, he had ordered broadsides to be printed, announcing the voyage and calling upon those Englishmen dissatisfied with their present circumstances and desiring to improve their prospects to come to London and sign on as passengers.

Carried over the length and breadth of the country by peddlers and tinkers, the broadsides were put up on the walls of taverns and distributed at innyards and marketplaces. They were read aloud by ministers to their congregations. Farmers, weavers, blacksmiths, bricklayers, and cobblers, stirred by the glowing descriptions of the vast new land to the west, had come swarming down to join the expedition.

Dirk had kept up a wide acquaintance among the captains he had known during his own seafaring days. He lost no time in hiring the most experienced and reliable of the lot, traveling as far as Plymouth and Bristol to get those men he wanted. Even now, he was still busy rounding up crews: experienced navigators and boatswains, gunners and carpenters.

Although he had delegated much of the work of provisioning the ships to others, he came down to the wharves to make sure that his orders were being carried out. Having spent months at sea, he knew the importance of decent and sufficient food and drink on a voyage that could take from eight weeks to several months, depending on the vagaries of wind and tide. He had insisted on going over every one of his ships himself, climbing down into the holds, inspecting the planks and riggings, to assure himself that the vessels were seaworthy.

Melora tried to be patient and understanding. But sometimes, after Dirk had spent the night with her in her chamber and she awoke to find him gone, she turned and buried her face in his pillow, breathing in his scent, wondering how it would be for her after he had sailed.

Her conflicting emotions tormented her. Although she was

relieved that he had not yet asked her to go with him, she was troubled, too. Slowly, reluctantly, she forced herself to face the possibility that he might not want to take her with him.

Was it because of the difficulties of the long voyage, the hardships and dangers that might await them after their arrival in America? Surely he knew by now that she could endure hardship and cope with danger, if she had to.

Or was it that, in spite of his love for her—and she did not doubt that he loved her—he could not bring himself to make her his wife?

He would be the proprietor of a tract of land so vast that, in spite of the crude maps he had shown her, she could not imagine the full extent of it. He would choose his private acreage and have it cleared. Afterward, when he had built himself a manor house as fine as his uncle's Ashcroft, when hired laborers had planted and harvested his crops, he would be ready to establish his own Grenville dynasty.

Perhaps he planned to wait for years, if necessary, then return to England to find himself a wife, the daughter of an illustrious family, a highborn young beauty who would preside over his home and bear his children—

Although the very thought filled her with anguish, her pride kept her from questioning him. She could only move from day to day, treasuring every moment they were together, keeping her misgivings locked inside her.

"Melora!"

Now, at last, he turned from the ship and caught sight of her. At his call, she came hurrying to his side. Indifferent to the stares of the waterfront idlers, he slid his hands under her cloak and embraced her, his fingers burning through the thin silk of her bodice. He was bending his head, and she tilted her face to him, but before his lips found hers, she heard footsteps close by and a man speaking hesitantly. "Ah—your pardon, my lord."

Dirk released her, and she turned to see a stout man in the plain but well-cut garb of a prosperous merchant. The man removed his hat and bowed. "I've come about those crates of oranges—" He paused and glanced dubiously at Melora in her elegant spring finery.

"My instructions were plain enough, Master Pratt," said Dirk. "I must have at least forty crates of oranges within the fortnight. Lemons, too, if you can get them."

"There's not that many in my warehouses, my lord."

"Then you must go to every captain who's returned from the Canary Islands, and find more," he said impatiently. "I'll not have my crews or passengers fall sick with the scurvy for want of proper victuals."

Melora's heart sank like a stone. Dirk had forgotten her completely, absorbed as he was in his conversation with the merchant. In spite of her resolve, she could not wholly control her resentment. His thoughts were already far away, aboard that flagship of his, now rising and falling gently with the tide, tugging at her hawsers, as if she shared her master's eagerness to be set free to catch the tide.

Melora touched him lightly on the arm. "I had best be on my way." There was a slight edge to her voice. But she could not remain angry with him long. "I've planned a special supper for this evening. Poached salmon with fennel—"

"Melora, forgive me," he said, with a contrite smile. "Two of my captains have arrived here from Bristol and I have promised to meet with them tonight. But perhaps tomorrow evening—"

"As you wish." She turned away to hide her disappointment, and slowly walked back to the waiting carriage. It was as if he had already left her.

The tall, erect gentleman with graying hair, clad in a plum-colored satin suit, confronted the manservant who had opened the front door of Pembroke's townhouse. "I am here at the earl's request, my good man. You may tell him Edmund Standish has arrived." He spoke with a deep, sonorous tone, and held out a folded parchment bearing Pembroke's seal.

The servant inclined his head politely. "His lordship is not at home."

"And my daughter, Mistress Melora Standish? She is staying here, is she not?"

"She is, sir. But she went out a few hours ago."

"I will wait." The visitor spoke with quiet determination.

"You may have a long wait, master," a familiar voice came from the shadows of the hallway. "Mistress Melora's gone down to the docks."

The servingman stepped aside and Standish found himself face to face with Bronwen, who, indifferent to the spring weather, still wore her gray velvet cloak with its arcane gilt-embroidered designs. "Well met, Master Standish," she said, with a smile.

The footman kept his face carefully expressionless. In the time he had served here, he had learned that the earl had all manner of visitors, who came and went at all hours. But this white-haired Welshwoman who had arrived with Mistress Standish and remained lodged in a small chamber on the top floor of the house was one of a kind.

Her face was wrinkled and weatherbeaten, but her bright blue eyes seemed to penetrate to the depths of a man's hidden thoughts with a single glance. The servingmaids swore that she had the most remarkable powers of foretelling the future with a handful of curiously marked stones, or a deck of fantastically painted cards, when it pleased her. She was held in high esteem, not only by the young lady, but by the earl himself.

"Come inside, master," Bronwen said, with the self-assurance that would have done credit to a duchess. "I've been waiting for you."

"But I sent no word as to the date of my arrival. The deplorable condition of the roads made it impossible for me to be sure how long my journey would take."

"Nevertheless, I knew you would be here today."

She turned to the manservant. "You may go now," she said.

The young man breathed a sigh of relief. Under his carefully

cultivated veneer of imperturbable poise, there remained the
superstitious lad who had come from Surrey less than a year
ago to enter the earl's service. There was something about the
old Welshwoman . . .

"You've had a long journey from Northumberland," Bronwen said, seating herself at a small table and motioning to
Standish to take the chair opposite her. "I will order refreshments, master."

When they had been served with Malaga wine and almond
cakes and the maid had departed, Standish could restrain his
curiosity no longer.

"The earl has sent me a most extraordinary message." He
drew out the letter and tapped it against the edge of the table,
then gave her an ironic smile. "No doubt you already know
what he writes."

"I can guess," the Welshwoman said. "His lordship's prepared to offer you his patronage, should you wish to establish
yourself here in London once more."

"Was it Melora who persuaded the earl to help me?"

"You might say so."

"How does it happen that my daughter is living here in his
house?" There was a hint of uneasiness in his voice.

Bronwen gave him an unflinching look. "She is not his mistress, if that's what troubles you," she said. "She had been
staying at Whitehall, but she finds these lodgings more convenient at present."

"Then Grenville spoke the truth when he asked my permission to bring her here to London. She has served as a performer
in the palace?"

"Ah yes, the court masque. Mistress Melora would have
made you proud, had you seen her," Bronwen assured him.
"But she has done a great deal more than that since she came
here." She gave him a peculiar smile. "Would you believe me

if I were to tell you that your daughter appeared upon the stage at the Fortune playhouse?"

Standish drew in his breath and stared at her in disbelief. "By heaven! What jest is this, Bronwen? You know as well as I that no female is permitted to perform at a public playhouse!"

"Nevertheless, Mistress Melora did so. And her performance was—memorable. Perhaps she will tell you about it herself, in her own good time."

He shook his head in growing bewilderment. "And what is she doing down at the waterfront?"

"She's with Lord Grenville. His lordship will be setting out across the sea to America within the fortnight. She spends as much time as possible with him."

Bronwen caught the searching look in Standish's eyes. "Yes, master," she said, before he could ask. "She loves him."

"A girlish infatuation, no doubt?"

"Your daughter's become a woman, since last you saw her," she told him. "She has given herself to his lordship, body and soul."

"He has declared his intention of making her his wife? She is to sail with him when he leaves England?"

"They have not yet spoken of marriage."

He struck his fist upon the table.

"So that's the way of it!" His voice shook with anger. "This arrogant young nobleman has taken his pleasure with Melora. But he feels under no constraint to marry her. She is an actor's daughter, while he—"

"You do him an injustice, Master Standish," Bronwen interrupted. "Let me tell you the way it is with him and Melora. Then you may judge for yourself."

When Melora returned to Pembroke's house early that evening, she was followed from the carriage by the footman, who was laden down with her purchases. She had tried to fill the hours by going from one shop to another, selecting an embroidered silk shawl, a fan of ostrich plumes, a pair of topaz earrings. She sighed, wondering how she would contrive to keep herself occupied during the long, empty evening.

"Poppet!"

She gave a start as a deep voice hailed her from the doorway. No one ever called her poppet except—

She lifted her skirts and ran to her father. She halted a moment, and her eyes swept over him: she felt a profound sense of reassurance, for he looked better than he had in years. His face had filled out, his skin was tanned, and he held himself with an assurance that she'd feared she might never see again. His plum-colored suit was cut to the newest fashion. He stretched out his arms and she flung herself into them, warmed and comforted by his touch.

After they had finished the excellent supper she was to have shared with Dirk, they walked together arm in arm through the garden that sloped down to the river.

"There will so be much for us to do," she said. "I will help you choose a site for your theater, and then we must seek out your new players. Osric and Caleb were about to set out on the road, but perhaps we can make a place for them, performing between the acts—"

"Melora, wait a moment."

But she went on as if afraid to stop speaking. She wanted to lose herself completely in planning her father's new enterprise so that she might shut out all thought of Dirk's sailing.

"With Lord Pembroke for your patron, you will have no difficulty in gathering the finest troupe in all London. He's one of the most influential men at court."

"Melora—"

"And we will call upon Master Inigo Jones to supply the new scenery. Master Jones is the most sought-after craftsman in the city. He designed a magnificent setting for the court masque—I played the role of Artemis—I wish you could have been there to see me—"

"Melora!" Her father's voice, trained to resound to the far-

370

thest corners of any playhouse, rang out and silenced her at last. He drew her down on a broad stone bench beneath the branches of an ancient oak. "I've something to tell you. Be still and hear me out."

Something in his tone made her faintly uneasy.

"It was most generous of the earl to offer me this splendid opportunity. I will be honored to accept his patronage. But I cannot return to the London stage."

"You cannot—but all the time we were traveling the roads, you spoke of little else. Is it your health, father?"

"I've never felt better," he assured her. "But so much has happened to both of us since we parted. I have made other plans for the future, poppet. The fact is—" He hesitated slightly, "I am about to marry."

She stared at him in stunned disbelief. "But who—when—"

"I have asked Mistress Frobisher to be my wife, and she has agreed. The banns will be read in the church at Kilwarren next month."

"Mistress Frobisher?" The name meant nothing to her.

"She's the widow who owns the Rose and Thistle. The inn where I have lived since I left the Leaping Stag last autumn." He put his arm around her shoulders and drew her close.

"You are going to marry again." Somehow, such a possibility had never occurred to Melora. And yet her father was a fine-looking man, still in his mid-forties, healthy and vigorous once more.

"She is a good woman, Melora. She's not like—my feelings for her are not the same as—" His voice shook slightly. "No one will ever take your mother's place, Melora. But Bess Frobisher is warm-hearted and generous, and well respected by her neighbors. Her inn's a large, well-run establishment of excellent repute, patronized by the gentry."

"But—surely you can't mean you would give up all thought of a future in the theater to become an innkeeper!"

He shook his head and smiled. "You know me better than that."

"Then how——"

"That's what I've been trying to tell you. I will use the innyard for my performances in spring and summer. It can accommodate a good-sized company of players and has plenty of space for the audience."

"But London is the very heart of the theater," she protested. "Why can't Mistress Frobisher come and live with you here?"

"She is a countrywoman. Her roots are in the border country. She worked hard to keep the inn going after her husband passed away. She built up a fine trade. And she is proud of her accomplishments, as she should be. The Rose and Thistle means as much to her as the theater means to me."

He took Melora's hand in his. "She loves me, poppet. No doubt she would leave Northumberland if I wished it. But I would not ask it of her, for her happiness means much to me."

It was plain from the look in his eyes, the tenderness in his voice, that her father was devoted to his wife-to-be. Before Melora could question him further, he said, "Now it is your future we must settle. Bronwen's told me of you and Lord Grenville."

He had caught her off-guard. "She had no right——"

He ignored her protest. "My daughter would not give herself lightly. You love him, don't you?" His eyes held Melora's.

"Yes, Father. But—I—"

"You were planning to let him sail off to America without you."

"How could I leave England for a wilderness across the sea? Nothing but endless forests, filled with savages and dangerous beasts. Why—after these months of living at Whitehall, how could I ever consider the hardships, the struggle to survive——"

She tried to look away, not wanting to meet her father's searching gaze. Never had she been able to conceal her feelings from him.

"So you choose to remain here because you lack the courage to face the perils of a new land? Or because you've been spoiled by the luxuries of court life?"

"Dirk has not asked me to marry him."

Her father's hand tightened around hers. "He will, poppet."

"You don't understand. The Grenvilles are a proud race—lords of the border since—"

"He wants you for his wife. He told me so."

"But how? When?"

"I spoke with him at a waterfront inn this afternoon."

"You should not have—"

"Be still, Melora. Perhaps I haven't been everything a father should be, dragging you about the countryside, allowing you to perform in taverns, letting you go junketing off to London with a stranger—"

"You were delirious with fever when I left you."

"That's as may be. But I was in my right senses when I spoke to Grenville today. I told him that no man, whatever his rank, would use my daughter for his pleasure and desert her afterward." She heard the innate pride in his voice. "But I had no cause to reproach him. He wants to marry you, Melora. To take you with him when he sails.

"He hasn't ask you before only because— But I promised to let him explain for himself. He's down there at the Red Boar, dining with his captains." He rose and drew her to her feet. "Go to him now, Melora."

She hesitated, trying to bring some semblance of order to her whirling thoughts. "But if I leave England—" Tears stung her eyelids. "When will we see each other again?"

"As to that, who can say? I'll not deny how much I will miss you. You cared for me with all the devotion a man could ask of his daughter. But now I'll have a good wife to see to my needs, a most distinguished patron to lend his name to my company,"

His voice rang with the dauntless optimism of earlier years. "I have great plans for the future. Bess—Mistress Frobisher—has already begun arranging the inn to suit my purposes. She has set aside a large chamber as a tiring room for my company, and an outbuilding where scenery can be stored. There is to be a wide path for the wagons, so they won't come rattling across the yard and distract the audience from the performance."

Listening to him, Melora felt a curious, hollow sensation. After all the risks she had taken to help him, to arrange his future, she could not accept that she was no longer needed. That another woman, loving and devoted, would be taking her place in her father's life.

"Who knows?" he was saying. "Perhaps Pembroke might arrange for me to visit London and perform at court during the winter season."

As she went on listening, her disappointment gave way to another, stronger emotion. A glorious sense of freedom rose up in her, spreading until it filled every corner of her being.

Seafaring men and merchants from a dozen lands filled the Red Boar. The low-ceilinged taproom, with its oaken beams, was blue with the heavy smoke from the long clay pipes that had become so popular, despite the king's diatribe against the smoking of tobacco. A couple of musicians, one with a lute, the other a flageolet, played a lively sailors' tune. Melora looked about, trying to catch sight of Dirk.

There he was, seated off in a corner, deep in conversation with two other men: his new captains, no doubt. They had their heads together over a large square of parchment, oblivious to their surroundings.

Melora's dark-blue cloak fell open to reveal her turquoise gown, with its wide skirt and close-fitting bodice; her pearl earrings and necklace glowed in the lantern light. Men stopped their drinking and stared up at her. Some were taken by surprise to see so fashionable a young lady in these surroundings; a few grinned in bold invitation.

A tall, bronzed naval officer in a gold-laced coat got to his feet, swept off his plumed hat, and bowed. "Good evening, madam. I should be honored if you would take supper with me." But she shook her head and moved past him.

By now, she had created quite a stir among the patrons—except for Dirk, who was still too deep in conversation with his companions to notice her.

Drat the man! She'd get him to notice her, one way or another.

A smile quirked the corners of her lips as she made her way through the crowd to the musicians. She spoke quietly to lute player. He nodded, then helped her up onto the nearest table and struck up the opening chords of a ballad.

One of Dirk's companion's touched his arm; he turned, stared incredulously, then surged to his feet.

Boldly, she threw back her head and gave her audience a dazzling smile. Her voice rang out across the taproom.

> I bought myself a bonny cock,
> The biggest I did see,
> I fed him 'neath the tree, boys,
> And the cock, he pleasured me . . .

The men grinned and pounded their tankards on the tables. "More, lass! Let's have the rest!"

But before she could launch into the next verse, Dirk was shouldering his way through the crowd, his eyes narrowed to slits, his face dark with anger. He reached her table and glared up at her. "Melora! What the devil do you think you're doing?"

"Entertaining these gentlemen, my lord," she told him.

He seized her about the waist, lifted her down, tossed her over his shoulder, and carried her toward the door. A shout of laughter went up from the crowd. The door swung open and the cool, spice-laden night air enveloped her.

"Put me down at once." He set her on her feet but kept a firm grip on her shoulders. "What right have you to use me so?" she sputtered.

"A husband's right," he said. "I'll not have my future wife making a spectacle of herself in a sailors' tavern."

Her heart leaped at his words. The riverfront street with its narrow buildings swayed before her eyes. The lantern lights from the ships glowed like stars through the swirling mist. She caught her breath and managed to speak.

"I don't remember your asking me to marry you, my lord!"

"I ask you here and now." He pressed her face against his shoulder., "I wanted to ask you that first night we came back to Whitehall—" She heard his low, rueful laugh. "For once in my life, I put aside my own selfish desires. I wanted to give you time to choose your future for yourself." His arms tightened around her, and he bent her back, his face looming above hers. "You will marry me, Melora!"

"Yes—oh, yes—"

He lifted her once more, but now he cradled her against his chest. Her arms went around his neck, and she made no further protest as he carried her down the length of the wharf to the tall flagship of his fleet. Those of his newly hired crew who were standing watch leaned over side and grinned at one another.

Up the gangplank he strode, and on along the deck to his private cabin at the stern. He kicked open the door, then set her on the bed. He kissed her, his tongue exploring the soft warmth of her mouth.

He let her go only long enough to strip off his clothes, then hers. She lay back on the bed, her dark hair fanning out on the pillow, and watched him from under her half-closed lids.

Gradually, she became aware of an unfamiliar movement beneath her, around her. The slow, sensuous rhythm merged with the swelling current of her desire. The rise and fall of the ship were becoming a part of her.

She looked up at Dirk, tall and bronzed, his body glowing in the light of the swaying lantern overhead. Her need swiftly grew, so that she could no longer wait. "Come to me, love," she said softly, reaching up to him. He lay down beside her, his arms encircled her, and his mouth claimed hers in a long searching kiss.

She drew him to her, parting her thighs to receive the first thrust of his hard, hot shaft. He moved between her legs, but delayed his entry. He cupped one of her breasts to suckle at the turgid nipple. A shiver of delight moved from the hardened peak outward, downward, until every nerve of her body tingled with the fire of her need.

She raised her hips and pressed her hands against his buttocks, drawing him closer. Then, with one swift movement, he was inside her, filling her, possessing her.

The first rosy light of dawn glowed through the half-open cabin window. He lay on his side, one arm across her body, which was now relaxed in sleep. The freshening breeze came sweeping in, and she snuggled closer against him, instinctively seeking his warmth. He drew a deep breath as he felt the pressure of her round bottom against his shaft. His loins began to throb with hunger.

Tightening his arm around her, he drew her closer. She awakened with a soft cry, roused by the touch of his hot shaft against her buttocks. He reached around her and his hands cupped her breasts. She raised her thigh and he slid his manhood between her legs.

One of his hands moved down and found her hard, moist bud, rubbing it gently. The friction of his fingers brought a cry of pleasure to her lips. Slicked with warm moisture, she opened herself to him. Slowly he thrust deep inside, then withdrew. She pressed her buttocks closer, rubbing herself against him in a wordless appeal for release from the aching need inside her.

His shaft invaded her once more, and a fierce tremor ran through the length of his body. As she felt him explode, emptying his seed into the center of her being, she joined with him in the swift, spiraling flight to a place beyond time and space—a place that would always be theirs to share.

Later—much later—he led her out on deck so that they might watch the sun turn the rooftops of London to soft, luminous gold. He showed her how to hold the wheel, while he stood behind her, his hands covering hers. She had not taken time to pin up her hair. The river breeze lifted the dark strands, blowing them backward, so that a few silken strands caressed his cheek.

"I wish we were ready to leave right now," she said. "I dreamed once of your new land. Now I long to see it for myself."

"You're sure, love?" he asked. "I've no doubt of your courage, your determination. How can I, when you've proved them a dozen times over? And yet—"

She turned her head and gave him a teasing half-smile. "Have you tired of me already?"

"Never, my love. Not while I live. But I have been thinking that this voyage will bring me all I've wanted. While you—since our first meeting, you've talked of your own dream. Will you be content to forget all that?"

She laughed softly. "What makes you think I have?"

"Melora—sweeting!" He moved his hand in an impatient gesture. "You've no notion of the hardships waiting for us once we've reached America. There'll be no playhouses there, not even a settlement you would call a proper town."

"But there will be." She turned to him, and her eyes began to glow with the fire of her own inner vision. "Crude cabins at first, then a small settlement, and another. The colonists will long for some respite, however brief, from their daily labors."

"They will have all they can do to survive," he told her, "to clear the land and build their homes, to grow food enough to sustain them through the winters."

"It won't be enough. They will need more." She looked out over the river at the city, then raised her eyes to his. He gazed down at her as he tried to take in her words.

"My father knows he has no need to stay in London to follow his calling. An innyard in Northumberland will be enough for him. And others, like Caleb and Osric—they will seek out a market square, a village fair, and the people will gather. For a few hours, their lives will be touched with wonder."

"Melora, my love . . . you mean to start a theater in a wilderness?"

"Not at once—not for years, maybe. I can wait."

"And in the meantime?"

She moved closer and pressed her body to his. "Why, I will give you tall, strong sons, to carry on your name."

"And daughters." He drew her close and she tilted her face upward. "I want girls with ebony hair, brave and loving—"

Her hands reached up and drew his head down, and his lips found hers. And she knew that wherever their journey might lead, she would never look back. The future lay before them, bright and glowing. Together they would build their new world.

PUT SOME FANTASY IN YOUR LIFE —
FANTASTIC ROMANCES FROM PINNACLE

TIME STORM   (728, $4.99)
by Rosalyn Alsobrook
Modern-day Pennsylvanian physician JoAnn Griffin only believed
what she could feel with her five senses. But when, during a freak
storm, a blinding flash of lightning sent her back in time to 1889,
JoAnn realized she had somehow crossed the threshold into another century and was now gazing into the smoldering eyes of a
startlingly handsome stranger. JoAnn had stumbled through a rip
in time . . . and into a love affair so intense, it carried her to a point
of no return!

SEA TREASURE   (790, $4.50)
by Johanna Hailey
When Michael, a dashing sea captain, is rescued from drowning by
a beautiful sea siren—he does not know yet that she's actually a
mermaid. But her breathtaking beauty stirred irresistible yearnings
in Michael. And soon fate would drive them across the treacherous
Caribbean, tossing them on surging tides of passion that tran-
scended two worlds!

ONCE UPON FOREVER   (883, $4.99)
by Becky Lee Weyrich
A moonstone necklace and a mysterious diary written over a century ago were Clair Summerland's only clues to her true identity.
Two men loved her—one, a dashing civil war hero . . . the other, a
daring jet pilot. Now Clair must risk her past and future for a passion that spans two worlds—and a love that is stronger than time
itself.

SHADOWS IN TIME   (892, $4.50)
by Cherlyn Jac
Driving through the sultry New Orleans night, one moment Tori's
car spins out of control; the next she is in a horse-drawn carriage
with the handsomest man she has ever seen—who calls her wife—
but whose eyes blaze with fury. Sent back in time one hundred
years, Tori is falling in love with the man she is apparently trying to
kill. Now she must race against time to change the tragic past and
claim her future with the man she will love through all eternity!

*Available wherever paperbacks are sold, or order direct from the
Publisher. Send cover price plus 50¢ per copy for mailing and handling to Penguin USA, P.O. Box 999, c/o Dept. 17109, Bergenfield, NJ 07621. Residents of New York and Tennessee must
include sales tax. DO NOT SEND CASH.*

PINNACLE BOOKS HAS SOMETHING FOR EVERYONE —

MAGICIANS, EXPLORERS, WITCHES AND CATS

THE HANDYMAN   (377-3, $3.95/$4.95)
He is a magician who likes hands. He likes their comfortable shape and weight and size. He likes the portability of the hands once they are severed from the rest of the ponderous body. Detective Lanark must discover who The Handyman is before more handless bodies appear.

PASSAGE TO EDEN   (538-5, $4.95/$5.95)
Set in a world of prehistoric beauty, here is the epic story of a courageous seafarer whose wanderings lead him to the ends of the old world — and to the discovery of a new world in the rugged, untamed wilderness of northwestern America.

BLACK BODY   (505-9, $5.95/$6.95)
An extraordinary chronicle, this is the diary of a witch, a journal of the secrets of her race kept in return for not being burned for her "sin." It is the story of Alba, that rarest of creatures, a white witch: beautiful and able to walk in the human world undetected.

THE WHITE PUMA   (532-6, $4.95/NCR)
The white puma has recognized the men who deprived him of his family. Now, like other predators before him, he has become a man-hater. This story is a fitting tribute to this magnificent animal that stands for all living creatures that have become, through man's carelessness, close to disappearing forever from the face of the earth.

Available wherever paperbacks are sold, or order direct from the Publisher. Send cover price plus 50¢ per copy for mailing and handling to Penguin USA, P.O. Box 999, c/o Dept. 17109, Bergenfield, NJ 07621.Residents of New York and Tennessee must include sales tax. DO NOT SEND CASH.

MAKE THE CONNECTION

WITH

Come talk to your favorite authors and get the inside scoop on everything that's going on in the world of publishing, from the only online service that's designed exclusively for the publishing industry.

With Z-Talk Online Information Service, the most innovative and exciting computer bulletin board around, you can:

- ♥ CHAT "LIVE" WITH AUTHORS, FELLOW READERS, AND OTHER MEMBERS OF THE PUBLISHING COMMUNITY.

- ♥ FIND OUT ABOUT UPCOMING TITLES BEFORE THEY'RE RELEASED.

- ♥ DOWNLOAD THOUSANDS OF FILES AND GAMES.

- ♥ READ REVIEWS OF ROMANCE TITLES.

- ♥ HAVE UNLIMITED USE OF E-MAIL.

- ♥ POST MESSAGES ON OUR DOZENS OF TOPIC BOARDS.

All it takes is a computer and a modem to get online with Z-Talk. Set your modem to 8/N/1, and dial 212-545-1120. If you need help, call the System Operator, at 212-889-2299, ext. 260. There's a two week free trial period. After that, annual membership is only $ 60.00.

See you online!